WHAT'S "WHOOPS" IN FRENCH?

"Monsieur Rosalez, we have a problem," said Maurice Aubuchon with his characteristic frown.

"What i- th-

"- -maturely on th- -hy. They shut - -een running - -ause. So far, w- -ot been successful."

"Well, keep troubleshooting and let me know when you figure something out."

"Yes, Monsieur, but there is another problem that you should know about."

"Another problem? What's that?"

"The astrodynamicists have been looking at the new trajectory of the asteroid. The one it was on when the thrusters failed. It doesn't look good."

"It doesn't look good? I would imagine not. Those thrusters were supposed to run another few months to put it on a trajectory that would make it accessible for us to mine. Other than costing me hundreds of millions of euros to build and perhaps costing me billions of euros in lost revenue, what else could be 'not good'?" Rosalez asked, now sounding more irritated.

"They think the asteroid is now on a collision course with the Earth..."

ON TO THE ASTEROID

Travis S. Taylor
Les Johnson

ON TO THE ASTEROID

This is a work of fiction. All the characters and events portrayed in this book are fictional, and any resemblance to real people or incidents is purely coincidental.

A Baen Books Original

Baen Publishing Enterprises
P.O. Box 1403
Riverdale, NY 10471
www.baen.com

ISBN: 978-1-4814-8267-7

Cover art by Sam Kennedy

First paperback printing, September 2017

Library of Congress Catalog Number: 2016018024

Distributed by Simon & Schuster
1230 Avenue of the Americas
New York, NY 10020

Pages by Joy Freeman (www.pagesbyjoy.com)
Printed in the United States of America

I would like to dedicate this book to the dinosaurs. If they'd have had a space program, they might have survived. Hopefully, we'll learn the lesson from their misfortune rather than repeat it.

—Travis

The women and men of the NASA MSFC Advanced Concepts Office. These are the people who can make dreams real.

—Les

PROLOGUE

SUMMER ALONG LAKE BAIKAL WAS A GLORIOUS TIME
for the boy and his family. The brutal winter was
over and the longer days of summer were upon them.
The lake was crystal clear and almost completely still,
reflecting the light of the sunlike gems set in an
expensive ring that might belong to a Czarina. The
morning was cool, about fifty degrees, and the boy was
outside doing his chores. His father was tending the
cattle and his mother was busy weeding the garden
they kept behind the modest house in which he and
his three siblings lived with their parents.

Not much happened during the all-too-short summers in Siberia. The snow and ice melted and the
darkness that seemed to define their lives for most
of the year took a vacation. The skies tended to be
clear and blue during the day and filled with the
mysterious stars at night. The boy's father would often
tell his children stories about his ancestors, whom he
claimed were nobles in exile, as they sat around their
cooking fire in the long twilight so typical of northern

latitudes. None in the family had received a formal education and they didn't expect that any of them would ever do so. They were farmers and farmers they would remain.

The boy had a few friends, and they planned to get together later in the day, after their chores were behind them, to go fishing and perhaps swimming in the lake—as cold as it was, it was far warmer and tempting now than at any other time of the year. He looked forward to these outings with his friends. They were a welcome respite from his work and the unpleasant habits of his older sister. Since she turned fourteen, she had become almost unbearable to be around. All she seemed to think and talk about were boys. The boy, himself only ten, promised himself that when he turned fourteen he wouldn't spend all his time thinking and talking about girls. NEVER.

He was clearing debris from the previous week's storm from the outer part of the field, near the lake, when the column of blinding blue light flashed across the sky to the north. It was brighter than the sun, and its light reflected from the surface of the lake was blinding. There was no sound and that, more than the light, disturbed the boy. He dropped the branches he'd gathered and began running toward the house. He could see his sister just outside the house staring dumbfounded into the sky. His father was emerging from the barn and appeared to be looking for the source of the light that had undoubtedly brightened its interior.

He had just reached his sister, the one about whom he had just been complaining, when the shock wave struck them. Time passed in what seemed like slow motion to the boy. He saw the debris at the front of the blast wave only moments before it reached him, yet it seemed like several minutes. Dirt, debris, and even water were being thrown into the air as what seemed like a wall of air reached them standing just beside their house. He had to cover his eyes to protect them from the dust and dirt in the air. He then heard the sound of the house being battered by the sudden gust of strong wind and saw parts of the roof flying off, along with the window shutters and much of the siding that covered the right side of the house. The sound was as deafening as the light had been blinding. He was terrified.

Simultaneously with the arrival of the shock wave, the ground trembled like in an earthquake. What the wind had not blown over, the shaking Earth did its best to tumble. The cook stand collapsed onto the fire that had been lit this morning to cook breakfast and much of the fence the boy's father was building shook out of the postholes and onto the ground.

After it—whatever "it" was—had passed, the boy and his family were all alive and mostly uninjured. The damage to their property was significant but repairable, and aside from there being some exciting tales exchanged with their neighbors, who had similar experiences, the most lasting effects of the mysterious light and ensuing storm were the stories.

Only a few hundred miles away it was a completely different story. Resulting from what scientists would later estimate was the equivalent of a ten-megaton nuclear bomb—or one about one thousand times more powerful than the atomic bomb dropped on Hiroshima but without the nuclear radiation—a meteor or a comet had crossed paths with the Earth, entered the atmosphere and exploded just before impact at an altitude of about five miles. The affected area beneath the blast was over eight hundred square miles, and, fortunately, it was mostly uninhabited. The boy and his family were in one of the closest villages to the impact zone and because they weren't within it, they survived. Eighty million trees and the animals living among them weren't so lucky. The damage within the zone where the object exploded was nearly complete.

The year was 1908, and it was just another day in the life of the solar system.

CHAPTER I

GESLING ESTIMATED THAT HE HAD LESS THAN TWO minutes to live. The status board in front of him was lit up like a Christmas tree, one decorated with all red lights, and if the klaxon didn't stop sounding soon, he thought he might die before the lander impacted the surface of the Moon in what company parlance would deem "a hard landing." To Gesling, the best he could hope for now was a just a "hard" landing. Unless he did something soon, he was going to crash.

Time did seem to slow down, though his life wasn't passing before his eyes. He wasn't thinking of his last night with his wife Carolyn, or of his parents and childhood. He was completely focused on saving his own skin and the multi-hundred-million-dollar investment that was the lander he was piloting to the surface of the Moon. There wasn't much time.

Just a few minutes before, the situation board was all green and he had initiated the main engine burn that would take him and the lander from lunar orbit to a powered descent and landing on the Moon. This test flight was part of Space Excursions' latest commercial space venture and one that would set the stage for landing tourists at the world's first hotel on the surface of the Moon with a year. He and his copilot, Bill Stetson, had rehearsed the mission for months and they thought they'd run through a simulation of just about everything that could possibly go wrong. Everything but whatever-the-hell had just caused the main engine to shut down after beginning the deorbit maneuver. Thanks to the laws derived by Mr. Newton, he and the lander were going to land on the Moon. The only question left at this point was just how hard the landing would be.

Gesling touched the screen in front of him and called up the latest engineering information about the ship's systems, frantically trying to isolate the problem and figure out how to recover. The engine had shut down suddenly and that meant that the computer had detected an anomaly that would have resulted in an explosion if it hadn't been shut down. The system was designed to prevent the worst case. In this situation, it may have avoided the worst case, but the second worst case replacing it was not much better.

"Paul, listen up. I'm seeing the same data as you and I think I've found the problem." That was the voice of Bill Stetson, his copilot for the mission, who was on the module that remained in lunar orbit after Gesling and the lander had separated from it. Stetson was not just Gesling's colleague, they were also friends. Bill had joined Space Excursions after retiring from NASA and was one of the few people in the world who had already walked on the Moon, albeit in a rescue mission just a few years ago. That had also been one that nearly ended in disaster.

"I'm all ears, Bill. What have you got? Be quick, I'm in a bad way down here."

"You need to restart the main engine and it should be okay. The sensors in the LAD showed that a gas bubble was in the fuel line and they shut the engine down to prevent an explosion. For some reason the backup sensor, which doesn't show any vapor, didn't kick in and keep you going. We need to figure out why, but that doesn't matter now. You need to cycle the engine and restart."

Stetson sounded cool and authoritative as he spoke. Gesling made a quick mental note that attributed his calm demeanor to his being an old school NASA astronaut who had faced crises like this before. Gesling felt anything but calm.

"Cycling the engine now. And you're sure there's no vapor in the line?"

"I give it a fifty-fifty chance. Seems to be a better chance than what you've got without the engine on and working."

"I'll take it," said Gesling as he completed the restart sequence on the liquid methane powered engine that would now either explode and end his life in a literal blaze of glory or provide him with a mere hard landing on the lunar surface.

He held his breath as the restart sequence completed and the red engine status light turned from red to yellow and he felt the harsh bump accompanying the engine's start. He didn't die, and he was relieved.

"Hot damn! Bill, you saved my skin."

"All in a day's work, my friend. Now just make sure nothing else goes wrong in the next few minutes. You've got a ship to land."

"Roger that," said Gesling. He looked briefly around the spartan command center of the lander, watching red light after red light wink from red to yellow to green. All except for the one that was monitoring his descent rate. He was still dropping much too fast; the engine hadn't yet had time to slow him to the speed at which he should be descending from this altitude. There was nothing he could do except wait for the burn to remove as much speed as possible before they touched the surface. In theory, when the landing gear touched the surface, the relative velocity of the lander should be zero. In theory...

Gesling looked out the window at the starkly grey lunar landscape as he monitored his descent rate out of the corner of his eye on the screen in front of him. He could clearly see, with acuity almost indescribable, the contrast between the lunar craters and surface features against the dark blackness of space. The sunlight reflecting from the lunar regolith was blinding, especially as the dust currently being kicked up from his ship's engine crossed his line of sight, obscuring the features he was previously admiring. The lunar dust danced with random Brownian motion and vortices and swirls creating a chaotic ballet of flickering sunlight.

A quick glance at the laser altimeter told him how high above the surface he was and from that how fast he was dropping. It wasn't a perfect descent but at least the sensor showed that the descent rate of speed and the altitude were close to converging on zero—which would be a good thing as long as that convergence happened above the surface and not below. In other words, he hoped it happened before he smacked into the Moon. But the numbers hadn't converged yet and that meant that he and the ship would touch the Moon, altitude zero, with a speed greater than zero—hopefully not too much greater than zero. On Earth, and in most casual conversation, this would be called a crash. On Earth, a crash you could walk away from and a bad landing you could still fly away from. A bad crash required an ambulance. Gesling was now hoping for a bad landing, but he'd settle for a crash provided it wasn't a bad one. There weren't any ambulances out there at four hundred thousand kilometers from Earth—at least none that could be there anytime soon.

The lander reached zero altitude while the speed indicator showed he was moving at five kilometers per hour. He felt the not-very-gentle *whump* of the gear taking most of the initial impact before the entire lander jolted, rocked and then settled into a full stop. Most automobiles had better than a five kilometer impact bumper. He wasn't driving a car.

I'm still alive, thought Gesling as he looked around the cabin and made sure it wasn't about to explode or have some piece of rock plunge through its skin. The ship stopped rocking and remained fully upright. The status boards showed that all systems were working and all of the red lights that had previously indicated his imminent death and doom were now green. It was then that he realized he was holding his breath and let out an explosive exhalation.

"Paul? Are you okay down there?" asked Stetson from high above, probably now flying over the lunar far side with his voice being relayed by one of the small cubesat communications satellites now orbiting and providing global communications and positioning information to anyone and everyone on the Moon. In other words, the cubesats were relaying the message to Paul since he was the only one there at the moment.

"Bill, I'm not only okay, I'm pumped. She landed hard, but there is no indication of damage. I'm walking through the shutdown sequence now."

"I'm glad to hear it. I know Mr. Childers and a certain Carolyn O'Connor-Gesling are also glad for that. I'm not sure, but I think they were both chewing nails back in Nevada as they watched your status board light up."

"I'll get on the private channel with them as soon as I make sure the ship is secure. What a way to end your career, eh? Were you experiencing déjà vu up there?"

"Hey, don't remind me. I may be retiring after this flight, but that doesn't mean I'm out to pasture yet. I was already running through options to get a rescue ship down there to you while you were restarting that engine. I did it once and I could do it again. But if it's all the same with you, I'd rather not."

"Not is fine by me," said Gesling as he went through the post-landing checklist on his helmet's heads up display. He couldn't help but muse at the fact that just five years ago, Bill Stetson had been the one piloting a NASA ship to the Moon's surface. He'd been on a mission to find and bring home the survivors of a wrecked Chinese lunar lander that Gesling had found on the world's first commercial lunar flyby. He'd brought them all home safely, despite what seemed to be an endless stream of mishaps, and now he was part of Gary Childers's private space company that would soon be bringing tourists for a week's stay at the company's lunar hotel.

Thinking of the hotel prompted Gesling to take his first real look out the window since the dust kicked up from his rocket engine had settled. He scanned the horizon, looking for it and found it almost immediately. Clearly not natural and standing out rather starkly against the deep grey of the lunar surface was the Out of This World, Space Excursions' lunar habitat and hotel, waiting on its first paying customers. From a distance, Gesling was able to confirm what the Out of This World's onboard cameras and those from orbit showed—that the hotel was in one piece and undamaged. Gesling would soon find out for himself. After securing the ship, he was going to exit the airlock and take his first stroll across the lunar surface to check it out. *Thank God he didn't put flashing neon lights on it*, Gesling thought as he continued working his way through the checklist.

About forty-five minutes later, Gesling finished powering down the lander and adjusting his spacesuit for his short stroll to the Out of This World. He was nervous without a doubt. Between him and the hotel was just about the deadliest environment humanity had ever decided to explore: an airless world bathed in unfiltered sunlight which would cause his ambient temperature to increase above two-hundred degrees Celsius if it weren't for the suit's built-in air conditioner. Accompanying the abundant sunlight was a steady stream of ionized particle radiation, the solar wind, and the risk of a sudden solar storm that could dose him with enough radiation to kill him outright.

A walk in the park, he thought as he opened the door from the lander to the airless lunar surface.

Gesling eased his way down the ladder from the lander to the surface and soon felt the reassuring solidity of the ground beneath his feet. It wasn't the ground he was used to, and that made his heart rate increase. He could hear the blood pumping in his ears and his rapid deep breaths as he took his first steps on another world. Unlike the explorers who had come before, the Apollo astronauts, the returning Americans that included Bill Stetson, the Russians and now the Chinese, he didn't make any pithy comments meant for public consumption. Instead, he chose to remain quiet and in his own thoughts during those first few moments.

"Paul, if you don't say something I am going to get in a rocket and come up there to beat some sense into you!" The voice on the speaker was that of his wife, and Space Excursions' very own media liaison, Carolyn O'Connor-Gesling. When they'd met about seven years ago, Gesling had no idea she would become his wife. At this moment, he wasn't sure if she was speaking as his mate or as the chief publicity officer for Space Excursions.

"Yeah, right. I guess I should," Gesling said, thinking of the words he'd rehearsed with Carolyn and Mr. Childers before he'd departed Earth just three days ago.

"This is Paul Gesling of Space Excursions, taking the first steps by a non-government employee on the surface of another world. Today is a new beginning for humanity. A beginning that will fulfill the promises made to a previous generation by opening up the space frontier to all of us. And I dare say, it is about time!" Gesling looked down at the footprints he was making in the dirt so that his headset camera feed would clearly image them for all back home to see. He continued, "These footprints aren't being made by some elite, out-of-reach and too-perfect astronaut. They're mine and you can add yours to them soon by signing up for Space Excursions' Ultimate Getaway—a week-long stay on the Moon. I may be the first to land here and walk this path to the hotel ahead of me, but I won't be the last. Join Space Excursion as we make space an affordable excursion for all. It may be only one small step for a man, but it most certainly is a giant leap that every member of mankind can take."

"Perfect," said Carolyn. "Now you can forget about all the PR stuff and get yourself safely into the Out of This World. I'll process the footage and get it out on the net before you can get settled in for your rest break."

"Carolyn, I miss you."

"I miss you too, but we've both got work to do," she said. After a brief pause she added, "And Paul, be careful."

"Right, careful. Always." Paul smiled though nobody could see it. He'd switched the interior helmet camera view off. He looked around at the lunarscape spread out around him. The landing vehicle and ascent system was like something out of the old science fiction movies he'd watched as a kid. Only, now, he was the would-be hero on a daring space adventure.

"Onward and upward it is," Gesling said to himself, wiping the smile from his face. He was already looking forward to being home and in his wife's embrace—but first he had a Moon to cross. Or, at least several hundred meters of Moon to cross. *Pinch me now*, he thought.

The walk on the Moon felt just like he'd thought it would. It was almost exactly like the bungee cord rigging system they had developed to simulate walking on the Moon back at Space Excursions on Earth. The training system would serve future lunar tourists well. There was a slight difference, though. On Earth, even though the bungees made his steps and jumps much longer, the full feel of one Earth gravity was still ever present. On the Moon, however, he felt light as air. Old aches and pains he'd had in his body just were no longer there. That slight catch in his left knee he sometimes felt ever since his football injury in high school, wasn't there. The stiffness he felt in his shoulder from throwing too many baseballs from centerfield in high school and then aggravating it at the company softball tournament, well, it simply wasn't there. The one-sixth gravity made him feel good. There was definitely a business aspect of that feeling he would have to relay further to Gary. Assuming a person could survive the launch and flight, a stay on the Moon might make them feel years younger. The longer-term health benefits or detriments would most certainly have to be investigated.

It took only a few minutes to cross the dusty lunar plain that stretched between the landing zone and the entrance of the Out of This World's airlock. But it was an exciting and surreal few minutes. Paul had to stop and scoop up a handful of the lunar dust and drop it just to get a feel of how different the gravity really was. As soon as he'd done that, he wondered if he should have. The fine grains of the lunar regolith stuck to his suit like Styrofoam peanuts do anytime they are used as packing materials. The electrostatic interactions between the dust and his suit were more than evident.

"Until you feel it you just can't truly understand it," he muttered to himself as the dust glittered and danced in the sunlight in front of him. The arch of dust descended to the surface, slowly throwing scattered shards of multicolored rays from the Sun in every direction. Paul stepped up in front of the airlock door of the lunar hotel and pressed a passcode into the keypad. The door cycled, opened silently, and he stepped in.

As the airlock repressurized, Gesling was aware of the strong airflow being directed across his spacesuit and sucked through the grate and into the floor beneath where he was standing. He could see that the air was doing its job of removing much of the pesky lunar dust that had attached itself to his suit during his walk. A considerable amount of the dust remained on the suit, looking like grey smudge prints, mostly on his pants and some around his gauntlets where he had picked up a handful of the Moon's surface. Childers knew the lunar dust was going to be a problem and installed the best cleaning system his engineers could provide to try and keep it at a minimum and Gesling was now providing the system its first real test. Since paying customers wouldn't want to spend a week in a dirty hotel, Childers had spared no expense.

"We'll have to think a bit more seriously about the air shower to clean off a little more of this dust. There is no way that tourists are going to come here without reaching down and playing with the Moon dirt," he said to nobody in particular, but he knew that his every word was being recorded for analysis. In essence, he was leaving himself a note. Satisfied that he was now as clean as the air shower was going to get him and that the air in the lock was safe to breathe, Gesling removed his helmet to take a deep breath before opening the inner door into the hotel proper. While he was still a bit dirty, he wasn't too dirty. The air was a bit stale, but otherwise good. Gesling took another deep breath and then keyed in the sequence that would allow him to enter the inflated habitat. The door opened and he stepped through.

The interior was more spacious than Paul remembered. He'd walked through the full-size mockup many times at Space Excursions' Nevada assembly plant, but it never seemed this spacious. And then he realized that it probably seemed big because he and Bill Stetson had spent the last three days cooped up in the *Dreamscape* together and that this was the most open area he'd had since before they launched. Paul laughed to himself at the thought of *Dreamscape* being crowded. He had studied in detail the Apollo mission and the previous mission that the Chinese and Stetson had flown on. The *Dreamscape* was a luxury liner compared to its predecessors. He told himself he was spoiled and to quit whining.

The *Dreamscape* was a reusable hypersonic spaceship made by Space Excursions that was able to take off and land like an airplane and, once refueled in space, make the six-day round trip voyage to the Moon and back. It could make the trip to loop around the Moon and return to Earth, without stopping there, and not need any modification or additional hardware. To stop at the Moon required additional fuel and the *Dreamscape* did this by carrying with it an expendable stage that was attached to its frame in Earth orbit before departure. The stage carried enough fuel to slow them down so they could capture into lunar orbit and then start again to boost them back home. Once they were on the way home, the stage would separate and fly into a million-year long solar orbit before it was likely to crash into anything else in space. But it wasn't just space trash at that point. Gary Childers was too much of an opportunist and businessman to let such a spacecraft go to waste. There were two payload packages aboard the booster stage. One of them housed small canisters, which were actually cremation urns holding the remains of several multibillionaires. The other was a small camera and transceiver package that allowed family members back on Earth to check in on the status of their departed loved ones as they traveled through space. The system was solar powered and was designed to last for at least one hundred fifty years. It was possible it would last even longer. For generations family members could sit with their long gone loved ones as they journeyed through deep space.

Paul took in a slow breath and made a full three-hundred-sixty-degree turn. He looked at the hotel space around him. Gesling made a mental note to share his perceptions with Carolyn and Gary Childers upon his return. After all, if the Out of This World seemed big to him, then it was bound to seem big for its future guests as well. The first thing he did was move to the hotel's command computer to personally check out its status.

Paul pulled the gauntlets and twisted them. The stiff gloves popped loose and he slid them off his hands. They were cold to the touch. He tethered them to his waist and then tapped at the controls on the computer touchscreen. The screen lit up with a bright blue dot that then expanded and filled the screen. There was a welcome icon and a login tab. Paul tapped the login and entered his username and password. The system screen opened up and displayed a welcome message to him.

"Welcome Mr. Gesling. Would you like to check in?" A female computer voice said. Paul laughed and then began inserting information that would allow him to check internal systems status as well as cycle on the entire hotel. He was relieved to see that every-thing was working as it should. Then he had to do the basic administrative tasks because it was a hotel. He had to check in before he could stay there. At least he didn't have to leave a credit card number for incidentals. Gary Childers would be picking up the tab for his stay.

"Paul, how does it look?" The disembodied voice of his boss, Gary Childers, came over the hotel's PA system and startled Gesling, as he was totally engaged in the checkout process. He was glad he was wearing a diaper in his spacesuit.

"Mr. Childers, you startled me," Gesling stammered before recovering.

"Sorry, Paul. We're on pins and needles here," Childers replied. "How does it look?"

"It all looks pretty good to me," Gesling said as he surveyed the two-room hotel and habitat. He was standing in the all-purpose room that contained the onboard control center, the galley, the entertainment center and the bathroom. Ahead and separated from the main room by only a curtain that was currently not drawn was the storage area and where the guests would sleep. Gesling wasn't yet sure how they would fare sleeping in hammocks they'd have to string up and take down every day. At one-sixth gravity, sleeping on the netting of a hammock shouldn't be uncomfortable, but it didn't quite fit the image of a multi-million-dollar getaway to the Moon. He would soon find out. He was to bunk here for the night, checking out all of the hotel's features, including the shower—which he thought should feel pretty good right about now—and report back any glitches that needed fixing before the first guests arrived in about a year.

CHAPTER 2

GARY CHILDERS WAS AN OLD-SCHOOL BUSINESSMAN running a multibillion-dollar energy company from his corporate headquarters in downtown Lexington, Kentucky, where he'd made his fortune mining, processing and selling coal. Then came the whole global warming thing and he'd diversified into solar, geothermal and offshore wind energy—making more millions in the process. Childers was one of those people who knew how to make money turn into more money, and he did it well and often.

At age sixty-five, Childers was also a frustrated space fanatic. As a boy, he'd seen the end of Apollo and the lunar landings that went with it. He lived through Skylab, the International Space Station and the slow rebirth of American piloted spaceflight after the retirement of the Space Shuttle. And the pace at which his beloved NASA was making progress pained him. It pained him so much that he had spent over half his fortune to build a commercial space company that would do more than the other, similar startups

19

that were ferrying wealthy businessmen on suborbital joy rides. He built a completely reusable spaceship capable of traveling from Earth to the Moon and back again. He built it with passenger seats and big windows. And the millionaires and politicians lined up to take their own five-day joyrides around the Moon and back. For the first few years, his Space Excursions company was a money loser. Then it broke even. Now it was turning a profit that stockholders would love, had there been any. But Gary Childers didn't want to be beholden to anyone, let alone a bunch of shortsighted investors that didn't know or understand the long view. That's why Space Excursions remained one hundred percent private and one hundred percent owned by Gary Childers.

It was the crew and paying passengers aboard Childers's company's spaceship, the *Dreamscape*, that had heard the call for help coming from stranded Chinese astronauts in their disastrous attempt to beat America back to the Moon just five years prior. His friend and chief pilot, Paul Gesling, had then once again come to the rescue by flying the *Dreamscape* into Earth orbit to bring home the Chinese crew rescued by NASA and stranded there by the actions of a rogue Chinese astronaut among the crew who had apparently thought it would be better to be dead than rescued by Americans. Now, he was about to make history again, hopefully in an equally dramatic but less dangerous manner. And it was this topic that he and his public relations manager, Carolyn O'Connor-Gesling, were discussing in his last minute pre-press conference cramming session.

"Carolyn, is the link with Paul up and running?"

Childers asked, waving off Carolyn's attempts to straighten his tie and make the lapel microphone a little less noticeable to the many cameras that awaited him on the other side of the door they were making their way toward.

"Yes, Paul's made himself presentable, tough as that is sometimes, and I think excitement of being on the Moon will more than make up for his lack of sleep."

"Its tough duty to have to sleep in a hammock...on the Moon," said Childers dryly, with sarcasm so thick that it would drip—had that been physically possible.

"He'll be fine, you know Paul. Now, here's the latest on who'll be in the audience for the press conference. You've got another six minutes before show time, can I get you anything?" Carolyn handed Childers a printed copy listing the press, media and new media outlets participating in today's press conference. The list contained the usual national and international news networks, the space bloggers and a few freelance journalists who covered events such as this for whoever hired them to do so.

"And the models?" asked Childers.

"The models are on the table to the right of the podium and within reach."

"Carolyn, don't let Paul take you for granted or he'll have to answer to me. You have got to be the best organizer I've ever had work for me. You haven't missed a beat since I hired you."

"Thank you, sir. I'll be sure to tell him after you let him come home from the Moon. For now, let's just settle for getting you through this press conference and then we'll worry about getting my husband back to me."

"Right." Childers smiled and opened the door to the auditorium on the other side.

He walked into the familiar surroundings of the company auditorium and the throngs of faces looking back at him. The antiquated-sounding click of high resolution camera shutters was the dominant sound as Childers walked from the door to the podium in front of the assembled media. Just as Caroline said, to the right of the podium were his "toys." Models of the *Dreamscape*, the *Dasher* and the *Dancer*, Childers's names for his lunar orbiter and lander, respectively, and the Out of This World, the lunar hotel in which Paul Gesling had spent his lunar sleep cycle. The sight of his toys evoked a smile, which in turn calmed his nerves and put him into his element—explaining the latest company milestones to a group of interested and anxious reporters.

"Ladies and Gentlemen, thank you for your attention. Today I am pleased to announce that Space Excursions has accomplished yet another space first and is preparing the way for a series of further successful firsts. Last night, Space Excursions employee and chief pilot, Paul Gesling, spent the night on the Moon, resting as the first guest in the company's lunar hotel while former NASA astronaut Bill Stetson, who accompanied him on the lunar voyage, remained in the orbiting *Dasher* module. Gesling will remain on the Moon for another day and night, and then he will return to lunar orbit to rejoin Mr. Stetson and make the homeward trip to Earth. You'll hear from Mr. Gesling, live from the surface of the Moon, in just a few moments." Childers paused to assess his audience. He was a gifted spokesman and, as with many similarly talented speakers, he knew that the key to making a good speech is to make sure that you understood your audience and that they understood you. Judging by his quick scan of the faces in the room, he was sure he was in a good place.

"Following the successful return of Messrs. Gesling and Stetson, and in about eighteen months, Space Excursions will relaunch the *Dasher* and *Dancer* spacecraft with their first party of tourists bound for the lunar surface and a week-long stay at the Out of This World, where they will experience first-hand both deep space flight and the thrill of actually walking on the surface of an alien world, in this case, our Moon."

"Before we transfer to the Moon and Mr. Gesling, are there any questions for me?"

Hands all across the room went up. Childers, not being a politician and therefore not really giving a damn if he ticked off a reporter or two, had his favorites among the crowd and he called upon one of them first. In this case, Doreen Davidson, not only because he liked the alliteration of her name, but also because he liked her blog, and that she had always written positively about Space Excursions in the past.

"Mr. Childers, we know there will be six paying customers on the next flight and staying on the Moon in your hotel. Can you tell us who they are?" she asked.

"As I think we clearly explained in our press release, we're not going to provide those names at this time. If the passengers want to make themselves known, that is up to them. But we all signed some fairly strict confidentiality papers that my lawyers advise me to stick with. I suspect you will know who they are by the time we actually launch, but again, that's strictly up to them."

Next, he called on the reporter from the BBC.

"Mr. Childers, you and your company are among a group of companies spending obscene amounts of money in space to dubious benefit. With at least five companies now working to mine asteroids for private gain, a recent poll in Europe showed that a majority don't approve of the world's rich elite taking extravagant trips to the Moon while so many on the planet are living in poverty and barely able to subsist. There's even been a discussion of banning European citizens from flying on your ship. How can you justify this overt display of excess?" The BBC reporter, a man in his mid-twenties with a clear upper-crust British accent looked at Childers with a smug smile and the arrogance that only a well-heeled Brit could possibly manage.

"Mr. Brighthall, the last time I checked, the United States of America is neither subject to European opinion polls nor its politicians. Furthermore, as a believer in economic freedom and the right of people to spend their money as they choose, I am inclined to tell the good people sampled in your poll where they can put their sanctimonious, better-than-thou attitudes, but I won't, since I am a gentleman and since I don't want to cause an international incident. And, most importantly, because I want to sell rides to the Moon to my many European friends." Childers looked, and was, annoyed. He continued, "Let's just say that in aggregate, the world is a much better and more affluent place to live today than at any time in history. Personally, I attribute that as the inevitable outcome of free people, in free economies, spending their hard-earned money as they so choose."

"Space technology is helping to lift the economies of the world in ways that were unimaginable just a few years ago and I won't even try to list them all. Instead, I recommend you do some reading. There are several great books out there that describe what I'm talking about. If you and your colleagues don't want to participate, then don't. And please keep your hands out of my pockets while you pursue whatever it is you decide to pursue." With that, Childers was through talking to the BBC reporter and on to the next.

"Mr. Childers, are you going to fly on one of your own rockets? And, if so, when?" The question came from a female freelance journalist that often wrote space-friendly articles for Space.com and other sites frequented by space advocates.

"Well," he paused in thought briefly at the question. Then Childers smiled and raised his left eyebrow just before he answered, "That's two questions. To answer the first, yes, I plan to go. The answer to the second question I will leave to your speculation."

After about ten more minutes of mostly benign questions, Childers walked toward a large hyper-resolution monitor that was displaying the Space Excursions corporate logo. He nodded to Carolyn and the image of Paul Gesling appeared on the screen. Gesling was in shirt sleeves and standing in front of one of the large viewing windows of the Out of this World showing the truly spectacular lunar landscape immediately behind and outside. The 3D image was stunning, giving those in the room the sense that they, too, were on the Moon.

"For your next round of questions, you'll be speaking with Paul Gesling from the surface of the Moon," said Childers, looking for all the world like a sixty-five-year-old kid on Christmas morning.

"Good afternoon and welcome to the Out of This World," Gesling said as he did his best not to smile like a kid in a toy store. He gestured somewhat excitedly as he began to walk through the interior of the habitat. The camera tracked his movement across the floor and faded into a different view as he approached a closer camera on the side wall. The automated camera system was working flawlessly. "This is where I spent the night and where our guests will spend their week on the Moon. Now, let me show you around..." The tour continued as Gesling moved around the habitat, stopping at each point of interest, including the toilet.

"Mr. Childers, it's time for you to leave for Nevada. Paul and Hami can take it from here," whispered Carolyn, trying not to be heard through the microphone as she spoke.

"Ladies and gentlemen, I need to get on the road. My associate, Hami Kunda, will answer any additional questions you may have." Childers moved toward the exit where waited Carolyn and the rest of his entourage that would accompany him to the airport and on the Space Excursions private jet to Nevada.

It was a beautiful Kentucky day and Childers stopped on the way to his limousine to admire the brilliant blue sky filled with jet contrails that contrasted with the ever-growing Lexington skyline. The sight conjured in his mind's eye the thought that had driven him since he was a boy. *One of these days, instead of jet contrails, those will be rocket exhausts and we'll be flying people to and from space by the hundreds each and every day.* The thought lingered in his mind as he started to move toward the limo and just as suddenly as the thought of rockets had popped into his mind the first 7.62x63 millimeter slug caught him in his right leg, shattering bone as it tore through his skin. Skin, bone, ligament, and muscle tissue flew from his leg in a spray of pink, red, and flesh-colored mist.

Childers was pushed backward and spun clockwise by the impact as the mist and tissue fragments splattered against the open limo door. He twisted sideways from the impact, knocking Carolyn off balance and directly into the path of the next bullet as he fell to the ground. The second slug caught Carolyn in her upper back, which was now facing in the direction she'd been walking just seconds before. The bullet passed through her like a warm knife through butter, perforating her left lung and making a large and bloody exit wound. She, too, fell to the ground. The wound gushed in red and made a wheezing and sucking sound each time her heart beat or she struggled for a breath.

Max Potter, Childers's longtime body guard was on Childers as soon as he realized what was happening. Moving as he had been trained, he only momentarily had the wherewithal to consider aiding the stricken O'Connor instead of his boss. Realizing that she had not likely been the primary target of the attack and likely not to be shot again, he moved toward Childers. Potter, outweighing the aging Childers by two-to-one, formed the perfect human shield for his boss as the next two slugs meant for Childers struck him. Even though the bodyguard was wearing a level four bulletproof vest under his sport coat, the very large and fast sniper rounds tore through him like the armor wasn't even there, killing him instantly. There were now three bodies on the ground; one dead and two who would be soon if nothing was done.

Childers's other assistants scattered, as did the pedestrians who just happened to be in the wrong place at the wrong time and in the line of fire. It was one of the pedestrians who called 911 from the safety of a doorway just behind where the bodies were bleeding out on the ground.

Just as instantly as the thoughts of rocket contrails had popped into Childers's mind and just as instantly as the sniper rounds had made life-altering and life-taking impact on them, the shooting stopped.

CHAPTER 3

PAUL GESLING AND BILL STETSON SHOULD HAVE been leaving lunar orbit for home with a sense of triumph. Both had visited the Moon more than once. Gesling had now piloted five of Space Excursions' commercial trips around the Moon and back to the Earth in the reusable *Dreamscape* spacecraft. Lunar tourism was Space Excursions' first commercial space venture. It was a resounding success and formed the financial basis that now enabled the company to build a lunar hotel. Stetson had walked on the Moon during the rescue of the stranded Chinese astronauts; now he was coming home with a fellow moonwalker.

They were not feeling triumphant. Instead, they felt powerless and, worse still, useless, especially Gesling. His colleague and friend was nearly a quarter of million miles from home, and from his wife, and there was absolutely nothing either of them could do to help her or to get home any faster. Orbital mechanics just would not allow it.

"I can't believe anyone would want to kill Gary

Childers," said Bill as he watched the ship's instruments, pausing only briefly to peer out the window at the rapidly receding Moon.

"I can't believe that Carolyn's been shot. Damn it all to hell, I feel so helpless way out here. When they catch whoever did this, I'll kill him. I swear I'll kill him."

Stetson knew his buddy was worried sick and blowing off steam, so he didn't bother reminding his friend that he couldn't hurt a fly and that he was a huge believer in the rule of law. It wouldn't serve any purpose to try and talk reason with someone in an unreasonable state, unreasonable distances from home, following such unreasonable and horrific acts.

"Who would do such a thing, anyway?" Gesling shook his head in disbelief.

"People are screwed up, Paul. Gary is a successful businessman in a time that people don't value the rugged individual like they used to. It doesn't help that he's so damned outspoken about what he believes," Bill said, hoping to reassure his friend. "They'll be okay. She'll be okay."

Stetson knew that Gesling and Childers were friends as well as colleagues. He was getting to know Childers, but he wasn't likely to ever get into the man's inner circle where Gesling resided. Only going together through the hard knocks of growing a business, being "in the trenches" together could grow the camaraderie that these two men shared. Stetson knew that he had to try and get his friend to think of something other than his critically injured wife, if that were even possible. Looking out the port at the black sky and the eternal gray sphere that was the Moon, he tried feverishly to come up with something to say that would change the subject, even if it were only for a brief few minutes.

"Wow, wouldya just look at that?" Finally, Stetson broke the silence, "Look at the Earth. Isn't it beautiful? I never get tired of looking at it. And from here you can see the whole sphere."

"No political boundaries visible from up here."

"It's hard to believe there are now over seven billion people. When I was a boy, there were fewer than four billion and we wondered then how we were going to feed them all." Stetson pursed his lips and continued, "But we managed. And now there are that many people in the middle class alone. Yep, it's a better time to be on Earth now than at any time in human history."

"But for how long? Four billion people consuming resources at the same rate as three hundred million Americans doesn't seem sustainable. And it isn't. Look at Africa. The South African War has been raging for nearly three years with no end in sight. Both sides are just proxies for the Chinese and the West, each backing their favorite dictators and warlords just because they want the mineral rights if their side is victorious." Gesling's mood was certainly sour. But Bill understood. If somebody had told him that a maniac shot his wife he'd be in an equal or worse fugue.

"Paul, I know you are worried, but I've never heard you be this pessimistic. I just can't believe you buy that 'limits to growth' crap. Look where you are. You're in space, where the resources are unlimited. There are more minerals on the Moon and in near Earth asteroids than there are accessible on Earth. That's why those space mining companies are coming to

Mr. Childers to build them their habitats. They have to have a place for their miners to live when they're out here getting the mineral resources ready to be sent back to Earth. Pretty soon those African warlords will look around and see that no one is backing them anymore because it's easier and more ethical to get the same resources from up here."

"Bill, do you honestly believe we can mine the asteroids on a scale that will make any difference? Right now that seems like it is millions of years away—science fiction. It can't be cost effective with today's technology."

"Yes, yes, I do." Stetson didn't blink. "And I also know that when Japan finishes their prototype space solar power station and starts beaming clean, zero greenhouse-gas emission power back to their resource-starved island that other countries will take notice and start building their own power stations. I'm angry that the first one will be Japanese and not American. But, hey, as long as someone is building it, that's just fine by me."

"Space solar power. I still don't buy it being cost effective. Or safe, for that matter. But who the hell knows? Cost effective or not, Carolyn would've loved to write the press release for something like that," Gesling said with an even darker tone.

"Stop talking like that!" barked Stetson, incensed that his friend was talking of his wife in the past tense. "She'll write press releases for things more exciting than that—like the first trip to Mars in a few years. She's alive and in the care of some of the best trauma surgeons in the country. They'll pull her through... and Mr. Childers to boot."

As if on cue, the radio beeped to alert them that someone from back home in Nevada wanted to have a conversation. Thus far, all of their musings had been made with the radio muted and all recording devices on the ship purposefully turned off. Bill had insisted on it. Gesling remained fixated on the view through the port while Stetson reacted to the signal and turned on the ship's radio. Stetson knew that his friend wouldn't be up for talking unless there was news about his wife.

"Stetson here, what's up?"

"Bill, we have some news. Gary Childers is out of surgery and it looks like he'll make it. One of the bullets shattered a bone in his leg and the other passed clean through his body without hitting a vital organ. He suffered a great deal of blood loss, but not enough to do any permanent damage. Fortunately, whoever the sniper was wasn't a very good shot."

"That's great news, but what about Carolyn? What do you know about her situation?"

"Carolyn is still in surgery and we don't know anything other than that she's alive and in the operating room. No word yet on the shooter either. The news reports say that whoever did it covered their tracks really well. We'll call back when we know something."

"Sounds good, out." With that, Stetson again turned off the radio, not wanting the ground crew or anyone else to hear the private conversation between him and Paul. That just wouldn't be *right*.

CHAPTER 4

USING THE GIFT GIVEN TO HUMANITY BY THE TWEN-
tieth-century Prometheuses who inhabited the Oak
Ridge and Los Alamos National Laboratories in the
1940s, the liquid hydrogen propellant flowed through
the core of the nuclear thermal rocket engine, heating
it to over twelve hundred degrees Celsius and giving
the unmanned stage a kick as it then accelerated out of
Earth orbit and into interplanetary space. There was no
smoke, not just because there was no air, but because
the heated hydrogen wasn't combusting at all. It had
merely been superheated in order to create an overpressure inside the rocket engine's "combustion chamber"
which wasn't really a combustion chamber at all. And
then the overpressured hydrogen gas was accelerated
due to the laws of fluid flow and thermodynamics down
a converging nozzle to a small opening that rocket scientists called the "throat" where it reached supersonic
flow speeds. From there the gas continued to accelerate out a diverging nozzle into space. At no point was
a detonation, deflagration, or combustion exothermic

reaction required. The nuclear core was simply there to heat up a liquid and turn it into hot gas just as it would if it were in a power plant back on Earth. But instead of using the hot gas to turn a turbine and generate electricity, this reactor was heating propellant to provide propulsion at twice the efficiency of any conventional chemical rocket, including even the most efficient and effective combustion based rocket engines ever built before such as the Space Shuttle Main Engines and the F1s of the Saturn V era.

No, this rocket wasn't like most of its ancestors. Instead of heating and expelling fuel through burning, it was being heated to much higher temperatures by the energy released from the splitting of uranium atoms in the core of the ship's engines. First conceived and tested by the United States in the 1960s, Nuclear Thermal Rockets required only half the fuel to get the same performance as chemical rockets. This was the breakthrough that was going to allow humans to make the journey to Mars affordably and the flight was scheduled to begin two years hence.

Launched into space by NASA's heavy lift rocket, the nuclear stage was designed to operate only once it was in space. The risks of using nuclear energy to launch rockets from the surface of the Earth was simply too great, or perceived to be, for anyone to suggest.

The news that the engine had started was greeted by shouts and cheers of joy in Mission Control, still located at the Johnson Space Center in Texas. While it was greeted by cheers, they were mostly preceded by the sound of people breathing after holding their breath too long in the adjunct control center at the Marshall Space Flight Center in Huntsville, Alabama. It was there that the engine was designed and no group of people could be happier that it worked. They knew all that could go wrong, the things they'd tried to design to mitigate, and sometimes knowledge can cause one to be pessimistic. Pessimism, and its cousin, Murphy, of Murphy's Law, were not around. The engines performed as designed and they worked flawlessly.

"Hot damn!" Exclaimed the Marshall Chief Engineer, Paula Downey. Downey was a graduate of Stanford and had worked for NASA nearly all of her twenty-five-year career. She'd cut her teeth working on new space propulsion technologies back in the early 2000s and quickly proved to her peers and to senior management that she knew her engineering and was better than most at getting to the root cause of many engineering problems encountered in "rocket science."

Downey began walking around the room, shaking hands, slapping backs and even hugging some of the engineers in the room who'd worked on the nuclear rocket project for these last several years. This was one of the reasons she was not only respected, for her engineering talents, but actually liked by her peers. She was a people person and knew how to relate to the many personality types that made up the workforce of NASA. It didn't hurt that, at age fifty, she was still a beautiful woman with a figure that turned heads when she walked through a room. Her black hair was salted with grey and no one really cared if that was its natural color. She was a pleasure to see, to talk to, and to work with.

"Paula, I guess this means that we're a go for Mars?" asked Dean Epperson, one of the systems engineers on the team.

"Dean, I guess it does. If the habitat and the lander

teams can meet their testing milestones like this team did, we'll be launching to Mars in just under two years."

"I never thought I'd see the day," he replied. "It seems like every time we think we're going somewhere, the politicians or the bean counters pull the rug out from under us."

"Let's hope that doesn't happen this time," she said with a false and overly emphasized frown. "There's too much at stake. Now that the Europeans, the Japanese, and the Chinese have signed on, I don't think that even the upcoming presidential election will be able to slow us down."

"Don't say that! I was here when the shuttles stopped flying and the program to replace them was temporarily shut down. If you'd told me then that we'd be testing the systems to go to Mars, I'd think you were nuts. Never forget that we're a political agency and all it'll take to shut us down is one anti-space person in the White House."

"That's a good point, but this time I think we'll make the transition. We've got the support of both parties in the Senate—strong support, I might add. It helps when you have former astronauts in each party handing the chairmanship of the Appropriations Committee back and forth every time the Senate changes hands. I don't mean to sound patronizing, but I think we've got it covered."

"I guess you're right. Good thing I'm a test engineer and not a manager. I don't see how you can stand it," Dean said, looking somewhat like a dog with his tail between his legs.

"I know I'm right." She smiled and replied, "That's why I'm paid the big bucks."

CHAPTER 5

IT WAS DIFFICULT FOR CEO ANACLETO ROSALEZ TO contain his excitement. Rosalez, called AR by his family and close personal friends, watched the launch of the Ariane V rocket take his baby, the spacecraft and payload he'd been working on for almost a decade, into the clear blue sky from the Guiana Space Centre near Kourou, French Guiana. The Ariane, towering over one hundred fifty feet tall as it blasted into the sky using its cryogenic main engines and environmentally unfriendly solid-fuel rocket motors, was the workhorse rocket of the European Space Agency and the industries in Europe that needed access to space. Ariane had proven itself to be a very capable and reliable rocket, and its predominantly French operators had shown themselves to be equally reliable and, in this instance, discreet.

Rosalez was CEO or on the board for multiple companies and his personal wealth was estimated at over five billion dollars, making him a rival of the wealthiest men in Silicon Valley, Shanghai, and

Dubai. Today, he was enduring the heat in coastal French Guiana to see the launch into space of his latest project. A project that, if successful, would change forever the way Europe viewed itself as a world power, how people on Earth viewed the use of space, and how his investors would feel about their ten-year, high-risk investment paying off. The spacecraft on the rocket belonged to Asteroid Ores, Inc., and he was not only the company's CEO, but also its number one shareholder.

"Monsieur Rosalez, the controllers are telling me that the rocket is working perfectly and that we should be off and on our way within the hour," said his personal assistant, Maurice Aubuchon. Maurice was very French, speaking in English only when the job required him to do so—as it did here when he was speaking with his boss. Rosalez, being Spanish, spoke English as his second language. Which, unfortunately for both of them, meant that they would have to communicate with each other speaking that language that most Europeans quite object to having become the world's *lingua franca*—English. Despite their preferences for their respective native tongues, both spoke English rather well.

"Maurice, can you believe we're almost there? Once we get into space and on our way, it'll only be another year before we start mining and selling almost ten thousand tons of platinum, let alone the literal mountains of other elements that'll come back with it. Even with the inevitable drop in prices that'll come with us flooding the market with the stuff, we'll be able to return our investors' money a thousand times."

That put a smile on the otherwise always-worried Maurice's face.

"You make it sound so easy. There's a lot that has to happen between now and then before we can start building that platinum-fueled vacation villa in Hawaii. The spacecraft has to separate from the rocket and get itself out of Earth orbit, coast for nine months and then dock with asteroid 2018HM5. And that doesn't even take into account the maneuvers required to stop the asteroid from spinning and getting its orbit changed to include the Moon at perihelion."

"Maurice, you worry too much. But then again, that's why I hired you—to worry so I won't have to. I'm sure you have things well under your control." Rosalez smiled as he made the comment, quite sure that his assistant had matters as under control as was humanly possible and equally sure that Maurice didn't believe that he did. Maurice was borderline obsessive compulsive and that was a trait that Rosalez needed in the person running the asteroid mining operation. It was rocket science, after all, and how anyone in the space business could survive without being or having access to someone with obsessive compulsive disorder was a mystery to him. Plus, it was just plain fun to tweak Maurice and make him nervous—something Rosalez did with alacrity.

The rocket was now completely out of Rosalez's sight and from what he knew of the mission profile, the spacecraft that would soon make him and his company a household name, was about to separate from the rocket and ignite its electric propulsion system so that it could reach the target asteroid on only one tank of fuel.

As Rosalez gazed wistfully at the rocket plume that was now being dissipated by the winds blowing off the Atlantic Ocean, he noticed out of the corner of his eye that another of his staff was approaching, the only Brit on the team, Jonathan Price. Price was his attorney. Rosalez wouldn't have ordinarily thought it important to have his personal attorney at the launch site, but this was a far from ordinary day.

"Monsieur Rosalez, may I have a word with you?" Asked Price. Like Maurice, he looked worried. For Price, this was unusual, though not unprecedented.

"Certainly, Jonathan. Maurice and I were just enjoying the moment. Well, one of us was anyway," Rosalez replied, hoping that he was overheard by Maurice. He noted that Maurice grunted quietly when he heard the remark, which meant he had been overheard.

"Monsieur Rosalez, now that the rocket is on its way, we need to come clean about what we're doing." Price was young and, according to conventional wisdom, might grow into a great attorney someday once he had some experience. Today, however, he sounded a lot like Rosalez's assistant, Maurice. He wondered if they'd been talking among themselves and quickly dismissed the thought. It didn't matter. This was not a new issue for Jonathan to raise; it was just an annoying one.

"Yes, yes, I know. We need to tell the world about our company, the rocket launch and our plan to divert an asteroid so that we can mine it. You've been telling me that for years, Jonathan."

"Yes, Monsieur Rosalez, I have been saying for years that we need to make our plans public. We've followed every applicable law and made sure we're not violating any space treaty, but nonetheless, we need to let the world know what we've done and what we're about to do. We're not only launching a rocket into space, but we're launching a rocket that will alter the trajectory of an asteroid and place it on a near-Earth orbit. That might make a few people more than a little nervous, and if I didn't know the people in this company and the lengths you've gone to make sure this all goes correctly, I would be nervous as well."

"Alright, alright already. We'll issue the press release tonight after the spacecraft successfully starts its engines and is on its way to 2018HM5. I know you've already had a chance to review it; are there any last-minute changes we need to make?"

"None. I've been reviewing it almost daily, hoping that you'd go public sooner and I wanted to make sure I was ready when you did. It's good to go."

"I was rather hoping that we could dispense with the boring '2018HM5' moniker and use the name I proposed to the International Astronomical Union. Have you heard from them?"

"No. Not a word since we submitted the paperwork last March."

"No matter, get the press release ready to go and hit send at six o'clock this evening. That way we'll inform the world of what we're doing on the same day we launched and began escaping Earth orbit so no one will be able to stop us, especially those tree huggers in Brussels."

"Yes, sir," said Price as he walked away from Rosalez and back toward the air-conditioned control room.

Rosalez was sweating, yet he didn't seem to notice it until now. The excitement of seeing the rocket launch and his dreams finally starting to be fulfilled had caused him to totally ignore his own physical discomfort. He resumed speaking, this time to himself, out loud, but without anyone else being close enough to overhear.

"Sutter's Mill. I really wanted to be able to call it Sutter's Mill." Rosalez was an American history buff. Because of this, he had long ago decided to call the asteroid they were going to mine Sutter's Mill in honor of the discovery of gold in California's Sierra Madre mountains near Sutter's Mill that spawned the gold rush of the 1840s. He, too, dreamed of starting a gold rush of sorts—this time leading to the capability of humanity settling the solar system by tapping the nearly infinite resources of space beyond mother Earth. He'd dreamed of this since he was a kid and was now using his fortune to make it happen.

Time until Asteroid 2018HM5 "Sutter's Mill" reaches near Earth: 609 days.

CHAPTER 6

PAUL GESLING AND BILL STETSON WERE ON THEIR final approach to the Space Excursions Nevada spaceport three days after they departed from the Moon. Despite Gesling's precarious mental state, being extremely preoccupied and worried about his wife's health after being shot, the flight controllers allowed him to pilot the *Dreamscape* back to the ground from interplanetary space. Stetson, having trained for most of his career with NASA prior to joining Space Excursions, was on standby to take the stick and land the craft if he or anyone in the control room had been concerned about Gesling's ability to perform the job. Truth be told, the ship's autopilot could have controlled the landing without any human input. Machines may not yet have been intelligent, but they were certainly capable of doing jobs like this extremely well.

The *Dreamscape*, a reusable winged spacecraft, was able to land at the Nevada facility with little fanfare. Landing and taking off, it resembled a conventional jet airplane. After attaining some altitude, the resemblance to a jet became vanishingly small as the ship's hypersonic scramjet engines propelled it to several times the speed of sound and the aft rocket engine kicked in to give the ship the final acceleration it needed to attain Earth orbit. On this trip, the *Dreamscape* arrived on a trajectory from the Moon that shot it directly into the atmosphere, allowing it to use friction to slow down and bleed off energy rapidly. The thermal protection system on the bottom of the craft glowed brightly and created a shell of ionized particles around the vehicle that prevented conventional radio transmissions from working at this critical time. After reaching subsonic speeds, the *Dreamscape* again resembled an airplane as it made its final approach for landing.

On schedule, and after the transition to subsonic, the landing gear on the *Dreamscape* deployed. Despite his worry and concern for his wife, Paul Gesling was in his element as he controlled the ship in its final moments of flight. The blackness of space was behind them and the beautiful blue of the Earth's atmosphere was ahead. Below was the eternal brown of the Nevada desert and to both Gesling and Stetson, under the circumstances, it was time to be home.

Moments later the landing gear made contact with the runway and the *Dreamscape* was home.

The irony of his and Stetson's safe return from the Moon was not lost on Gesling as they rapidly worked through their checklists so they could soon disembark from the *Dreamscape* and get to the hospital. If anyone had asked who would be at greater risk of death at the beginning to the mission just barely a week before, who would have considered Carolyn to be the one at risk? Everyone thought Paul was the one who would be more likely to die. Everyone, except, of course, the shooter. Gesling had been wondering for days if the police had any leads or had perhaps already captured the shooter.

The ground crew, led by Hami Kunda, met Stetson and Gesling as they opened the door and came down the stairs that had been rolled up to the front side door of the *Dreamscape*.

"Hami, is there any news about my wife or Mr. Childers?" asked Paul as he rushed down the stairs and started walking toward the waiting SUV that he had been told would take him to the hospital to visit his wife for the first time since the shooting. Gesling knew that Hami had been at the scene of the shooting and was thankful that it was he who had been in the ground crew and designated to meet and take him to the airport.

"Paul, there's been no change. Carolyn is still unconscious, but her overall status appears to be stable. Mr. Childers is awake, eating and generally making a nuisance of himself," Hami replied.

Kunda and Gesling got into the SUV while Stetson hung back.

"Are you coming, Bill?" asked Gesling.

"No, not yet. One of us has to work the paperwork and make sure the ship is properly stored for the next time. I'll do that and then come down to the hospital later. Okay?"

"Okay by me," Paul replied.

He quickly got into the vehicle and closed the door. But he didn't do it so quickly as to avoid looking and marveling at the beauty of the *Dreamscape*.

"Look at her," he muttered to himself. "She's a

beauty and I am going to take my wife with me to space in her before this is all said and done. Carolyn, I promise you that."

REUTERS—PRIVATE COMPANY LAUNCHES CRAFT TO DIVERT ASTEROID FOR MINING

(KOUROU, FRENCH GUIANA) *The European company, Asteroid Ores, Inc., today launched a spaceship that will divert an asteroid so as to allow it to be mined, company executives announced today. The asteroid, designated 2018 HM5, is thought to contain thousands of tons of rare elements, including platinum, and weighs well over two billion tons. Once the asteroid is in its new orbit, the company has a fleet of robotic miners it plans to launch in order to extract the platinum and other elements for a return to Earth and the commercial market. The company's CEO, Anacleto Rosalez, says the company's long-term strategy is to "make space mined minerals price competitive to those mined on Earth" so as to make them a "viable alternative to mining techniques that are destroying the planet."*

CHAPTER 7

GARY CHILDERS WAS BACK IN HIS LEXINGTON OFFICES for the first time since the shooting. Though still walking with a cane, to the staff around him he looked fit and ready to resume most of his day to day duties running his coal company and Space Excursions. The bullet had shattered a bone and almost caused him to bleed out. Had his bodyguard not thrown himself in the way of the succeeding bullets, Childers would almost certainly be dead. Childers felt terrible that Max had sacrificed his own life in order to save his, and that was why he'd set up a fund that would take care of Max's wife and children for the rest of their lives. It wouldn't replace Max, but it would at least minimize the economic pain that accompanies losing a parent and a spouse.

He was working at his desk when the door to his office opened, admitting both Paul Gesling and Bill Stetson. Stetson was wearing his usual cowboy hat—a Stetson, of course.

"Gary, we hope you don't mind us stopping by. We just left Carolyn at the nursing home and thought we'd check on you while we were out," Stetson said as they entered.

"Not a problem. Come on in and take a seat."

"Thanks."

"How is Carolyn? Any change?" Childers intentionally addressed the question to Gesling, who looked like he could use some engagement.

"Well, she's still unconscious. She hasn't regained consciousness since the shooting. The doctors did say that the brain swelling caused by her head hitting the pavement has mostly gone away, but they can't say when or if she'll wake up," Gesling said.

"They also said that her lung is healing nicely. She's a strong woman and the bullet wound doesn't appear to have caused permanent physical damage," Stetson added, removing his hat.

"Well, that's some good news anyway," Childers said, pausing only briefly before continuing, "The police don't have a clue about the shooter. They found some evidence that whoever it was used the top of the McAlister Building while they waited for me to come out the front door. The shooter didn't leave much to be found. The police have advised me to take extra precautions in case he tries again. I'm already tired of getting in and out of cars in garages and behind a wall of body guards. But until the guy's caught, I guess I'm stuck."

Sensing that they needed to change the topic of conversation, Childers continued, "Bill, we just signed a contract with Asteroid Ores to provide them with the space habitats that'll house their astronauts as they begin mining the rock they're bringing back."

"Well, that's good news. They've been so secretive

that I kind of thought they would try to do it all themselves. Are we going to sell them a variant of the orbital hotel?"

"They've got some unique requirements, but I think our Mod #2 can meet most of their needs. They're offering a good price."

"I have to admit I was stunned to learn of their plans for the rock. I'm a big believer in us eventually mining asteroids, but the speed at which they're moving almost makes my head spin. They came from nowhere with that launch of theirs. How did they keep what they were doing such a secret?" Stetson said.

"Bill, I've known Anacleto Rosalez for years and I knew he was up to something big, but even I didn't know that it would be asteroid mining. There have been many companies come and gone promising a big return from mining the asteroids, but until now they've all failed. It's an expensive, time-consuming and risky business proposition. Most public companies don't have the stomach for a ten-year investment without any returns. That's why only humble billionaires like me can make things like this happen. We don't have to answer to anyone other than ourselves if we fail."

REUTERS—ASTEROID MINING COMPANY ANNOUNCES SPACE MILESTONE

(MADRID, SPAIN) *Asteroid Ores, Inc., the company that two months ago launched a super-secret ship to rendezvous with an asteroid for future mining, announced today that they have achieved a milestone in their project with the robotic craft successfully attaching itself to the asteroid. The company CEO, Anacleto Rosalez, told Reuters "Today we successfully guided our robotic prospector to the surface of the Sutter's Mill asteroid and attached to it, meeting one of the key success criteria for the mission." According to Rosalez, the next step will be for the spaceship to use its super-efficient electric rocket engines to nudge the asteroid from its current orbit into one that will take it to an orbit around the Moon where Asteroid Ores can send future ships to mine it for rare metals, including platinum.*

Their plans are not without opposition from the European Parliament, however. Delegates from Mr. Rosalez's home country of Spain have joined several other European nations in calling for an international treaty to ban asteroid mining by private companies since the resources of the solar system are considered the "common heritage of all humankind" by previous international agreements. To date, only Germany and France appear to oppose the call for the treaty from within Europe. The United States has made it known that it would also oppose such a treaty on the grounds that it would wreck the emerging economies within near-Earth space. A spokesman from the US State Department defined the space economy to include numerous commercial and governmental satellites in Earth orbit as well as space tourism.

CHAPTER 8

ELECTRIC ROCKETS LOOK FUTURISTIC, LIKE AN advanced space propulsion system should. As the xenon gas fuel is stripped of its outer electron and accelerated toward the rocket's exhaust by carefully designed electric and magnetic fields, the entire engine emits a brilliant blue glow. There is none of the fire and smoke that would be seen from some conventional chemical rocket engines. Chemical rockets are a brute force approach to moving things around in space and the only realistic way to get off the surface of a planet, deep in a gravity well, and into space. But once you are in space, highly efficient electric rockets are an excellent alternative.

Chemical rockets produce all the thrust they're going to produce in their first few minutes of use by providing spectacular acceleration—the kind an astronaut can feel as he is pushed back into his seat while the rocket begins to speed up. Electric rockets produce a continuous, very small thrust that might not even be felt by a person. But it is a continuous thrust, and, given enough time, an electric rocket can accelerate a spacecraft to much higher speeds using only a fraction of the fuel required by a chemical rocket. Such was the case with the electric thrusters bound to the surface of the Sutter's Mill asteroid.

The gentle push began as soon as the thrusters were turned on. Sutter's Mill, which would weigh just over two billion tons on Earth, didn't have any weight in space. It still had mass, so it still required a significant total force in order to alter its motion so that it would go where the mission planners from Asteroid Ores wanted it to go. The entire operation was similar to a swimmer pushing a barge off its original course. A single swimmer couldn't make any abrupt changes to the course of a multiton ship. But if that swimmer could swim sideways into the barge for a very long time, then the barge would drift slowly onto a different path.

The electric thrusters were designed to operate continuously for the entire two years it would take to nudge the massive rock from its current course to one that would make it accessible for Earth-based miners to exploit, including an Earth flyby in just another eleven months. With each day of operation, the asteroid would be on a slightly different course on its billion-year journey around the Sun. To bring it where its operators wanted it to be, two full years of thrusting would be required.

Bill Stetson and his wife Rebecca had just enjoyed a rare weekend away at Galveston Island as they pulled into the driveway of their modest suburban home in the Houston suburbs near Clear Lake. Though Stetson no longer worked for NASA, he still considered Houston to be his home.

"Too many good memories were made here to sell it and move," he told her as he patted her thigh lightly and ended it with a gentle squeeze. Bill had often told himself and his family that very same statement word for word. In fact, she was pretty sure he had said it every single time that she had suggested to him that they move closer to either Nevada or Kentucky for better proximity to his new employer, Space Excursions. For whatever reason, she could never convince him that they should move. She smiled inwardly, thinking of just how set in his ways her husband was. Her wonderfully heroic husband who had walked on the Moon and flown into space on countless occasions.

Their home was built in the 1990s and had all the hallmarks of a suburban "McMansion" that seemed to dominate construction in that era. It was all brick with a roofline broken by many separate gables and lots of skylights. Next to the road sat a mailbox made from matching brick with a simple name plate that said, "Stetson." Rebecca had suggested they do something more to the mailbox like putting a rocket or something on it. But Bill had always rejected doing anything much different than the others in the neighborhood. Bill was a humble man and didn't care much for showing off.

The sun was about to set as Bill pulled the car into the driveway. The secure proximity sensor in the garage had already sensed that the car was approaching and the garage door was therefore already on its way up as they approached. While Bill wasn't much for showing off, he was certainly one for having the latest gadgets. Since their children had long since moved out of the house, and with only the two of them making the trip, there weren't too many bags to be unloaded after their weekend away.

"I set the alarm for while we were gone," he said and nodded to the system's keypad on the garage wall. The little off-white keypad's secure light was glowing a steady red color, meaning that it had not been triggered in their absence. Becca didn't really give it any further thought. As far as she knew nobody had been robbed in their neighborhood as long as they had lived there. And they had lived there a really long time.

"Bec, I've got the bags. Can you get the mail?" Bill asked her.

"Sure," Rebecca smiled at her husband and then turned and walked to the mailbox. On her way to the box, she was distracted by their next-door neighbor, Denise, who was leaving her house, Irish Setter in tow. Denise often took evening walks with her dog and this evening looked to be no different. She and Rebecca had chatted at the end of the driveway on countless occasions but they were just neighbors, not seriously close friends.

Rebecca stopped short of the mailbox, standing to its side, so that she could chat with Denise without the bulk of the mailbox being between them. Luckily for her, this meant that the bulk of the massive brick mailbox was between her and the aluminum front door of the box as she opened it. Had she been standing in front of it, the explosion that sent densely packed ball bearings and nails would most likely have killed her. Instead, the shrapnel from the bomb that was triggered by the door opening tore into her left hand, nearly severing it, and sent the bricks surrounding it outward—knocking her to the ground and burying her legs and feet under a pile of mortar and shattered masonry. A dust cloud of powdered mortar mixed with dust and brick settled about the destruction. Rebecca was stunned and the world seemed to be moving in a strange swimming and blurry slow motion to her. Voices and sounds were nonexistent. The only thing she could hear was her heartbeat pounding like a big bass drum inside her head and chest. She watched red blood spurt from what was left of her hand with each pounding of the drum. Her head fell more than turned to the side and she could see Denise holding her ears and screaming in terror. Still there was no sound. Nothing but the pounding drum in her head and chest. Rebecca was most certainly in shock and was losing blood very fast. Her mind drifted even deeper into the surreal swimming slow reality around her.

As far as Becca could grasp, Denise and her dog were only momentarily deafened by the blast, the shock of which had caused Denise to loosen her grip on the dog's leash, setting the dog free. Rather than run away, the dog immediately began barking and then sat by her side looking feral and protective of his mistress. Rebecca thought to herself that he was such a good dog. But the thought faded as a shadow blotted out the sun above her and then lowered over her. Consciousness drifted away from her.

Stetson heard the explosion from inside the garage. He dropped the bags he was carrying and ran to the street, only to see a cloud of smoke and the remains of his mailbox collapsed on top of his wife's body. His heart nearly stopped as he assessed the scene and then began running toward her, hoping and praying that she was all right.

"Becca?!" he shouted. "Honey, are you all right?"

Stetson kneeled beside his wife and turned pale when he saw the blood squirting from her hand with each beat of her diminishing pulse. He understood almost immediately that she was bleeding out.

"Hold on, Bec!" he shouted as he yanked his belt free from his pants. Bill quickly slipped the belt around his wife's wrist and fumbled nervously with the buckle for a second or two. "Get a grip on yourself, Stetson. Stay calm and focus."

Bill took a deep breath just as he would in any flying emergency and then calmed his mind. He slipped the belt through the buckle and pulled it tight until the bleeding went from gushing to a slight trickle with each pulsing of her heart. His own heart was racing. He pulled his outer shirt off over his head, not worrying about the buttons. Then he slipped his undershirt off quickly and started to carefully wrap it around his wife's mangled limb.

"Hang in there sweetheart," he said fumbling through his pocket for his cell phone. He calmly but quickly dialed 911. He held the T-shirt firmly in place around her hand as it became soaked red with his wife's blood.

Paul Gesling was having dinner with Gary Childers at his Lexington home. Childers was dining weekly with Paul and had done so since the shooting. The meals weren't strictly social, with Gary Childers there was no distinction between "shop talk" and casual conversation. He lived for his work and his work defined his life. Until the shooting, Childers would have assumed the same was true for Gesling, but not now. Gesling was clearly in mourning for his wife, now in a coma for well over two months, although the doctors were saying that she could wake up at any time.

Intentionally avoiding any mention of the shooting or Carolyn O'Connor-Gesling, Childers and Gesling were engaged in a discussion about all that was happening within Space Excursions.

"I'm telling you they'll love it and not really care that they're sleeping in a hammock. They'll be on the Moon, for God's sake." On this point, Paul was passionate. He'd been there. He'd experienced the thrill at being on the surface of another world and he knew that people would pay a lot of money to have the same experience.

"I'm sure you are right, but I just can't help but think we need to start planning to bring more conventional bedding. There are customers who are telling me they plan to do more than sleep while they are there, if you catch my meaning."

"Well, yeah, sure. Who wouldn't want to screw on the Moon? But I wouldn't worry about the logistics and expense of sending beds. Those who want to do some lunar hanky-panky can find some privacy in one of the curtained areas of the habitat and go at it. I'm sure one sixth gee will open up some innovative approaches to that sort of thing." Gesling came close to leering as he finished the thought.

"Well, if zero gee is any indication of libido, then I'll have to agree. Just last week, two of the guests in the What-A-View sneaked into the viewing cupola during the middle of the night shift to make love with the nearly full view of the Earth beneath them. They would've been fine if they hadn't forgotten that the only places in the hotel with complete privacy are in their sleeping areas. Once they moved from behind the curtain to the cupola, they were on camera and in view not only of our mission controllers but the webcam that's streaming for the entire world to see. It wouldn't have been so bad had they been young and beautiful movie stars out for a romp. That might have boosted bookings. But no, these two had certainly seen better days and we had viewers from all over the world asking us to shut off the camera feed before they became ill." With that, both men laughed.

"Gary, I hate to change the subject away from something as interesting as sex in space, but how is the NASA Deep Space Habitat progressing?"

"It's going well. It's mostly fabricated and going through quality inspection now. After the environmental testing, she'll be ready for launch. The Mars mission departure is only about six months away and they want all the hardware at the launch site four months out so they can begin the final integration into the launch vehicle," Childers said.

"I'm glad we're going to be part of the mission. I just wish Bill or I were on the crew."

"Paul, the work you're doing will open up space travel to far more people than NASA ever will. Yes, they'll get the glory for being the first to 'explore strange new worlds,' but it'll be us that bring those to follow."

"Speaking of which, have you thought about how busy space will be in half a year? We'll have two hotels in orbit and one on the Moon, all full of paying customers. NASA will be launching a crew to Mars and Asteroid Ores will have their rock halfway back. Not to mention the new Chinese and Russian lunar base," Gesling said with his characteristic zeal as he spoke.

"Yeah, I've thought about that. And I think..." Childers was interrupted by Gesling's phone vibrating and playing a tune he didn't recognize.

"It must be family or something about Carolyn. I have the phone set to send everyone else to messaging," Gesling said as he looked at the incoming message on his phone. He began to read the message and frowned.

"Damn! Someone just tried to kill Bill and his wife!"

"What? Are they okay?" asked Childers, nearly spilling his drink onto his plate as he heard the news.

"Yeah, well, no, not really. Bill's okay but his wife was nearly killed by some sort of bomb in his mailbox. She's lost her left hand and suffered some burns. They're at the Clear Lake Medical Center. He said he'd call with an update as soon as he knew more."

"Text him back. Tell him that we'll pay for whatever they need. I'll get my personal physician on a plane to Texas to advise and see if there any specialists we need to hire. And we need security there, now!" Gary slammed his fist against the table rattling the dishes and silverware.

"What is going on? Why would someone put a bomb in Bill's mailbox? It's got to be related to your shooting. It is too coincidental to be anything other than related." Gesling had gone from his stunned and emotional reaction at hearing the news to a more analytical mode.

"I fear you're correct. We have to assume that whoever tried to kill me also tried to kill Bill. Or at least harm him by killing his wife. They're still out there and until we know otherwise, no one working for me can be safe." Gary tapped away at his phone sending messages to his personal security teams.

"Has there been some sort of recent business deal that went bad? Do you have any enemies out there that might have gone over the edge like this?" Paul searched his memories for anything that might offer insight on what was happening.

"Not that I know of. But for someone to go after me and Bill, it's got to somehow be related to Space Excursions. I think there is no doubt about that now."

"I agree. But who?"

Childers pondered the question and replied, "And why? What could we possibly have done to cause someone to try and kill us?"

"Both attempts have resulted in innocent people being injured; first Carolyn and now Rebecca." Paul rubbed at his chin feeling the days' growth of whiskers there. "This person is sloppy or doesn't care who he hurts or how he hurts Space Excursions."

"We can't let that happen again. From now on, you, Bill, your families and all of my personal staff are going to have twenty-four-hour protection."

No longer hungry, both Childers and Gesling moved from the dining room table into the living room. Noticing the massive glass window on the front wall of the room, they silently stopped before crossing in front of it, wondering who might be on the other side looking in. Childers walked to the right side and pulled the curtains closed.

Time until Asteroid 2018HM5 "Sutter's Mill"
reaches near Earth: 338 days.

CHAPTER 9

THE ELECTRIC PROPULSION SYSTEM'S SMALL BUT relentless push on asteroid Sutter's Mill was slowly altering its trajectory. Had the high-voltage power supply that fed the thrusters not shorted out, there is no doubt they would have placed the rock on a path that would take it safely into a lunar orbit, making it accessible for Earth's resource-hungry population to mine. But the power supply did fail, and the beautiful blue glow of the thrusters winked out, stopping before the asteroid was placed in the desired orbit, leaving it on a path that no one had planned or even yet knew. But soon the smart people back on Earth would know where it was heading—and they would be terrified.

"Monsieur Rosalez, we have a problem," said Maurice Aubuchon, with his characteristic frown.

"What is the problem, Maurice?"

"The thrusters have shut down prematurely on the asteroid and we don't know why. They shut down late yesterday and we've been running diagnostics to try and find the cause. So far, we have not been successful."

"Well, keep troubleshooting and let me know when you figure something out."

"Yes, Monsieur, but there is another problem that you should know about."

"Another problem? What's that?"

"The astrodynamicists have been looking at the new trajectory of the asteroid. The one it was on when the thrusters failed. It doesn't look good."

"It doesn't look good? I would imagine not. Those thrusters were supposed to run another few months to put it on a trajectory that would make it accessible for us to mine. Other than costing me hundreds of millions of Euros to build and perhaps costing me billions of Euros in lost revenue, what else could be 'not good?'" Rosalez asked, now sounding more irritated.

"They think the asteroid is now on a collision course with the Earth . . ." Maurice let the final words of the sentence trail off, as if he were hoping they would not be true if he didn't say them loudly.

"What? Are they sure? How can that be? I thought we'd shown that the new trajectory would pose no risk of an impact."

"We did show that; if the system had remained on and functional, we are certain the new trajectory posed no risk to the planet. But they shut down prematurely and, well, now it looks like we have a big problem."

"Oh. My. God. Don't tell anyone about this until we're sure about the analysis. Let me talk to the people who made the calculation and get them someone to double check their results."

"Yes, sir. Right away. We'll have them ready to speak to you about their calculations within the hour," Maurice stammered as he hurried off.

"Great. Just great. Not only will I lose billions, but I might be responsible for killing millions of people if this thing hits..." Had anyone been looking at the dark-skinned Rosalez, they would have seen him turn distinctly pale.

Time until Asteroid 2018HM5 "Sutter's Mill" reaches Earth: 271 days.

CHAPTER 10

THE NINTH-FLOOR CONFERENCE ROOM AT NASA Headquarters in Washington, DC was filling up fast. The main event, Vice-President Alexa Faulkner, hadn't yet arrived, but even without her, the room was filled with enough "important people" to make even the most jaded of the Washington cocktail party scene take notice.

Gary Childers was used to being around the wealthy and connected, but this, he thought, was *ridiculous*. He saw at least five senators, the presidents of Boeing, Northrop Grumman, and Lockheed-Martin, as well as several other major aerospace companies. Settling in at the head table were a group of nervous-looking men and women with touchpads who looked totally out of place compared to the others assembled in the room. *Must be scientists or engineers*, he thought.

Childers had received an invitation to the meeting only three days before, in the form of a personal call from the NASA administrator, no less. All she would say was that there was a "situation" that required his expertise and that there would be a meeting in Washington during which she would explain. He was even promised reimbursement for his travel expenses, as if he cared. He was clueless about the topic, but he could tell it was important by looking around at his peers. That, and the fact that everyone in the room except the scientists at the table had been asked to leave their electronics at the door.

Vice President Faulkner walked briskly into the room, accompanied by NASA Administrator Tara Reese-Walker. The women were engaged in lively conversation as they approached the podium, with Reese-Walker only briefly introducing Vice President Faulkner and taking a seat on the front row.

"Ladies and Gentlemen, thank you for adjusting your very busy schedules to join us here today. This meeting was called at the request of the president and he's asked me to personally lead the effort I'm about to describe. I realize many of you, though not all, have security clearances of various levels. Today you are going to be briefed on a national security situation and my handlers have asked me to ask if anyone in the room objects to being bound by national security regulations, under penalty of fine and jail, for revealing what is about to be discussed. If so, then you are free to leave. All who remain are implicitly accepting these conditions." She paused for effect and scanned the room to see if anyone would get up and leave. None did.

"Very good. What we have is a national, dare I say, global emergency. As you may be aware, several months ago the company Asteroid Ores launched a spacecraft to rendezvous with an asteroid now called

Sutter's Mill with the intent of diverting its course through space so as to bring it back to the Earth for mining purposes. According to the company, the mission was all going according to plan until their propulsion system stopped functioning late last week. It was supposed to continue operating for another several months in order to place the asteroid in a safe lunar orbit. When the propulsion system stopped working, the Asteroid Ores team did all they could do to get it working again—without success. When their analysts looked at how much they'd already altered the asteroid's path before the system failed, they discovered that the two-billion-ton asteroid is on a collision course with Earth. It will impact in just under eight months."

The room was so quiet that Childers could hear the person next to him breathing.

"Administrator Reese-Walker, can you inform the group what the effects of the impact are likely to be?"

"Yes, Madame Vice President. Ladies and Gentlemen, the experts tell me that the Sutter's Mill asteroid will enter the atmosphere at seventeen kilometers per second, roughly fifty times the speed of sound. It should begin to break up in the atmosphere at an altitude of about fifty-four kilometers, assuring that it will reach the ground in multiple pieces, each still traveling at about sixteen kilometers per second. The combined energy at impact of the fragments will total about fifty thousand megatons. That's about one thousand times more energy than the most powerful hydrogen bomb ever tested. If it hits land, then, at a minimum, it will make a crater fourteen kilometers across and half a kilometer deep. Those five hundred kilometers away will feel an earthquake of magnitude seven point eight on the Richter Scale and be pelted with ejecta from the impact. Those that are within one hundred kilometers will momentarily see a fireball twenty-five times larger than the Sun—before their clothing ignites and they die. If it strikes water, the resultant tsunami will be between twenty and two hundred meters in height. High enough to wipe out complete cities along the coastlines of whatever body of water it strikes. And the experts in this field tend to argue about what the longer-lasting impact on humanity will be. Needless to say, things will be bad on the scale of apocalyptic."

The stunned silence in the room quickly gave way to chatter as participants talked to themselves and each other about what they'd just heard. Childers remained silent.

"Now, let's dispense with the Hollywood theatrics. We don't have Bruce Willis waiting in the wings with a super-shuttle and a hydrogen bomb ready to go and blast this rock to smithereens. Though using nuclear weapons to divert it is an option that remains on the table. We also need to let everyone know this is not, I repeat, is not an Extinction Level Event. If it hits, then millions of people will die. Millions. There will be long-term implications to mankind. But it won't wreck the entire planet and people will survive," Reese-Walker continued.

"The next thing I need to dispel is the belief that someone in the government has the responsibility for this sort of thing. No one does. No organization wanted the job of protecting the planet because they knew that no new money would come with the added responsibility. NASA's Office of Planetary Protection is only chartered to consider biological cross contamination, not diverting asteroids. No one in DoD or at DARPA has the job either. All we've been funded to do over the last few years is to identify and track new asteroids. Period. Now, there are some bright people here and across the world who have done some thinking about the problem on their own time and they've already come up with what we believe is a workable solution. One that has a chance of avoiding catastrophe."

Reese-Walker looked around the room, making eye contact with some key people she apparently recognized, including Childers.

So why are we here? Childers thought to himself.

As if reading his mind, she continued, "You're here because you or your organization has critical hardware or skills that will be needed to divert the asteroid and prevent it from hitting in the first place. We have a plan and today we're asking you to help make it happen." She stopped and pointed to one of the men, a scientist type—with the requisite mustache and chin-only beard—sitting at the table. He arose and moved to the podium.

"Good morning, I'm Colin Dachwald. I'm a small-body scientist from the NASA Goddard Space Flight Center and it looks like I'm the one elected to fill you in on the plan that we think will keep the beast from hitting the Earth. This has come together rather fast, and I am sure there are holes, so please make notes and be ready to put us on the right track if need be."

"The key to diverting Sutter's Mill is to subtly change its trajectory. Most people incorrectly think that the rock is going to hit the Earth because it is aimed at us. They're wrong. It's going to hit the Earth because two bodies are going to occupy the same volume of space at the same time. That volume of space is currently empty. It's where the Earth will be in a few months as we travel around the Sun. It's also where Sutter's Mill will be at the exact same time, and that's the problem. To prevent the strike, we need to make sure Sutter's Mill passes through a slightly different volume of space than the Earth at that time so that we won't run into each other. Either that, or cause it to pass that point before or after we get there, which is much harder to do."

"Why not just blow it up?" asked one of the men seated near the front. Childers didn't know the man.

"A good question. First of all, Sutter's Mill is about two kilometers long and has a mass of over four billion metric tons. We don't have a bomb big enough to vaporize or even completely shatter something that big. If we were to try, we might just break the big rock into a few smaller rocks, all still headed on a collision course with Earth. So instead of the planet getting hit with a bullet, it would get hit with a shotgun blast, which might be just as bad or worse. That doesn't mean we couldn't use a nuclear weapon to divert it, however."

"I don't understand," said the man who asked the question.

"When a hydrogen bomb detonates on the Earth or in the atmosphere, most of the effects are caused by all that energy being deposited in the atmosphere. In space, the bomb would release neutrons and x-rays among other things, which would dramatically heat up the surface of the asteroid, causing some of the surface to boil off. The material that boils off would act like a rocket, with the ejecta going in one direction, pushing the rock in the other direction. It should work, but I would call it a last resort choice because of the possibility that it would shatter the rock into pieces."

"We don't have much time. The longer we delay in diverting the asteroid, the smaller our chances of success. A small change in course while it is still far away will result in a much larger miss distance later on. If we wait too long, then we won't be able to give it enough of a push to put it on a course that will avoid hitting us. Given that we don't have time to build and test new hardware to deflect it, we're opting to take existing hardware and use it. We're going to go to Sutter's Mill and repair or replace the electric propulsion system that failed and caused the problem to begin with. We estimate that the system Asteroid Ores put on the rock could still give it enough of a shove to miss the Earth if we get there while it is still several months out."

"Why don't they go out there and fix the damned thing? Are they going to pay for it?" asked the CEO of Lockheed-Martin.

"They simply don't have the resources to pay for sending a crew to the asteroid to effect the repair, which is what we believe is the best approach to solve the problem. I really don't want to comment any further on Asteroid Ores' legal liability. Believe me when I say that the attorneys are all over this as we speak," Reese-Walker chimed in from her seat near the speaker's podium.

Dachwald signaled for the first slide to be projected on the screen at the front of the room. It showed a cartoon of a space vehicle departing Earth orbit. Childers immediately recognize the parts shown in the figure and smiled. *These guys have been busy*, he thought.

"We propose to use NASA's heavy lift rocket to take the recently tested nuclear thermal propulsion stage, the one planned for the upcoming Mars mission, to an assembly orbit around the Earth where it will mate with Space Excursions' inflatable, the one they are building for the Mars mission, which will serve as the crew's deep space habitat. The crew will then launch on one of the commercial space planes, rendezvous with the assembled ship, and be on their way to the asteroid." He then advanced to the next slide.

"When they arrive, they'll rendezvous with Sutter's Mill near the location of the malfunctioning electric propulsion system, go EVA and repair or replace the electric propulsion engines that failed. Once they restart the engines, the crew will remain for a week or so and then depart for home. The timing of their return will depend on too many factors to know it exactly now—the date they arrive, the length of time it takes to repair the existing system, the alignment of the asteroid with Earth to minimize the fuel requirements, etc."

"How many people will be going?" asked another member of the audience.

"That's to be determined. We believe it will be between three and five, depending upon the final logistics that can be worked out. These people will be together in deep space for months and we need to make sure that all of their physical needs can be met as well as their psychological needs. This is going to be a high stress and high risk mission. Crew selection needs to be very carefully thought-out."

"Isn't the rock spinning? All the studies we've done show that it'll be risky to try and rendezvous with a rotating mountain in space," asked the Lockheed-Martin CEO.

"They attached two small spacecraft to the asteroid, one on each side, each containing a long cable—a tether. Think of an ice skater when she pulls her arms and a leg in in order to speed up. She's conserving angular momentum. As she reduces her rotational inertia by pulling her arms and leg in, her rotation speed must increase to maintain constant angular momentum. Now do it in reverse with a spinning rock and extend five-kilometer-long tethers instead of arms and legs. The rock stops spinning. Cut the tethers and you're ready to go."

"Surely you're joking," the CEO smirked.

"Not at all. We've seen their data and confirmed it by radar imaging. The rock was rotating and now it isn't."

"What about the Mars mission?" The question came from the CEO of Northrop-Grumman. Childers knew that they were the prime contractor for the Mars Lander, a piece of hardware that didn't look like it was going to play a role in the mission.

Reese-Walker stood to answer this one. "Mars can wait for another launch opportunity. They come roughly every two years and by then this will have been resolved. Hopefully." She added the laugh.

She's telling you to sit down and be patient, you dope. She truly believes that you'll get your money and that you just won't get to fly as soon as you'd like,

Childers thought. *Clearly she has been in government her entire life and has no clue what it is like on the outside. The big concern for Northrop-Grumman would be,* Gary thought, *if they got money to string them along until the next launch time. Otherwise, there would be layoffs. The CEO would likely lose his job and it could actually kill the mission. Government contracting was always touchy because the government made all the rules and could bend or break them whenever they needed to with no required compensation. There were way more implications to this thing than one would think. There would be a new Congress before the next launch opportunity. Northrop had better hope the election goes their way or Mars will fall out of favor and Northrop-Grumman will be out a few billion dollars that had been promised to them by legal, apparently nonbinding contracts.*

"Were it me," Gary mumbled to himself, "My lawyers would be looking at who caused this mess to be paying for my layoffs."

The director continued, "Now, for the details. First..."

The meeting continued until they broke for lunch at 1:00 p.m.

Time until Asteroid 2018HM5 "Sutter's Mill" reaches Earth: 251 days.

CHAPTER II

CHILDERS'S FLIGHT BACK TO THE NEVADA SPACEPORT was uneventful. For Childers, who always flew first class, that was the best kind of airplane flight—on time, boring and otherwise uneventful. During the flight, he mentally reviewed the outcome of the meeting in Washington and gave his silent thanks that he had opted to invest in space tourism instead of asteroid mining. He knew Anacleto Rosalez and thought highly of him. He also knew this accident, even if the asteroid were diverted, would be the death knell of his mining company and perhaps even mean Anacleto's personal bankruptcy. Fortune sometimes favors the bold. Sometimes one can be too bold to be favored.

Childers was met at the airport by Hami Kunda and his newly enlarged security detail. He and Hami slid into the back seat of his modified SUV and departed McCarren Airport for the spaceport. The Nevada sun was unrelenting and, as usual, Childers had to squint in order to admire the countryside despite the tinted windows of the vehicle.

"Mr. Childers. I've assembled the habitat management team as you requested. They'll be in the conference room waiting to hear from you as soon as we reach the building."

"Excellent. What's the status of the testing? Have we shaken her down yet?"

"Not yet. That's planned for later this week. The thermal vacuum testing is complete though. No major problems. One of the heaters near the reaction control thrusters failed, but the backup kicked in and there was not a real issue."

"Good. We've got a few minutes; let me fill you in..."

Twenty minutes later, Childers was in the conference room briefing his assembled team on the new mission for their Mars habitat. The engineering team, though mostly populated with "can do" types, was nonetheless full of questions and technical concerns about the new mission and the amount of analysis that would be required to make it happen.

"Mr. Childers, the environments are mostly the same, but we don't know what we'll encounter at the asteroid. Some of these rocks have their own atmosphere of dust and debris around them." The comment came from one of the materials experts.

"The power system should be able to function just fine going to an asteroid instead of Mars. That's beauty of having our own nuclear reactor to work with. It doesn't care if the sun is shining or not," said another.

"Yeah, but that'll make the heat rejection problem even worse. We've already stretched the radiators to their maximum capacity. Where's all that extra heat going to go?"

The comments were coming rapid-fire. They were coming too fast for Childers, who was not an engineer, to keep up. He decided to leave and let Hami keep the team focused on the new job at hand.

As he left the room, the path to his office had him walking along the upstairs corridor that overlooked the assembly area where *Dreamscape*, the Out-Of-This-World and now the Deep Space Habitat were assembled. The latter two were in a clean room on the west side of the floor, separated from the area where the *Dreamscape* was being serviced, by a wall that served to keep dust, dirt and the heat of the Nevada climate from contaminating the sensitive mechanisms and electronics within them. The *Dreamscape* needed none of that. It was designed to operate like an airplane and that meant it had to tolerate all of the inconvenient environments that nature, and humans, could send her way. The side of the walkway overlooking the high bay was covered with glass to keep down the noise and to prevent the accidental VIP from dropping something, usually a camera, on the heads of the workers down below. He paused to admire the activity below him on the floor.

The five-story-tall door on the East side of the building was open, probably to allow the free flow of parts to and from the *Dreamscape* service area and, if Childers were to hazard a guess, to allow the sunlight to illuminate the room. It had long been his opinion that people work better in natural light.

And it was from there that he had a bird's eye view of the small airplane-like vehicle that flew into the high bay from outside. It flew high above the floor and close to the top of the door. Childers squinted to get a better look and saw that it appeared to be a remote-controlled toy airplane. The realization that something was amiss was only beginning to dawn on him and among some of the workers on the floor below. He reached for his phone to sound an alarm, but before he could do so the explosives packed in the plane exploded, showering the room below with deadly bits of metal that had been packed within the body of the craft.

Childers saw the glass in front of him buckle and then shatter, taking on the spiderweb appearance characteristic of automobile safety glass before shattering into literally thousands of small glass shards. The spiderweb shatter pattern saved Childers's life by absorbing most of the pressure wave resulting from the blast. That, and the fact that the shrapnel packed in the remotely piloted vehicle was shaped to eject downward, not up and out, so as to maximize the damage to those below it on the ground. Despite all this, Childers was thrown backward and onto the floor and covered with thousands of tiny glass pieces that had once been his observation window.

The alarm sounded among the mayhem that had been an orderly, high-tech assembly plant only moments before. As Childers brushed himself off and rose from the floor of the catwalk, he saw that there was a lot of smoke and, through the haze he could see a gaping hole in the tail fin of the *Dreamscape*. Closer to the ground, he saw several of his technicians lying on the floor, apparently injured from the blast or the shrapnel.

Without saying a word, Childers worked his way down the hallway toward the far exit. He glanced out the window and into the clean room below. He noticed that the wall of the room had not been breached and that the Deep Space Habitat had not suffered any apparent damage. The workers there were following their safe shutdown procedures and evacuating. For the moment, at least, Childers could see no evidence that the explosion had caused any sort of fire.

He was met at the stairway by the plant manager and two security guards.

"Mr. Childers, we need to get you out of here," said one of the guards. He was a "typical" security guard, all muscle and no neck. In other words, not someone to trifle with. Except that Childers was the boss and used to trifling.

"Not now. I need to see to my people. Have the police been called?"

"Yes, sir. They're on their way."

"Alright then," he said looking at the plant manager. Childers continued, "Great. Now do your job and don't worry about me. I'm sure these two gents can keep me safe while I'm out there doing something useful until the medical professionals arrive." With that, Childers continued down the stairs and exited into the high bay on the first floor.

The smell was the first thing he noticed. Unlike the somewhat antiseptic smell of the building under normal circumstances, the air in the high bay smelled like sulfur—like the aftermath of a Fourth of July fireworks celebration, but without the celebratory feeling among those nearby. To Childers's surprise, there wasn't much noise other than the fire alarm wail. People were either seriously hurt or in the process of rendering aid.

Childers ran to the first unattended victim he saw, a woman whom he recognized as one of the newest employees of the company. He'd personally interviewed and hired her last week. Reaching into his short-term memory, he recalled that her name was Maria and that she was an electrical engineer just graduated from Purdue. Her clothes were tattered, her face covered in soot and the right side of her body bleeding in several places from the shrapnel that had come from the bomb. There was a lot of blood, but none was gushing—a good sign. She was conscious and trying to raise herself up with her left arm—another good sign.

"Mr. Childers. What happened? There was an explosion and the next thing I remember is now," she said, only just beginning to realize that something terrible had happened. To her credit, though she exhibited signs of being in shock, she didn't panic.

"Maria, isn't it?"

She nodded.

"Maria, help is on the way. You are injured, but it doesn't look like you're going to be on the company's disability plan for very long," Childers said with a forced grin, trying to put her at ease. He could tell she was in a great deal of pain, but her wounds didn't look immediately life-threatening.

"No, sir," she said.

"Good. I'm going to see if there is someone more seriously injured than you that needs help. If you can get yourself up and out of the middle of the floor, it will make it easier for the emergency medical people to get here and move around. Can you do that?"

She again nodded.

Childers stood up and started to move down the floor to the next injured person when he heard a sound that was out of place among the chaos. It was coming from the direction of the open high bay. A buzzing sound. He looked up and saw an object, a flying object, approaching the high bay from outside. He wasn't yet sure, but it appeared to be another remote-controlled airplane headed their way.

Childers stood and grabbed the sleeve of one of the bodyguards that was still with him. The other had moved to help Maria get on her feet and moving to the side of the high bay. He pointed at the airplane.

"It's another bomb. The bastard who did this is sending in another one to take out the survivors and the emergency personnel," Childers said.

The plane's engine got markedly louder as it crossed the threshold into the high bay. It was thirty feet off the ground and flying directly toward the wall at the back of the room. The targeted wall was the one that had protected the Deep Space Habitat and the engineers working on it from the initial blast. Childers estimated that the remotely piloted plane would reach it in less than fifteen seconds.

Childers began running toward the largest group of people who would most likely be affected by another blast. Unfortunately, this meant he was running toward the area where the bomb would explode. He was shouting for people to take cover and pointing excitedly at the plane now flying directly overhead.

Bang! Bang!

Childers heard the sound of his bodyguard's sidearm as he fired at the plane. Childers wasn't a gun aficionado, but he knew that hitting something that small and far away was a challenge for anyone equipped only with a handgun. The guard was standing with his knees slightly bent, shooting with his right hand well supported by his left.

Bang! Bang! Bang! Bang!

Finally, one of the shots hit the plane and knocked it off its path toward the back wall. The left wing appeared to have been hit, causing it to begin spiraling toward the ground which was, unfortunately, exactly where Childers and at least seven other people were standing. Too late, those that were still mobile began to move away. Childers watched the plane approach, wondering if this was how his life was going to end.

The small plane, not much larger than a backpack, just big enough to carry enough explosives to cause some serious damage, hit the ground and broke into pieces a mere ten feet from where Childers was standing. There was no explosion. Just the thud of the plane's mass hitting the concrete floor of the high bay.

Once Childers realized he wasn't dead, he recovered his wits and again began directing those that were uninjured to help those that were, if they were able, and urging the rest to get out of the building. The emergency medical personnel were now coming in through the open high bay doors and tending to the seriously injured. There was no sign of an additional plane or any other sort of attack.

"Mr. Childers, we have to get you out of here. That's an order sir." Childers's bodyguard was back at this side and firmly taking him by the arm.

"I get the message. I'm all yours. Let's get out of here and let these people do their jobs."

"Thank you, sir."

"No, thank you. That was a great shot. It looks like you took out the wing and whatever he might have been using to detonate the bird. It was probably radio controlled."

"I use a Sig Sauer 229. It's a 9 mm with a 3.9 inch barrel. I've been training with that gun since I was a boy and it has never let me down. When I was in Special Forces, we'd train shooting at drones with our sidearms. I guess it's like riding a bike; once you learn how to do it, you don't ever really forget."

"We were all lucky to have you here today." Childers nodded at the bodyguard.

"Thank you sir, but I'd rather give the credit to my training. Now let me do my job and get you out of here, okay?"

"You've got it. Take me to my office. I should be safe there."

"If it looks safe, then that's fine with me. Otherwise, we're going to get you in a car and as far away as possible."

"Sounds like a plan," Childers said as he took one last look at the remains of his assembly facility and the damaged *Dreamscape* that stood in the center of the room.

CHAPTER 12

"THE EUROPEANS AND AMERICANS ARE RESPONSIBLE for this mess and now they want us to join with them in a foolish attempt to fix the very system that caused the problem to begin with?" Evgeni Golov, the Director of NPO Energomash responded to the speaker who had just delivered the same story, the Russian version, that the NASA Administrator had provided to Gary Childers in Washington just days before.

"You are correct, Evgeni. The American president called President Lazarev just yesterday explaining the plan and inviting us to send a cosmonaut on the journey to the asteroid," said Makariy Loktev, Chairman of the Planetary Protection Committee of the Russian Academy of Sciences and, more importantly, the man President Lazarev placed in charge of coming up with the Russian plan to deflect the incoming asteroid.

"Why would they believe that they can repair the failed system and that it won't break again? Given that it will take precious time to send astronauts to the asteroid in the first place, and then additional time

84

to repair or replace the electric thrusters, they surely realize that doesn't leave much time to actually deflect the asteroid in the first place." Evgeni Golov was now speaking to the other twelve assembled engineers and scientists in the room, as if their affirmation of his comments would help convince the chairman that he was correct.

"We don't have much confidence in their proposed solution. It is very risky and we may not know whether or not it works until it is too late to do anything about it. Nonetheless, President Lazarev has decided to accept the American offer. Russia will fully cooperate with the American team," said Loktev.

"This is madness. To place the lives of millions of people in the hands of those who believe a space propulsion system that emits the equivalent of mouse farts will be able to deflect a two-billion-ton piece of rock is sheer madness."

"Yes, Evgeni. It is madness. And that's why we've been instructed to put in place Plan B. Should the American effort fail, then we will be ready to launch our own rocket to deflect the asteroid." Loktev pursed his lips as he spoke.

"And what approach are we going to use? You know better than I that the academy has studied this problem for years and found very few satisfactory approaches to divert something this big. The answer always seems to be the one nobody wants to hear."

"The nuclear option," said Loktev, answering Evgeni's unspoken question.

"Yes, the nuclear option. We need to detonate a hydrogen bomb just in front of the asteroid. Perhaps detonate two, just to make sure we're successful."

Evgeni spoke in a hushed tone, as though he didn't really want to have the other attendees of this meeting to hear what he had to say.

"The president has given us the authorization to proceed with the approach you suggest. We're to begin immediately to modify a Proton rocket to carry one of the military's 8F675 twenty-megaton warheads and place it on an intercept course with the asteroid." Loktev spoke of using a nuclear bomb with the off-hand authority of someone used to being in the halls of power where such things are casually discussed.

Evgeni, pleased that the chairman agreed with his position, was unprepared for the remark from Loktev that came next.

"This plan is considered to be classified above Top Secret. You will not discuss it with anyone outside of this room and as far as the engineers who will be working on the project know, it is simply another doomsday weapon that we are prototyping at the request of the president. Lord knows we've done more than a few of those over the years. We're holding this in reserve and it will only be launched if it looks like the American plan is going to fail. It will then be our right and obligation to do what is right—and what should have been done in the first place."

"What about our member of the team going to the asteroid? Will this person be told?"

"No. We cannot risk allowing the plan to be known before we are ready to launch."

CHAPTER 13

PAUL GESLING WALKED INTO THE CONFERENCE ROOM at the Johnson Space Center with a sense of anticipation and a bit of pride. Since he learned that he would be the commander for the international mission to intercept and divert Sutter's Mill, he was once again filled with a sense of purpose. Carolyn was still in a coma and he thought that fact alone would disqualify him from being selected for the flight, let alone being selected as the person in charge. He was certain that Gary Childers and all of the money and leverage that his boss had played a role in the final decision somehow. It paid to have friends that were powerful and connected.

Paul had only briefly thought about declining the offer because of Carolyn's status. But that thought had been quickly dismissed. He knew what she would say to him if he had declined and that was enough to push him firmly into the mindset of being away from home, and her bedside, for the better part of a year.

Glancing at the people milling around in the room, Gesling made a mental note of those in attendance.

He saw NASA administrator Tara Reese-Walker and
Paula Downey, the chief engineer for the nuclear propulsion system that would propel their spacecraft. He
recognized several other NASA types as he scanned
the room, but the appearance of the dark-haired
woman near the front of the room actually startled
him. It was the Chinese astronaut and commander
of the ill-fated lunar mission that he and Bill Stetson
had rescued, Hui Tian. He'd heard that a Chinese
astronaut would be joining them on the mission, and
he was now wondering if she was that astronaut. He
hoped so. She was dedicated, and had proven herself
capable in the face of extreme adversity when she and
her crew had crashed on the Moon and were facing
almost certain death.

He knew that NASA astronaut Melanie Ledford was
also to be among the crew. She was a space veteran
who had flown multiple missions to the aging International Space Station. She hadn't yet been beyond
Earth orbit, but that didn't worry Gesling. For the
most part, space was space. They weren't going into
a significant gravity well, like the Moon, so her experience would be just as relevant as his, if not more
so. He'd heard she was to be the commander of
the upcoming Mars mission and he wondered if this
change of plans would have any effect on her mindset
and motivations. They'd met a few times at various
conferences, but had never actually worked together.

"Paul! Over here!" he heard a familiar voice.

Paul looked toward the person calling his name and
was pleased to see Gary Childers motioning for him
to join him at the front of the room. He was standing
with Administrator Reese-Walker, no surprise there,

and Hui Tian, who had joined them in conversation while Paul had been scanning the rest of the room. He moved toward them.

"Good morning, Commander Gesling. I'm very pleased you accepted the offer to lead the expedition. Bill Stetson speaks very highly of you," Reese-Walker said.

Paul was now convinced of just how his name was nominated for commanding the mission. The combination of Childers's business power and Stetson's connections at NASA were certainly the reasons. Childers, well, was Gary Childers. And Stetson's reach and influence in NASA, despite being retired from the organization, never ceased to surprise him.

"We're just getting ready to begin. I understand you already know Ms. Tian. She will be the taikonaut joining the crew from China."

Gesling bowed toward Tian and smiled, "It will be a pleasure to work with you again, Hui. I saw you when I came in and I am extremely pleased to learn that you are on the team. We need someone with your ability to think on your feet and keep calm under pressure. This is not going to be an easy mission."

"The pleasure is mine, Commander Gesling. The Chinese government has pledged full support and any resources needed to this mission. We're counting on it to be successful as are the rest of the world. The consequences of failure are too dire to even be considered."

"I agree," Paul said.

"How is your wife? I was so shocked at the news of the shooting and only recently learned that she was so seriously injured." Hui nodded in respect as she asked.

"She's still unconscious. The doctors tell me that's

not unusual from such a serious brain injury, but they're also telling me it could be a long, tough road to full recovery." Gesling looked pained as he shared the news of his wife's condition.

"I'm so sorry. Please let me know if there is anything I can do."

Administrator Reese-Walker moved to the podium and called the meeting to order.

"Today the crew of the asteroid diversion mission begins the training that will enable them to repair the propulsion system on Sutter's Mill and prevent a catastrophe. To begin, I'd like to introduce the crew and then send them off with the technical team we've assembled to begin their rushed orientation and training. There is not much time. I'd first like to introduce the mission commander, Paul Gesling of Space Excursions. Paul has extensive experience..."

"Paul, hey Paul?" While Reese-Walker was speaking, Childers whispered in Gesling's ear, "Paul, you need to know that there are several on the crew that didn't think you should be in command. Mikhail Rykov, the Russian standing over next to the wall, was the other candidate. He had the support of Russia, of course, the Europeans and Japan. Hui and the Chinese supported you being the lead, as did Administrator Reese-Walker— thanks to Bill Stetson. And, of course, I really lobbied on your behalf."

"I kind of figured. What was the main issue?" Paul asked.

"Carolyn. They said you'd be too distracted being away while she is in the hospital. Personally, I think that was just their excuse. It was all politics, as one would expect," Gary continued to whisper.

"Harrumph." Gesling wondered what the interpersonal relationships among the crew might be like under these circumstances. Though he had to admit that he had considered that his predicament with his wife's condition might keep him from the mission entirely. He didn't really blame others for having any of the opposing arguments.

Childers leaned back to again listen to Reese-Walker as she completed her introduction of Hui Tian. Paul wasn't sure if their conversation was done or not.

"Ms. Tian is a valuable addition to the team. Next, I'd like to introduce Mikhail Rykov, from Russia, who will be responsible for repairing the electric thrusters on the asteroid that malfunctioned. He is an advanced propulsion expert, and the designer of the electric thrusters that Russia is planning to use for their upcoming Kuiper Belt Explorer mission. He's flown in space three times, most recently on a mission to the Moon where he served as the commander of their first crew in the Russian outpost now established there."

Rykov, with his characteristic Russian swagger and exaggerated charisma, stood and nodded his head toward the attendees. He then broke out with a big smile.

"Reudiger Hahn, of Germany, is the European Space Agency's member of the crew. Reudiger is one of those overachievers; if there aren't any more in this room I will be utterly shocked. He earned a doctorate in advanced propulsion, specializing in electric propulsion systems, and another doctorate in planetary geology. He will be able to work with Mikhail in repairing the broken thrusters on Sutter's Mill and, if time permits, gather a few samples of the rock to bring home for analysis."

Hahn was tall and thin. To Gesling, he didn't look

like he weighed over 140 pounds. He, like Rykov, stood and nodded toward those in the room. Unlike Rykov, he didn't exude a sense of machismo. Rather a sense of quiet competence that Gesling liked.

"Last, but certainly not least, I'd like to introduce Dr. Melanie Ledford. Melanie is a three-time Space Station veteran and was named the commander for the now-postponed mission to Mars. Dr. Ledford has her Ph.D. in aerospace engineering and is a practicing physician, an M.D. specializing in internal medicine. Dr. Ledford, welcome aboard."

Unlike her male counterparts, Dr. Ledford remained seated, smiled and only slightly bowed her head to acknowledge the introduction. She was a redhead and Gesling knew that her temperament was sometimes stereotypical with what people have come to associate with redheads—fiery.

"We don't have the time for any speeches or further introductions. I'd like to get them started in their orientation by sending them off with Paula Downey from NASA Marshall. Paula is the agency's chief engineer for the nuclear thermal propulsion stage that will send the crew to Sutter's Mill," Reese-Walker concluded, nodding to Downey who now stood near the side exit to the room.

"If the crew will come with me, we'll get started," Downey said as she motioned to the door.

"I'd best be off," Gesling said to Childers as he rose and began to move toward the exit.

"Good luck and take good notes," Childers said, sounding more like a boss giving an order than a friend cheering him on.

❖   ❖   ❖

"Now that they're on their way, we do have a few more items to discuss. First of all, I'd like for Gary Childers of Space Excursions to tell us the status of the Deep Space Habitat after the unfortunate events that happened at the company's Nevada spaceport last week." Reese-Walker walked away from the podium and motioned for Childers to take her place.

"Thanks, Tara," Childers used the administrator's first name to reinforce the fact that they were good friends and to let everyone know that he was not to be taken lightly. "Last week, our facility in Nevada was attacked by remotely piloted drones carrying high explosives. The first drone flew into the high bay where we were servicing the *Dreamscape* reusable orbiter and exploded. The explosion sent shrapnel downward toward the engineers and technicians servicing the ship. Three people were killed and about fifteen others were injured. The *Dreamscape* too suffered significant damage and we're considering just scrapping the ship and building a new one to replace her. The damage to the ship's airframe was significant."

"The clean room where the Deep Space Habitat is being tested was not damaged in the first attack. If it hadn't been for the quick thinking and skill of my bodyguard, more people would have died and the habitat damaged by the second drone which flew in shortly after the first one exploded. He shot it down with his sidearm. And we were lucky. The bullet clipped the wing and the cable that connected the explosives with the radio antenna that controlled both the plane and the detonation of the explosives. When the crashed plane was examined by the FBI, they found that the perpetrator didn't rig it for any sort of impact explosion. There was a small camera used to steer the drone and we suspect that a signal was going to be sent to detonate the device when it was in position to do the most damage."

"Mr. Childers, isn't this the latest in a string of attacks on you and your team that began with your being shot just a few months ago?" The question came from one of the managers attending from the European Space Agency.

"Yes. It was. Someone tried to kill me and ended up injuring me and my associate, Carolyn O'Connor. Following that, there was a bomb attack on Bill Stetson and his wife in Houston. This bombing at my Nevada facility was the third event in the series."

"Do you or the police have any idea who was responsible?"

"No. There are a few leads, but very little evidence. Whoever is behind these attacks is a professional and very, very technically savvy. The experts tell me that the Houston bomb and those on the drones in Nevada were made by the same person using the same explosives. Both were highly sophisticated devices. The drones were purchased commercially but they were heavily modified to serve as flying bombs. Whoever is behind this is not stupid. He, she, or they appear to be highly trained and very capable. And they are still out there."

"Do you think the attacks are related to this mission?" asked one of the NASA managers sitting on the front row. Childers recognized him, but couldn't for the life of him recall his name.

"No. The first attack, the shooting, occurred before the whole Sutter's Mill activity began. Before the

Asteroid Ores rocket to Sutter's Mill was even launched. No, whoever is behind this has a motivation that isn't connected."

The next question, from Reese-Walker, surprised Childers for its bluntness. "Will Space Excursions be able to fulfill its commitment and maintain schedule in light of this attack? And, do you think having your hardware and your team as part of this mission will jeopardize it?"

"The Deep Space Habitat is complete and almost ready to be shipped here for launch. So, no, the hardware we're under contract to deliver shouldn't be an issue. As to my company being somehow a detriment to the project's success, I cannot answer. We've beefed up security at all of our facilities and this project already has the highest level of security possible. We know there is someone out there gunning for us, but I don't think that will be a risk to the mission going forward."

"Thank you, Gary, for your candid answers," said Administrator Reese-Walker as she rose to retake control of the podium.

Thank you my ass, thought Childers as he sat down. *You set me up and then after I recovered to your satisfaction, you get all chummy again. Typical politician . . .*

CHAPTER 14

"WITH THE *DREAMSCAPE* OUT OF ACTION, HOW ARE we going to get into space to rendezvous with the ship that'll take us to Sutter's Mill?" Melanie Ledford asked. She, Paul Gesling and the rest of the crew were dressed in clean room clothing, the so-called "bunny suits" that covered them from head to toe just like a child's bunny costume at Halloween minus the ears and fluffy tail. Paul couldn't see Melanie's mouth, but he could see the paper facemask vibrate as she spoke.

They'd just finished their final walk through of the habitat they'd be calling home on their journey to the asteroid before it was to be broken down and shipped to the launch site for integration into the rocket that would take it to space. The bunny suits were standard issue for everyone working on sensitive space hardware—worn to minimize contamination from "dirty humans" prior to being launched. They were standing in the clean room looking at the outside of the habitat while similarly clad engineers were completing their final technical inspections.

"We're working on that. We can get you a ride from the Russians or one of the other commercial space companies, if they have a vehicle that will be ready in time. Alternatively, the Chinese government has offered a ride in one of their Long March rockets. We'll go in whatever vehicle is available and that our leadership signs up to," Paula Downey responded. As NASA's chief engineer for the project, she was well versed on the technical as well as management and political issues associated with the asteroid diversion mission as well.

"And I wouldn't count Mr. Childers out just yet. He is moving heaven and Earth to get the ship rebuilt as fast as possible. But there isn't much time, I agree," Paul added.

"What is our launch window?" Mikhail asked.

"Well, it isn't set in stone yet." Paula frowned as she responded. "We have a window of about ninety minutes each day for a week. After that, we need to rerun the Earth departure trajectories to find another one that will close and allow you to reach Sutter's Mill in time. Unfortunately, the planets and this damnable asteroid aren't sitting still as we try to put this ship together. Though, the nuclear engines will make the job a lot easier on us."

"How so?" Reudiger Hahn asked with a tone in his voice that sounded offensive. The tone was accentuated by the arching his back, making himself appear taller and more like an alpha male trying to gain control of the tribe that was his fellow astronauts.

Gesling recalled that Reudiger was an outspoken critic of using anything nuclear-powered in space, whether it be fission-powered rocket engines like the ones that were about to take all of them on an intercept trajectory with the Sutter's Mill or the plutonium power packs that were routinely used on deep space robotic probes. His reaction to the word, "nuclear" was clearly personal and a conviction that was not to be swayed by any real data.

"First of all, they provide a slightly higher thrust than a chemical rocket engine. This allows us to trade payload mass for trip time. With less mass to push, the higher thrust engines will accelerate the ship to a higher speed. They're also much more efficient, meaning that we will only have to carry about half the propellant weight we'd require if this were a chemical rocket mission."

"But at what cost? Look at Fukushima and Chernobyl. The ecological destruction from nuclear power is great. We could accomplish this mission with only chemical propulsion and be much better off because of it."

Reudiger was ready for a verbal brawl and Gesling wasn't one to take the bait. Paul was decidedly in favor of nuclear propulsion for deep space travel when it made sense, and he believed it made a lot of sense for this mission and certainly for one to Mars. He was hoping no one else would respond so they could get on with their briefing. There wasn't much time and this debate wouldn't settle anything related to their mission. But it looked like his desire was not going to come true. The Russian seemed as eager for a fight as the German. He, too, arched his back and then pulled his face mask off to the side so his face could be clearly seen.

"Reudiger, pardon my Russian bluntness, but you are full of shit and simply wrong. Physics of spaceflight is the driving factor, not silly European green nonsense based on emotional and political arguments and zero factual science. The only way we can get the trip times and payload mass we need to send people to Mars is by using nuclear propulsion. We've done the studies for decades and while chemical propulsion is certainly viable, it is a dead end with regard to human exploration of deep space. We need nuclear rockets to take us to Mars and there is no other option if we choose to go further. You should know that as well as I do." Mikhail grinned as he taunted the more reserved Reudiger.

"Gentlemen. We must put a stop to this debate. The available hardware and the schedule are what drove us to making nuclear propulsion the baseline for the intercept mission. If NASA weren't building the Mars mission hardware right now, which is nuclear, then we wouldn't even have a shot at reaching Sutter's Mill in time to fix the propulsion system and avert a global tragedy." Paula stood as she spoke, placing herself between Mikhail and Reudiger, and looked back and forth between them expectantly. "This debate just isn't helpful and we have millions of lives hanging in the balance."

Neither of the men responded. Both looked like schoolyard bullies about to kick the crap out of each other behind the gym.

"Now that that is shelved, let me continue. You'll be launched into space by someone's rocket, perhaps by two rockets, depending upon what is available. Once in Earth orbit, you'll rendezvous with the Deep Space Habitat and the nuclear thermal propulsion stage that will take you to Sutter's Mill. Once the Earth departure burn begins, you'll have approximately three months of flight time before you reach Sutter's Mill. Once there, you'll spacewalk to the asteroid's surface and repair or replace the electric thrusters that malfunctioned. We've allowed up to a week for the repair mission with up to two three-hour EVAs each day. Once the repair is complete, you'll remain near the asteroid to make sure the repaired hardware is working properly before you restart the engines and return home. If all goes well, you'll get home about a week before the asteroid flies by Earth."

"That's not much time for the electric thrusters on the rock to change its course," Paul said, trying to keep the conversation technical and away from the almost-fistfight over using nuclear power in space. To help with the topic change, he began walking toward the exit from the cleanroom. The others followed.

"The astrodynamicists tell me that that will be enough time to nudge it so that it will be a clean miss and pass somewhere between the Earth and the Moon. I'm sure they will share their analysis with you or anyone else. They want to make sure they're right just as much as we do," said Paula.

"And a week between our arrival home and the flyby isn't exactly what I'd call a comfortable safety margin," said Gesling.

"I agree. But the motion of the planets, and in this case the asteroid, is what it is and we can only nudge it a little bit." Paula waved her hands as she spoke, pretending that her right fist was Sutter's Mill being deflected away from Earth, her left hand.

"I understand, but it sucks nonetheless."

"I agree." Paula nodded in affirmation, smiled and then said, "From what I know about each of you,

you're accustomed to being in high pressure, no scheduled margin for events and making the best of them. That's why you are here."

The group of astronauts looked at each other as they exited the clean room and began taking off their protective gear. Some of them grinned as their egos enjoyed the stroking. Others felt placated and only gave a nod or a shoulder shrug as their egos were less vulnerable.

"We'll keep this rock from hitting the Earth," Melanie said.

"Do we really have a choice?" The Russian added.

"The only other choice has abysmal consequences," Gesling noted. The others all nodded in agreement.

The team had dinner at a local steakhouse, followed by ample drinking at a nearby bar. One thing hadn't changed in the selection of astronauts since the Mercury 7 crew—they knew how to work hard and how to party hard. The nuclear debate between Mikhail and Reudiger began again after the second post-dinner drink and continued unabated until Hui Tian had to excuse herself.

"Comrades," she said and nodded directly at Mikhail as she began, "I must be off. As much as I enjoy the company, and the drinks, I'm still a bit jet-lagged and I really must turn in."

"Good night, Hui. It's great working with you again," Paul said.

"Good night, Paul," she said as she put on her jacket and left the bar.

Hui didn't drive, so she asked the cashier at the bar to summon a taxi to take her to her hotel. She was a bit tipsy and didn't pay much attention to the ride from the bar to her hotel, only taking in the sights of suburban Houston when she forced herself to focus, usually at a stoplight.

Tian traveled light, and was able to get ready for bed quickly. Her room lights were out and she was asleep within twenty minutes of the taxi letting her out at the front of the hotel. She was exhausted and deep sleep was what she desired.

After what seemed like only a few moments of sleep, Hui awakened with a start. She turned her head to look at the ubiquitous clock radio on the hotel's night stand and saw that it said 3:44 a.m. The room was otherwise dark and she was trying to figure out what awakened her when she suddenly realized she was not alone. She wasn't sure how she knew that someone else was in the room, but she was certain that there was someone else nearby.

She frantically ran through her options. She could pretend to be still asleep and hope they left. She quickly discarded this option because why would anyone break into a room to just sit and stare at a sleeping person? She was of course afraid of rape, and that thought alone got her adrenaline flowing and her heart rate accelerated. She thought about quickly leaping out of the bed and running for the door, but discarded that idea also. There was no way she could get out from under the covers and to the door before the person, whoever it was, could stop her. She could scream, but she knew that no one would hear her. Hotel rooms were too well soundproofed. Calling 911 was also not an option because it would take too much time. Instead, she took a chance.

"Who is there?" Hui asked into the darkness.

No response.

"I know someone is there. What do you want?"

"I came to warn you," the male voice said in Chinese from just to her left, near the room's balcony.

"Who are you? Warn me about what?" Hui asked. The voice was familiar to her and since he was speaking in Chinese, she had to assume she knew the person. After all, what's the chance of a random Chinese burglar in Houston breaking into a Chinese person's hotel room?

"I came to warn you to not be part of the mission if it involves Space Excursions, Paul Gesling, Bill Stetson, or Gary Childers."

She did know the voice. She had trained with him for months and even been on the Moon with him. She decided to not let on that she knew who it was, at least for the moment.

"Why are you warning me of this? And why are you in my room, in the middle of the night?"

"You know why. And I am sure you now know who I am. Hui Tian, if you don't remove yourself from the mission, I cannot guarantee your safety."

"Zhi Feng. Why would you want the mission to not succeed? If we fail, millions of people will die."

"They can find another way to divert the asteroid. But I won't let *them* get any more credit for anything. The glory should have been ours, but they stole it. They humiliated us and I will now humiliate them."

Hui rose up in the bed and slowly began to slide the covers off her body to allow more rapid movement, should she need to move fast in the next few minutes. She was still worried about her safety, but not so worried that she wasn't going to try and get out, if the opportunity arose.

"Them? You mean Stetson and Gesling?"

"And Childers. I've missed them twice and I won't miss them again. I just don't want you to be injured when it happens."

"You know this is wrong. They saved us on the Moon. If it weren't for them, we wouldn't be having this conversation right now—we'd be dead."

"Better dead in glory than alive in shame," Feng said with an intensity that caused Hui to believe her former colleague had lost his sanity.

"You must stop this madness. Our mission will save the lives of millions, perhaps the lives of millions of Chinese. If you do something that causes us to fail, the shame of murdering millions will be much greater shame than you perceive from what happened on the Moon."

"Perceive? *Perceive?* Is that what you call it? I call it international humiliation of the backward Chinese, once again being rescued by Yankee innovation. No, I will put a stop to this and I will try to protect you from harm, but it cannot be guaranteed."

Hui heard Feng moving, and it sounded like he was moving toward the balcony door, which she now concluded was ajar. She noticed a slight breeze coming from the direction of the door and now knew how he'd managed to get into her room.

"Good bye, Hui Tian. You were my commanding officer and I have the highest respect for you, except for your treasonous actions on the Moon with Bill Stetson. But that respect won't stop me from reclaiming the honor that is rightfully ours. You have been warned."

Hui heard his footsteps rapidly approach the balcony's open door and the soft metal-on-metal sound of the sliding door closing as he left the room. She bolted from the bed and locked the door behind him, quickly drawing the curtains across the entire wall. She turned on the lights and sat on her bedside, shaking. It took only a few moments for the tears to flow as she realized how close she had just come to death, or worse.

After only a few seconds to regain her composure, she went to the hotel phone on the bedside table and called the front desk, seeking their help in summoning the police.

CHAPTER 15

PAUL GESLING WAS SPENDING EVERY SPARE MOMENT in front of the 3D holographic projector studying the schematic drawings and performance specifications for all of the systems that comprised the spaceship that would carry them to Sutter's Mill. The newly named *Tamaroa* would be their home for the next several months and he was determined to know as much about her as he could before they left Earth.

Named after the U.S. Coast Guard cutter made famous in the book *The Perfect Storm*, their *Tamaroa* would also be a rescue ship. Instead of rescuing the crew of sinking sailboat and then a swamped National Guard helicopter, they would hopefully be saving an entire city... or more.

At least the original Tamaroa *looked like a ship*, Gesling thought to himself.

The nuclear-powered rocketship didn't look much like a traditional spaceship to Gesling. To him it appeared ungainly and fragile. Designed and originally built to carry a four- to eight-person crew to and from Mars over a two- to four-year period, the *Tamaroa* was essentially two spacecraft connected by a long truss. Gesling walked the length of the scale-model projection of the *Tamaroa*, stopping occasionally to change his viewing angle and memorize one surface feature or another of the craft that would have taken the first humans to Mars had it not been commandeered by Gesling and his crew to save the Earth.

"Amazing, isn't she?" Paula Downey's voice startled Gesling, who hadn't noticed her walk into the room from the door to his right. She walked crisply toward Gesling, her head held high and facial expression showing all the pride a parent would wear had their offspring just been accepted at Harvard. Only the *Tamaroa* was her child—and it was going into deep space, not Harvard.

"Amazing isn't the word I would have used, but it'll do," replied Gesling.

"You'll think she's amazing when you ride her and feel her thrusting.... I mean, when you're inside her and... and, well, that didn't exactly come out like it should have." Downey turned red.

"That's okay. I know what you mean. I've been to the Moon, remember? There's nothing like the thrill of feeling the engines ignite and leaving Earth orbit." Paul laughed.

"I've been told its better than sex." Paula blushed a bit more.

"I wouldn't go that far but that's a discussion best left to another time—and with someone else." Paul didn't want to come off as a prude but at the same time he was a married man and didn't want to get into an uncomfortable situation with the engineer.

"Right. I'm sorry. I wasn't thinking. What do you know about the truss?"

"Not much. Tell me." Paul was glad she was changing the subject.

"Well, at one end of the truss are the nuclear rocket engines and the propellant tanks. Toward the middle are the radiators. At the opposite end is the crew module. Most importantly, the truss keeps the crew safely a tenth of a mile away from the fission reactor which powers and propels the ship. Without the truss providing all that separation, she'd have to carry a lot more shielding mass to protect you from the reactor's stray neutrons. It's made of composite materials and is stronger than steel."

"I understand why it's built the way it is, but that doesn't keep me from thinking that it doesn't look like a nuclear rocket ship should look." Paul shrugged his shoulders and gestured with his hands realizing he was sounding a bit like Captain Kirk the way he was speaking. He paused and took a breath then changed his mannerisms a bit. "I mean, a nuclear ship should be big, yes, but not spindly. It looks too fragile. It should have the physical dimensions of an ocean liner with a proper—big, strong, looking and capable. This looks like, well, like a ship designed by committee."

"Well, parts of it were designed by committee." Paula almost sounded annoyed but he wasn't sure. "You know that. Everything we've sent into space has been designed by committee—a committee composed of engineers, scientists, technicians, welders, electricians..."

"Okay, I'll drop it. But please build the next one to look more like a rocket and less like the ladder of a fire truck." Paul surrendered the argument.

"Deal. Now what questions can I help answer? Is there anything you don't understand about her?"

"The radiators. They're huge. Why are they so big?" Paul was used to rockets, chemical ones, with regenerative cooling and such.

"Ha ha, that gets a lot of smart people," Paula teased him. "A nuclear reactor puts out a lot of heat. A lot of that heat is transferred to the propellant, that's how the engine works. But there is a lot of heat that doesn't get carried away by the rocket exhaust and some of it is used to generate electrical power for the ship. It's called a bimodal nuclear reactor—it is operated in two modes. One mode produces rocket thrust, the other produces power. But even that doesn't use up all of the heat generated when the uranium atoms split in the reactor. It's that waste heat that the radiators have to dump into space."

"Can't we use it for something else?" Paul asked.

"Not easily. And unfortunately, unlike here on Earth where we have water to carry away most of the waste heat from a nuclear power reactor, in space we can only radiate. And radiating heat takes a lot of surface area; hence the large radiators."

"What happens if there's an accident? Like Fukushima or Chernobyl?" Paul was suddenly thinking of disaster in space and any number of scenarios he'd seen in science fiction movies.

"First of all, that won't happen. This reactor is designed to fail 'safe' and shut down if something goes wrong," Paula reassured him. "It's triple redundant. No, if the reactor shuts down, you will have plenty of other things to worry about instead of radiation from the reactor."

"Explain." Paul wished he could just fly a rocket he understood, like the *Dreamscape*, but he knew better.

"Without the reactor, you can't fire your engines to go anywhere and you won't have power to keep you warm and the air circulating. If the reactor fails, you're dead."

"Oh. Okay then, let's just make sure that doesn't happen." Paul noted the important safety tip.

"We did our best." Paula raised an eyebrow in a very cocksure way.

"What about solar storms? The *Dreamscape* has portable shields made of hydrogen-rich plastic that we set up around us if the Sun decides to send a burst of radiation our way. It's my understanding that you use a water wall around the crew quarters to absorb the radiation and keep exposure low during sleep. But I don't see that the skin in this model is any thicker around the core module than anywhere else. What gives?"

Paula smiled and motioned toward the core module.

"Hal, show us the magnetic shielding please," Paula said, enunciating more clearly and certainly speaking louder than previously.

"Deploying now," came a calm, male and oddly familiar voice from speakers hidden somewhere in the room. Downey was apparently talking to the display computer.

Within the holographic projection, around the core cylinder and the habitat and deploying from the truss were six booms, each with a large black box attached; three on each side of core module and habitat section.

"Did you just call the computer Hal?"

"Yes, I did. I'm a big fan of old science fiction movies. We thought it would be fun."

"And the voice, you even used the same voice?" Paul got the humor. He liked it, actually.

"That took some doing, but yes. Why not?" Paula asked him.

"Well, for starters, you know that bad things came of that computer. You didn't program the one on the ship that way did you?" He wasn't seriously concerned but the lighthearted tone relaxed the two of them a bit. It was something for pilot and engineer to lightly bond over.

"Of course not. The psychs would never have allowed it. Though we were tempted. . ." Downey said with her disarming smile in full bloom.

"So, tell me more about these magnetic shields. I've been reading about the concept for years but I didn't know it was mature enough to use yet."

"They wouldn't be, if you were on a solar-powered spacecraft. But with the nuclear reactor, you've got plenty of power available, so why not?" Downey then walked up to the 3D image of one of the deployed booms.

"In this box is a superconducting magnet. It's made from a new class of high temperature superconductors that don't have to be kept at liquid nitrogen temperatures of minus 452 degrees. Keeping something near absolute zero is pretty tough. These can operate at temperatures of up to 150 degrees without degrading. And, unlike most other superconductors, they don't lose their ability to conduct current if the ambient magnetic field is too strong. That makes them perfect for making magnets."

"Together, when current is flowing, these magnets can shield against all but the most energetic of the galactic cosmic rays and completely shield the crew against radiation in the solar wind and from solar storms. It's our version of a deflector screen." She pointed first at the box in front of them and then waived her arms to include all six boom and magnet sets. "The magnets each are capable of producing a three-tesla field. The total combined is a whopping eighteen teslas. That is, like, particle accelerator strong."

"So the solar radiation gets bent around the ship and doesn't pass through to the crew?" Paul asked.

"That's right." Downy seemed happy that he was following her so easily. "Most of it is deflected back into empty space. The only things we can't stop completely are the galactic cosmic rays. They are so massive, mostly carbon and iron, and moving so fast that we just can't build a magnetic field strong enough to stop all of them. Maybe the third or fourth generation system will be able to, but not this one."

"I bet that saved a lot of weight on the ship," Paul said.

"Tons. Mostly water. If we had gone with the more traditional approach, we would have needed to put up to three meters of water around the habitat to act as shielding, making it pretty darn heavy to launch or move around."

"What about the artificial gravity? The ship is designed to slowly spin along the truss axis to simulate the gravity on Mars and there hasn't been any mention of me training to perform the spin-up and spin-down maneuvers."

"You won't be using it much. We designed the ship to include the capability to simulate Martian gravity for the duration of the trip by spinning, but you're not going to Mars and you won't be in space long enough to suffer the worst of the biological effects resulting from being in a close to zero gravity environment. So, you will only need to spin up a few hours a week to help prevent any medical issues. This trip will be a short hop for the *Tamaroa* and the engineers just don't believe it is worth the risk. We may let you test it on the way home to make sure it works and reduce the risk for the first Mars mission."

"Having a little gravity would be nice," Paul argued.

"I wish I could say I understand. I would love to go where you're going but I wasn't selected for the astronaut program. Funny, they never really said why."

"What else have you got to show me?" asked Gesling.

"Lots. Let's start with the new oxygen regeneration system. It can..."

Paul and Paula spent the next two hours reviewing all the major subsystems in the *Tamaroa*. At the end, Paul didn't feel as overwhelmed as he had before. Having the ship's chief engineer provide a personal, though virtual, tour went a long way to alleviate his concerns.

Now all he and his crew had to do was get from the surface of the Earth and into space so they could board the *Tamaroa* and start the mission.

CHAPTER 16

"IT DOESN'T REALLY MATTER IF WE ARE A DAY LATE, but a week late might mean the difference between losing millions of lives or just having a wild fireworks show in the upper atmosphere," the NASA Administrator explained to the vice president.

"I see," Vice President Faulkner nodded knowingly.

Stetson simply stood calmly over the mission control console doing his best to pay attention to his job with one hundred and ten percent attention and at the same time make note of how the politicians reacted as they watched over the room. Stetson, in other words, was doing his best not to be distracted. The NASA administrator should have known better than to bring the "guests" into the control room. They sure as hell didn't need to stand right behind him jabbering the entire time. Bill did his best to put the chatter out of his mind and focus on the task at hand.

"Downey?" Bill opened a channel to the chief engineer of the nuclear thermal rocket system that had been intended for Mars originally. "Status of our ride?"

"Uh, the same as it was ten minutes ago. All systems are nominal and the reactor is inactive, safed, and will stay that way until long after the docking procedure," Paula Downey replied. Bill looked across the room of the mission control center and found her head looking over the sea of consoles back at him. He simply nodded as he made eye contact. He scanned the room continuously making note of who was on console and who was missing. He'd have talks with anyone who didn't tag-team out and put a highly trained butt in their seat before taking a coffee break or a bathroom run.

"Paul, is the habitat fully rigidized yet?" Stetson turned to his right to find Gesling sitting at his console monitoring the health and status of the Space Excursions Mars Habitat Module as it was being deployed. He thought about the name for a second and realized they were going to have to drop Mars from the title.

"Negative, Bill. The inflation pressure is still at one point zero one atmospheres and the thermal sensors imbedded in the epoxy layer are still at exothermic temperature. She's gonna need one more lap," Gesling replied.

Bill completely understood that the Mars Habitat Module had been inflated to full size once it made it to low Earth orbit. After it had been inflated, multiple layers of epoxy resins and hardeners were released over and within the skin. As the Habitat Module was exposed to direct sunlight while maintaining a Sun-synchronous orbit, the ultraviolet energy from the Sun cured and hardened the epoxy. The hardening process was an exothermic reaction that could be monitored with on-board thermal sensors. As soon as the epoxy was completely cured, the exothermic reaction would end and the surface of the habitat would heat and cool based on solar exposure and radiative cooling. The long cylindrical module rotated like a pig on a barbecue rotisserie so that all of the surface would get equal solar exposure. Once the exothermic reaction stopped, the surface temperature distribution would fluctuate with the rotisserie. For now, the temperature seemed pretty much constant.

Bill looked at his watch, an old astronaut habit, then back at the main screen showing the habitat's orbit. The nuclear thermal rocket stage was chasing it a few thousand miles behind, but was gaining. Autonomous rendezvous and docking of the two should happen on schedule provided that the habitat surface cured on time. It was up to Bill to make the call if the docking maneuvers had to be delayed or not based on the status of the habitat.

"Orbital?" Bill called to the orbit and trajectory expert console. A young girl that Bill thought couldn't be more than twenty-three looked over her shoulder back at him from her console. He knew she was sharp as they come, but, call it ageism or not, Bill would have felt more comfortable with someone a little more, well, seasoned sitting in the seat.

"Yes sir? Orbital here."

"We assume we are on schedule until Habitat tells us otherwise, but I want you to have several burn solutions for one, two, and three orbit delays loaded in and on standby." Bill thought about his statement for a minute. He knew that they had orbits calculated for all sorts of delays and contingency needs, but he also thought about the politicians behind them. This was his chance to show how hard working in space was with visibility all the way up to the White House. Bill had long grown tired of the forever shrinking budget the American space program had and he knew, or at least hoped, that every little bit of public relations couldn't hurt.

"Uh, yes sir. Ready to go on those if we need to," the girl at the Orbits console replied. Bill realized he had no idea what the young woman's name was. He made a mental note to find out as soon as the docking procedures were complete and they had a bit of a break before the nuclear thermal rocket engines were brought online.

"Good." There was really nothing for him to do but wait until the Habitat hardened. Bill turned to the administrator and the vice president behind him. He did his best to muster up a good old-fashioned astronaut hero smile. It was more of a forced grin, but it would have to do.

"Ma'am, not much is going to happen for about an hour to ninety minutes, it seems. If y'all want to go get some lunch I'll have somebody chase you down so you don't miss the rendezvous," Bill said through his fake smile while motioning toward the big screen showing the two spacecraft playing chase around the Earth.

"Thanks, Bill," the Administrator nodded. "Do that. In the meantime I'll introduce the vice president to the rest of the team and perhaps lunch is a good idea."

"Affirmative. Madam Vice President." Bill shook her hand as the politician smiled at him. "Hopefully, we'll have more excitement for you in a bit."

"Space is big. It takes time. I understand." The vice

president continued to smile as she nodded knowingly. Bill decided that he liked the lady. As far as politicians were concerned, she seemed more aware of reality than most he had met. Or at least she was good at appearing that way.

The epoxy hardened as the manufacturers said it would and, after several orbits being exposed to the direct sunlight, the once floppy inflated balloonlike structure was now a hardened carbon composite space-age vehicle. The habitat walls rigidized into a material that could withstand the buckling forces that would be generated by the huge thrusts of the nuclear thermal rockets once they were kicked on. The habitat would also have to withstand impulses from hard docking impacts, and if it were to go on to Mars someday, would have to hold up to the aerobraking reentry maneuvers in the upper Martian atmosphere. But for now it just needed to handle docking, the trip out to the asteroid, and the trip back all the while maintaining an atmosphere and livable conditions for the astronaut crew.

Paul couldn't wait to climb on board the habitat and test it out for the first time, but that would be a few weeks out. Putting first things first required that the autonomous docking procedure be completed successfully and then the engines being brought online and tested. The rendezvous so far looked flawless, but they were still a few minutes from actual impact.

"Paul, I'm picking up some periodic modal vibrations on the structure, are you seeing that?" The engineer covering the structures and telemetry console noted. Paul chuckled to himself lightly. He'd rather the engineer overreact rather than not react at all.

"Roger that, structures. We saw this in the sims. Even though the structure has been rigidized it is still somewhat flexible and each time we hit the thrusters it's like squeezing an air bag. Nothing to worry about, she's just breathing."

"Makes sense. The structure seems to ring following each position correction. They are all within tolerance," the structures engineer replied.

"Bill, everything is looking good. We are ready to hand over the docking process to the autonav," Paul said.

"Roger that, Habitat," Stetson replied. "You heard the man, Nav. Go for autonav."

"Affirmative, Capcom. Nav is go for autonomous docking procedure engage," the navigation console engineer replied.

"Nothing to do now but to sit back and watch the computer do its thing." Paul leaned back in his chair and put his hands behind his head. He took in a slow quiet breath and hoped and prayed to the computer navigation gods that all would work out as the engineers had planned.

"Autonav is engaged. Thrusters are firing."

"Hab, go to audible countdown to dock," Stetson ordered Paul.

"Roger that, Capcom," Paul leaned back to his console. "Contact in T minus twenty-six seconds."

"Lidar, radar, and video alignment are dead on," the Navigation Engineer added.

"Seventeen seconds, sixteen, fifteen..."

"Universal docking system shows green across the board."

"Docking contact in five, four, three, two, one, contact!" Paul said urgently. He quickly checked all the data flowing through his console screens to make certain nothing unexpected happened. The habitat was ringing like a bell but there were no signs of structural integrity failures.

"Capcom, Nav shows docking ring locked!"

"Hab?"

"Capcom, Habitat shows docking ring locked, fully engaged, and all systems are in the green." Paul sighed relief and let out a brief cheer. "Sutter's Mill, here we come." The *Tamaroa* was now intact. All that was left was to test her engines and get a crew on board her.

CHAPTER 17

GESLING LOOKED AROUND IN THE CRAMPED CAPSULE and once again lamented the damage done to the *Dreamscape*. With the reusable space plane out of commission, the mission planners decided to take the Chinese up on their offer to provide the international team going to Sutter's Mill with a free ride to space. The capsule was small and extremely uncomfortable. The chairs were crammed together so close that Gesling could feel Melanie's breathing to his left and Mikhail's obnoxiousness to his right. The thought made him chuckle, which was a relief under the circumstances.

"What's so funny?" asked Melanie, who had evidently noticed Gesling's guffaw.

"Oh, nothing, really. I was just wishing we were in the *Dreamscape* where we'd have a lot more room for the flight."

"You're not in your comfy little private space plane, *Commander* Gesling. Get used to it."

Gesling was taken aback at the harsh tone of her rebuke. This wasn't the first time Melanie had been short with him, but it was the first time she'd done so in public. And this was very public. They were on the launch pad in the *Shenzhou-X* capsule that the Chinese regularly used to send taikonauts to their base on the Moon. Liftoff was planned to be in less than thirty minutes and the world's eyes were upon everything happening at the Chinese launch site.

"Oh, I realize that, Dr. Ledford. And I won't forget it," was Paul's acerbic reply. Paul was only now starting to realize that Mikhail probably wasn't the only other member of the crew who resented him being named mission commander. It must have been a significant blow for Melanie to not be named commander of the asteroid redirect mission when it supplanted Mars—she was to have commanded that mission, after all. Paul looked around the cabin and realized that he was the commander of a team of commanders: Hui was in charge of the Chinese Moon mission a few years ago, Mikhail led the first crew in the Russian lunar base, and Melanie was to have been commander of the Mars mission. *Oh boy, why didn't I realize that before?*

The crew was soon to launch into Earth orbit and dock with the rest of the *Tamaroa*—the ship that would take them to Sutter's Mill. The nuclear propulsion system stages and the Deep Space Habitat were launched successfully over the last ten days and all that was missing was themselves—the people who would fly to the rogue asteroid and divert it from a collision course with Earth.

Gesling was again running through the pre-launch checklist on the touchpad before him when he began to hear more than normal chatter on the radio. Unfortunately, it was almost all in Chinese. From the tone, even Gesling could tell that something unexpected was happening.

"Hui, what's going on?" Gesling asked.

"I was just tuning in. They're saying that something has appeared on the radar flying inbound from the East and it's only five miles away. They're diverting one of the fighters to intercept it."

Gesling knew that in China, just as in the USA, the airspace near a rocket launch was closed. And to make sure it remained closed, especially on a launch involving people, there were always a few fighter jets on patrol. He didn't like the fact that whatever was coming toward them was so close already. Surely their radars could, and should, have picked it up from much further out.

More Chinese chatter came through the radio, sounding even more excited than before.

"They're saying there is another one, coming from the South."

"Do we evacuate?" asked Reudiger.

"Evacuate just because we're sitting on a few tons of liquid hydrogen and oxygen waiting to be lit? Why ever would you think we'd need to do that?" replied Mikhail, trying to not sound too nervous himself.

"No, we sit tight until ground control tells us we need to do something," Gesling replied.

"Paul, this is Bill." Stetson's voice came over the comm channel from mission control to Gesling's headset. It was the command channel and only he could hear what was being said.

"The Chinese have picked up what appears to be two small drones coming toward the launch complex. They're not moving very fast, so the jets are probably going to be able to intercept both of them before they pose a significant danger to you. The information we're getting is sketchy, but they sound like the same kind of drones that damaged the *Dreamscape*."

"Zhi Feng," Gesling muttered.

"That's what I'm thinking. The leadership here is scrambling trying to figure out if we should abort and get you guys off the rocket." Stetson stopped speaking and Gesling heard someone telling him something, but it was too muddled for him to pick out what was being said.

"Paul, we want you off the bird now. We think the drones might be a diversion."

Gesling didn't hesitate. He punched the emergency abort button just below his right fingertip as he spoke to this crew, "They want us out of here now. This is a hot abort."

All had been trained for an on-pad abort, but none had ever before experienced it. Mikhail opened the capsule's hatch and grappled with the basket that was latched to the side of the top horizontal stabilizer bar on the launch tower. The bar was designed to remain affixed to the capsule and rocket until just thirty seconds before launch, a time limit they were currently well within.

Gesling saw the crew board the basket in the order in which they'd trained: Hui Tian first, because of where she was sitting with respect to the hatch; Then Reudiger, followed by Gesling and Ledford. Mikhail would be last, since he was the one designated to help the others board the basket. In less than sixty seconds, they were all in the basket.

"Release!" Mikhail shouted as he unlatched and sent the crew careening away from the rocket in what felt like an out-of-control roller coaster ride. The stark landscape of the Gobi desert and the bubble of civilization that was the Jiuquan Satellite Launch Center momentarily distracted Gesling. But his attention was diverted for only for a moment. He knew that if they didn't get distance between themselves and the rocket, then they could all die a fiery death.

As the basket accelerated, Gesling noticed a plume of smoke coming from the north. He realized at once what he was seeing—a missile. And it was coming straight at them. He couldn't tell if it came from an aircraft or from the ground, but that didn't really matter. It was coming.

He tried to keep his eyes on the plume, and the missile that was presumably creating it, as the basket passed sixty miles per hour and approached the hopeful safety of the bunker on the ground below. Gesling was gauging the progress of the missile against their own toward the bunker. It was going to be close.

The basket began to slow as it passed through the door of the bunker. Once they were past the opening, the massive concrete and steel doors began to close.

Gesling took one last look at the rocket that was to have carried them into space. He was still looking at it when the missile struck just below the capsule, about 175 feet above the ground. At first, Gesling thought there might be no effect from the impact, but he quickly learned that was not to be the case. The explosion and ensuing orange and white fireball quickly filled the sky as it and the pieces of the rocket consumed by the blast moved toward the almost-closed door of the bunker. Gesling and the rest of his colleagues could only watch the explosion as they slowed to a stop in the cavernous bunker. A red light just inside the door flashed continuously as they approached. There was no place else for them to go and no time to do anything other than gasp.

The door closed and a solid green light replaced the red flashing one. There was a huge audible *clang* as the door shut just as the blast wave reached the ground, causing the entire structure to vibrate and ring like a very low frequency bell. A bell they were inside of. Paul wished he could cover his ears or shake his head in order to alleviate the ringing in his ears, but he was in a spacesuit and he didn't have time. The five astronauts scrambled from the halted basket and threw themselves to the ground, hands over their heads, in a position to hopefully protect themselves from any falling debris within the shelter. There was none. The door held and the bunker remained intact following the blast.

"Is anyone injured?" Gesling asked.

In response, he heard a chorus of murmurs but no positive answer, for which he was grateful.

"Zhi Feng. That son of a bitch. How did he manage to get that much hardware into China, for God's sake? Two drones and a missile?" Mikhail exclaimed.

"He is a very resourceful and well-connected engineer. Remember, he managed to create a heating system to keep us alive in our damaged spacecraft when we crashed on the Moon. He knows how to build things and make them work. And, well, he is Chinese. He didn't have to get anything into China that likely wasn't already here," Hui Tian replied.

"Hell, everything is made in China nowadays," Melanie Ledford grunted.

"Well, your resourceful engineer friend may have just condemned millions of people to death," Reudiger said.

"At a minimum he just cost your people hundreds of millions of dollars," Paul added, thinking of the business end. Too many years with Gary Childers had shaped his thinking along those lines.

"The ship is fully assembled in orbit and waiting on us," Mikhail said as he flipped the visor open on his helmet. "Understand the physics of our situation. The ship's liquid hydrogen fuel is slowly boiling away and unless we launch and depart within a week, there won't be enough fuel to get us there and back remaining onboard," Mikhail said.

No one said a word in response. Gesling knew that what Mikhail said was true. Now that both the *Dreamscape* and the *Shenzhou-X* were damaged, how would they get to space in time?

CHAPTER 18

"THEY FOUND THREE MORE CRAWLERS, EACH WITH a missile just like the one that destroyed the *Shenzhou-X*." Stetson was briefing Gesling and the rest of his team on what had happened in the Gobi the day before. They were sequestered in a Chinese army base several hundred miles from the Jiuquan Satellite Launch Center, protected by nearly five thousand Chinese troops garrisoned there.

"This guy is a veritable arms dealer," Melanie said.

"Two remotely piloted drones and four remote-control toy trucks armed with homemade missiles. The attack was brilliant. And I think some Chinese military heads are going to roll as a result. They never imagined that an attack like this could happen on Chinese soil." Stetson was scrolling through projected slides showing the remains of the hardware that had nearly killed them all.

"Mr. Childers confirmed that the drones were identical to the ones that damaged the *Dreamscape* in Nevada. It looks like they were going to fly themselves directly into the rocket. The trucks, each the size of an ottoman, were clearly modified versions of a commercially available radio-controlled survey vehicle like those commonly used to identify property lines in remote regions throughout the world. There are serial numbers, so the FBI and others can hopefully track them back to where and when they were purchased."

"Any sign of Zhi Feng?" Gesling asked "He had to be close by in order to control the drones and the trucks."

"No sign of him. The transmitters on the devices had enough power to broadcast a signal up to a hundred or more miles away. He could have been anywhere, watching his toys and steering them our way by remote control. But the Chinese authorities assure us that he will not escape to continue this personal vendetta of his. I think they were severely embarrassed by this event on a very global scale."

"What now? Is there a Plan B?" asked Gesling.

"You mean, plan C? The *Dreamscape* was the original plan. The Chinese were the backup," Melanie corrected him.

"You know NASA." Stetson surveyed the room's occupants before he explained. "Yes, there is a Plan C, but you aren't going to like it. The NASA Commercial Crew Office can have a modified Falcon 10 ready to go by the end of the week. But there's a catch."

"And that is?" asked Melanie.

"It can only carry three of you. It's designed to take replacement crew to the Space Station. The next crew was scheduled to go up later this month, but the bird is already on the pad and they just moved up the timetable. The trajectory can be easily modified to allow it to rendezvous with your ship."

"What about the other two of us?" asked Reudiger.

"Grounded. There's no other rocket available."

"Wait, my friend. You are forgetting about Russia. I have it on good authority that NPO Energomash is readying a rocket for launch as we speak. I am not sure of its destination, but it is the same rocket we use to send crew to the Moon. I've ridden on it personally and it can easily take the remaining crew to space for the rendezvous," Mikhail boomed in reply.

"Mikhail, we checked on that. The Russian Academy said that the rocket is being readied for a national defense mission and cannot be modified to carry crew in time to meet our schedule." Stetson frowned, wishing that Mikhail's option would work. He didn't like the thought of only three of five astronauts making the trip to the asteroid.

"Have you checked with ESA?" asked Reudiger.

"Yes, of course. They don't have anything that can be readied in time."

"And none of the other commercial launch services companies have anything that we can use?" asked Melanie. "What about Sierra Nevada or Blue Origin?"

"None. And we looked everywhere. I'm sorry, but only three of you will be going to make the trip."

"Which three?" asked Melanie.

"Gesling, Tian, and Rykov. We're flying you to Florida on a plane that leaves in three hours. Melanie, you and Reudiger are being added to the ground team. I'm sorry, but that's all we can do."

"Hell no!" Ledford quickly stood and nearly shouted. "You are not going to take this away from me. My team was ready to launch for Mars and then this whole crisis scrapped those plans because of the stupid so-called commercial space industry! The result of the stupid barnstorming and reckless space business put millions at risk and destroyed years of training making me second fiddle to this bus driver," she said, pointing at Gesling. "And now you're telling me that I'm to remain on Earth while these three take on a job that we all know will require at least all five of us to accomplish safely? This is total bullshit!"

"Wait a moment." Reudiger raised his hand before he finished speaking, "Surely Mr. Gesling should be dropped from the crew to eliminate the terror threat from our mission. As Hui told us, these actions aren't directed at the rest of us, merely the members of the team that are somehow affiliated with Space Excursions and you, Mr. Stetson."

"Melanie, Reudiger, I hear you. But the decision has been made and it cannot be changed if we are to not miss our launch window. Paul is going on the mission," Stetson said forcefully. He'd expected some disappointment and pushback, but not an outright attack on his friend Paul.

"This is *not* the end of the discussion, by God!" Melanie shouted as she stormed out of the room while punching numbers on the touchscreen of her smartphone. "We will see about this."

"No, I suspect it isn't the end of the discussion. But while we're discussing, we have a mission to accomplish and little time to make changes if we are to be successful," Stetson said frowning and shaking his head.

"Not much time at all," he reiterated.

CHAPTER 19

THE *TAMAROA* WAS FAR MORE SPACIOUS THAN THE capsule that brought them to space, and for that Paul Gesling was immensely grateful. Though it wasn't exactly what he'd call "roomy," it was actually adequate for the mission before them. Of course, part of the reason it felt spacious was due to the missing crew members and their gear. The ship was designed to take up to eight people on a two to three-year voyage to Mars and back; for this trip, there were just three.

Located at the end opposite the propulsion system, the *Tamaroa*'s habitat was similar to the one Space Excursions had placed on the Moon. The core of the module was quite solid, cylindrical in shape, and would alone have afforded them more room than the three Apollo astronauts had on their journey to and from the Moon. Located behind the habitat was the transfer capsule that brought them up from Earth and that would return them safely there upon the successful completion of their mission. The airlock separating the capsule from the habitat remained open should an emergency arise that forced them to quickly evacuate into it for safety. At the front of the capsule was another cylinder about twice the diameter of the core. It had been inflated and rigidized once the vehicle had reached orbit. That forward cylinder was the command capsule for the mission—were it a naval ship or a starship from most science fiction it could have been designated as "the bridge."

Gesling currently sat strapped into a chair in the middle of the command cylinder mindlessly looking at ship systems and functions on a large touchscreen in front of him. Pulling up the schematic for the ship, he zoomed into the sections just aft of the command cylinder where there were three hatches. Once the core had reached orbit the command cylinder and three separate inflatable rooms had been deployed on the outside of each hatch. The rooms were inflated from packed dimensions of five feet by eight feet to a room over fifteen feet long and twelve feet high, each new room dramatically increased the space available for the astronaut crew to live and work. It was these inflatable rooms and the command cylinder that had been cured and hardened, also known as "rigidized" by the sun's light. It was a very clever design.

The central core had been launched packed with supplies and equipment that was moved into these new rooms once the crew docked the launch capsule and emerged into their new home. None of the equipment to be moved was heavy—there is no weight in space—but each piece did have mass and therefore inertia. Due to Newton's law of inertia an object at rest stays at rest and an object in motion stays in motion unless it is acted on by a force. The force had to be applied by the astronauts themselves. So, moving the gear required both muscles and coordination. It took nearly a full work day to unpack and then move the gear to its new home. It took another day to test and make sure all the systems were working properly. It wasn't until after those system checks that the ship's nuclear core could be brought online to full power. Then the crew could begin the long voyage to Sutter's Mill.

Paul tapped a few more icons on the screen, bringing up the latest data from the ship's nuclear engines. As far as he could tell, the *Tamaroa* was purring like a kitten. He hoped it continued to do so. Once he was satisfied the ship was in good shape he opened up the latest downloads about the status of the asteroid. It was still there, looming toward Earth. Their mission had to be successful. They had to stop the devastation and death on such a large scale that the Sutter's Mill would cause. He had to keep it from harming Carolyn. He hadn't been there to protect her from the crazy bastard that had shot her. He had to protect her from the asteroid. He knew he had to do something.

If he wasn't there holding her hand and doing all he could to help her regain consciousness, he had to be out here in space doing all he could to stop the asteroid. At least that was what he told himself to justify the guilt he felt for not being there for her when she had been shot and not being there for her now. The justification didn't seem to be enough. He felt guilty just for being there. Hell, Dr. Ledford was probably much better prepared to lead a mission like this. Paul did his best not to dwell on it, but he couldn't help but feel just a bit out of his league, and guilty for just being there.

"Well, the mission clock is at five weeks, three days, four hours and twenty-some-odd minutes." Rykov grinned as he muddled the English with thick Russian accents and something in Russian that probably shouldn't be translated anyway. "Only another thirty weeks to go before reaching Sutter's Mill, comrade."

"If you continue to tell us how much further we must go, then this will turn out to be a very long trip," Hui Tian said deadpan in response. Her Chinese accent was much less distracting than Rykov's Russian. "I trust the engine systems are all well and good."

"*Bozhe moi.*" Mikhail Rykov laughed deeply and overacted his amusement. "Computer shows the ship all in the green. And there is not really anything to do with them unless something goes wrong. You know, you should lighten up, young lady. I could think of worse places to be for the next five weeks."

"Ah," Hui Tian grinned. She wasn't certain but Rykov's tone almost sounded flirtatious. "I'm very light, Mikhail. In fact, I'm nearly weightless."

"That's the spirit, Hui." Rykov looked back at her as if he'd had a serious thought. "We actually need to hit the spin cycle soon. Then you'll get heavy."

"Right." Hui looked to her right and tapped a touchscreen a few times. The mission day timeline and scheduling application opened. "Spin cycle is not for another hour and seven minutes. So, if you have this under control, I think I'll wander up and check on Paul."

"Good here, I think."

"Till the spin cycle then."

Since launch, Gesling had spent the bulk of his time at the ship's flight controls, which were located in the command capsule upship. Hui had to pass from the aftmost section of the ship, where engineering and the docking hatch was, then go through the core cylinder where they each had small private areas and where they would enter into the spin section later, and finally pass through the forwardmost hatch to the command capsule. The command capsule housed the main flight controls, computer systems, sensor interfaces, communications equipment, and in general all the things needed to run the ship.

As she moved past the various parts of the otherwise sterile ship, she couldn't help but wonder if Rykov had been flirting with her. Not that she was interested in him; not at all. But it had been a long time since a man had shown any real interest in her physically and, well, even if it wasn't reciprocal, it felt kind of nice.

Paul sat in the command chair, his chair, scrolling randomly and almost unconsciously through the daily feeds from home. There was no real news there about anything he was interested in. Bill had mentioned that Carolyn had displayed no changes for the better or worse. No changes at all. It had been months now and still nothing. He couldn't get his mind around that so he focused on anything else.

Bill also told him about how his wife Rebecca was going through an experimental trial procedure that Childers had managed to arrange. Apparently, they were hoping to use some magic stem cell matrix mixture, bone grafts, titanium, and 3D-printed muscle and tendon tissue to rebuild the hand she had lost in the explosion. Paul was mostly fascinated by the procedure's details and was typing up a response to Bill about how amazing that was.

"How are you?" Hui asked as she entered the five person sized capsule.

Paul startled. He didn't notice that Hui was in the room until she spoke. It was easy to get around unheard in the spacecraft since there were no floors to walk on and the loud air circulation system created a not-so-subtle white noise background sort of like a washing machine running in the distance. And being preoccupied with Rebecca's amazing medical procedure had his mind elsewhere. He settled himself and thought for a brief second that he was glad he hadn't screamed like a little girl. He hit the command chair unlock and spun around to face her.

"Not too bad, once I recover from being scared out of my wits. I might need to change my shorts though. It might not hurt to wear a cowbell from now on, either."

"Cowbell?" Hui paused not quite sure she understood the reference for a moment but then Paul could see a slight nod of her head and a smile as she finally got it. "Very funny. Sorry about that."

"That's okay. We'll have to get used to everyone out here being on silent. On second thought, the cowbells might not be a bad idea." He paused with a half-hearted chuckle, then continued, "I was just catching up on things back home. Nothing to speak of."

"I see," Hui replied and made her way to a chair and then strapped herself into it. "I'm not bothering you, am I? If you'd prefer to be alone I can—"

"No, no. Come in. Have a seat." Paul had been sitting in the capsule alone for the past hour, he felt he could use a real person to talk to for a bit. "How about you? Any great news from home?"

"Not really. My youngest sister's daughter just had a baby girl. I am now a great aunt, as you Americans would say."

"And you will be a great one I'm sure! Congratulations," Paul said. "Do you have a picture?"

"Not yet." Hui looked around at the capsule and then out into space. Paul could tell she noticed the small red star almost abeam of what would be the ship's three-nine line if it had wings or were a clock.

"Mars," Paul noted. "I can't look over there and not think about Melanie not being out here with us. I feel very bad about that."

"Yes, both Doctors Ledford and Hahn should be here with us or should be going there instead of us doing this," Hui Tian agreed. "It would be fun to go there some day."

"I was thinking that earlier when I first saw it this morning. Heck, I've pretty much thought about it every day as it seems to be right there taunting us. How different it would be if we were on our way to Mars instead."

"Very different and less, what is the right word..."

"Somber? Morbid? Scary?" Paul wasn't sure what the right word was either.

"No, not those. But, something along those lines perhaps. Serious maybe?" Hui shrugged.

"Serious? Nah, going to Mars would be serious, but in a different way. I'm not sure what the word is. But I can't help but think about how this ship was supposed to be carrying the first human mission to Mars and now we're out here, running on a skeleton crew, trying to deflect an asteroid that should never have been moved in the first place."

"I'm surprised to hear you say that. I thought you were in favor of mining asteroids. Didn't you tell me that we would have to be mining asteroids in order to help save the planet?"

"Well, yes, I did say that. And I believe that. I just don't think we were ready to start altering the orbits of flying mountains unless we have a backup system in hand to stop things like this from happening. All things considered, I'd rather be going to Mars." Paul pointed at the red dot in the sky to their right.

"You know I agree with you. But whether we like it or not, we have a pretty important job to do out here. And, don't forget, neither of us would have been going to Mars. I was still training for the next Chinese mission back to the Moon and you were planning on taking tourists to that lunar hotel of yours. So, neither of us would be going this deep into space doing something this important."

"Important. You used it twice. Maybe that is the word?" Paul wasn't sure there was a perfect word to describe their mission. One thing he did agree with was that they were supposed to be doing other things at the moment and not on such a deep space mission. "Well, you know what? I feel guilty about our important mission."

"Guilty?"

"Guilty. I feel guilty because I like being out here. I like the fact that we were the ones chosen. I like the fact that we have a job to do that is taking us into deep space to someplace no human being has ever been before. I often find myself asking, 'why me?' Why am I the one lucky enough to go to space? To the Moon? And now to an asteroid? Why not someone else? Certainly Dr. Ledford or Reudiger would have been better suited or more qualified to be here than me. I was lucky, or had the right connections, I don't know what, but I do feel guilty about it."

"I've asked myself the same question, but I don't feel guilty about it. I worked hard to get here. In China, there are more qualified candidates for the astronaut corps than there are engineers in the United States. With a population over one billion, the competition is tough, but I did it. I know I am qualified to be here and I don't feel one bit of guilt over it."

"Yeah, but you don't have to feel the guilt of not being there for Carolyn, uh, some family member who needs you there. She's lying in a hospital bed, unconscious, and I should be there." Paul choked back the emotions welling up and threatening to overcome him as best he could. He turned as a yellow appointment icon popped up on his screen. He tapped the snooze button closing it.

"Doing what? I mean, you are not a medical doctor. You are an engineer and a spacecraft pilot."

"I don't know, I mean, well, I should be at the hospital, maybe? Holding her hand. Talking to her. Maybe that would help her come out of the coma faster."

"Do you really believe she would rather you sit by her bedside and mope than fly into deep space on a mission to save millions of lives, perhaps even hers? Really?" Hui's expression was one of incredulity.

"Yes? I mean, I don't know. She's much more pragmatic than me, so probably no, not really. She would probably be mad at me were she to wake up with me by her side and then learn I turned down this mission." Paul seemed to hear those words for the first time and truly understand them. Carolyn *would* be mad at him if he had not done everything in his power to save the world, or at least the lives that were in danger.

"So stop feeling guilty. Take pride in what we're here to accomplish. Know that your loved one will understand. I wish I could have been there to see my grandniece, but I'm also very glad to be here. You should be guilt free. I know I am. I will see my niece when I get home and will give her a hug as you will your wife."

CHAPTER 20

"WHAT? IT'S LOUD, I CAN BARELY HEAR YOU." PAUL'S mind was still wrapped deep into the dream he was having. He and his wife were holding hands watching others in their group play in the waterfall. The Jamaican Dunn River rushed off the large rocks all around them, creating a beautiful spectacle and a very loud rushing sound. He could feel the spray on his body and enjoyed the warm heat of the Jamaican sun as it filtered through the greenery all around the river.

After only a couple days following their wedding, the Dunn River Falls Excursion was an ideal honeymoon activity. Paul knew he'd been there a couple years ago with his wife, but it seemed like he was there all over again. The dream was quite lucid. He turned so that his back was to the falls. His wife's hair eclipsed the sun behind her, leaving faint rays of gold sunlight filtering through. Paul smiled, thinking how much like a halo it looked and how angelic his wife appeared to him. In his eyes she was perfect.

"Paul, dear?" Carolyn looked into his eyes. The

rushing of the falls was very noticeable and the noise of one of the tourists screaming behind him was distracting. The movement of her hair with the slight moist breeze killed the halo effect behind her head.

"What is it?" he asked. She seemed more distraught than he recalled. He reached out to take her hand in his.

"Paul. Get up," she told him. The sound of the waterfall was more than just rushing water noise. It almost sounded like the squeal of a balloon deflating when its neck is being pinched tight. And the scream was periodic, not like a person screaming at all. "Paul!"

"What!" Paul startled so abruptly that his floating right arm jerked and he backhanded himself in the face. He quickly gained his composure while rubbing at the red spot on his forehead with his left hand. He then realized that an air pressure alarm was sounding, along with several other secondary alerts. He shook his head and began unzipping and unfastening himself from his bag.

Paul turned to the panel in his sleep cube and tapped at the screen of his handheld tablet that was Velcroed to the wall. There was a drop in cabin pressure. The leak was so large that it was causing a fluting action making the noise that rang through the crew area in the central cylinder. The noise was damned near earsplitting.

"Paul! Are you awake?" Rykov's voice shouted through the zippered door of his rigidized cube. "We have an emergency situation."

"Yes, I'm on my way. Do you know what is going on?"

"Only that there is a severe loss of pressure in the cabin nearest the command capsule," Rykov explained.

"Is everybody okay?" Paul unzipped his door and forced himself through it. Rykov and Hui Tian were both exiting there cubes respectively. He pulled up the ship schematic on his pad. There were several red dots blinking on the command capsule's port side. "The command capsule integrity is lost. Hui, close the hatch to it and start up the secondary command center in engineering. I'll shut down the air handling system to that section of the ship. Mikhail, suit up and grab the patch kit. I'm right behind you."

"I'm on it, comrade." Mikhail turned and kicked off the wall, pushing himself aftward toward the airlock.

"I've got the hatch," Hui noted.

Paul filtered through the icons on his pad until he found the air handling system. He shut down the vents, both intakes and outtakes, in the command capsule. The he backed out of that menu up a couple levels to the alert systems menu. He shut off the klaxon noise. He realized he felt fairly lightheaded so he then checked the cabin pressure.

"Jesus, we're already at six pounds per square inch!" he said. "Less than half an atmosphere."

The hatch closed with a *kathunk* as Hui pulled it to. She dogged the door down, which attenuated the screeching fluting sound of the leaking air. Then Paul watched Hui as she kicked from the wall and then zipped past him toward the aft of the ship. He could feel vibrations from the motors in the intake and outtake vents just forward of them in the command cylinder cycled closed. The pressure in the crew cabin began to rise slowly.

"Well, that's good. Means there are no leaks in here, but if we're going EVA we need to pull the pressure down to five psi anyway. We just weren't supposed to do it so quickly," he said to himself as he adjusted the cabin pressure settings. He put in the final EVA pressure goal and the computer calculated the safe rate of drop that could be implemented. It would be an hour or more before they should go outside. Paul checked his heart rate and hoped that they weren't all going to get a bad case of the bends based on their rapid decompression. The computer would cycle the pressure back up and then down at the most appropriate rate with hopes of avoiding that.

"Hui, as soon as the secondary system is up we need to send a communication to Earth," Paul ordered. "And let's get our vitals sensors taped on. We decompressed too quickly."

"We may be in deep space but we were hit by debris," Hui Tian told them as she brought up a radar image on the main screen in Engineering, which was for the moment acting as the bridge. The three astronauts were each in spacesuits with their helmets off but nearby. Until the leak was fixed and they knew what was going on, Paul had ordered it just to be safe.

"Holy shit!" Paul didn't like what he saw. The radar image showed a debris cloud as big as Texas that they had passed through. They were already more than ten thousand kilometers from it, and they had been lucky. It looked like there were several chunks in the cloud that were as big as automobiles. There was no way to know if they were solid or gravel piles but the relative velocity between the *Tamaroa* and the cloud was on the order of ten kilometers per second. It could have been devastating. Fortunately for them, the density of the cloud was very low, making the odds of a hit much lower than was intuitive from looking at the radar image. The devil was in the detailed resolution and the radar wasn't that accurate at the distance between the ship and where the debris cloud currently was.

"Is the radar at max power?" Rykov asked.

"Uh, not sure," Hui Tian tapped the screen and adjusted a slidebar control. "It is now. I assume power is not a problem?"

"Not at all, comrade. The reactor supplies us all the power we need and then some." Rykov sort of smiled.

"Sweep the beam across our path up front and leave it on that sweep. I don't care about what we have behind us." Paul pulled himself closer to the screen and then realized he'd passed the "too far" point. He extended his arms until the screen came back into focus. "Damn, gonna have to get reading glasses before long," he said under his breath.

"For now it is clear between us and Sutter's Mill," Hui replied. She pointed at the blue and red trajectory lines of the *Tamaroa* and the asteroid respectively.

"Can you back up the trajectory of the debris field based on the measurements we have?" Paul asked. He had a hunch that he hoped wasn't correct.

"Yes, hold on a minute." Hui continued tapping away at the touchscreen for another moment. It was a good time to turn to Rykov and work out their repair plan.

"Cabin pressure is just under five point seven psi," Paul started. "Mikhail, once we know we are clear from further debris for sure we'll go ahead and start chasing down the damage outside."

"Ready when you are, Paul," he replied.

"Trajectory extrapolation complete," Hui interrupted. "Not sure how but it looks like the cloud came from Sutter's Mill."

"That doesn't make sense, does it?" Rykov asked. He rubbed at the beard starting in on his chin. "Why would some of the asteroid be moving faster than the rest?"

"It was spinning." Paul pulled himself up close enough to tap at the screen. "When they despun the thing I'll bet you a dime to a donut that this debris field broke off and was slingshot forward converting the angular momentum of the spinning asteroid into acceleration. I'd love to have the despin data from the mining company."

"Makes sense," Rykov nodded. "Where is it headed now?"

"To Earth," Hui zoomed out on the screen showing the red line intercepting with Earth in a couple of months. "Eighty-eight point three seven percent likelihood of impacts."

"We need to warn them and we need to fix the command capsule." Paul pulled his helmet from its tethered location on the wall by him and pulled it over his head. The visor still up, he turned to his Russian engineer. "You ready?"

"Ready when you are, comrade!" Rykov said playing up his accent as he so often did with them.

"Hui, hold down the fort. See if you can get a warning message back to Earth as well."

"Roger that, Paul. We were lucky. It looks like the long range antenna is still lined up," she said.

"Yes, I'd say we were lucky we didn't hit one of those larger chunks. Good thing for us that space is big," Paul added. The other two just nodded in agreement.

CHAPTER 21

A MONTH LATER, THE TEAM WAS IN THE COMMAND capsule looking out the windows and at the many touchscreens that covered its interior surfaces. Paul Gesling was strapped into his command chair. He preferred it to floating around. It made him feel more in control of himself and like he was actually flying. He had noted over the months of flight time that Hui preferred to be tethered in as well, but Rykov almost never strapped in. The Russian had spent several months on the International Space Station and Paul just assumed that he'd gotten used to not being strapped in on the station. That triggered him to make a mental note if Gary ever decided to do an orbiting hotel. Some people might prefer to be strapped in and others might not.

Sutter's Mill didn't look the way Gesling had expected. Rather than the odd-shaped potato or roughly spherical ball that so many asteroids seemed to resemble, it looked more like a skipping rock, the kind he used to select for skimming across the water when he was a boy. Were he a giant and had a big pond at which to throw the thing, he was sure he could get five or even six skips out of it. But then he thought that it reminded him more of a cookie than a skipping rock.

The large two kilometer in diameter and half kilometer thick cookie-shaped asteroid wasn't randomly tumbling either, as he'd expected. The initial maneuvers performed by the Asteroid Ores' tether system had taken any residual rotation out of the rock. It almost looked flat enough to be used as a space-based aircraft carrier. He, Mikhail and Hui were crowded around the viewport looking at the asteroid as they progressively got closer, slowing their relative motion with respect to the rock, so that they would soon be stationary. Stationary in respect to the asteroid, which was careening madly towards Earth at about seventeen kilometers per second.

As they drew closer, they discerned a fissure running roughly down the middle of the asteroid's flat surface. They weren't able to tell how deep it went, but it was clear that something had caused the massive rock to nearly cleave into two pieces. Near the limb of the asteroid farthest from their present position there was another crack that looked more like something had taken a bite off the edge of the giant cookie than it did a missing chunk of asteroid.

"I'm bettin' that missing chunk over there is what hit us a month ago." Paul pointed at the image on the screen as he whistled. "Looks less solid there according to the lidar."

"I suspect you are correct, Paul. But until we take the radar data and reconstruct the debris field and then compare it to the surface of the asteroid we will not know for certain," Hui replied.

"Leave it for the Ph.D. students back at university," Mikhail Rykov added.

"Right, whatever. I'm just glad Asteroid Ores' tether system worked to despin this monster," said Gesling. "Otherwise, this mission would be way more complicated."

"And dangerous," Rykov said.

"Yes." Hui nodded in agreement. "We didn't believe it would work. My country has had engineers looking at the asteroid tumble problems for years. They looked at using tethers to remove the angular momentum and then promptly put it near the bottom of the list calling it 'too risky.'"

"Us too. We always concluded that the tethers would break. That's why we baselined electric propulsion for both the propulsion system to move the rock and to despin it," remarked Rykov.

"I guess this just goes to show that sometimes simpler is better," Paul commented.

"Look! There! I can see the EP module," Hui almost shouted.

Just coming into view as the habitat passed the asteroid's flat surface on its first slow flyby was the propulsion module containing the malfunctioning electric propulsion system. As far as he could tell there was no light coming from the exhaust nozzle. There was no glow of plasma. There were no blinking running lights. There was basically no sign of anything functioning. But they were still a bit far off to see much detail.

"I see it, but we're too far away to see if there is any damage—if there's anything to see. It could be an internal problem. I need to get into it to see what's wrong," Rykov said.

"One more pass and then I think we can bring the ship in close enough to dock. How far away do you want me to take her before you try the harpoon?" Paul asked Hui as he turned to look at Mikhail, who was floating behind and to the left of him. He wished the Russian would put his butt in a seat. The floating around was seriously distracting. Paul was more used to sitting in a seat and flying. That made sense. How the hell could anyone be able to reach all the buttons and switches and controls while floating about?

"I should be able to set the harpoon to within a hundred meters of the propulsion module. I don't want to risk having the harpoon miss and cause more damage to it," Hui replied. Paul turned back and looked at her strapped into the seat to his right.

"A hundred meters is pretty close. I can do that," he reassured her. "How many times were you able to rehearse harpooning?"

"Not enough. And they were all VR simulations. There wasn't enough time to get any real experience on the ground, not that it would have done any good. We're so used to gravity that we automatically adjust for its effects when we shoot arrows or guns, or throw balls for that matter. We aim high, allowing for the ball or bullet to fall while in flight. Out here, the gravity will be negligible so it'll be totally different. The simulator is probably better."

Two hours later, Gesling had adjusted the ship's velocity and orientation so that it was relatively stationary above the edge of the rock. Even though they were moving through space at about seventeen kilometers per second relative to the Earth, no one would know it from looking out the windows of the habitat. With no objects moving past and only the dark emptiness of space providing background, there was no reference to show motion and it looked like they and the rest of the universe were at rest.

Hui was velcroed in front of the laptop computer station and monitor that controlled the harpoon that would spear the asteroid. She'd been there with the VR goggles strapped on her face for the past hour practicing with the harpoon gun simulation, now that they had the actual visual map of the real asteroid to use in the simulation. She wanted to practice with as real a target as possible since she only had two chances to make it work. They were only able to outfit the ship with two harpoon guns and winches and if she wasn't able to make one or the other stick tightly enough to reel the ship in and keep it in place, then they'd have to risk stationkeeping by constantly adjusting the ship's position with the attitude control thrusters to repair the broken divert system, dramatically increasing the risk to the crew.

"Hui, are you ready?" asked Gesling.

"Yes. I've targeted a spot that looks like the harpoon should be able to penetrate. From what I can tell, the part of the rock I've targeted is integral with the main body of the overall rock and not a clinger."

"A clinger?" asked Rykov.

"A smaller rock that is barely gravitationally bound to the main rock," Paul explained to the Russian.

"Ah yes," Rykov muttered something that sounded like "ahh-stah-va-sir veer-a-nim." Paul guessed it was a Russian translation for "clinger."

"If we try to pull this ship into a rock that's not part of or connected firmly to the main asteroid," Hui continued. "Then we'll pull a small boulder toward the ship instead of the ship toward the rock. That would be bad and we won't know until we start the winch."

"And if it is a rock that pulls loose? Won't it be coming right toward us?"

"Yeah. That's why I'll be watching with one hand on the thrusters and the other on the button that will cut the cable to the harpoon. If a rock starts coming toward us, I need to be able to get us out of the way quickly."

"That's great. I feel so much better." Rykov didn't sound convinced to either Gesling or Tian. "Bozhe moi, don't mind me. I think I'll go sit by the nuclear reactor where it is safe."

"Here we go," Hui said as she tapped a series of commands into the keyboard.

The crew heard a low frequency *thump* as the rocket-powered harpoon fired from what looked like a cannon mounted just below the cylindrical hull of the habitat. Attached in Earth orbit by astronauts during one of the many EVAs required to assemble the overall deep space vehicle, the harpoon canister did look a cannon but functioned more like a rocket-propelled grenade launcher—one that fired a depleted uranium tipped tungsten spike propelled by a fast-burning solid rocket motor. Derived from the latest generation army anti-mortar intercept rockets meant to protect ground troops in combat from enemy mortar rounds, the harpoon sped toward the rock accelerating at about thirty-two gees. But since it was a rocket and not a cannon, there was very little recoil to the larger spacecraft.

Gesling and Rykov watched the impact through the window while Tian was still in her VR goggles. Paul suspected she was using the camera mounted on the harpoon, riding with the projectile until the moment of impact.

When the harpoon hit, a shaped charge in the nosecone fired, forcing the barbed grapple contained within it further into the rock. If it worked as designed, the cable would be firmly embedded in the asteroid. As far as Paul could tell, the harpoon hit the asteroid and kicked up small shards of rock and debris that flew out into space within roughly a forty-five-degree angle from the vertical. The debris cloud expanded outward from the asteroid, creating a plume that in the sunlight flickered like fireflies. He kept his hands near the thruster controls, just in case he had to perform a quick maneuver to avoid any debris.

"I didn't think about the debris. Will any of it hit us?" Rykov asked.

"It shouldn't. The harpoon was designed to not kick debris straight back at us. And the shaped charge in the nosecone concentrated most of the force produced by the explosion into setting the grapple," Hui replied. "Besides, the relative velocity would be very small compared to what the multi-layer insulation blankets the ship is wrapped in are designed to stop."

"I guess I'm used to the Moon. Even though the gravity there is only one-sixth gee, rocks blown into the sky will still fall back down. We've been mining there for a few years now and none of our explosions looked like that one," Rykov said.

"If any of it were going to hit us, it would have done so by now," Gesling said as he entered a few more commands into the console before him. "As far as the lidar and ground penetrating radar are concerned, we're locked in."

"Let's hope so," Rykov agreed nervously.

"I'm starting the winch," he added. Hui pulled the goggles off and nodded to him that she was good to go.

Hui and Mikhail both looked up as the vibration from the winch starting produced a low rumbling sound throughout the habitat. The habitat briefly jolted and then the vibration stopped.

"We're connected. I pulled us in a few meters to check the strength of the connection—making sure the grapple held—and it all appears to be fine. I'll slowly pull us in to within about fifty meters of the surface. Then we can relax and sleep. Mikhail, tomorrow will be your day. All I have to do is sit up here and watch."

Two hours later, they were each in their personal spaces, zipping themselves into their sleeping bags along the outside wall of the habitat with their heads toward what they all agreed would be the ceiling. The nightly banter between them, even after several months in space, often sounded like that of kids in a college dormitory.

"Mikhail, we were thrown together so quickly for this mission that I never had a chance to ask you how you picked up your electric propulsion expertise. You spent over seven months on the ISS and commanded three tours at your Moon base, not something a typical electrical engineer has on his resume."

"I studied at the Moscow Aviation Institute where I worked with the chief architect of the *Coeus* Titan sample return mission. I actually designed the electric thrusters used to bring back the samples. Shortly after the hardware was delivered for launch, I joined the Russian Air Force with the goal of becoming an astronaut. By the time the *Coeus* reached Titan, I was in astronaut training and when the samples made it back to Earth I had been on the ISS for months. Before the samples were fully analyzed I was on the Moon for my first turn of duty."

"That's an impressive career path, Mikhail," Hui said.

"Fifteen years. That's how long it took *Coeus* to fly from Earth to Titan and back again. That's also how long it took me from the time I joined the air force until I was walking on the Moon. We mustn't forget how close the Moon is and how truly far away the planets are."

"Anyone looking at our flight path would have to agree with you," Gesling replied.

"Three months is a long time to be traveling, isn't it?" Hui said.

"I'm just glad we're not at each other's throats by now. Our market research for the hotel shows that some of the crews that spent this much time together on the International Space Station weren't talking to each other at this point," said Gesling.

"It is better than fifteen years," added Rykov. "And I can tell you that after seven months on the ISS that, well, uh, tempers often flare up."

"Paul, how is your wife?" Hui, asked. Paul couldn't see her through his privacy curtain, but he was sure she had asked with sincere interest.

"No change. The report today was the same as it was yesterday and the day before that. Her brain is functioning, they believe she is dreaming. But she's totally unresponsive." Paul thought about her dreaming and in some way imagined that she had managed to connect with him in his dreams since he'd been out in deep space. He knew that was just a fantasy, but sometimes it was good to believe in a fantasy, at least for a little while.

"Don't let that dampen the mood. I try to be an optimist and at least her condition hasn't worsened. If I'd remained at home, I'd be a basket case worrying that you guys were going to screw it all up and let this rock kill half a billion people." Paul did his best to be the upbeat commander.

"That shall not happen, comrade," Mikhail said. Paul knew he probably never said "comrade" in his daily life until he became the only Russian on the mission. It had become sort of a mark of national pride with Mikhail so he had humorously hammed it up. So much so that it had become an unconscious habit in his speech pattern. "We will stop the damned rock."

"I agree. It shall not hit the Earth," said Hui.

Within only a few minutes, both Hui and Mikhail were asleep, leaving Paul to ponder his own thoughts as sleep eluded him. Paul had seen her sleeping with her cube unzipped and he imagined how she must look now with her arms outside of the sleeping bag's netting. Hui seemed to prefer her arms floating freely in front of her as she slept. Paul imagined that she looked like a sleepwalking zombie from some hundred-year-old Hollywood movie. He smiled. He had no clue how Rykov slept and had no desire to interrupt him.

The hum of the fans used to keep the air recirculating throughout the cabin usually lulled Paul into sleep, but not tonight. His mind was racing through what the next few days would entail. He always felt this way the day before a big flight or mission event. All the times before, it was usually only himself or possibly a tourist or two that would die if he screwed up. This time millions of people, and maybe even his wife, were at risk. He knew he couldn't screw up.

First, they had to get Rykov down to the surface to examine the electric propulsion thruster that was malfunctioning. There were not enough self-diagnostics built into the spacecraft for them to ascertain its health status—*a very piss-poor design by the mining company,* Paul thought. The only way to figure out what was wrong with it was to go out there and dig into it. That is why they had brought *the* expert on spacecraft electric propulsion, Mikhail Rykov. If there were papers written in rocket and propulsion journals that didn't reference his work you could just skip them and look for the ones that did.

Rykov was, in this case, the best man for the job. That was why he was out there with them. He had to decide whether or not the electric propulsion engine could be repaired or if he would have to emplace the spare they brought with them. Once they had an engine that was working, the flight plan called for them to loiter at the rock for a few days to make sure the systems were working as they should before performing the burn that would bring them home safely ahead of the rock. His mind was racing through all of the things that could go wrong and how they would respond.

Dammit. I hate it when this happens. How do these guys fall asleep so quickly?

It took the better part of an hour, but Gesling eventually fell asleep.

CHAPTER 22

THE EXPLOSION HAPPENED TWO HOURS AND SEV-
enteen minutes into the spacewalk. Rykov and Tian
had long since exited the airlock and used their tether-
free Autonomous Maneuvering Units, or AMUs, to fly
themselves "down" to the broken electric thrusters
on the surface of Sutter's Mill. They had just opened
the casing containing the thruster to begin repairing
the thruster when all hell broke loose in the habitat.

At first Paul didn't know what was happening. The
pop he heard wasn't terribly loud, but it shook the
entire length of the habitat, causing it to vibrate like
a person's stomach might standing next to the snare
drum in a marching band. Then several of the status
lights on the control panel began to blink red and
buzzers sounded throughout the Command Capsule.

"What the hell?" muttered Gesling as he pushed
himself through the air and over to the control panel
to see just what the hell was going on.

The vibration continued and all he could tell from
the instrumentation was that attitude control thruster

number four had failed. He again glanced around the habitat's interior and his eyes settled on the window facing the asteroid to which they were anchored. It was starting to rotate. Rather, he was starting to rotate relative to the asteroid and that shouldn't be happening. The ship was a behemoth and it took a lot to get her rotating. Not to mention accelerating.

He timed how long it took for the image of the asteroid to come back into the same relative position where it started and took a mental note. In the meantime, he was quickly running through the checklist necessary to run a diagnostic of the propulsion system to figure out what was happening. Precious seconds went by with no useful information coming from the instrumentation. He again looked at the window and timed how long it took the ship to rotate three hundred sixty degrees. It took three fewer seconds than the first one he measured. Whatever had gone wrong was still happening and his spin was accelerating.

"Mikhail, Hui, listen up. Something's happened up here and I've lost attitude control. The ship is spinning. Can you see anything from where you are?"

"My God, we hadn't noticed. We were so intent on the thruster that we hadn't looked up. Yes, you are spinning and you've got slack tether," replied Mikhail.

"And I think I see number four thruster firing. That must be what's causing the spin. You've got to shut it off," added Hui.

"I knew there was a problem with number four but I didn't realize it was stuck on. All I can tell from in here is that it failed."

"You'd better do something pretty quick. The tether is getting more slack. You're not only spinning, but you're thrusting yourself closer to the surface with every rotation. Pretty soon you'll tangle in the tether and rip off the communications antenna or one of the radiator arrays."

Inside the habitat, the altimeter alarm sounded. Gesling *was* spiraling in toward the asteroid and at an accelerating rate. He had to do something to stop the descent and the spin or the ship would be seriously damaged.

Paul entered the command to stop all of the ship's attitude control functions which successfully shut down thrusters one, two and three—but not number four.

Dammit. Dammit. Dammit. He thought.

"The thruster won't shut down. It's failed open for some reason. I'm going to try to slow the spin and boost altitude with the other thrusters."

Gesling's hand flew across the glass touch screen that controlled the ship's functions with lightning speed. He shut off all the displays except for the ones showing the fuel levels in the thrusters he was about to use, the altimeter and the relative attitude. The four attitude control thrusters were situated around the center of the habitat's cylinder at ninety-degree angles from each other, each had four nozzles, also separated from each other by ninety degrees. This gave the pilot the ability to control the orientation, or attitude, of the spacecraft by precisely firing the thrusters needed to roll, pitch, and yaw the craft as needed.

With thruster four firing continuously in the positive roll direction, Gesling would have to counteract the spin it was inducing by firing the other three thrusters in unison in the other direction to counter the acceleration the damaged thruster provided. He'd have to be careful to not overcorrect and start the ship tumbling in three directions simultaneously—a situation difficult to correct under the best of circumstances. He'd also have to watch the propellant levels to make sure there would be enough attitude control propellant to control the ship for the flight home. Most importantly, he had to buy himself some time and then get that damned stuck thruster turned off.

He began pulsing the number two thruster in the opposite direction; then numbers one and three, in that order, over and over, giving with each a small impulse bit that, taken together, should stop the ship's roll. The altitude loss was more troubling. Without knowing precisely how much thrust was being used to push the ship downward, it would be difficult, if not impossible, to know which of the other thrusters to use, and when to use them, until the spinning stopped. Firing one of them at the wrong time could accelerate the movement toward the asteroid by mistake, making the situation much worse. For this reason, Gesling decided to stop the ship from spinning and then deal with the descent problem. He hoped he would have time to do that before the habitat hard-landed on the surface of Sutter's Mill.

The number four thruster must have been firing so that it gave the ship a kick toward the asteroid and not purely along the ship's rotational axis. This could be caused by two of the number four's minithrusters simultaneously malfunctioning or by a break in the feed line, causing a purely random propellant leak. Gesling assumed it was the latter, given what little data he had.

The exact cause was no matter, except for the fact that unless he found a way to stop the thruster, it would totally deplete its fuel tank, leaving the ship with only whatever remained in the other three tanks for controlling the ship's attitude. And each of those would be roughly thirty-three percent additionally depleted trying to slow the ship's roll.

In only a few minutes, which to Gesling seemed like hours, the ship started to visibly slow its roll. The vibration stopped, causing Gesling to guess that the malfunctioning thruster's propellant tank must be empty. By tapping a new firing sequence into the flight control computer, Gesling was able to bring the spinning to a stop.

"Paul, you've stopped the spin, and a good thing too. The tether is completely wrapped around the high gain antenna." The voice in the radio was that of Mikhail.

"But you really need to stop the descent. At the rate you're coming in, you'll impact in no more than three or four more minutes. Hui and I are safely out of the way but if you crash, I don't relish the thought of dying out here in my spacesuit."

"Got it. I'm going to fire the numbers one and three thrusters now to give me some altitude. Let me know how I do," Paul said, his voice not betraying the tension and fear that he was now feeling. It was the voice of training.

Gesling made a quick mental calculation and then commanded the two thrusters to fire. The thrusters were located on opposite sides of the habitat, and each orientated so that their exhaust would go toward Sutter's Mill and propel the habitat up and away from it.

Gesling looked toward the radar altimeter and saw that his rate of descent was slowing, which was what he was trying to do. But he didn't want the course reversal to happen too quickly lest the communications antenna with the tether wrapped around it be broken or damaged. What he wanted to do was to stop the descent and not begin an ascent. He wanted to stabilize the ship at whatever altitude it was in so that the tether could be safely removed from whatever it was entangled.

Too late, Gesling muttered as he heard a muffled thud and felt the ship briefly shudder. Something had broken or was.

"Shit! That's not good," he said to himself.

He switched the display from digital to analog mode. He hated seeing numbers click by. It didn't give him a feel for the rate of change in the altitude the same way a moving needle or gauge did. The digitally created gauge replaced the numerical counter as he continued to pulse the small hundred-pound class thrusters, decreasing the total impulse, by decreasing the burn time, with each pulse.

The rate of the ship's descent slowed to zero and remained there. Only then did Paul realize he was sweating like he'd run a marathon. The ship had lost more than half its initial altitude, but it was stable and not spinning or moving closer to the asteroid.

"Mikhail, this is Paul. I think I've got it stopped but I heard something snap. What do you see from out there?"

"Paul, you did great. But we have some work ahead of us. The tether is thoroughly tangled in one of the radiators and it looks like it snapped the high gain antenna off the hull. It's still tangled in the tether so it won't go anywhere. I think Hui and I can clear both, but not on this EVA. It's going to take some time."

"Unless you think the ship is in imminent danger, get back to your repair of the electric thruster on the asteroid. Fixing that is far more important than fixing the ship right now. I'll run some diagnostics from in here and try to figure out what happened. Mission Control was yapping away trying to get my attention until the antenna snapped. Now there's nothing. The telemetry they were seeing was probably nominal as we are at a four light-minute distance from Earth right now. I have no idea what they wanted. If I get a chance I'll hit the playback. They won't know we had a problem for another minute or two, assuming the low gain telemetry feed is still working."

"Comrade, it looks like from here the low gain antenna is gone. I don't see it anywhere."

"Well, then, they may have no idea we had a problem and if they did, then they might not know I was able to stop the descent in time and may think the we crashed." Paul pulled up the telemetry feed transmission log on the touchscreen and noted where it terminated. The rate of decent was accelerating when the telemetry stopped transmitting. Mission Control back home would think they crashed.

"Sounds like you have your hands full up there. Don't worry about us. We'll get back to what we're doing and let you know when we're ready to come back in. But, Paul, do me one favor."

"What's that?"

"Please don't drop the ship on our heads out here. For a few minutes, I thought we were going to have to ride this rock all the way back to Earth."

Gary Childers was paying for 24/7 care of Carolyn O'Connor as she lay in her Lexington hospital bed in a coma. Despite the time she'd been unconscious, the doctors told Gary that she still had a chance of recovering. She wasn't totally unresponsive—her pupils and ears responded to stimulation and she was observed to react reflexively to stimulation. Childers visited her regularly, as did Bill Stetson and several of those who worked with her at Space Excursions. As time wore on, though, the time between visits grew.

The night shift nurse, Krystol Russell, was in the middle of her shift and changing the urine collection bag attached to Carolyn's catheter. Krystol's friends and family often chided her about her chosen profession, asking her how she could stand taking care of otherwise helpless patients, many of whom might never be able to thank her or even know who had helped take care of them in their time of need. She minded the chiding and the questions more than she did her actual work. She became a certified nursing assistant because she wanted to help people and to make a difference. And going to school for four years to become a nurse was out of the question, at least for now. Ever since she could remember, she was rushing to her momma's side when a younger sibling had a cut or scrape, assisting in the cleaning of the wound and application of the band-aid. It was a natural thing for her to attend a community college and become a CNA after graduating high school. Here she was, taking care of a very pretty lady in her early forties that had almost been killed by a shooter. She didn't know Carolyn, but she knew that some very important people wanted her very well cared for.

She reached down to remove the bag, which first meant removing some tape that affixed the bag to Carolyn's leg. Carefully peeling back the tape so as to not damage the now-sensitive and soft skin of her

leg—a product of being bedridden for months with
only periodic adjustments to prevent bed sores—when
she heard Carolyn draw a deep breath. At first she
was alarmed, thinking that something was causing her
patient to be in pain and she looked around to make
sure that none of the medical equipment affixed to
her had been inadvertently bumped. The IV was still
in place, as were the blood oxygen monitors and other
diagnostics. Krystol sighed and went back to her task
of removing the now-filled urine bag.

She paused. There was something different. Looking quickly back from her work to her patient, she
saw that Carolyn's eyes were wide open and looking
around the room. Krystol nearly tripped and dropped
the collection bag as she rushed to the side of her
patient and pressed the hospital bed's call button.

"Welcome back, Miss Carolyn. I'm Krystol and I'm
here to take care of you," she said in a soft, soothing
voice to her now-awake patient.

Krystol could see that Carolyn wanted to say something, but all that came out of her mouth was unin-
telligible gibberish. Her patient hadn't been able to
speak for months and even though she was no longer
intubated, her mouth and throat were undoubtedly
dry and uncomfortable from disuse. She leaned closer.

"Miss Carolyn, I can't understand you. Take it easy.
You're going to be okay and I just called for the doctor. We're taking care of you."

O'Connor tilted her head toward her nurse and
said, "Where is Paul?"

CHAPTER 23

MIKHAIL AND HUI RETURNED FROM THEIR SEVEN-hour EVA with trepidation. Mikhail had bad news to report about the nonfunctioning thruster on Sutter's Mill, but he was substantially more worried about whatever news Gesling was going to have about the ship. He and Hui shed their spacesuits quickly and joined Gesling, who was floating in front of the cooking station. Gesling didn't say a word to them as they entered.

Paul handed them their drink containers, freshly filled with instant iced tea, and started the conversation by providing a status of the ship. The sound of his voice was somber.

"The number four thruster is completely out of commission and I had to eat into the reserve propellant on the other three to stop our rotation and the descent. I don't know if there will be enough to keep the ship in a stable attitude on the way home. I'm pretty sure spinning up the habitat will eat up our fuel reserves."

Mikhail and Hui both knew what that meant. If the ship couldn't be pointed in the right direction every time they fired their engines, then they couldn't target the ship to move in the direction they needed to get back to Earth.

"And we've lost communication with Earth. Without the high-gain antenna, there's no way to let them know we're still alive out here." Paul shrugged his shoulders, which felt weird to him in microgravity. "We need to fix that ASAP."

"What about replacing the low-gain antenna? We could put together a very simple Yagi or a makeshift dish with a dipole and use it to at least send a message and let them know we're okay?" Hui suggested. "Rykov, you're the electrical engineer. You can build an antenna out just about anything, I bet."

"Absolutely," the Russian engineer agreed.

"We can, but we'll have to burn attitude control fuel to do it. Remember that everything out here is in motion and we can't point any smaller antenna we rig up back at Earth without constantly adjusting the ship to direct it. The high gain antenna was gimbaled so it could track the Earth and point itself. The low gain antenna can't."

"So if we let them know we're okay now, then we'll use up some of the fuel that we will need later on to make sure we are okay and don't get lost in space somewhere on the way home," Mikhail said.

"That sums it up. We need to fix the thruster and get this asteroid on a new trajectory. Once they see that, they'll know we were successful and still alive."

"Or that we lived long enough to finish our mission."

"Yep," Gesling agreed.

Mikhail, Paul and Hui silently sipped their drinks, looking at each other for another ninety seconds before Mikhail spoke.

"The control electronics in the thruster are totally fried. And I think whatever shorted it out also caused damage to the cathode. The entire assembly is useless. I need to use the flight spare we brought with us and hope that the problem wasn't a fundamental design issue. The spare is a duplicate of the one that failed and if the problem is not random, then it, too, might fail."

"Can you replace it and untangle the tether from around the radiator array in the same spacewalk?" asked Gesling.

"I cannot. Replacing the unit will take every minute of at least two more all-day spacewalks. It wasn't designed to be repaired or replaced and that means it will take me some time to get the job done. If I damage the replacement unit while installing it, then we will have real trouble," Mikhail said.

"And if that tether breaks or jams the radiator, we won't make it home for sure," said Gesling.

"Hui can untangle the tether while I replace the thruster. I can do it by myself."

"Are you okay with that, Hui? I could go out and help, but had I not been on the ship before when something went nuts we'd be in a very bad situation."

"Absolutely," she replied. "I think it wise for you to stay on the ship."

"That's it, then. We have our plan. Let's get some rest and back to it."

"One moment, comrades," Rykov said.

"Yes?"

"Well, the transmitters should still be functioning. They are modern software defined radios. We could put a simple omnidirectional dipole antenna on them and start sending out signals. It is quite likely that with our disrupted communications that NASA will point its Deep Space Network of radio telescopes at us. They could still detect the Voyager spacecraft's weak signals even after they left the solar system, using the big dish in Puerto Rico."

"Of course NASA will do that." Paul knew that their mission was the most important one mankind had going and all eyes and ears would be on them. "How long will that take to rig up?"

"A day or so inside then a couple hours outside."

"Fifty-two hours we don't have until that engine is up and running and pushing that asteroid away from hitting Earth," Paul said.

"Perhaps, I can rig the antenna during downtime over the next couple of days," Rykov added.

"I can emplace it," Hui added.

"We will do that, but not now. Engine first." Paul made a command decision. "Back burner it and let's get some sleep."

Evgeni Golov was asleep in the Moscow apartment he rented for his mistress. After an evening at the symphony and a late-night stop for dessert at her favorite restaurant, they had made their way to her apartment and hurriedly made love. The act itself was almost perfunctory, making Golov wonder if his relationship with his mistress was getting as predictable as with his wife. But the thought was only fleeting because a wave of overwhelming tiredness was not far behind and he quickly fell asleep, with his mistress's head gently placed in the crook of his left arm.

He was roused from a deep and satisfying sleep by the ringing of his cell phone. The ring tone was not what he recalled setting; it sounded like one of those terrible new songs so beloved by his teenage daughter. As he fumbled to answer, he realized she had probably taken his phone and changed all sorts of its settings the last time he was at home with his family. Elena, his mistress for the last five years, stirred but didn't awaken as he finally found and answered the phone.

"Yes?"

"Evgeni? This is Makariy. The Americans have failed. We just learned that their ship crashed into the asteroid and they are most likely all dead."

The news caused Golov to become instantly awake.

"And the asteroid?" he asked.

"They didn't have time to repair or replace the thruster before the crash. Its course is unaltered."

"Are you at the Institute?" Golov asked, already reaching for his shirt from the floor beside the bed. He glanced only fleetingly at his mistress with little concern that he was about to run off. Important men often had to make hasty exits. Wives would sometimes complain, but mistresses had no say in the matter.

"Yes. You need to get here as quickly as possible. You know what we have to do."

"Yes, yes, of course. So you have the approvals required?"

Elena stirred as Golov switched on the light. He motioned for her to remain quiet.

"President Lazarev was informed and gave his

consent. He intends to have a press conference and announce our plans to intercept it."

"I can be there in an hour."

Elena, now also fully awake, sat up in the bed, not making any effort to cover herself in the process. She slipped from the bed and began gathering Golov's remaining clothes into a pile near the foot of the bed, presumably to make it easier for him to find them.

"Get here sooner if you can. We have much to do."

"On my way," he said as he nodded approvingly toward Elena, acknowledging what she'd done to expedite his departure rather than her fully naked body. *Maybe she's worth keeping around after all*, he thought.

CHAPTER 24

PAUL GESLING WAS AGAIN ALONE IN THE SPACECRAFT as both Hui and Mikhail exited the ship using their AMU's. Hui was going to untangle the radiators from the tether holding them in place above Sutter's Mill while Mikhail began replacing the faulty electronics in the asteroid divert system. As Gesling ran through the diagnostics and monitored both astronauts using the external cameras, he found his thoughts drifting toward home and his stricken wife. This was the first full day that they'd been out of contact with Earth and the first day he didn't receive an update on her status in the morning brief. Not that he expected anything different that he'd received every other day since they'd left—a simple one line message from Bill Stetson saying that there was "no change."

Somehow, not receiving that simple two-word message was unsettling. Even though Gesling knew that today's message would have likely been the same, not receiving it gnawed at him more than anything that had gone wrong so far on their trip. He felt . . . *isolated*.

Paul, he thought to himself, *there's nothing you can do except what you're here to do and save a few million lives in process.* He found himself chuckling as that fleeting thought registered in his consciousness. *There are millions of Carolyns back home that are counting on us and they must be terrified thinking that we've failed since they lost contact with us.*

In addition to feeling isolated, Paul now found himself engaged in second thinking the decisions they'd made so far—including the one to send him on the mission in the first place. *Did I cause the thruster failure? Could I have done anything differently to keep it from happening? Get a grip, Paul.*

"Paul?"

He'd barely finished that last thought when he realized that Hui was speaking to him on the short-range radio.

"Paul, can you hear me? Paul, please respond," Hui called.

"I'm here. Is everything okay out there?" he asked.

"I'm glad. I was starting to wonder. I've been trying to get your attention for at least a couple of minutes."

"Sorry about that. Everything's okay. I was just a little distracted thinking about our predicament."

"You will have to tell me about your thoughts when I get back inside. In the meantime, you might want to reel in a little cable so the array doesn't get tangled again."

Gesling looked at the monitor that showed both Hui's spacesuit silhouetted against the darkness of deep space on her left and the stunning gray asteroid on her right. He touched the screen and the gimbals on the camera responded accordingly, tracking toward his right and her left toward the radiator. He immediately discerned that she'd been successful and freed the array from the errant cable. He also quickly scolded himself for letting his focus drift while the crew was on an EVA. He *was* the right man for this job, but he *had* to get his head on straight. Hui was being very polite. Paul could only imagine how Melanie Ledford might have responded since he'd knocked her off the mission command spot and then she'd been cut from the mission altogether once their rides had been destroyed. Paul scolded himself again. Ledford would have been pissed at his performance. He would not let himself get so distracted again. He owed that to Ledford, his crew, himself, and the millions of lives at stake back on Earth. There was no internal chuckle this time as he thought about it.

"Good job, Hui. I'll pull it in a few meters so we don't have any more snags."

Gesling's challenge was to retrieve enough of the excess cable to prevent it from tangling again on the radiator array or some other external system, but not allow it to come under significant tension, lest it again pull the spacecraft toward the asteroid and make him expend yet more attitude control propellant to get back on station. He touched the virtual button on the display screen and watched the camera as the slack tether was slowly rewound onto the reel inside the spacecraft. Just before it would have become taut, he stopped the motor and waited.

The tether recoiled, slightly, as the reel stopped pulling it in, but otherwise there were no discernable effects from the maneuver. The ship and the asteroid each had enough inertia that the mass of the cable had little impact on their relative positions.

"Hui, that's it then. You can come inside and join me for a late lunch," Gesling said.

"Thanks, Paul. I look forward to it," she replied.

Paul watched Hui pause and then fire the minithrusters on her AMU, beginning her slow flight back to the ship and Gesling's company.

"Mikhail, how is it going with you?"

"I thought you'd never ask. I'm ahead of schedule and might be able to get the electronics box completely replaced today. If so, then all I have to do tomorrow is run some diagnostics and restart the system."

"That's good news. Keep me informed up here. I feel a little useless."

"Just keep that ship working so you can fly us home."

"That's the one thing I can do."

"Paul, are you confident that the radar systems back home will be able to see the change in the asteroid's velocity from the thruster going back on line? How quickly will they be able to tell, do you think?"

"Mikhail, your guess is as a good as mine. You're the electric propulsion expert. What's the thrust on that thing? A newton? Two newtons? I could probably give that asteroid more of a push by kicking it than that thruster will in the first few hours it is back up and running."

"A few days then," Mikhail said, sounding himself somewhat distracted.

"A few days, or even a week or so. The radars simply aren't that accurate and that thruster will have to operate a long time to give this piece of rock enough of a nudge for them to know it's working."

"That's what I'm worried about."

"Well, I know you don't want your family and friends

back home worried about you out here. Neither do I. But they'll not give up hope right away and once they see the rock changing course, they'll figure out that we're okay and coming home. And, by then we'll have fixed the radios like you said."

"Paul, when I finish this repair, we need to talk. But I don't want to be distracted any more right now. Let me finish what I've started so at least this part of the mission can be successful."

"Roger. Out."

The liftoff was perfect. From the frozen steppes of Kazakhstan, the Russian rocket took flight from the Baikonur Cosmodrome on its way to space. Baikonur was the hub of Russian spaceflight and had been since the beginning of the space age with the launch of both Sputnik, the world's first artificial satellite, and Vostok 1, which carried the first human into space. The primary difference between those payloads and the one on the rocket now making its way heavenward, was the payload. Sputnik carried a radio. Vostok carried Yuri Gagarin. This rocket carried a fifteen-megaton nuclear warhead and was bound for the asteroid Sutter's Mill.

CHAPTER 25

"GARY, YOU'VE GOT TO DO SOMETHING. THOSE MANI-
acs have launched a nuclear weapon. They didn't even
wait to see if Paul and the rest of the crew had repaired
the thrusters on the asteroid. Those trigger-happy
bastards just decided to launch a nuke because they
could." Bill Stetson, standing in his Houston driveway,
shouted into the weblink appended to his collar.

To Stetson, it was surreal. He was standing in a
tranquil Houston neighborhood on a beautiful sunny
day that wasn't either too hot or too humid, a rare
event in Houston, talking to Gary Childers, who was
currently over a thousand miles away, about events
on the other side of the planet that would soon have
implications for his friend who was currently several
million miles into deep space.

"Bill, I've got a call in to the administrator and
one to my lobbyist who is trying to get me on Alexa
Faulkner's calendar for later today. I'm as concerned
as you are about Paul and the rest of that crew,

but you saw the video and telemetry. The ship was spinning out of control and going straight down on a collision course with Sutter's Mill when we lost their signal and we haven't heard anything since then. There is a very real possibility that they all died in a crash and that Sutter's Mill is on a collision course with Earth."

"But, you know as well as I do that..."

"Bill, hold on and listen to me. I'm actually amazed that we didn't launch our own nuke as soon as we lost contact."

"Gary, I know that. But shouldn't they have waited to see if the asteroid started veering onto another trajectory before they made that call?"

"That's the case that Administrator Reese-Walker took to the president and that's why a missile wasn't launched out of Vandenberg," Childers said.

"Don't the Russians care about Rykov? He's one of theirs."

"Gary, the Russians have a history of sacrificing one of their own for the good of the many. Remember communism? Or Stalingrad? For them it was all a risk calculation and I must admit that I understand why they did what they did."

"Dammit, Gary, I do too. It's just that, well, I don't want to condemn my friend to die unless there's a damn good reason and I don't think we know enough yet to make that decision."

"I'll do what I can do. But I wouldn't hold my breath if I were you."

"Shit."

"My sentiments exactly."

❖　　　❖　　　❖

Mikhail was back in the ship, out of his suit and again sipping tea provided by Paul. Hui was tending to something in one of the lockers on the other side of the inflated habitat that was their "home away from home." Gesling, also sipping tea, was floating near the communications console and making adjustments that Mikhail couldn't quite make out.

"Paul, you and Hui should come over here. I need to tell you something," said Mikhail, gesturing with his arms for both to come closer as if somebody else might hear what he was going to say. There was nobody else for millions of miles, but habits die hard.

After the American and the Chinese astronauts joined their Russian counterpart, Mikhail cleared his throat and began speaking quietly and calmly.

"I believe we are in great danger."

"Us? Out here a few million miles from home riding a killer asteroid on a collision course with Earth on a crippled ship that may not be able to steer us home; we're in danger?" Gesling's attempt at humor fell flat with the Russian.

"Yes, we are in great danger. I believe my government will have launched a nuclear rocket to intercept this asteroid as soon as they lost contact with us."

"You're kidding," said Gesling.

Mikhail looked at them and said nothing.

"Paul, I don't believe Mikhail is joking," said Hui.

"I'm not. That was their preferred method of dealing with this crisis from the beginning and it was only through strong intervention from both of your governments that they didn't launch such a missile strike already."

"Holy shit," Paul said almost completely under his breath.

"Holy shit is right my friend," Mikhail nodded in agreement.

Zhi Feng learned about the Russian missile launch while scanning the news feed on his CompUEye. The image of the rocket launch in Russia caught his attention as he sat in the lobby of the Tokyo Hilton where he was accessing the FreeNet via their "secure" guest access network. Hotels and other public places made it too easy for him to elude being tracked by offering access to the FreeNet to their guests—paying and otherwise. Their antiquated password protection protocols were pathetically outdated and he was able to access them with ease.

He looked around the lobby at the mixed crowd of Japanese citizens and Westerners, who, from the sound of the conversation, were mostly American. He heard snippets of Chinese from around the room and briefly wondered how many Americans could tell the difference between someone from Japan and China.

Probably not many, he thought.

The thought left his mind as he read the article scrolling across his field of view. To anyone looking at him, he would look like a hotel guest staring at the wall or studying the painting there. The more tech savvy might guess he was on the FreeNet, but that would be the end of their observational curiosity. This was just fine with him and what he counted on. He didn't want to be noticed.

Ah, the American bastard Gesling was killed in space! Feng thought gleefully. *That's one less person*

I'll have to kill. It's a pity about Hui Tian, though, he mulled. He liked Hui and even at times imagined that they would become a couple. If only she hadn't been so afraid of him when he was in her room and warned her to stay away from Gesling and Childers. *If only...*

He wasn't alarmed, as most readers were, by the logical consequences of the crew's failure and apparent death. He'd studied Russian rocketry extensively, and was even privy to some of their stolen design data from his days at the Chinese National Space Agency. That, and just about all the design information from every other country's rocket programs. He smiled at the thought. *We stole from the best.*

He knew that the Russians could build a rocket capable of carrying a nuclear warhead into deep space and having it do what it was designed to do—even if the original intent had been to blow Beijing or Washington to bits. The thought that the Russian missile would miss or that the explosion wouldn't divert the asteroid was considered such a low probability to him that he simply ignored it. Unlike most other readers of that particular news feed.

With Gesling gone, that left only Stetson and Childers to kill. Both had so far eluded his efforts and he considered that a personal affront. It was almost as if they were challenging him to try harder. And try harder he would. He knew he was smarter than they or any of their minions. He knew that he had to avenge China's tarnished integrity so she could assume international preeminence in space. And he knew that job was his to accomplish. He just had to figure out the next steps toward achieving that goal.

It was at that moment that Feng decided he must return to the USA in order to have a chance at killing them. Some time had passed since his last attempt and they might start to let their guard down since he'd been quiet for so long. Part of him hoped so; part of him didn't. He liked a challenge and the challenge of killing an enemy who has been forewarned *and* scared appealed to him. He briefly toyed with the idea of sending the dog Childers a message, but decided against it. *A warning would make it more of a challenge,* he thought, *but a surprise attack is far more likely to succeed.* And their deaths were more important for him, and China, than any thrill he might feel knowing that they were running scared.

He turned his attention back to the FreeNet and found airline schedules for flights leaving Narita airport bound for the USA. There were several to choose from. Now all he had to do was decide which person whose identity credentials he'd stolen he would impersonate for the trip. Feng could hack into the most secure computer systems of any commercial airline and become virtually anyone he wanted to become. The thought of impersonating a Japanese businessman caught his fancy and he began scrolling through the possibilities.

CHAPTER 26

"MIKHAIL, I'VE BEEN THINKING ABOUT THAT NUCLEAR missile that you believe is headed toward us," said Hui as she looked up from her tablet computer where she had been diligently working for at least the past hour.

"All of us have been," replied Rykov. While Hui was busy at her computer, Mikhail had been running diagnostics on the newly replaced thruster electronics, which weren't yet performing as they were designed. He'd been grunting and cursing to himself for the better part of that last hour as he tried to figure out why the new thrusters weren't showing voltages in the desired performance ranges. Without high voltage, the ions which served as propellant for the small thrusters wouldn't accelerate to the right exhaust velocity and therefore wouldn't divert the asteroid as planned.

"Remember the fissure we saw on the way in? It was pretty deep. Deep enough that whatever caused it nearly cut this big rock into two pieces. I've been running some simulations looking at what will happen when a multi-megaton nuclear weapon goes off at or near the surface of the asteroid and it doesn't look good."

"How so?" Paul asked and was now giving his full attention to Hui instead of thinking, again, about his wife back home.

"Remember that a nuclear bomb in space doesn't produce the same effects as one detonated on Earth and in its atmosphere. First of all, there won't be a mushroom cloud or blast wave. In the Earth's atmosphere, the air is dense enough to mostly absorb the nuclear radiation, the neutrons and gamma rays, producing the blast wave and lots of thermal radiation. That's how buildings are obliterated and people are burned to a crisp. Out here that won't happen."

"I've seen the videos of the testing from the fifties and sixties. They were part of my training in the Air Force. I was qualified on planes that carried nukes we were going to drop on Moscow," Gesling said, adding, "Sorry about that Mikhail. Nothing personal."

"No offense taken. I am sure we, too, have our pilots trained to drop similar bombs on New York and Los Angeles. Or whatever would be better planned military targets. I do not know, I'm an engineer, not war planner," Mikhail said in broken English with added Russian thickness. Then he smiled a toothy grin at his comrades.

"Out here, the effects will be quite different. Without the atmosphere to absorb all that radiation and in turn creating superheated and fast moving air, the radiation will only decrease with the square of the distance as it spreads out from the detonation. Any ship nearby will receive a lethal dose of gamma rays, neutrons, and other radioactives."

"So how does that deflect an asteroid?" asked

Gesling. He knew. They had all read the alternative mission briefs months before they had left Earth.

"They've probably targeted the missile to strike just above the surface of the asteroid, hoping that the explosion and radiation will heat the rock, vaporizing some of it and turning it into ejecta, which would act like a rocket exhaust and push the asteroid onto a new path. The ejecta would go one way, the asteroid the other."

"I remember most of that from our preflight briefings. If they vaporize enough of the rock, it moves into a completely new orbit and misses the Earth entirely," Gesling said as he moved closer to Hui, whose voice had grown softer while making her explanation.

"Except that in this case, the bomb will likely vaporize enough rock to cause the asteroid to split into two pieces instead of diverting. It's like trying to hold a cookie that is cracked along the middle. You must carefully pick it up or it will break off before you can eat it. Then the crumbs fly off in different directions. We're in the same situation here. When the nuclear device detonates on our cookie"—she pointed out the window at the asteroid—"our cookie is going to break in half and then the smaller piece of the asteroid may get enough delta-vee to miss hitting the Earth, but the big one may not be moved enough to cause it to miss the planet. Without knowing the mass split between the two, the yield of the bomb, when the bomb will get here, and several other factors, there is simply no way to know for sure."

"If it does split, and either piece hits the planet, a lot of people will die."

"Wait a minute. The missile Mikhail thinks they've launched won't arrive for another two months. That's plenty of time for the asteroid to be nudged into a new orbit. It won't be where they think it would be when they launched and the missile will miss us entirely, flying through empty space instead of hitting the rock. I've been running trajectories for our return home and looking at what will happen to the rock once the thrusters begin working. Even with the small thrust the electric propulsion system provides, this rock will be on a different course than when we got here," Gesling said.

"Paul, that's all well and good. But what if the missile is not a fire-and-forget type weapon? Which I highly doubt it is. It likely has its own sensors and navigation capability. It will use some sort of onboard radar or optical sensor to find the target and remain locked onto it until the mission is complete. This is all standard technology for either of our countries' missile defense programs."

"Even if it is in a new orbit and obviously not a threat?"

"It may have sensors and be smart, but it likely isn't smart enough to run all the orbital mechanics calculations and determine that it doesn't need to strike. I know my government. They prefer simple systems with few options. Systems that usually get the job done."

"In this case, the job is likely to kill us in the process. We need to stay close by as long as possible to make sure those thrusters keep working."

"That is certainly likely."

"Then we need to contact them and have them stop the missile. Surely it can be detonated or diverted if commanded to do so," said Hui.

"I'm sure you are correct. My government would not launch such a weapon without the ability to turn it off."

"Then we need to contact them and tell them to call off the missile strike." Hui looked expectantly at Gesling.

Gesling would have squirmed had he been in a seat and able to do so. As it was, he could only grimace. He didn't have good news.

"Hui, we don't know for sure that the electric thrusters are working yet. And it will be several more days, or even weeks, before we know that they are working well enough to actually divert the asteroid. With the high-gain antenna destroyed and only the low-gain antenna to work with, we'll have to boost away from the asteroid and point the ship in the correct direction to beam a radio signal to Earth. That will take propellant. I don't believe we should do that until after we're sure the thrusters are working well enough to be left behind and operate on their own. We are so low on propellant we may not make it back home as it is. If we go out far enough to send the signal home, then we might not have enough fuel to return here and fix or adjust the electric thrusters and then get home. Once we leave this rock, we'd better be darned sure we don't need to come back. Or we'll end up riding it all the way to Earth the hard way. That being said, Mikhail is almost finished with the omnidirectional antenna and we will start broadcasting soon. Hopefully, they will hear us sooner than later."

"Paul, that should still be okay if they don't pick up the low power omnidirectional signals. Even if it takes three weeks to be sure the electric thrusters are working well enough to leave, that would still give us several weeks to radio back home and tell them to call off the missile strike." Mikhail sounded optimistic about their situation for the first time since realizing that a missile strike was likely on its way toward them.

"Mikhail, I wish I shared your optimism. Even if everything is working as it should and we stop the missile strike, if there is one, I'm still not sure we have enough attitude control propellant to get home. I've been plotting various trajectories and almost all of them will likely require too many small correction burns, each requiring that we use propellant to adjust the ship's attitude before performing to make sure we're pointed in the right direction. Even if we save the planet, we may very well go into permanent orbit around the Sun instead of heading home to be in the Rose Bowl parade."

The three astronauts were silent as they looked at each other in the cramped confines of their suddenly, seemingly, smaller spacecraft. Mikhail was the first to respond.

"Paul, you said almost all of the possible trajectories require too many burns. That implies that there are some that don't require as much. What of those?"

"The only ones I've found that fit somewhat into our projected capabilities all require that we stay on the asteroid until about a week before it flies by the Earth, or hits it, whichever the case may be. If we depart then, we should have enough propellant to get home."

"Does that include the propellant we'll use to call off the missile strike?" asked Hui.

"No. That assumes we don't do anything until we're ready to depart for home. If we hop off, radio home, and then come back, the margin gets less. My best guess in that case is that we'd have to wait until one or two days before closest approach."

"In both of those cases, you're assuming that the new electronics works and the electric thrusters do their job as designed. Based on the data so far, I can't assure you that will be the case."

"Then I suggest you get back to it," Gesling said.

CHAPTER 27

PAUL LOOKED OUT THE SMALL WINDOW INTO THE blackness of space. As the Sun vanished behind the bulk of the massive rock that was Sutter's Mill, the star field burst upon his awareness as his eyes grew accustomed to the darkness. For Paul, who frequently stargazed in the Nevada desert near where the *Dreamscape* took off and landed, it was a magical and spiritual experience. When he looked at the stars, he could almost feel the vastness of empty space separating him from the stuff out of which he and all life was made. He felt connected and disconnected at the same time—to him, it was a fleeting glimpse of eternity. And it was meant to be savored.

Paul hadn't heard anything from home about Carolyn's condition in the three weeks since they lost radio communication with Earth. While Mikhail had built a low-gain dipole antenna and Hui and he had done an EVA to attach it, they had not yet received any word back. It was possible that the low-gain antenna couldn't pull a signal out of the background noise all the way from Earth, but Paul wasn't sure. He was an aerospace guy, not a radio guy. Mikhail had assured him that if they were listening with the big dish in Arecibo, Puerto Rico that they would hear them. At least maybe Earth knew they were alive. Maybe not. He couldn't assume any of it.

Paul's mind was continuously busy now with figuring out how to get them home safely. He had less and less time to let himself dwell on the fact that he had no idea how his wife was. He still missed her, but he wasn't spending as much time being morose and thinking of her constantly. When he realized he hadn't thought of her in a while, he immediately felt guilty. When he was thinking of her, he felt as if he was neglecting the rest of the crew and indulging in self-pity. It was a truly no-win situation.

As Paul looked at the stars and momentarily thought of Carolyn, he took satisfaction at having proved the psychologists back home wrong on at least two points. The first was his ability to lead and function on the mission with his wife being injured and comatose back home. He'd talked to the psychiatrists extensively before departure and he was confident that they'd recommended against sending him on the mission. But someone, probably Childers, had used his influence to overturn that inevitable recommendation, to assure that he was on the trip. The second was their sometime stated, but mostly implied, belief that a mixed-gender crew couldn't manage to be in deep space away from home without some sort of sexual liaison occurring. So far as he knew, Hui and Mikhail had not "hooked up" during the voyage, and given the fact that there was virtually no privacy to be had on their small ship, he was fairly certain he would know if they had. Hui was an attractive and assertive woman. He and Mikhail were both red-blooded heterosexual males. The psychologists tended to believe that their sex drives would overcome their intellect and ego. What the experts didn't fully appreciate was that they were all three professionals who placed the importance of the mission far ahead of personal satisfaction, whether it was physical or a matter of ego. If the impulse was there, they were exceptionally good at controlling it. Or maybe they just weren't into each other in *that* way. Psychologists didn't know everything about how personalities work even if they thought they did. Paul didn't care one way or the other as long as it didn't impact the mission negatively.

He didn't have long to let his mind wander before he moved his head out of the small shadow and back into the sunlight. The glare of the sun obscured the stars and brought him out of his reflection. He looked around and saw Hui behind him, and, from what he could tell, mostly by her silence, she was having a moment of deep thoughts as well. Or maybe they were both just really bored or going stir crazy. They'd all been in space a really long time now and only Mikhail had experience like that.

Mikhail, as he had done every day for the past few weeks, was looking at lines of data, software code and engineering specifications. He'd installed the new electronics in the electric thrusters that were to divert the asteroid and they weren't working as designed. From what Paul could tell from the ship's instruments, they weren't working at all. It was at this moment that Mikhail broke the news.

"I cannot fix the problem. I know what's wrong but I don't know how to fix it."

Hui was the first to respond. "What's wrong with them?"

"The unit is drawing power from the solar arrays, processing it and sending it to the thrusters. But the voltage is far too low to provide the acceleration needed to meet the propulsion requirements. It's only about twenty-five percent of what they need to operate. The performance of these systems isn't linear. You can't run it at twenty-five percent power and get twenty-five percent of the thrust. If you run it at twenty-five percent or even fifty percent power, you get zero net thrust. They simply aren't going to work."

"Would another EVA help? Is there anything you can do to them physically that will get them to a hundred percent?"

"No. I've looked at that. These are complex electronic circuits, fabricated in clean room conditions, and there is no way I can rewire or jump start them. Something is wrong with the hardware and there is simply nothing else I can do. We'd get more thrust out of them by throwing them off the asteroid a piece at a time!" Mikhail sounded frustrated and at his wit's end.

"Well, then, we're screwed," said Gesling, being uncharacteristically negative.

"The rock isn't being diverted, so Armageddon is still on. The people back home still think we're dead as far as we know and there is the hypothetical nuclear missile that may be headed our way. I guess I now hope they did launch it. And in fact, hope they haven't heard our signal yet so they don't feel like they are sentencing us to death."

"We can still leave, can't we?" asked Hui.

"Not until a week before the impact. Remember we don't have enough attitude control propellant to leave now and get safely home. If we do, we may get away from the missile strike, but we'll be entombing ourselves in solar orbit for the next several million years. I'd just as soon not do that." Gesling was feeling the weight of hopelessness bearing down upon him as he looked at the also-helpless looks on his colleagues' faces.

"But what if they didn't launch a missile? Then this rock will hit and kill millions. We can't just give up and sit here."

Paul looked again at his colleagues and saw the faces of defeat. He, too, felt defeated.

Silence.

"Paul, Hui, I have an idea. What if we land, and I mean physically land and tie down the ship to the asteroid and then fire our main engines while we are attached to the asteroid? The thrust would provide an impulse to the rock and perhaps get it to move enough from its path to miss Earth. I wasn't going to suggest it unless it looked like we had no other choice and it is certainly starting to look like that now," Mikhail suggested.

"Wow, that's a Hail Mary play if I ever heard one," Gesling replied, taking a deep breath before continuing. "It's a long shot, but it might just work. I ran the numbers just after we arrived. When Bill and I were on the Moon and working to get Hui and her comrades home, we were always thinking of alternatives should what we were doing not work for some reason. I always want to have a backup plan. We're still far enough out that we should be able to nudge the asteroid off course enough to miss Earth—if we can find a way to attach the engines to it."

"What about after? How do we get home?"

"We don't. Once we light up the engines and push this rock out of the way, we're here for the duration. We'll have one hell of a view of Earth as we pass by."

"So we'll be stranded and just remain here until we run out of air."

"Most likely. If the people back home knew we were alive, then they might be able to mount a rescue effort. Maybe they could get something out to get us before we suffocate, but it would be another long shot. And it's a longer shot since they don't know we're still alive. I would bet no one is planning a mission based on a small chance we're still out here and stranded."

"Can we move the ship to another part of the asteroid so we can get our signal back home?"

"We keep broadcasting the omni and hope they hear us. Otherwise, it'll be long ride." Gesling waved his arms, manipulating the virtual control panel in front of him, and the 3D projection of Sutter's Mill momentarily vanished and reappeared with it and the *Tamaroa* now clearly visible. On the asteroid, about two hundred meters aft of the ship, their appeared a white flashing "X" with an arrow emerging from it and canted about seventy degrees off the normal.

"According to the geometry of the asteroid and the trajectory we're on, the best hope we have for pushing it in the right direction means we need to have our thrust vector pointed in the direction of that arrow. And we need to do it as soon as possible. Every minute we wait decreases the probability of successfully diverting the asteroid. This kind of thing only works if you thrust as far away as possible from the impact point."

"Show us the Earth," asked Mikhail.

Gesling again manipulated the wispy virtual control panel and the 3D image of Earth appeared on the other side of the cabin.

"And the geometry of where we are now, the thrust point and the Earth are all correct?"

"Yes. The rock will be between us and home almost all the way in," Gesling said as he moved his hands above the virtual controls. A fraction of a second later, the holographic projection was in motion. Sutter's Mill slowly followed a curved path toward a point in space well ahead of Earth, which was also moving toward the same point. In a few seconds, they were both converging on that point in what looked like it would be a collision, but at the point of almost impact, Sutter's Mill moved across the path of the Earth moments before the two could collide.

"That's the best case. And you can see that we won't be in a line of sight and have enough power to use the low gain antenna to communicate with Earth until after we pass and are on our way into deep space. By then it will be too late for anyone to come after us."

"But we'll be able to let them know we're alive and what we've done," said Mikhail.

"Yeah, we'll be able to do that. And say our goodbyes."

"And there is a chance that they'll notice the asteroid is no longer on a collision course, call off the nuclear strike and send a rescue ship. Or pick up the omni signal, but it is likely the asteroid is blocking it and will be until it is too late." Hui tried to sound optimistic but was having a hard time doing so. There were just too many variables working against them.

"That's a lot of miracles but we can always hope. I suggest we take one step at a time and if a miracle happens, or multiple miracles, then all the better," Gesling said and immediately thought of the miracle he was still praying for each day—that Carolyn would wake up and return to a normal life. Yes, he did need multiple miracles. "Mikhail, is there any chance of finding enough cabling that we could walk the low-gain antenna around the asteroid and point it at Earth?"

"Sorry, Paul. While we might find that much cabling in the ship, it would take salvaging it from almost every system and rigging it all together. Not sure it would work then anyway."

"What about just taking a radio around the asteroid?" Hui asked.

"Maybe we could pull one from the ship, but that would take some time."

"Okay, okay, I get it." Paul stopped them. "We might come up with a fix later for a radio communication, but right now we have to divert this rock. So, let's get started."

"The *Tamaroa* is six hundred feet long. How in hell are we going to get this monster anchored so that it won't take off when we fire the engines?" Asked Mikhail, who, in characteristic fashion, seemed to already be working to solve the immediate problem facing them.

Gesling knew that there was nothing better to get people out of depressed mood than giving them a sense of purpose and a challenge. And *this* was going to be a challenge.

❖   ❖   ❖

Gary Childers was in his North Carolina mountaintop cabin enjoying a book while sitting in front of a real wood fireplace warming the otherwise chilly mountain air. He was reading a traditional book, meaning that it was printed on paper and not displayed in front of him on some screen or projection system. He had tried the gamut of book alternatives over the years, from reading primitive unformatted books in text format on a glowing cathode ray tube computer monitor, to the early e-book readers promulgated by online booksellers, into and through the next generation of e-readers that appeared on nearly every possible electronic device developed. He even tried the virtually projected books that came as an option with his recent corneal transplant—"read your favorite authors anywhere, anytime and in complete privacy!" the advertisements had said. None were for him. He still preferred black ink on white paper bound with glue or thread into an honest-to-goodness physical book, though he almost never got to read anymore for leisure. One of the drawbacks to being a multibillionaire mover and shaker was that you had to keep moving and keep shaking if you wanted things done your way. Every now and then he would find a fleeting few moments of down time. Sometimes, and not that often, he could actually sit down, pull a book off the shelf, and disconnect from his world. But then usually his mind would spin up at full throttle on things he needed to get done. It took real effort for him to actually sit still and read and enjoy it. As it was, this night, his reading was making him tired.

He'd escaped to his mountain retreat to get away from all the frantic activity in Washington and at his

Nevada headquarters. With only a miraculous nuclear strike by the Russians standing between Earth and a disaster of truly historic proportions, it seemed that everyone was putting into place disaster survival and preparedness plans—and for good reason. If the nuclear strike failed, then a lot of people were going to die and, in all probability, entire nations might cease to exist. And as hard as he had tried, with all his reach and resources, he had been unable to stop it from happening.

The models of where the impact would happen were still evolving, but the best guess was somewhere in the Pacific near Hawaii. If that were to occur, then the United States could expect extreme damage all along the West coast, as would every other country bordering the Pacific Ocean. Nations like Japan, Korea and the Philippines would vanish under a tsunami like the world hadn't seen since the end of the reign of the dinosaurs. Billions would die and the world's economy and ability to respond to the disaster would be crippled. Even those nations and regions untouched in this scenario, such as Europe, Russia, and much of Africa, would see their economies collapse as the supply of oil, raw materials, and manufactured goods simply vanished. The world's economy was truly global and interconnected. Like no other time in history, the nations of the world actually depended upon one another, making the likelihood of a major war very small.

Childers ruminated on that thought as he put his book aside on the mantle above the fire that kept the chill of the night air out of his bones. No matter how hard he tried, he simply couldn't just sit there and read. He finished off the last of the bourbon in the glass next to him on the end table. The ice clinked in the glass, almost echoing in the quiet. Gary sighed as he closed the book.

He couldn't help but continue to reflect on the world's woes. The only threat to international peace that remained in the world was centered on the Middle East and revolved around people who hadn't learned how to get along with each other since the dawn of civilization. The irony was that the civilization that had evolved to be interdependent and somewhat resistant to the nationalistic and tribal tendencies that often led to war no longer was centered where it was born. No, that area still harbored hatred going back thousands of years that no one has been able to resolve. And they would remain virtually untouched by the disaster that was about to befall humanity—if the models were correct. Childers wondered if they would take a break from hating and killing each other to notice that a billion or so of their fellow human beings had perished, or, if they'd see it as a sign from their god that they had been right all along. Gary physically shook his head with a sad inward chuckle at the thought.

The impact, if it were to happen, was still a few months away and so far there didn't appear to be mass panic. Unlike in the movies, people weren't rioting. At least they weren't rioting *yet*. He knew that the psychologists predicted this sort of panic wouldn't set in until (or *if*, he reminded himself) the Russian missile launch failed. Sure, there were doomsday cults popping up all over the place and churches of all types were seeing attendance they hadn't experienced since the early twentieth century. But, in general, humanity believed in its respective governments overall, and assumed they'd be taken care of. In essence, the planet was in denial as long as there was an inkling of hope. The Russians still offered that inkling.

The U.S. government was developing a contingency plan to relocate to an undisclosed location somewhere in the middle of North America, well away from vulnerable coastlines facing any ocean. Companies and individuals were hyping the sale and construction of "survival shelters" of dubious quality and effectiveness, of course, and others were making serious plans to themselves relocate to safer regions as doomsday potentially approached.

Childers had his own contingency plans. His corporate offices, and most of his employees and production facilities, were already in the middle of the country—far enough away to not worry about a tsunami reaching them. Sure, being away from the water wouldn't do much good if the models were wrong and central North America took a direct hit, but the chances of that were small. He would make sure that all of his employees, and their families, would be safely inside the bunkers he was having made just outside Lexington and in the Nevada desert. With enough food and water to last half a year, he felt like he was doing all he could to take care of his people. As for himself, he would be watching things from the best possible vantage point—in space.

The *Dreamscape* was being repaired and readied for flight. The damage done in Feng's one-man terrorist attack was severe, but Childers had the resources, mostly the money, required to repair the mangled spaceship and get it spaceworthy. He and six others would launch into space a few days before the impact—or the near-miss, trying to be optimistic—and see what happened from there. In either case, it would be spectacular: An impact would be horrific on the ground, but most likely quite awesome and interesting from space where the dead could not be seen. It would also allow him to choose a place to land that was untouched by disaster, maximizing his and his companions' chances of survival. A near miss would also be interesting if he could phase the orbit so as to be in the correct side of the planet to witness the asteroid skim the outer atmosphere and fly back into deep space. He briefly wondered if, in this case, he would be able to discern the damage done to the surface of the asteroid from the nuclear explosion. It was the first time in his life that he hoped a nuclear bomb would be exploded.

Childers shook himself out of the state of reflection on upcoming days and strolled outside onto his porch and into the night air. Looking down into beautiful Maggie Valley, just a few miles away from Asheville, it was difficult to believe that something big could soon strike the eternal-seeming planet with force enough to completely wipe mountains such as these off the face of the Earth. He looked skyward and frowned. It was an overcast sky and looked as if it might begin raining any minute. He'd hoped to catch a glimpse of the stars to calm himself down. When Childers was troubled, he could usually count on either a good bourbon or a starry sky to cheer him up. Tonight, neither was able to do so.

CHAPTER 28

"THE ENGINES PRODUCE MORE THAN A HUNDRED thousand pounds of thrust. They'll burn for about twenty minutes and then that's it. We'll have taken all the kick this baby can give," Gesling explained—he was almost giddy. Solving this problem was right up his alley and it got all their minds off their predicament. He gestured toward the back end of the holographic projection of the *Tamaroa* as he spoke. Moving forward toward the central truss, he continued, "The truss isn't designed to take that kind of compressive load. It was built to fly a ship in space, unrestrained, with only the mass of the ship itself to support. If we don't have some way to transfer the load from the truss to the asteroid, then she'll snap like a toothpick."

"We're too large to do this," said Hui.

"Yeah. NASA sent us out here in their deluxe Mars space yacht instead of a repair truck. Nevertheless, it's what we've got and we'd better figure out how to make it work."

"From the thrust angle you showed, it won't be as

simple as just getting the ship to touch the surface. It will have to sit so the main engines point upward at least twenty degrees from the surface." Mikhail pointed at the holographic display, waving his hands about as he explained.

"And unless we're firmly anchored, the ship will skid and then bounce rapidly into space and away from the asteroid. Remember we're not landing on the asteroid. It's too small to have much gravity. This will be more like a rendezvous and docking maneuver. Once we dock, we'll have to securely tie her down to keep her there when the engines light."

"What's our length?" Mikhail asked although Paul was sure he already knew it.

"Six hundred feet," Paul answered.

"About a hundred eighty meters, right." Mikhail nodded.

"Sorry about that Mikhail, I use metric in my day job but when I'm working problems I tend to revert to the familiar English units."

"Yes, you and the people of Liberia have that in common," Mikhail said with a smile. "Not to worry comrade, I can convert."

"Can we break the truss?" asked Hui. Paul noted how her hair floated about her head almost like a fluid. She typically had kept it in a ponytail or up in some way, but today she was letting it float free.

"You mean intentionally? Yes, I suppose we can. We might even be able to take it apart. The truss was assembled in Earth orbit in pieces. There isn't a rocket on the planet that could loft it in one piece. Let me pull up the assembly schematic."

The holographic image of the *Tamaroa* changed,

this time showing the elements of the great ship that were individually assembled in space to make her whole. Gesling, Tian and Rykov pushed off to float near the aft end of the ship near the engines, the nuclear reactor and the propellant tanks.

"The reactor and thrusters were evidently launched in one piece and attached to the truss here so they could be mated easily with the fuel tanks," Gesling said as he motioned toward the projection.

"And up here is where we are," said Hui, pointing toward the front of the ship and toward the habitat.

"Here are the water tanks coded in blue, the empty clamshell that would have carried the Mars lander, and the logistics module here in yellow," Paul said, motioning back toward the middle of the *Tamaroa* and highlighting each component as he pointed them out.

"I just don't see how this will work. The ship is simply too big. If we take her apart before we land, then we won't have control over her. The attitude control thrusters are located all along her length and are integrated into one computer-controlled system. I barely was able to regain control of the ship when we lost the number four thruster. And don't forget we owe the reactor back there for all our power. If we take her apart we lose that. And without power, we're dead."

"So we cancel that idea and find a way to dock the ship with the asteroid and then break the truss to reorient the thrusters," Mikhail said confidently. Paul liked the Russian engineer's "can do" attitude. To Rykov it was just another engineering problem that could and would be solved. And they would be the engineers that did it.

Gesling tapped a few times on the control panel and

the image of the asteroid reappeared. He zoomed in to the area where the ship would need to land. The zoom revealed an area filled with boulders and debris.

"I don't think we'll need to worry about the truss not breaking when we touch down. The ship is simply too large and fragile to land here without ending up on top of a few boulders. I can bring her down, but I won't hazard a guess as to how well she'll be performing afterward. Look at those boulders."

The crew stared silently at the image in front of them, seeking in vain an area free of rocks large enough to safely accommodate the length of the *Tamaroa*. There were none.

"So assuming we land in one piece and don't break containment on the nuclear reactor, the fuel tanks, or the habitat, we still have to go out and disassemble the truss to orient the engines in the correct direction," Hui said with more than a tinge of sarcasm in her voice. Her Chinese accent only made it sound more solemn.

"Don't forget about the water tanks and the engine bells," Paul tapped at them in the hologram.

"Why is nothing in this business straightforward?" asked Mikhail.

"That's why they call it 'rocket science.'" Paul didn't really mean it as a joke but it got a chuckle out of Hui.

"Indeed, comrade," Rykov let out a deep belly guffaw and slapped at Paul's back. The motion spun Paul just enough that he had to stabilize himself with his hands against the touchscreen.

Mikhail repositioned himself to look at the truss segment that in its assembly sequence terminated just above the water and propellant tanks but below the now-empty Mars lander casement. After a few minutes staring at the drawings, he looked at his companions and frowned.

"I just don't see how we're ever going to get this to work," he said. "Especially not with the tools we have and the time within which we have left to do it."

"Mikhail, I don't either. The numbers work from a propulsion point of view, but the engineering challenge is unsolvable. Maybe if we had the bright people back home helping us, we'd have a chance. But I just don't see a way to make it happen."

Hui moved away from the projection of the *Tamaroa* and was staring intently at the image of the asteroid. After a few minutes, she looked up and cocked her head slightly.

"Paul, take a look at this," she said as she pointed to the massive fissure that bisected the asteroid.

"What have you got?"

"An idea. Look at the width of the fissure and the slope of the walls. Can you fly us into it and touch down with the engines pointed in the correct direction, or close to it?"

"Let's look at the dimensions," he said. Paul's fingers flew across the control panel tapping at the screen and occasionally at the attached keypad.

The image of the asteroid and the ship vanished and was replaced with a close-up view of the portion of the asteroid bisected by the fissure. They'd flown across it on their way to the site where the electric thrusters had been positioned and taken very good photographs and radar data in the process. They could see the dimensions of the opening and somewhat into its interior before the image faded into the darkness created by the shadowing of the fissure's walls.

"Our imagery only goes down about four hundred feet and it looks fairly smooth—at least up to that point. The radar data looks good beyond that down to about five hundred fifty feet; at that point it gets a little murky. The returns past that showed some scattering that could be due to boulders or a closing of the fissure. I have no way of knowing with what we have."

"What if you fly us into the fissure and then fire the thrusters?"

"Hui, you know that the habitat is on the front of the ship and that we'll be at the bottom of the stack down inside the rock when we do that."

"Yes, but can you do it?"

"Hell yes, I can fly us in there, but I can't say whether or not we'll be pointing in a direction that will push the rock such that it'll miss the Earth. I also can't say what will happen to us. This is an inflatable habitat, not one made of steel. My first thought is that when the nuclear engines fire we'll be pushed even farther in the hole and this thing will burst like a balloon."

"Paul, my friend. You are a fine pilot and a good engineer, but you're not a materials scientist. Be glad the habitat isn't made of steel or some other inflexible material or it would burst. Your company made this out of the finest and toughest flexible material they could find that was suitable for space travel. It even has triple redundant skin to allow for resistance to micrometeors or orbital debris impacts, as we have seen firsthand. If we can wedge the ship in the fissure, and if we don't find the habitat up against a solid rock wall, then the flexure may keep us intact."

"Okay, let's assume I can fly us in there without running into a rock on the way down; we don't know what's beyond five hundred fifty feet. Let's also assume that we can wedge ourselves in there without cracking open the fuel tanks or the habitat. And from what I can tell about the width of the fissure, that may just be possible. It seems to narrow close to where the clamshell is on the truss. The habitat can squeeze through, but if we stop with the clamshell just under the rock outcropping, then we might be able to anchor ourselves there. Whether or not it will hold when the engines fire is anybody's guess. And I still don't know if it'll nudge us in a useful direction or not. I need to look at the possibilities and figure that out."

"While you are doing that, Hui and I will start looking at ways to anchor the clamshell and the truss to the rock outcropping. Perhaps the 3D printer can be of help."

"And the harpoon!" exclaimed Hui, now looking energized for the first time since the conversation began.

"Damn, I forgot about that. We have another harpoon and cable. Between that, whatever-the-hell else you come up with, and the outcropping, we might be able to stay in one place long enough to make this work," Gesling almost cheered.

"I'll check out the harpoon and make sure it's still usable while you get started making your calculations," Hui turned toward the harpoon controls.

"I'll look at the schematics of the *Tamaroa* and see where the best places to tie off to might be," Rykov said.

Bill Stetson and his wife were looking at their Houston home and wondering if it would be there after the impact. Stetson was all too familiar with Houston's geography and though it was technically several miles from the Gulf of Mexico, it wasn't far from the bay that connected the city to it. Any major rise in seawater would quickly move up the bay and flood the city. They should know, several homes on their street were flooded when Hurricane Ike hit back in 2008 and homes one street over flooded from some near-miss storms since then. They found that out when they were forced to buy flood insurance for their current home.

"Rebecca, the likelihood of the Gulf of Mexico being hit isn't big, but it isn't zero. The fact is, they don't know exactly where Sutter's Mill will strike, if it strikes at all. I'm more worried about what will come if there is a hit—anywhere. I've been with Gary in some of the meetings with the disaster preparedness panels in Washington and it doesn't look good. Even if the asteroid misses the USA entirely, there will be a worldwide depression. We're all so interconnected now that any major disruption to global trade will cause extreme shortages of the stuff we need to function as a society. We would be able to keep the essentials working—water, power, and probably food, though the selection at the grocery store will become extremely limited until international commerce gets going again. But things will be fragile. With our phones, medicines, car parts and replacement parts for the infrastructure made of parts from all over the globe, there will be shortages."

"At least we'll be able to eat," she said.

"Yes, but that might become a problem as well. Depending upon where the rock hits, it might put so much ash and debris into the atmosphere that it will block sunlight and cause the planet to cool."

"Like the Maunder Minimum?"

"The what?"

"When I was studying agronomy at Sam Houston, one of the professors went on and on about 'the years without a summer' back in the late seventeenth century. If I recall correctly, there were a few years without very many sunspots, which reduced the amount of heat and light reaching the Earth. This caused the climate to cool and produced a few decades of very short summers—short seasons for growing crops—and led to famine in much of Europe and elsewhere."

"I think that would be a good parallel. You've heard about people wanting to artificially pump sulfates and other particulates into the upper atmosphere to combat global warming? Well, our meteorite friend here might just do it for us. I'll have to look up this Maunder Minimum thing tonight. It sounds interesting. Heck, the only thing interesting from that period I recall is from my music appreciation elective I had to take as senior. That era was called the Baroque music era and all the music was weird and out of rhythm if you ask me. Maybe they were all depressed because the dang winters were so long."

"Well, if that happens, there will be a lot of hungry people. The world is a lot farther away from its food sources now than in the seventeenth century. And there are a lot more of us. Combine that with a depression and the likely end of global trade, at least on any sort of large scale, and you've got a recipe for disaster even if the country isn't touched by the asteroid."

"Is that why Gary is taking all his employees in to the Kentucky and Nevada facilities? Is he stockpiling food?"

"Yeah, that and a lot of other things. I'll say this for Gary, he cares about his employees and their families. He's filthy rich and he's sparing no expense to get prepared for the worst. He's got a huge horse farm just outside of Lexington that he's turning into a massive shelter and another is being built in Nevada. At both he's stockpiling food, medical supplies and... guns."

"I'm glad to hear that he's doing something. If what you describe happens, then it could get pretty rough around here."

"That's why I don't want to be near any big cities, including Houston, when the rock gets close. Hopefully the Russian nuke will do the job. But, if not, then I will feel a lot better being near people I know and trust. And Gary's doctor just in case we need one." Bill didn't say anything, but Becca's new hand was still healing in a bizarre-looking halo cast that stretched from her wrist to the tips of her fingers. It would take a real doctor to remove the pins and screws when the time came.

"Do you know yet where we'll be?" Becca looked at her hand but didn't comment on it.

"Kentucky. It's Gary's home and, well, if the worst does happen, Kentucky land is better for growing food than the sand in Nevada. Plus that's where Carolyn is. I promised Paul that I'd be there for her and I plan to live up to my word." Childers knew he should tell his wife about Childers's plan to be in space aboard the *Dreamscape* when Sutter's Mill arrived at Earth— especially since Gary asked him to be the ship's pilot. But he decided to wait.

"That's one of the reasons I love you," Rebecca said, taking her husband's hand and gripping it with her good hand.

"I know," he said, feeling guiltier.

CHAPTER 29

I CAN'T BELIEVE I'M DOING THIS, THOUGHT PAUL.

Using the remaining functional attitude control thrusters, Gesling was slowly maneuvering the massive *Tamaroa* along the surface of the asteroid, approaching the fissure which nearly bisected the massive rock into two pieces. He had done the math over and over and over again. He then had both Hui and Mikhail walk through it with him. The calculations showed that if he placed the ship nose down into the fissure and settled her on the "left" side of the fissure, then the thrust from the ship's engines would be oriented close to the optimal direction for diverting the asteroid. They'd lose about twenty percent of the directional thrust they needed, but it should be enough to have Sutter's Mill give the Earth a close shave instead of impacting. They'd get a bird's eye view of Earth as the rock flew past—but they'd be too far down in the hole to see it. *If we live*, he added.

The *Tamaroa* was now hovering just above the fissure. Using nothing but gentle puffs of gas, he reoriented the ship's nose downward toward the fissure.

Hui and Mikhail were now positioned beside him at the control panel. Neither spoke as they hovered in the air to his left and right, watching intently out the main cabin window and peering into the darkness that awaited them.

Paul turned on the ship's running lights and directed those on the front to illuminate the hole before them. Allowing them to see only a few more feet into the darkness, the lights were just not bright enough to penetrate further.

"Here we go," Paul said as he commanded a series of thrusters along the outer hull of the ship to begin moving the ship downward toward the rock. The movement was so slight that none of the crew could feel the acceleration.

"Warning, warning, proximity alert!" An audible klaxon warned. Pilots often referred to the warning as the "Bitching Betty." "Warning, warning, impact imminent."

"Shit, Hui, do me a favor and turn Betty off, will ya?" Paul concentrated on what he was doing—flying the very large spacecraft into a very tight place.

Hui switched off the audible alert, but the altimeter and laser ranging data displayed across the panel in front of them. They could see their progress, however, as the darkness and the fissure moved closer, and closer shadows made visual ranging tricky. Paul made certain to keep at least one eye on the laser ranging data, one eye on the radar, and one eye on the viewscreen. He had at least four more eyes looking out windows. He was running out of eyes but not things that needed eyes on them.

A few moments later, the nose of the *Tamaroa* inched into the fissure. The fissure was wide enough at its opening to allow five ships the size of the *Tamaroa* to enter. Paul noticed that the radar returns from opposing sides of the ship showed that he was right on the mark; the ship was flying into the middle of the fissure and as far away from the edges as possible—for now.

Visibility ahead of them was now completely limited by how far the ship's forward facing lights could illuminate, which was not far. Gesling estimated he could see perhaps twenty-five to thirty meters into the gloom.

"With us moving at about a half-meter per second, if we see an obstacle ahead of us, there won't be much time to react. The best I'll be able to do is move us sideways. It'll take us a good minute to bring this beast to a standstill." Gesling spoke to no one in particular, his thoughts vocalized more for himself than his compatriots. He knew what he had to do, but giving himself the reassurance of saying what had to be done was tantamount to the checklists he was used to operating with. Pilots like checklists. At least the good ones do.

As he spoke, a rock outcropping to his left became visible in their headlights.

Gesling tapped the touchscreen on the virtual control panel before him and the ship slowly responded by moving its nose slightly rightward. Given the length of the ship and short reaction time available, Gesling had to fire more than the attitude control thrusters in the ship's nose. He had to fire all the left side thrusters simultaneously so that the ship moved uniformly to the right as it continued to plunge forward and downward. But he couldn't overcorrect, so only a few seconds after activating the left-side thrusters to move the ship laterally rightward, he had to then fire the right-side thrusters to stop the ship from moving too far to the right and into the far wall. Newton didn't make his job any easier. He noticed that the width of the gash was now about half what it had been when the ship first entered the fissure. As far as he could tell, when all was said and done, about two-thirds of the ship would remain above the surface of the asteroid.

"We found a cave on the Moon that reminds me of this," said Mikhail. "The opening is about fifty kilometers from Korolev Base. We marked it for future exploration. I wonder if anyone has gone down into it yet."

"Since all three of us have been on the Moon, we should compare notes sometime," said Hui. "But I don't think now is the time."

"It's odd we haven't done that before now," said Mikhail.

"Not now, please. I may make it look like flying this giant toothpick is easy, but it isn't and your chatter is distracting me." Paul forced his mind and body to focus on nothing but putting the thread in the needle—the really big thread with a nuclear reactor in it.

"I am sorry, my friend," replied Mikhail, looking somewhat embarrassed.

Gesling hadn't wanted to silence his friends, knowing that they were talking out of nervousness, but it was beginning to affect his concentration. He noted that the ship was now fifty percent inside the fissure and the gap ahead of the ship had narrowed considerably. It was now less than twice the width of the ship that was entering it.

"We may not be able to get past that," he said as his head motioned forward toward the illuminated cavern hole before them. Just becoming visible in the darkness was a large rock covering what looked like at least half the opening that was now thirty meters ahead of them. Gesling hurriedly reoriented the side-mounted thrusts on both the left and right side of the ship so that their exhaust would go forward when they fired. It was his solution to maneuvering the ship without the thruster that had failed and nearly caused them to crash into the asteroid shortly after they first arrived. The forward thruster, which would have been ideal to use for slowing their forward motion, was the one that no longer worked. Once they were turned, Gesling wasted no time in telling the revectored side thrusters to fire and stop their forward motion.

Slowly, the massive ship decelerated.

The boulder inched closer as the thrusters fired full throttle to slow the ship.

Finally, Paul realized he was holding his breath and likely had captured his underwear a foot up his rectal sphincter. He forced himself to relax and then he exhaled, triggering a similar reaction in both his shipmates. He now looked away from the forward window and viewscreen and instead focused on the numbers ahead of his eyes showing the ship's forward velocity and acceleration. The velocity was falling as the radar counted down the distance to the outcropping. The goal was for the forward velocity of the ship to reach zero before the radar reached the same number. Paul wasn't quite sure what would happen if the reverse occurred.

He found out.

"Brace for impact!" Gesling heard himself shout.

"What the hell does that mean?" Mikhail shouted back as he grabbed one of the handholds on the empty experiment rack up and to the right from where he was floating. Gesling saw that Hui attached herself to one of the straps holding equipment in storage just over her head.

With the sound like that of a wet rubber ball being rubbed by an annoying two-year-old, the fore end of the habitat began to deform as it was pushed into the rock outcropping that Paul had been trying to avoid hitting. Equipment on the wall rattled, popped free in some cases, and flickered on and off. With tons of mass moving slowly forward behind it, and the thrusters still firing to slow the ship's overall forward momentum, the inflatable habitat bulged inward.

The bulging continued to worsen, snapping support struts, splitting plasma displays that until moments ago were showing the exterior of the ship at various points along its long axis, and bowed menacingly toward the crew that was now only a few feet from its closest point.

Gesling heard Hui scream something in Chinese as she lost her grip on the strap to which she had been clinging and plunged in slow motion toward the bulge. The virtual control panel in front of Gesling that he was using to control the ship began to waver in the air, fading in and out of existence like a ghost. Sparks now flew from the bulging wall of the habitat, commanding his attention just as urgently as Hui's fall—fire was a danger in any spacecraft and now his was in imminent threat of being engulfed by it.

From out of the corner of his eye, Gesling saw Mikhail launch himself from the wall, pushing off like an Olympic diver trying to win a gold medal, and hurtling across the open space in the ever-shrinking cabin toward Hui. He reached her just before she would have impacted the bulge and they both "bounced" from the opposite side of the cabin and back away from the front, where their home away from home was quickly collapsing.

Gesling launched himself toward the rightmost experiment rack, the one nearest his location to which a fire extinguisher was mounted. As objects in the habitat began to be knocked loose from their moorings and the screeching sound of the inflatable habitat's skin rose in pitch to nearly unbearable levels, he one-handedly grabbed the fire extinguisher, spun around to point it at the sparks, which were now dangerously close to becoming a continuous stream bound to ignite something inside the now-smaller ship, and anchored his feet against the base of the experiment rack that Mikhail had moments ago been holding onto. With his feet firmly anchored, he squeezed the handle on the fire extinguisher and sprayed the electrical fire with flame retardant.

The sparks faded as the retardant chemical coated the entire area until finally there were no more. The air in the cabin had a faint burned plastic smell about it.

It took Gesling a few seconds to realize that the ship was quiet. The ear-piercing sound of the habitat being crushed against the rock outcropping had stopped—as had the forward movement of the ship.

The habitat was a mess. The forward third was now grossly deformed by the rock around which it was neatly plastered and none of the display screens were still functioning.

"Is everyone okay?" asked Gesling as he positioned the fire extinguisher back into its mount.

"Yes," said Hui, "Thanks to Mikhail. I don't know how I lost my grip..."

"Shh. Everyone be quiet. Do you hear any air leaking?" asked Gesling.

The crew of the *Tamaroa* floated motionlessly as they listened for the telltale hiss that would indicate their habitat had been punctured as it collided with the massive rock that was now part of their interior decoration.

"All I can hear are the fans," said Mikhail.

"Thank God for that," said Gesling. He knew that if the fans had stopped working, then they would have a whole set of other problems, including the possibility of suffocating on their own used and stale air.

"I can't believe the skin didn't burst when we hit the rock," Hui said. "You were right, Mikhail!"

"I'll thank God for that one also—and the materials experts back home who designed it. If we get the chance."

Paul turned his attention back to the virtual display that was reforming in the air in front of him. Several indicators were glowing red but he was able to quickly discern that none were immediately life threatening. He did frown, however, when he saw the position of the ship relative to the opening of the crevasse into which they'd flown the ship.

"The back of the ship is about thirty feet more exposed than we'd planned. Fortunately, our tilt angle is fairly close to what I'd calculated, which means when we fire the engines, they'll be pointing in the right direction to give this hunk of rock the kick it needs."

Mikhail was inspecting the front of the ship which, at least from the inside, now looked like someone had tried to kick the front in on itself and got their foot stuck in the process. Gesling noted that he was frowning.

"What's on your mind, Mikhail?"

"When you fire those engines, it's going to push the ship further into the hole, and this rock. With a hundred thousand pounds of thrust meeting the fabric of this habitat wrapped around this rock, it isn't going to be pleasant. We will not survive it."

Hui moved to join Mikhail near the bulge and said, "The harpoon won't help in this case either. It will break when it encounters that amount of force."

Both looked expectantly at Gesling, as if he would have the answer to the problem. He didn't.

"Well then, let's get busy and figure out a Plan B. We have to make the burn soon or the window of its effectiveness will close. The further out we change the direction of this rock, the more likely it will be to miss Earth."

Now only a few days from fulfilling its mission, the rocket carrying the fifteen-megaton warhead performed its final course correction maneuver that put it on an intercept course with Sutter's Mill. The rocket was nothing particularly special; it was similar to the many upper stages Russia and the former Soviet Union had flown in space many times before. Using chemical propulsion, its rocket engines were barely evolved above what carried Russian probes to the Moon in the 1960s and 70s. Its payload, however, was very high-tech.

With the dissolution of the Soviet Union in the late 1980s, the nuclear arsenal of the USSR, once the bulwark of the defense of the Russian homeland, had fallen into obsolescence and disrepair. In the late teens and early 2020s, Russian engineers and scientists went to their leadership and explained why the deterrent force upon which Russian depended, was no longer... dependable. The response from the Kremlin was quick and decisive: fix the problem.

The fix resulted in cannibalizing half of the nuclear warheads that had been sitting in storage to make modern, lighter weight and physically smaller warheads capable of being deployed and used within minutes of being needed. And some were made space ready. The near-miss of the Chelyabinsk meteor convinced the military that they needed a nuclear weapon capable of being used in deep space for the very purpose that this particular weapon was now on its way to Sutter's Mill to fulfill.

The "physics package," as some in the business wanted to call the nuclear bomb, presumably to make it sound less barbaric, was completely untested. Nuclear Test Ban treaties constrained treaty signatories from conducting above or below ground nuclear tests. Instead, multiple very expensive supercomputer simulations had been completed. Each simulation more complicated and requiring more computer power than was available in the world—combined—for the first fifty years of the nuclear age. The simulation gave the bomb's creators confidence that their creation would for once be used in a positive way—preventing a global asteroid impact catastrophe.

In three days, the "physics package" would unleash the most devastating force developed by humanity. Nuclear physics was going to be used in conjunction with Newtonian physics and alter the trajectory of an asteroid.

CHAPTER 30

"HUI, YOU TRAINED ON THE SIMULATOR FOR THE Crew Transfer Vehicle didn't you?" asked Paul.

"Yes. It's not dissimilar to the one we use. The controls are a bit more modern, but the control architecture is basically the same."

Gesling looked at the virtual display showing the *Tamaroa* within the fissure and pointed at the small crew-carrying Crew Transfer Vehicle docked rearward. "I've looked at the geometry of where we are in the fissure and the CTV should have enough room to fly you out of here."

Hui and Mikhail floated near where Paul was pointing and looked at the ghostly 3D image showing their ship and the mountain of rock that surrounded them on all sides.

"Paul, you said 'fly *you* out of here.' English isn't my first language, but I know enough to understand what you said and I don't like it."

"Someone's got to stay here and make sure the thrust maneuver happens as it should. But there's no need for more than one to take that risk. You and Mikhail can get safely out into space away from the fireworks and then come get me afterwards."

"What's the point? The CTV only has enough supplies to keep us alive for the next two weeks. We'll perish before the rock reaches Earth. We might just die sooner if we remain in here with you," Mikhail said.

"Mikhail, get your Russian pessimism off my ship. We aren't dead until we're dead. And there is no reason for you or Hui to take the risk of being in here with me when you have a better chance at surviving out there."

"Mikhail, I agree with Paul on that point. There is still a chance we will survive all this and we need to take it. I learned that on the Moon with my crew. Every minute of life counts, and adding two weeks might make some difference to the possibility of our being rescued."

Gesling looked at Mikhail without any hint of satisfaction at having Hui side with him in the debate. His fate might be sealed regardless of what his companions decided to do with the CTV.

"Paul, can you control the ship remotely from the CTV?" asked Hui.

"Not a chance. I need to be here to adjust the attitude control thrusters in case we veer too far out of alignment and monitor the ship's systems to override them in case we have a premature engine shutdown. I need to stay right here."

"What about the auxiliary control room in engineering further back?" Hui asked.

"The control room back there is minimalistic and simply doesn't have the monitors and windows I need to do this. This has to be done right here on the main control in the main flight deck." Paul shook his head no as he talked.

"We could rig something—" Paul cut Rykov off midsentence.

"How long would that take?"

"A couple of days, maybe?"

"There is no time. We're doing it this way. End of discussion," Paul ordered.

"Well then, before we leave, we need to make sure we do everything we can to make sure you get through this. I designed some clamps that I can use across the truss to anchor it onto the rock. But I haven't figured out how to anchor them. If we were home, I would use an explosive anchor like the navy developed back in the 1970s. They needed a way to quickly and reliably anchor large ships so they came up with one that was essentially blown into the seafloor with high explosives. 'Boom' and their ships were secure."

"Explosives aren't exactly in abundance on a ship designed to go to Mars," replied Gesling.

"No, but we do have something that can be made to explode with fairly significant force," said Mikhail.

Paul and Hui looked toward the Russian as he continued to explain.

"We can use the compressed air from the spare spacesuits. The ship was designed and outfitted for eight people to take a trip to Mars and back. We are only three. There are five unused spacesuits with oxygen canisters ready and waiting to be used. I can easily configure them to explode electrically. Getting a 'shaped' charge will be the challenge. I want them to drive the anchor bolt around the truss and into the rock. I don't want to shatter the truss."

"I've discovered another universal truth about engineers," said Hui.

"And that is?" asked Paul.

"No matter where an engineer may be, no matter what the technical challenge they are facing, they always find a way to blow something up. It is universal—in China, the USA, Russia and now on an asteroid."

"Well said. Mikhail, go ahead and start cannibalizing the spacesuits for their oxygen tanks. If you think they'll provide enough force to anchor the ship, then I'm all for it. Hui, are you still going to use the harpoon?"

"I'm not sure how much good it will do, but that is my plan."

Gesling watched Mikhail and Hui return to the ship after an extensive four-hour EVA during which they'd kludged eight anchors and compressed oxygen explosive charges around the parts of the *Tamaroa* truss that were adjacent to the rock wall of the fissure.

Each of the five spare spacesuits on the ship had two full oxygen tanks. They didn't want to use all the spare suits, keeping one in reserve seemed like a good idea, so they only used tanks from four. Getting the tanks out of the backpacks was easy and Paul had taken care of that part of the task while his colleagues suited up and prepared to go outside the ship and into vacuum. Under direction from Mikhail, Paul then used the suits' battery packs and radio systems to create a radio-controlled short—and a complete battery discharge—into one side of each tank near the valve that regulated the oxygen flow into the tubing that was designed to feed the suit's wearer with life-giving oxygen.

Once the makeshift explosive charges were wired and ready to go, Paul helped Mikhail get them into the airlock and then he watched and waited while they painstakingly positioned them on top of the anchors Hui had printed with the ship's 3D printer. The anchors had a printed cusp at the top that was perfect for positioning the air tanks.

Paul did his best to choke down his nagging fear as he watched them place the charges for the appropriate directionality. His scuba diving instructor had told him about an air tank rupture that sent a diver's tank flying through the air and through a concrete block wall. The last thing their ship needed was one of these tanks to rupture and instead of the force driving the anchor into the rock wall of the fissure, having it fly off and through the skin of the ship. That, he thought, would be a bad day.

As Mikhail and Hui reentered the ship, Paul went through his calculations again and found no errors. Minutes now mattered if they were going to deflect the asteroid. As the rock flew closer to the Earth, the miss distance grew smaller even if they were a hundred percent successful in their attempt to deflect the rock. And he knew that the margin of error in this calculation was probably larger than the calculated deflection angle. He'd hoped they could get some sleep before firing the engines, but that was now impossible. They'd been awake and working for nearly twenty-four hours and they couldn't afford an eight-hour break for sleeping.

Hui was the first to remove her helmet after leaving the airlock.

"We got them all placed and ready to go," she said.

"I need food and some sleep," added Mikhail.

"I'd really like to give you guys a break, but I can't. I've relooked at the numbers and all we have time to do is recharge your suits and get you into the CEV and off the ship. I'll suit up in the meantime so we can start the engines as soon as you are a safe distance away."

"Paul, are you sure? I don't like making decisions on no sleep. They usually don't turn out well," said Mikhail.

Gesling looked over his crewmates and knew that they'd been giving the mission their all for the last several days and more than that in the last twenty-four. He also knew that the laws of physics were working against them and that they were out of time.

"We can't stop now. Once we make the burn, then we'll have a feast and catch some sleep. Until then, we've got to press."

"When do we fire the anchors?" asked Hui.

"As soon as we're all suited up with recharged air tanks and all of our helmets on. I don't want an errant oxygen tank depressurizing the habitat with us unprepared. Or God only knows what else."

An hour later, all three astronauts looked like astronauts. They were fully in their space suits with helmets locked and in place. Mikhail had opened the hatch connecting the habitat to the egress tunnel leading to the CEV. If something were to go wrong, they could theoretically move from their duty stations in the habitat to the CEV within two minutes. Theoretically.

"Mikhail, let's trigger the first anchor and see what happens," said Paul.

Mikhail didn't verbally respond. Instead he waved

his gloved fingers over the virtual keyboard floating in the space before him. From Gesling's vantage point, it looked like his Russian colleague was drawing in the air—the keyboard was not visible from where he was.

"Anchor 1 is in place," Mikhail said.

"That's it? I knew there'd be no boom, but why no vibration?" asked Gesling.

"My friend, be glad you heard and felt nothing. This is a big ship and it would take a big explosion for you to feel something striking the ship two hundred feet away while resting against solid rock. And if you heard something, then that would mean the skin of the habitat had been breached."

Looking toward the front of the habitat, which was still ballooned inward from the rock upon which they rested, Gesling only nodded.

"I can't take any more badness today. Let's get on with the next one and hope it's just as uneventful."

Mikhail returned to waving his hands above the virtual keyboard and grunted. He looked up and toward Gesling. "The fourth unit didn't fire. I tried twice. So I'm going on the final four before I try to figure out what happened."

The hand waving continued, interspersed with long pauses, presumably to confirm that the charge had fired, or at least that's what Gesling assumed accounted for them.

"All of the anchors are set except for the fourth one. I just cannot get it to ignite."

"It'll have to do. You and Hui go ahead into the CEV and be on your way. As soon as you get far enough away from the *Tamaroa*, then let me know and I'll get the show started."

Mikhail and Hui floated over to where he was positioned and, as best they could encumbered with their two-hundred-pound spacesuits, gave him an awkward group hug. With their helmets touching, both of the departing astronauts gave Gesling a look that conveyed the very real possibility of never seeing each other again. With that, they moved themselves toward the hatch and the passage that would take them to the CEV.

Gesling made his way to the controls and began running through the checklist that would enable him to start the ship's nuclear engines. As he began to configure the system, he noticed a new warning light. The radiators were running hot. Very hot. And as Gesling read through the data, he swore, *Dammit. I didn't think of that. Too late now. If the ship survives the next twenty minutes*, then *I'll worry about the damn radiators.*

CHAPTER 31

HUI THOUGHT OF HER FIRST FLIGHT IN SPACE ABOARD the Earth-orbiting Chinese space station as she and Mikhail undocked from the *Tamaroa* and oriented the CEV so they could traverse the open spaces between the massive ship that had brought them to the asteroid and the walls of the asteroid fissure that now swallowed most of that great ship. As the backup pilot, she was confident there was enough room separating the two to get them safely out of the hole and into space. But only if she didn't lose her focus. And thinking of that first spaceflight was dangerously close to distracting her.

It was on that flight that Hui had met the man who would become her husband, if only temporarily. He, like her, had been a first-time-in-space astronaut, or taikonaut, as was the proper Chinese term. *Funny*, she thought, *how over time I'm not only speaking in English, but thinking in English as well.*

His name was Kalok and though they'd trained in the same complex, they'd never crossed paths. He was older than she and had been through the training program in the class just ahead of hers. They became fast friends and before their first tour at the space station was complete, lovers. Four months later, they were married. Six months after that, he left her for another woman.

Hui had to rapidly shake herself from her memories to avoid sideswiping the cavern in a particularly narrow part of the passage. Fortunately, Mikhail didn't notice her momentary lapse and she expertly guided the small craft through the narrow opening and out into space. She flew alongside the back portion of the *Tamaroa* that extended out of the crevasse and into open space. It was a strange sight and reminded her of an ostrich, the back of the *Tamaroa* being its legs protruding from the sand.

"Paul, we are in open space," Mikhail said into the microphone.

"Good. Tell Hui I admire her piloting. She should have been the one that flew us out here. Let me know when you are a safe distance away and I'll start the countdown."

Hui guided the small ship laterally away from the *Tamaroa* and stopped several hundred yards away near a rock outcropping behind which she assessed they could safely perch. There wasn't enough gravity to land so her maneuvers were more like what they'd had to do with the *Tamaroa*—hovering and stopping all motion relative to the rock.

The surface of the asteroid looked as alien as the first time they'd seen it. Perhaps more so. There was simply no way a person could become accustomed to seeing the surface of another world, albeit a small one. For Hui, the novelty would likely never wear off.

Again, she cursed the designers of the CEV and their decision to include only a short-range radio capability within it. Had they equipped it with something a bit more powerful, they could have gone to the other side of Sutter's Mill and let those at home know they were safe.

"Tell Paul we're safely away and ready for him to begin."

"Paul, you're good to go."

Hui and Mikhail didn't power down the small ship's systems because they fully expected to soon be flying back into the fissure and rejoining Paul in the habitat. They kept all critical systems up and running with Hui's hands poised above the handle that would reignite the main engine and allow her to quickly throttle it up to gain speed and out of harm's way should the worst case happen with the *Tamaroa* and it broke apart. It was impossible for the *Tamaroa*'s engines to explode in a nuclear explosion, the physics would not allow it. It was possible, however, that the stress on the ship's truss could cause it to buckle, allowing the engines to crash into the asteroid, rupture the fuel tanks, and produce a grand non-nuclear chemical explosion that might send debris cascading toward them. Hui was hoping for the nominal case and prepared for the worst.

For the next several minutes, nothing happened.

Then the nuclear engines ignited. The great ship shook as tons of liquid hydrogen began to flow around the multimegawatt nuclear reactor, producing just over a hundred thousand pounds of thrust. The long spacecraft pushed against the cookie-shaped asteroid, translating vibrations from the engine through its structure and into the rock. Surface regolith from Sutter's Mill shook and vibrated like sand on a speaker cone. A fine cloud of dust began to rise from the surface as the engine pushed against the asteroid and not the cloud. The cloud rose to about a meter in height.

Hui and Rykov watched the dust occasionally sparkle against their onboard ship lights and lighting from the engine and secondary reflections from the sun. It wasn't so much a dense cloud as it was the dust particles she had watched as a kid floating and dancing as sunbeams warmed the air through a window of her home.

So far, the makeshift tie-down anchors along the length of the ship below the asteroid's surface appeared to be holding. The engine bells were glowing from the intense heat of the reactor-heated propellant but the ship wasn't moving further down into the hole. This meant that Paul was very likely okay and not squashed against the rock outcropping that already dented the compartment in which we he was working.

For twelve minutes, the engines burned without event. The dust cloud continued to rise and trail about the ship. Static electricity attracted a considerable amount of the dust debris onto the surface of the *Tamaroa*. But other than the ship getting dirty, there was no discernable side effect of the engine firing and pushing the ship against the asteroid.

Both Hui and Mikhail were now breathing sighs of relief that the anchors had held. Or at least they were holding.

"It appears to be working," Rykov noted.

"Yes. So far so good. Reach out to Paul," Hui ordered from the pilot seat of the CTV.

"Right." Rykov tapped the microphone activation icon on the touchscreen in front of him. "Paul, please give a status report."

"It's a little tight in here right now. I'm not sure the command capsule can compress any further. I've got fires everywhere! But I can't deal with that right now." Paul sounded overwhelmed and under extreme stress.

"Hang in there," Hui almost whispered.

Then, they noticed the change. The ship lurched to the left and moved and then to the right.

"Paul! The ship is moving. Is everything okay?" Rykov asked. There was no response for several seconds. Several long seconds.

The ship listed a bit once again but this time one of the attitude control thrusters fired pushing it back in the right direction.

"Did you see that, comrade?"

"Yes, he is flying the ship." Hui felt her heart jump into her throat. "Why is he not responding?"

"Perhaps the radio in his suit is down?"

"Maybe," Hui didn't like not knowing his situation. "Keep trying him."

"Right," Rykov agreed. "Paul, are you okay? Come in Paul."

Thirteen minutes.

CHAPTER 32

THE CLOCK SHOWED THIRTEEN MINUTES AND ELEVEN seconds into the burn. The capsule was so compressed against the rock outcropping that there was barely enough room left for Paul to stay safely inside. Monitors and equipment were popping loose from their mooring points and were being flung about the capsule like shrapnel from a land mine.

"I'm adjusting the vector angle with the attitude control thrusters," Paul said. "Mikhail, can you tell me if it appears to be working or if it is stressing anything?"

Paul continued to adjust the attitude of the ship as best he could without overdoing it. Too much lateral thrust and he might pop loose the cables and tie downs.

"Mikhail?" He looked at the radio package on his wrist display and noticed a red icon on the screen. He then looked down at his chest and realized there was a metal bolt protruding from his suit that wasn't supposed to be there. Then something popped and rang like a bell in the cabin and a monitor came loose from the wall just in front and to the right of him and flew past his head at several tens of kilometers per hour. Paul flinched as best he could in his suit, which wasn't very much. He quickly checked the integrity of his suit. At least he wasn't leaking air. Then something hit the back of his helmet from behind, but it was moving fairly slowly. He didn't have time to figure out what it was, as the capsule rang like a bell again and popped. Sparks and orange white flames began to form on the panel to the left of him. In the microgravity the flame appeared like the glow about the mantle of a camping lantern and only flickered as sparks popped or the capsule walls shook.

Paul reached over with his left hand and one-handedly fired a couple of bursts from a fire extinguisher at it. The off-white colored material appeared to stick to the flame like a blanket and then it smothered it out.

A beam that went from floor to ceiling that was used as an equipment rack bent and flew free of its attachment points. The capsule squashed in closer around him. Paul could just imagine the view from the outside of the capsule. It must look like a pancake by now.

"Shit! I don't like this."

"I don't like this, comrade Hui," Rykov said. "Who knows what is going on down there? We have no way of knowing he is alright."

"His radio is just down. He is fine."

Then one of the attitude thrusters fired again.

"Look!"

"See, comrade Hui, like I said, nothing to worry

about. He is still controlling the ship," Rykov said with nervous humor.

"Keep calling him," Hui said.

"Affirmative." Rykov tapped the microphone icon again. "Paul, do you read me? Come in, Paul."

Nothing else happened a moment. Whatever had given way earlier apparently wasn't enough to knock the ship loose from the hastily placed anchors. Or the combination of the anchors and Paul's continued attitude corrections were enough to keep the *Tamaroa* in place. The dust cloud continued to dance off the surface and about the ship. The exhaust poured from the nuclear rocket engine and the asteroid was being pushed. The big question was if Paul was going to survive the effort.

"Fourteen minutes, Hui," Rykov noted. "Nothing other than a few attitude thruster burns so far. It looks like the structure is still intact."

"Come on, Paul," Hui muttered to herself.

"Fifteen minutes." The correction burns had continued. Paul was still alive.

At just after sixteen minutes, the ship lurched again. This time it moved to the left and then it did what they'd feared. It moved forward into the hole. It moved significantly forward into the hole.

"The anchors came loose," said Hui.

"Or the truss broke," Mikhail said.

"Either way, it's going to affect the thrust direction and it's got to be bad for Paul."

"Let's hope he can keep the engines operating for the full twenty minutes. We need to give this rock whatever push we can," Mikhail said. "Comrade, this is nuts. The capsule cannot withstand this strain. It must be flattened completely by now. Or at a minimum ruptured."

The ship moved forward several meters and then stopped again, the engines still running, making the back portion of the craft sway back and forth, looking all the more like a giant match stuck in the sand, and burning.

Finally, after just over twenty minutes after the engines ignited, they stopped. The ship still swayed, ever more slowly, until it came to rest.

Mikhail didn't wait long before he activated the radio. "Paul! Are you okay? What happened?"

Still no response. The silence was unnerving.

"Paul. This is Mikhail. The engines appeared to work flawlessly from out here, but we saw the ship lunge. Are you safe? Come in Paul."

Silence.

"He's not able to answer for whatever reason."

"We need to go in. He may need our help."

"Before we do that, let's check the radiation level to make sure that when the ship lunged, it didn't damage or crack open the reactor." Hui turned back to the flight controls and made a few adjustments before she pointed toward the graph now displayed on one of the forward display screens.

"The radiation levels haven't changed. At least over here. I'll ease us back toward the *Tamaroa* while you watch the radiation levels. I'm not too worried about a small change here or there on the way over, but a big spike would be bad news."

Mikhail watched the evolving graph of radiation levels while Hui concentrated on piloting the ship back in the direction from which she'd come less than an hour before. She was tired and could tell that her lack of sleep was affecting her ability to simultaneously monitor the various ship's systems as she normally would. Only her limited hours of training on the specifics of the CEV systems and her years of experience with similar Chinese systems kept her from making a mistake from her near-exhaustion.

Slowly, she brought the small capsule and its attached deep-space service module back toward the fissure and the *Tamaroa*. So far, there was no indication from Mikhail of a radiation problem.

That is good, she thought.

They were finally hovering just over the fissure from which they'd emerged and into which they must now return if they were going to be reunited with Gesling. No word from him could mean a million different things. In several of those options Paul would still be alive and well. In most of the others however, well, she didn't want to think about those.

"The radiation levels are stable," Mikhail said. "We must go to him quickly."

"Unfortunately, the ship moved and the path we took to fly out is now blocked by the ship. We don't have the radar that the *Tamaroa* has so if we go in, we'll be doing it by sight only. And the forward lights on us aren't that great."

"Hui, he's at least five hundred feet below ground and we don't know yet what happened to him and the habitat after the anchors broke. We're going in, right?"

"We're going in. I just need to figure out where to start and hope that the path I pick will let us get all the way down to where we started. We might have to go part way in the ship and then EVA for the rest."

"Then so be it. Let's go."

Hui looked at the barren landscape surrounding the tail end of the *Tamaroa*, pitched her tiny ship forward, turned on the forward lights and flew straight down into the darkness.

CHAPTER 33

"AR, A SUBPOENA FROM CONGRESS IS ONE YOU CAN'T ignore. The committee chairman is adamant that you testify and they're looking to crucify you for the panic and, God forbid, the damage Sutter's Mill may cause when and if it actually hits. They're not going to go away," Jonathan Price told his client.

Anacleto knew that Asteroid Ores would soon be bankrupt from the costs associated with the Sutter's Mill debacle. What he hadn't counted on was being held personally liable—fiscally, and potentially criminally. He'd been hearing the news pundits talking about him being tried for "crimes against humanity" should the asteroid actually impact and kill people. And now this, being subpoenaed to testify before Congress. Anacleto saw his world crumbling around him and there didn't appear to be any way out.

"This is a witch hunt. They should be going after Trivek, not me. They're the ones who made the damned thrusters that failed, not us."

"Oh, I'm sure they will go after Trivek. After they

get through trying and convicting you in front of Congress. AR, there is simply nothing I can do to prevent this from happening."

Anacleto wasn't one to accept defeat easily, but in this case he could see no easy way out. He'd tried something audacious and risky—and lost. He knew the company and fortune he'd amassed were in jeopardy, but this was the first time he'd really come to grips with the fact that he might actually also go to jail.

He walked away from Price and toward the window of his office and looked out upon the grand vista that was New York City. It was midday and the sun was shining. On the streets below, thousands of bright yellow e-taxis moved about, looking like a child's toys from his thirty-fourth-floor view of Manhattan. It could at least be raining, he thought. If I'm going to be miserable, then so should everyone else.

"Jonathan, pull together something for me to say. I'll need a draft by noon tomorrow."

"You could take the fifth and not say anything," offered Price.

"I could, but that's the coward's way out. We didn't do anything wrong, and I'll be damned if I'm going to admit guilt over anything and go down without a fight. We're trying to help the planet, for Christ's sake. Mining this asteroid would save thousands of square miles of wilderness that would no longer have to be mined. I can't let these pricks ruin that dream while they ruin me and my company."

"AR, we screwed up. We should have had a backup plan. I know that, you know that, and just about everybody in the space business knows that. But you didn't and here we are. They are going to make you out to be a villain and this will set back your vision for decades. No one will do this again anytime soon."

"Jonathan, we've been friends for years. You've worked for me longer than that. But sometimes I just want to punch you in the face, and this is one of those times. And it's only because your pessimism is more than I can sometimes bear."

"You pay me to be pessimistic. That's how I've saved you millions, if not hundreds of millions of dollars. I look at the worst case and then help you steer clear of it."

"I know. But in this case, it looks like your worst case might be the reality and I don't like that."

Anacleto continued staring down at the traffic as he spoke. He was saying the words that people, especially Price, expected him to say. "Be optimistic; be bullish; look to change the system" were the management-style buzzwords that everyone expected him to embody. What they didn't know was that all he was really thinking about was how to end the ordeal. And jumping off the roof of his office building was sounding more and more appealing. *Let's hope it doesn't come to that*, he thought.

CHAPTER 34

SUTTER'S MILL WAS ONLY A LITTLE MORE THAN three weeks out and try as they might, humanity had yet to do anything about it that appeared to have worked. As far as anyone on Earth knew, doom was still on its way. Millions were going to die. Millions more would be displaced from their homes. The world economy was going to be devastated. Life as most people knew it was going to change. But there was still one last hope. The last hope would be that the Russian nuclear missile would engage the asteroid within the next two days. The hope was that the missile would do all it needed to do to save humanity.

But none of that really mattered to Zhi Feng. His mind was singularly focused on one thing. It had been so focused since his fateful trip to the Moon. Rather than focus on the fact that he had gone to the Moon, he focused on his misplaced hatred. He was one of the first of the Chinese people to go to the Moon, and return home safely, but he chose to be bitter.

His personal psyche would not allow the Americans to outperform his beloved China.

As a child, Zhi's mother and father had made several deals and arrangements to have him placed in an advanced school in Beijing. His family was from a region thousands of miles away from the capital city and for all intents and purposes and in every definition of the word, his family were peasants. They were literally dirt poor. Zhi Feng recalled the dirt floor of their home and how he and his brother and father had often gathered discarded cardboard boxes and scraps of plywood from garbage heaps and abandoned or burned-out buildings. They used the cardboard as flooring in the room that he and his brother shared. It helped keep dirt out of the bed they had built. While he was only a toddler at the time, Zhi Feng recalled those days vividly. He recalled hating the cold and wet seasons. It was always cold and wet, or at least that was how he remembered it.

But Zhi was exceptionally bright for a child and one thing China had been good at for centuries was finding its talent and giving it a chance to grow. One could argue the ethics and humanity of the way China did it, but the facts were that young children with talent were often identified and given the opportunity to grow that talent for China's greater purpose.

Once Zhi had turned six years old he had scored very high on mathematics and logic exams given to all the kids. He had scored so high in fact that his parents were made an offer they couldn't refuse. China offered them a chance for their son to be taken to the best schools in the world and to be cared for by the state. It would be one less mouth for his family to feed and it would bring honor to the Feng household.

Before he had turned seven, Zhi Feng was taken to the new school where he would eventually learn his deep rooted national loyalties. Unbeknownst to the young Zhi, it would be the last time he would ever see his parents. At the time he recalled not wanting to leave. Zhi had cried bitterly and he recalled his mother crying and his father standing thin-lipped, choking back tears, but proud and looking down at him.

"Make China proud of you, son."

Zhi had lived to that last thought his entire life. As he excelled in math and science he pushed himself to be the smartest in every class. By the time he was thirteen he had been accepted at the university. Zhi was becoming one of the most brilliant engineers in the country and if he could maintain his performance he had a shot at getting into the space program.

His life had been on track to make China proud. He had been chosen to go to the Moon on the first Chinese mission there. He was going to fulfill his father's wishes and all was as it should have been. The sacrifice of a normal life, of not knowing his family, of not having a mother to hug when he fell and skinned his knee, of not having his brother and father there to teach him how to be a man, all of the sacrifice he had made for China was going to pay off in the end. He was going to the Moon and he would "make China proud." He would make his father proud. Zhi could barely even recall what his father looked like, but he would make him proud nonetheless.

But then the mission had gone from good to bad. Then there was still the chance that Zhi would have the chance to make an even greater sacrifice for China and give his life, until the damned Americans stole

that from him. Bill Stetson, Gary Childers, and the
now dead Paul Gesling. He smiled inwardly thinking
about Gesling's death. They had taken away the chance
for him to add the ultimate sacrifice to his long line
of sacrifices. They would pay for that. They would
pay. Gesling was dead, though not by his hands. But
he was dead.

It was time for Stetson and Childers to pay.

Zhi Feng looked at the immigration agent behind
the window at the desk. Los Angeles International
Airport was no more exciting than the typical flurry
of activity as far as he could tell. Feng did his best
to act like an impatient tourist as the customs agent
scanned inattentively at his documents.

"What is the purpose of your visit?" The man looked
up from the passport at him.

"Business," Zhi Feng said. The agent looked at
the picture on the ID and then back at Feng. The
agent stamped the form and handed it out through
the hole in the window.

"Very well. Welcome to America."

"Thank you." Zhi Feng took his customs paperwork and then made his way to the turnstiles into
the United States.

He passed through the corral and into the gate
area. As he scanned around, there were people sitting scattered about the gate and there was a woman
struggling with her luggage, a baby in her arms, and a
toddler tugging at her and crying. It was a very typical
airport scene. Very typical except for the three men in
suits and the two security agents looking right at him.

One of the men approached him and showed him
a badge.

"Hello, sir," the man said. "I'm Agent Reed with the Federal Bureau of Investigation, would you mind coming with us for a moment?"

"Uh, what is this about? I'm actually in kind of a hurry," Zhi said. He looked to his left and then his right. He wasn't sure he could outrun these men in the airport. He decided to play it calmly for now.

"I must insist, Mr. Feng," the agent said.

CHAPTER 35

PAUL COULDN'T BELIEVE WHAT HE WAS SEEING. HE was having a damned hard time believing what had just happened. The command capsule had been so flattened that he had his legs already outside the entry hatch preparing to make his escape when the rock outcropping that was holding the ship in place must have given way. He had realized at that moment that the anchors that Rykov and Hui had put in place were doing little to hold the *Tamaroa*. It was all the rock outcropping pushing against the command capsule. Once the rock gave way the ship lurched forward. The rocks shot free like missiles, crashing through a wall of rock just ahead of the ship at what he had assumed was the bottom of the fissure.

At the same instant the pressure was relieved from the highly compressed command capsule, which popped back into shape almost instantly. Violently. The immediate elastic retraction of the capsule snapping back to its minimum energy position, well, it released a hell of a lot of energy. Paul was knocked backwards by something, he wasn't sure what. But whatever it had been hit him hard enough that his helmet slapped into the wall behind him making him see stars, and not the ones out in space. His body recoiled and was flung forward and inward toward the nose of the capsule.

The walls continued to oscillate and ring out the energy that had been released like a tuning fork that had been struck by a hammer. They lurched inward and outward and back and forth and tossed equipment about, ripping it free from its mooring points with ease. Paul was slung arms and legs akimbo into the foremost section of the ship only to be flung immediately backwards into the bulkhead by the exit hatch where he'd just been. As debris peppered him, he grasped for a handhold—anything would have done, but he was having no luck. Several pieces of the debris cut into his suit and something hit his faceplate, leaving a spiderweb crack across the left side of it.

Paul managed to pull himself together and finally grab a handhold on one of the seats that was still in place. He waited for the debris to float to a reasonable velocity and for the walls to stabilize. Once everything reached a minimum energy position he let out a short sigh of relief.

"The engine seems to still be working," he tapped at the one control panel still functioning. "There is no way to tell what direction we're pointed though."

About a minute later he could feel the vibration of the engines stop. He floated himself to the window at the front of the capsule and looked out. There was daylight in front of him about a half a kilometer out. As far as he could tell the fissure in the asteroid went all the way through it and he had poked through a weak spot.

"I wonder if the exterior lights still work," he said to himself. He fumbled around the capsule looking for the controls and then finally switched them on. The exterior of the ship in front of him lit up with an almost too harsh white light. Brilliant sparkly gold reflected back at him from almost every direction.

"Holy shit!"

"Holy shit. Will you look at that?" Rykov pointed out the window of the Crew Transfer Vehicle at the main body of the *Tamaroa* and the rocks that had wedged between it and the hole that it had created.

"It looks like an arrow sticking through a target," Hui noted. "It is almost like it poked a hole all the way through the rock wall. Shouldn't our short-range suit radios pick up at this range?"

"Possibly, though that is a lot of rock," Rykov said.

"Paul," Hui keyed her suit mic. "Paul, do you copy, over? I repeat, Paul, do you copy? Over."

There was a long silent pause that gave Hui a sinking feeling in the pit of her stomach, but then the radio crackled and there was a digital connection made. The voice came through loud and clear.

"Roger that," Paul replied. "My long-range radio and suit are fried, so I'm using the wireless on my tablet. You two need to get in here. You're not going to believe what we've found."

"I'm glad to hear your voice. It looked like a rough ride from out here," Hui said.

"Believe me when I say that it was a helluva rough ride that I never want to ever have to repeat." Paul's voice sounded tired, but excited.

"Is it safe to come aboard, Paul?" Rykov asked.

"We show no radiation level increases. How is the air integrity?"

"As far as I can tell we have no leaks. You were right about the capsule material. Believe me, it is flexible as all hell. I actually could use some help figuring out where things stand in here. I need to check the habitat module and engineering."

"We're on our way. The hab entrance is blocked by rocks," Hui said thrusting the CTV in for a closer look. "I think we'll have to dock as normal in the aft section and then make our way forward from there."

"Affirmative. I'll be waiting for you."

CHAPTER 36

DR. MELANIE LEDFORD HAD GONE THROUGH MUL-
tiple emotional states over the past year. She had
been on top of her game as the newly appointed
commander of the first ever mission to Mars. It was
going to be historical. It was going to be nothing short
of difficult, amazingly hard, and unexplainably exciting.
A truly once in a lifetime event was coming her way
because of all the hard work she had put in for her
entire life. As far as the American space program was
concerned, she was the top astronaut.

Her doctorate in aerospace engineering and her two
master's degrees in geophysics and astronomy meant
that she was more than qualified academically. She
had over five thousand hours in complex aircraft as a
pilot, mainly from test flights at the Boeing Phantom
Works, some from flights back and forth between
Houston and other NASA centers, and some from
flying various Crew Transfer Vehicles to and from
the International Space Station. She also had about

a thousand hours on board the International Space Station. Her space resume was pretty good to boot.

But then some idiots attempted to capture an asteroid and bring it closer to Earth. Well, they had succeeded in the worst way. In doing so, they cost Melanie her trip to Mars, at least for now.

She had gotten angry when a civilian space tourist pilot was made commander of the mission to save Earth over her, but at that point she was at least still going on the mission. Then that idiot Zhi Feng blew up their ride, her ride, into space and she was stuck back on Earth doing support work. She, America's top astronaut wasn't going on the most important mission in space in her lifetime. Had she gone they might still be alive. But the mission had gone silent and remained that way for weeks now. They must be dead. The mission had failed. She should have been there.

It had taken her almost a month to get a grip on her situation and let herself reach the understanding that things "were what they were" and there was nothing she could do to change that now. What she had decided to do instead was to be the irreplaceable asset that she was. Being petty and moody wouldn't help anybody. And if it wasn't her turn in the flight rotation, then she knew she had to simply accept that and move on. Her turn would come. Or, at least she hoped it would before she aged out of the rotation completely.

Melanie looked out the window at the mountain and the huge radio telescope dish beneath her. The Arecibo, Puerto Rico dish was the absolute largest single dish radio telescope that mankind had ever put together. And ever since the *Tamaroa* had sent a message back to Earth that there were chunks of rock a month or so ahead of the Sutter's Mill asteroid she had been putting her astronomy degree and her knowledge of astrodynamics to work.

The large radio telescope could also be used as a transmitter, and therefore as a radar with which to map space. In fact, it had been used as such for many decades since the system had been constructed. Planetary scientists had used it to make radar maps of Mars, the Moon, Mercury, Venus, Saturn, Jupiter, and several asteroids and comets.

Melanie was currently searching the orbital trajectories ahead of the asteroid and along the track of the rescue mission to hopefully get a handle on just how big the "chunks" of the asteroid were that might be headed their way. She had been searching for months, but the debris was so far away that much detail had eluded her. And even with such a large dish, three hundred five meters in diameter, there was still barely enough return signal to map subasteroid-sized chunks much farther out than halfway to Mars. It took patience to collect the very weak radar return signals over long integration times and then waiting for the computers to crunch and analyze the data seem to take forever. She couldn't imagine how the astronomers back in the 1970s and 80s, with their slow computers, could stand the waiting. The dish had been there a very long time.

"Dr. Ledford," the young graduate student running the equipment looked out from behind his console. "The data analysis is coming in now. Would you like me to bring it up for you?"

"Sure thing, Mike. Let me see what we've got."

Melanie picked her coffee cup up from her desk and sipped it. It nearly turned her stomach as she spat it back into the cup. "That's cold. And just plain nasty. Can't we get better coffee up here?"

"Yes ma'am. Here we go." Mike tapped at his console and brought up the first algorithm enhanced images from the radar return data. "Holy shit."

"Holy shit is right."

"Yes ma'am, that's right. It's a debris field spread out about the size of Texas in its planar cross section orthogonal to Earth's orbital plane and it is spread out over several hundred thousand kilometers. It is roughly four hundred times longer than it is wide. We estimate the volumetric envelope of the cloud to be about two hundred eighty billion cubic kilometers total. And of course, the astrodynamics of the situation will allow it to continue to spread out even more, which is actually a good thing, sort of. There are some chunks that are as big as a hundred meters across. The *Tamaroa* is lucky they didn't hit one of the larger chunks. They must have just passed through the tail of the cloud. They were damned lucky, uh, ma'am," Melanie Ledford explained to the NASA Administrator, Dr. Tara Reese-Walker.

"Let me get this straight, there is a debris field the size of Texas on a collision course with Earth and we are just now figuring this out? When will it hit and where?" Reese-Walker didn't like what she was hearing.

"Well, ma'am, it is just now close enough that we are getting much radar return from it. One hundred meters is about the smallest size we can resolve at the current distance, but the general return from the debris cloud is quite large. Also, we need to keep in mind that it is fairly sparsely populated. I don't have to tell you that space is big. The data shows about four micrograms per cubic kilometer. So, less than can be seen with the human eye every cubic kilometer. That's the up side. The down side is the cloud totals a mass of well over a million kilograms of material and some of it is in big chunks. Doppler data shows it will hit Earth's atmosphere with a relative velocity of about fifteen kilometers per second. As of now we still don't know if it will be a direct hit, a glancing blow, or a near miss. But it is so expansive, I can't believe we'll miss it completely."

"What do you know?"

"What we do know is that it is about one million kilometers from Earth right now and will begin hitting in the next twenty-two hours or so. If the cloud impacts Earth head on and we drive through the complete cloud, tip to tail, the impacts could last for as much as eight hours. If we just pass through it crossways they will last about two hours or so. Then, depending on other variables, the timescale is somewhere between the two. As our trajectory data gets better we'll have a better answer for that, but we'll know about the time it hits us, so the analysis is almost a moot point."

"Jesus Christ!" Reese-Walker cupped the microphone of the desk phone and leaned her head over to look out her office door. "Samantha! Get me the President's Science Advisor on the phone right now!"

"Uh, yes, Dr. Walker."

"Melanie, keep crunching the numbers. I need as much info as possible. Can you narrow down where we might get hit first?"

"Well, in twenty-two hours the Atlantic Ocean will be pointed toward the cloud and the East Coast will start rolling by. We're likely to see the United States pounded from coast to coast. Hopefully, the debris is loose and it will just be a really big light show. But there are several large blobs in the data that scare the hell out of me."

"Ma'am, I've got the White House on the line!"

"Keep on top of this Melanie! I'll call you back."

The hot topic of the moment at the Arecibo Observatory was the impending meteor impacts. Priority was to determine: what was going to hit the Earth, how big it would be, how many of them there were, and when and exactly where it would happen. But the observatory had multiple systems running around the clock for multiple scientific experiments. There were multichannel radio telescope systems listening to space all the time. Some were looking for signals from black holes, supernovae, hydrogen gas clouds, and even aliens. Whatever their mission, they were running, nonstop, across the frequency spectrum. Computers would record the data and at some point somebody would do an analysis of it. Some of the data was automatically analyzed but most of it was not.

So, while the entirety of the staff at the observatory were looking at the coming meteors, nobody happened to notice that a radio signal from space was detected and stored away in the digital database to be found, hopefully, later, by somebody. The signal was weak, but detectable by the large dish. It was manmade and was continuously repeating itself.

"This is the spaceship *Tamaroa*. Our high and low

gain antennas are inoperable at this time. We are broadcasting from a makeshift omnidirectional patch with hopes that you will get this message. The electric propulsion system repair has failed. We are still alive and well on the asteroid Sutter's Mill and are attempting to push its trajectory using the nuclear engines of the *Tamaroa*. Please acknowledge and advise."

CHAPTER 37

"YOUR SPACESUIT HAS LOOKED BETTER, MY FRIEND," Rykov patted Paul Gesling on the back with his gloved hand. He and Hui floated through the hatch into the command capsule. The spaceship had been in much better shape as well.

"What a mess!" Hui looked at the debris floating about and the extensive damage to the ship's bridge. "We'll never get it working again."

"Not so sure we need to. We're out of fuel anyway," Paul replied. He tapped at his handheld tablet. "Most of the systems that are still functioning are controllable through this pad or the consoles in engineering. Looks like we have atmospheric integrity. Who knows, a coat of paint and a plant or two might be all it needs. Definitely a fixer-upper though."

Paul popped his facemask on his helmet. It was getting hard to see through anyway with the spiderweb cracks in it covering most of the left half. Paul took a deep breath of the cabin air and then motioned out the front windows of the capsule.

"Look what I found," he said, pointing out at the very large vein of sparkly gold in the rock wall surrounding them. There was an equally impressive dark red vein nearby. "And, if you look carefully, you can see all the way through this beast. See that bright spot out there. I think it is Earth!"

"Holy..." Rykov whistled. "That has to be gold. Probably billions of euros worth! Sure looks like it."

"I'm more concerned with the view through our soda straw here. Is that truly Earth?" Hui asked. "If it is, we'd better hope it starts drifting out of view over the next few days."

"We need to figure out if all this worked," Paul started. "And, we need to assess our life-support systems and supplies."

"Where do we start?" Hui shrugged her shoulders as best she could in her spacesuit. "We need trajectory data, but I suspect the systems on the *Tamaroa* are of no use stuck down here."

"Well," Paul removed his gauntlets and then rubbed his nose. "Man that feels good. We need to get in the CTV and get topside so our star trackers can start getting some position data. Sure would be nice if we could talk to someone from mission control."

"Yes, the CTV could collect the data easily," Hui agreed. "However, it will take several days most likely to have enough data points before a Kalman filter can map a new trajectory for us."

"Right." Paul blinked his eyes and rolled his head left and right and couldn't stop himself from yawning.

"Comrades, I know there is much to do, but I am literally about to pass out from hunger and exhaustion. We must stop and rest and refuel." Rykov rummaged through a compartment on one of the twisted and flattened equipment racks and pulled out some meal bars. He offered them to his colleagues. Paul took two. "It will do us no good if we are so tired that we make some fatal mistake in the process of saving ourselves."

"Mikhail is right. We must rest," Hui said, accepting a meal bar herself.

"Agreed. Let's take eight hours break and see where we are then." Paul tapped at his pad and set an alarm clock. "Till, uh, morning then."

"Are we sure we are safe in here?" Hui asked. "I mean, the ship has taken a beating."

"The aft section is basically no worse for wear, Paul. We came through the aft docking port. The damage is up here," Rykov said.

"Well the pressure alarms seem to be working. We have power and plenty of it. The reactor is working with no signs of damage." Paul read the status of the ship's systems on his pad. "The radiators are actually in the green and that's probably because they are in contact with some of the asteroid now and have a big heat sink touching them."

"That settles it, then?" Hui asked as she started to unfasten her spacesuit.

"I think we are fine in here. Keep your suits close and know that we can always make a run for the CTV if things go bad. If we have a leak, then it will likely be up front in the command capsule, or what's left of it. So, we can always just shut this hatch," Paul said as he turned his helmet until it clicked and then he pulled it free. He looked at the crack on the faceplate.

"Why don't we do that just to be safe?" Hui said.

"Agreed." Paul nodded at her. "Go ahead."

"Might I also suggest you swap out your suit with the spare, Paul?" Rykov suggested. "Uh, yours has seen better days, comrade."

"Right. Good plan."

Hui and Rykov got quiet very quickly. They were so tired that it didn't take long before they were out. Paul had made his way to the aft airlock and docking port where the spare suits were stored. There were several suits, but only one of them still had air. They'd used the oxygen bottles for explosives to tie down the *Tamaroa*. Paul shook his head at the thought. He knew now that the tiedowns hadn't helped at all and they had just wasted both the oxygen and the time. He didn't see any reason to tell Hui and Mikhail that, if they hadn't figured it out by now.

Paul grabbed the good suit and started the process of dragging it back toward his sleep cubicle. By the time he got back he was drifting in and out of consciousness. Somehow he managed to tie his suit down, crawl into his sleeping bag, and then zip himself in. That was the last thing he could remember doing until the alarm went off.

CHAPTER 38

THE RUSSIAN MISSILE WAS GUIDED BY OPTICAL SEN-
sors. A telescope in the nose of the "science package"
kept the bright spot that was Sutter's Mill in the center
of the image, and if the onboard computer detected
the bright spot in the center moving off-center, then
a correction signal was sent to the appropriate attitude
control thruster, which would then fire and push the
missile back on target.

What the Russians hadn't accounted for was that
several weeks prior the missile had passed through
a very large debris cloud. The very same cloud that
was now threatening the Earth had taken its toll on
the modified Russian missile.

The rocket had been peppered by several micro-
meteorites at very high relative velocities. One micrometeorite in particular had impacted with the clear
bubble over the optical sensors. Very little damage had
been done to the missile and its "science package,"
and as far as telemetry data being sent back to Earth
was concerned, the missile was perfectly healthy. The

mission control team back in Russia had no reason to think that the missile would not perform as planned. Diagnostic systems and telemetry data sometimes just weren't enough to tell the entire tale. The people on Earth hadn't panicked yet because they were assured that the Russian missile was going to save the day.

But in reality that wasn't the case at all. The micrometeorite impact against the protective optical bubble had left a divot in the aerospace hardened glass. The divot just happened to be in the right spot as to diffract the incoming light from the asteroid by three pixels on the image plane of the camera. While three pixels were only about one hundred millionths of a meter (one hundred microns) in distance on the image plane sensor, that translated into thousands of miles in actual space. By the time the astrodynamics experts back at the Cosmodrome realized that their missile was thousands of kilometers off track, it was already so far away from the asteroid that there was not enough fuel on board to bring it back on target. The missile would miss the asteroid by a distance larger than the diameter of the Earth and there was nothing anybody could do about it.

The mission's chief engineer had a call to make to the Kremlin. In return, the defense minister would have a call to make. In either case the news was politically devastating, as the Russians had announced the missile as the mission that would save the Earth from desolation by the near-Earth object. But now the Russians were going to have to eat crow and announce failure. Russian politicians didn't like to eat crow. In fact, they usually only ever ate crow once and then were never heard from again. But, in the end, there was no way around it. Millions of lives were in the balance. Perhaps there were still actions that could be put in place that would help minimize the loss of life. But it was very late notice for major preparations. The asteroid was only a few weeks out.

The Russian president had some phone calls to make.

CHAPTER 39

MIKE HAD BEEN WORKING AT ARECIBO FOR MORE than three years. He had hoped to finish up his doctoral research soon and get a real job, but at the same time he liked living in Puerto Rico. The pace of life was much less hectic than that which he had been raised in back home in the Bronx. And it was always nice and warm somewhere in Puerto Rico. He didn't miss New York City at all.

When he'd first gotten to the observatory he had no idea how any of the systems of the largest radio telescope in the world worked. In fact, he'd accidentally fried a very expensive amplifier for the S-band radar transceiver on his first day on the job. He continued to believe that it hadn't been his fault and that they should have trained him on it before letting him touch it.

Since that time he'd more than made up for his mistake. Mike became the guy that kept the systems running even when some new software upgrade brought all the computers crashing down. Once the graduate student who was there before Mike had passed along the torch on to him, he became the senior engineer for the planetary radar equipment. He had operated and maintained most of the planetary radar amplifiers and transceiver systems for more than two years now. When the planetary astronomers and scientists showed up to do an experiment they quickly realized that Mike was the man they needed to talk to first.

Mike had other interests in astronomy as well. While his expertise was the equipment used for making astronomical measurements with radio waves, he was very interested in the detection of extremely weak signals and the Search for Extra Terrestrial Intelligence or SETI. Not that he believed they'd ever pick up signals from aliens, but the technology needed to detect extremely weak signals pushed the state of the art in amplifier signal to noise capabilities and he was fascinated by it. He had been building low-noise amplifiers since he was a teen and he always felt like he could tweak the technology just one more bit and get a little more gain out of them. Many times that led to him blowing them up, but sometimes he made incremental improvements. Those improvements and some of the failures would make for a great doctoral dissertation—if he could ever get time to finish writing it.

So, in his spare time, of which he shouldn't have any because he should be writing, he hung out with the SETI astronomers and learned how their equipment worked. Most of it was funded through private grants, since NASA and the NSF no longer funded that type of research. And in some cases the owners of the equipment were very "hands-offish" until they realized that Mike was an asset, who, for the most part, would help them for free.

As far as the meteor cloud was concerned, there was little left for him to be doing. The big dish was on the wrong side of the planet now and wouldn't be able to help ascertain details of the debris cloud until it was too late. NASA, the Strategic Space Command, and whoever else were using other dishes scattered about the globe to pin down those details. And all of that effort was apparently above his pay grade. Mike was officially out of the loop on the whole debris cloud tracking effort.

The computers were running analyses as Dr. Ledford had requested, but most of those efforts needed much more computing power and were therefore being done elsewhere on supercomputers. For all intents and purposes, Mike was sitting idle for what might prove to be a good while. Dr. Ledford had gone home for the evening and wouldn't be back until morning. Like most graduate students he was a night owl by necessity and he had other work he could do. But he was more in the mood to just hang out and do fun stuff.

So he decided to look at the data that had been stored away over the past few days by the SETI transceivers. After all, the dish was focused on part of the sky the asteroid was in, which also happened to have several nearby star systems in the very distant background. Who knew? Maybe there would be something there. In reality, there would be almost no way he could find such a needle in the haystack, but he liked watching the data flow across the screen. Sometimes he even played an audio representation of one of the channels.

Mike started a digital strip chart across the S-band spectrum and watched as the "waterfall" of multiple colors representing signal strength and multiple millions of frequencies filtered down the screen. There was mostly the general noise of space. There would be an occasional blip that the filters missed but for the most part there was nothing but white noise. And the blips that got through always turned out to be some manmade satellite or a burping star or some such thing. There was never an alien signal, at least not to his knowledge. Then the autocorrelator filter grabbed onto a part of the waterfall. An alert box popped up on the screen.

"Signal detected," he read to himself. "What the..."

He zoomed in on the channel and looked closer at it. The signal had structure. It was digital. It was very, very weak but it was a signal. He quickly started the strip chart markers and sped up the flow speed of the waterfall until he found the end of the signal. It had lasted for almost an hour. That seemed impossible.

"Okay, I don't know enough about this to understand what I'm looking at." He looked at the screen for another second and decided to find help. He toggled open his video chat software and clicked on the username for the signals engineer from the SETI team. A sleepy-looking young lady answered the message.

"Mike? It's late," she said.

"I know, Lynne, and I'm sorry. But I think you found a signal," he replied. "Look at your email." He tapped at the keyboard and sent her a copy of about ten seconds of the waterfall chart.

"Okay, hold on," Lynne told him as she fiddled with her computer on her end. Mike could see her staring intently back at her computer and then she looked up wide-eyed. "It can't be an alien signal."

"What is it then?"

"I'll have to come in and look, but the Doppler shift is all wrong. It looks like signals we see from space probes inside our own solar system."

"What does that mean?" Mike was confused.

"Just hold on. I'll be there in thirty minutes."

"Alright then, I'll see you in a bit." Mike toggled the video chat software off and went back to looking at the signal. "Inside our solar system?"

CHAPTER 40

GARY CHILDERS ENTERED THE ROOM WITH A BOX of chocolates and a very large pink fuzzy teddy bear. It would be the first time he had seen Carolyn since she had regained consciousness. Bill and Rebecca Stetson were in the room already and were talking about the light show they were all expecting in a couple hours. Carolyn still had tubes coming out of her chest, presumably to drain her lungs as needed, and had oxygen flowing in her nose from smaller tubes, but otherwise she looked good.

"Gary!" she said with a scratchy voice as he entered. "Come here!"

"Carolyn, you look great," Gary told her as he handed her the teddy bear and set the chocolates aside. "Don't know if you can eat these yet but I had them imported from France just for you when you can."

"The nurse says she can eat whatever she wants," Rebecca Stetson said. Gary noticed the halo cast on her hand but did his best to act like he didn't. He was sure she was getting tired of being asked about it.

"I'm glad you are all here. I've got news," Gary said somewhat excitedly. "I just got a call from the FBI. They have apprehended Zhi Feng. He is now being questioned and will soon be transferred to a federal holding cell."

"That is great news!" Bill replied.

"And I'm also glad you're in one place. That'll make our move easier," Gary looked at his "family" as he thought of them. And he thought about how banged up they all were and how they had lost some of their best people. He did his best not to think of Paul. Gary had done everything he could to make certain that Paul had gone on the mission to the asteroid where he would end up losing his life. The amount of guilt he felt was almost beyond his capability to handle. But Gary was a survivor and right now he had to make sure that his "family," at least what was left of it, were going to survive the rest of the asteroid ordeal.

"Move? Where are we going?" Bill Stetson leaned back on the private hospital room's sofa.

"Well, in about thirty minutes we are all moving to my bunker in western Kentucky about three hundred kilometers from here. My jet is waiting right now to take us to my hanger at the Paducah Regional Airport. From there we'll go to my estate on the banks of the Ohio River. We're transferring Carolyn and Rebecca there until after this is over." Gary cringed for a second, realizing that Bill might not have told his wife yet about flying the *Dreamscape* into space for him when the asteroid approached. He could tell by the dirty look Bill gave him that he was right.

"Well, damn, sorry Bill."

"Now is as good a time as any, I guess, Gary," Bill replied.

"What is as good a time as any?" Rebecca asked. The tone in her voice was flat.

"Bill, let me." Gary held up a hand. "Rebecca, I need your husband to fly the *Dreamscape* into orbit for me. I have several paying customers that are paying handsomely to be in orbit when the asteroid hits the Earth. And, well, Bill is the only pilot I've got."

"You mean the only pilot you've got left," Carolyn said gruffly. Gary noticed the tears forming at the corners of her eyes.

"I would never say that, Carolyn." Gary squeezed her hand and continued. "I'm hurting too. Paul was the closest thing I've had in years to a true friend."

"I just hate that he gave his life not knowing I was still alive," Carolyn started sobbing. As she sniffed it choked her and made breathing difficult.

"Carolyn, you need to stay calm, honey," Rebecca rushed to her side and stroked her arm. "Just breathe as easy as you can."

"I'm sorry." Gary didn't know what to say. He was saved by his phone ringing. Bill Stetson's phone started ringing at the same time.

"What the?" Bill looked at Gary and then his phone. Both men answered.

"Hello?" The two of them echoed.

"When?" Gary asked. He couldn't tell what Bill was saying. "Now? Alright then." He hung up his phone and then looked at Bill.

"Right now?" Bill asked. "Okay. Will call in five minutes, then."

"You first," Gary told Bill.

"The NASA administrator is having a teleconference in five minutes with the rescue mission team," Bill said.

"Same here. And there was no hint as to why." Gary turned to the women and frowned. "We will go ahead and start getting the two of you moved to my plane. Bill and I will teleconference in while you two get packed and on the plane. We will be right behind you."

Rebecca only nodded at the two men. Gary wasn't sure if she was angry or not. Rebecca had been an astronaut's wife most of her life. She understood the territory.

"Stand by for the NASA administrator," a voice announced on the speaker. Gary and Bill had commandeered one of the offices in the hospital for the call while the women were being moved to the airport. Gary had staff taking care of that. Bill and he would catch up with them as soon as this thing was over. Besides, he figured it would take a little longer for them to move Carolyn anyway. They needed to hurry, though, as the asteroid debris cloud was expected to start hitting the east coast of the United States within the next two hours. Within three or four it would be in range of Kentucky.

"Hello, this is Tara Walker. I realize that most of you are making preparations for the pending impacts, so I will not bother with going around the room, so to speak, and getting a conference call list of names. If you have something to say, chime in and tell us who you are. That being said, the information I'm about to announce cannot wait any longer. There are two bits of news. I'll start with the bad. About one hour ago the president received a phone call from the Russian president wherein he was given the word that the rocket carrying the nuclear bomb to the asteroid has for whatever reason flown way off course and will miss the asteroid by more than twelve thousand kilometers."

"Holy cow," Bill whistled. "What do we do now?"

"Shit, Bill, I'm not sure there is anything left to do," Gary told him, double checking to make sure the speakerphone was on mute. The administrator continued.

"We are assessing the situation and hoping for a third solution alternative, but as of right now we are starting the beginning stages of developing an evacuation of the central latitude regions of the planet to minimize loss of life. The president is expected to make a statement within the hour."

"Jesus!" Gary looked at Bill. "That would take weeks."

"Is something like that even possible?" Bill sounded skeptical.

"If anybody has any possible solution scenarios please contact me as soon as possible." Administrator Reese-Walker sounded totally flummoxed.

"And now for the possible good news," she continued. "At approximately two-thirty a.m. Eastern Standard Time this morning, the team using the Multi-channel Extra-Terrestrial Array broad-spectrum radio equipment attached to the large Gregorian dish in Arecibo, Puerto Rico detected a signal from deep space. That signal was detected for approximately an hour before it was lost. After further analysis it is clear that the signal came from the *Tamaroa* spacecraft. Listen carefully to the following recording of the signal."

There was a short pause and then the message began.

This is the spaceship Tamaroa. *Our high and low
gain antennas are inoperable at this time. We are
broadcasting from a makeshift omnidirectional patch
with hopes that you will get this message. The electric
propulsion system repair has failed. We are still alive
and well on the asteroid Sutter's Mill and are attempting to push its trajectory using the nuclear engines of
the* Tamaroa. *Please acknowledge and advise.*

"That's Paul!" Bill almost shouted.

"I knew it," Gary said excitedly. "Listen. Listen."

"The message repeats itself from there. We have
no way of knowing what has happened up there and
as far as we can tell the trajectory of the Sutter's
Mill asteroid has not changed a detectable amount.
We have been responding to the signal for the past
several hours, but have gained no response from the
Tamaroa. The spacecraft, if it is on the asteroid, is
about twenty-seven million kilometers from Earth and
is at about a ninety-second speed of light delay for
communications. Hopefully, they are still alive and we
will get a further response from them soon."

"I'm texting Rebecca right now to tell Carolyn,"
Bill said as he thumbed his phone.

"Wait, Bill," Gary looked like somebody had run
over his dog. "Not yet. We don't know that this isn't
an automated message that is somehow still going after
they were killed or something. No, let's wait until we
know for certain. We can't put Carolyn through thinking
he's alive again and then finding out something else."

"Dammit!" Bill slammed his phone on the coffee
table in front of him. "You're right, but dammit."

"As soon as we get Carolyn safe, we need to get
involved with this," Gary said.

"I agree."

The two men listened to the closing statements of the NASA Administrator, but there was little more information. The NASA Deep Space Network system had been brought online and was continuously broadcasting at the asteroid. But for the past several hours there had been nothing but the repeated signal.

"But for now, we need to get to the bunker and wait out the next few hours." Gary checked his watch and realized they needed to get moving.

CHAPTER 41

THE EARTH AND THE DEBRIS FIELD CONTINUED TO approach one another at a hefty fifteen kilometers per second relative closing velocity. The outer edges of the atmosphere had just started brushing the outer edges of the debris field. Shooting stars had begun to flash brightly across the night sky off the eastern coast of the North American continent. A giant fireball streaked across the sky, visible from cities as far north as Jersey City. The explosive boom was so loud that windows burst all along the coastline from Richmond, Virginia to Jacksonville, Florida. Millions of dollars in damage grew to tens of millions as the wave of destruction from near Earth spread westward. And this was just the beginning.

As the small pieces that had been slung forward off of the Sutter's Mill asteroid during the despin operation tracked across the globe, they left a wake of damage ranging from broken windows to power outages. But that was only the small-scale debris. The largest so far had been a fireball that exploded at approximately five miles high above Memphis, Tennessee. The blast wave from the meteorite's airburst had an epicenter about fifteen kilometers southwest of downtown and was more destructive than an EF-5 tornado. It wiped several older office and commercial buildings off the map. Homes in the suburban area showed extensive damage as far south as Arkabutla Lake. The casualty toll was expected to be close to two hundred people. The emergency responders were working diligently to rescue those trapped in the rubble. And firefighters were engaged with fires and gas leaks over an area of more than a hundred square kilometers.

The hopes were that Memphis would be the worst of it.

At least, those were the hopes.

CHAPTER 42

"I DON'T CARE WHAT THE FAA IS TELLING YOU. THIS is my plane and we are leaving here now. That's why we're on a smaller regional airport instead of Blue Grass Airport at Lexington. Take off and get us to Paducah and it will be worth your while. I'll take care of the FAA," Gary told his pilot. The man was new. Gary's previous pilot had quit once all the shooting had started and it was clear that someone was doing their level best to see him killed. Gary didn't blame his former pilot. Who knew? That rat bastard crazy SOB Zhi Feng could show up anytime and start taking shots at him again. All of Gary's employees had pretty much demanded a higher level of pay or protection.

The new guy had come with high praise from the same organization that supplied his bodyguards. Gary hoped the man understood that when he worked for Gary Childers sometimes you did what Gary Childers wanted and not what the federal government "recommended." He'd learn that or Gary would be forced to find someone else that would.

"Yes sir, Mr. Childers. I just wanted to make sure you understood the risks we are taking. The commercial boys have stopped flying already. And the FAA is telling us we shouldn't take off," the pilot warned him.

"Are they saying we can't take off by law?"

"Uh, not yet, sir."

"Are they saying it is a no-fly zone and they'll shoot us down?"

"Uh, no sir. They are not."

"Are you afraid to fly in this?"

"No sir, the odds of getting hit by something have to be ridiculously low. And the Gulfstream 650 is the best plane there is. But I'm just warning you that there could be legal flak and there is the extremely remote possibility of danger."

"I understand. Now let's get out of here." Gary was finished with the conversation.

"Roger that, sir." The pilot toggled a switch and radioed to the control of the airport, alerting them that they were taxiing and taking off whether they advised it or not. "Just go relax, sir. This will be a short flight."

"Good. Thank you for understanding." Gary nodded and turned to the rear of the plane. He made a mental note to do something nice for the pilot in the future.

Carolyn's gurney had been strapped into the plush couch on the left side of the cabin and Bill and Rebecca had taken seats flanking her. Rebecca was by the window near Carolyn's head and Bill at the window by her feet. The nurse practitioner caring for her was seated behind them but was keeping a watchful eye on both Carolyn and the sensor readings being routed to her touchpad via wireless. There was no flight attendant, as Gary typically liked to take care of things like getting a drink for himself. Sometimes on longer flights he'd have an attendant or two, but this was a simple up and down from the middle of Kentucky to the western edge of it.

"Whoah! The sky is starting to light up to the east of us," Bill said. "We should get on with it."

"We are," Gary said just as the plane started to move. "We'll be in Paducah in thirty minutes or so and my place is only minutes from there. I have an ambulance standing by to transport us."

"Don't worry about me, Gary. I don't think I need an ambulance," Carolyn grunted hoarsely. "Too much fuss."

"Well, yes and no," Gary started, just as the jet pushed him back into his seat as it accelerated for takeoff and pitched up to climb to altitude. He could see a slight grimace on Carolyn's face. The nurse looked up at him and gave him a thumbs up. Carolyn might have some discomfort, but nothing major to worry about.

"You okay, Carolyn?" Becca asked her. "You need anything?"

"I'm fine. I'm fine," Carolyn reassured her. "Now what do you mean by 'yes and no,' Gary?"

"Well, I meant that an ambulance can travel faster than normal vehicles on the road so we are all going to ride with you to my place by the river," Gary replied. "It will be faster."

"Y'all have to see this!" Bill sounded excited as he motioned toward the windows. "Better than the Fourth of July!"

Gary unbuckled his seat belt and climbed partially over Bill to look out his window even though there was an empty window seat right behind him. Just as he looked out there were several bright green streaks across the twilight sky leaving long burning and sparkling trails through the atmosphere against the blue and pink sky background.

"Jesus!" Bill said, sounding like a kid on the fourth of July. "What fireworks!"

"We're safe from them, right?" Rebecca Stetson asked her husband.

"The odds of one of those meteors hitting this airplane are so astronomically small that you can't even imagine the number. For all intents and purposes the odds might as well be zero chance of a hit," Bill told his wife.

"That's right," Gary added. "Nonetheless, I'll feel better once we get safely to my place. Besides, Bill, we've got some phone calls to make."

Just behind several bright streaks of green zipping across the sky to the north and east of them a fireball appeared that was much, much brighter than the ones they had seen so far. The green and white streak filled the sky and then, as far as Gary could tell, it impacted or exploded. A mushroom cloud of fire was thrown upwards and the twilight sky turned as bright as noon.

"Oh my God!" Becca shouted. "What is that?"

"Something just impacted maybe fifty to a hundred kilometers north of us. Maybe further," Stetson exclaimed. "Gary, does this thing have a live television feed?"

"I'm already ahead of you, Bill," Gary said as he sat back down in his seat and ran the remote controls in the chair arm. A flat-screen was revealed on a forward bulkhead. Gary switched it on and it took a few seconds to negotiate with the digital satellite system and then they were watching a twenty-four-hour news channel. "There. They're showing it already."

"...first reports are that a large impact has occurred just south of Cincinnati, Ohio. As of now we have little information other than the live video feed you are seeing from our affiliate there. Oh my God, this looks devastating... you can actually make out the mushroom-style cloud. It looks like a nuclear bomb was dropped on Cincinnati. Oh my God, our prayers go out to the families of the people there... We are going to go now to..."

"...*Ding*... Uh, sir, this is the captain speaking. I'd suggest everyone buckle up as we are about to experience a very serious shear layer. Please remain seated and remain calm."

No sooner than the words had filtered through the intercom and Gary had managed to process what he was saying the plane started to buffet and rock. Gary lost his balance and grabbed for a handhold but missed. Fortunately, Bill grabbed him by the right arm and steadied him just in time.

"I'm good," Gary told him. "You can let go."

"Everybody, hold on and stay buckled!" Stetson shouted as he let go of Gary and turned to look at Carolyn and his wife.

The blast wave of the impact at the distance they were from ground zero might not have been threatening to buildings and trees and houses, but to an airplane the nearly two hundred kilometer per hour winds started tossing the plane like a toy.

Updrafts and vacuum pockets following the initial blast wave impact forced the plane to lurch upward and then fall dramatically. Gary could feel his heart sink to the pit of his stomach and then jump into his throat almost instantaneously. Gary looked over at his companions. Bill Stetson, astronaut extraordinaire had his body pressed into his seat and his head turned slightly so he could see out the window. He seemed calm, but Gary was guessing that Bill wished he were in the cockpit.

Rebecca Stetson was holding onto the seat arm, white-knuckling it, and appeared to be clinching her jaw to hold back bile. Carolyn had a grimace on her face, but being strapped in she could do little more than just lie there.

The jet continued to rock wildly and was thrown left and right and up and down randomly for the next several minutes. There appeared to be no end in sight until Gary felt the jet turn nose up and could feel the engines burning full throttle. The plane climbed for several minutes through the rough weather and then seemed to be clear of it.

"There are still lots of streaks across the sky," Bill noted. "We really need to get this thing on the ground."

"Agreed," Gary said. "I'll call..."

Then the plane peaked in its climb and nosed over. For a very brief instant Gary felt his stomach float into his throat and realized they must be close to microgravity, and then the plane completed the nose over and the pilot threw the throttle all the way to the stop, pushing them into a steep dive. The Gulf-stream G VI class aircraft picked up speed and jetted through the upper boundary layer of the rough winds. The jet jerked and jumped, but it pressed on through and gained speed. Gary looked out his window and could see lights ahead and beneath them that were rushing up quickly. He'd seen the same lights before.

"Paducah is just ahead. We're moving really fast, though," he said.

"He's punching through the winds. Your pilot knows what he's doing, Gary." Bill nodded, then smiled. "Or at least I hope he does. Gonna be a helluva flare at the bottom of this dive."

Just then the motors for the flaps kicked in, vibrating the plane as it tore into the high speed winds traversing the wings. Noise from the friction of the high speed airflow made the interior of the jet sound like a low dollar carnival ride. Then the flaps bit deeper into the wind as the motors drove them up higher. The plane started to flare out slightly and the speed began to drop rapidly. The plane was coming in very hot—too hot for a landing.

"We're very hot!" Bill shouted. "Stall this baby!"

The nose of the plane continued to shift up and up and the noise inside the cabin continued to sound like nuts and bolts in a blender on frappé. Then the *kathunk* of the wheels dropping out underneath them and the motors whining as they locked them in place. The wind friction against the wheels added to the noise. Gary thought the wind against the landing gear sounded like a thousand rivers rushing through the cabin, but it also slowed the plane dramatically.

Altitude dropped quickly and then the plane righted itself at the last moment and set down on the runway almost unnoticeably. Almost instantly the brakes kicked in and squealed and it sounded as if the jets had been turned around backwards and were firing at full throttle. There were a few jerks as the brakes grabbed and continued to squeal, but the aircraft slowed to a manageable speed just in time to turn at the end of the runway onto the taxiway.

"Ladies and gentlemen welcome to Paducah Regional Airport. Sorry for the bumpy ride. Mr. Childers, I've notified the ground crew we're here and your ride is waiting for us in the hangar."

"So, let's hope this is the final show," Gary said. "And not the precursor to something bigger."

CHAPTER 43

ZHI FENG SAT WITH HIS HANDS CUFFED IN FRONT of him. The FBI had put him in the back seat of a nondescript black sports utility vehicle with plans to move him from the airport. The vehicle was currently traveling south on Interstate 405 toward the main FBI office near El Segundo. Agent Reed sat in the seat to the left of Feng and two other agents were in the front of the vehicle. The traffic along the interstate was crawling at a snail's pace.

"This is just what happens when the governor goes on television shouting the sky is going to fall," one of the men in the front laughed.

"Yeah, all the Chicken Littles are running around, well, like chickens with their heads cut off." The agent driving responded with a half-hearted laugh. "But after what happened in Memphis and in Cincinnati it's hard to blame them."

"I agree," Reed commented from the back seat. "Hopefully, the worst of that is over."

"Hey, look at that," the man in the front passenger seat pointed out in front of them. "A shooting star!"

Zhi Feng remained quiet. He had nothing to say to these idiots and he was ashamed of himself for allowing himself to get caught. He was also tired. The airport security and the FBI had interrogated him for hours at a holding room at the airport. And that was after the awful overcrowded flight from Japan.

Zhi Feng wasn't sure why, but they had held him at the airport for the better part of an entire day. Finally, they were moving him to a so-called "better location." Were he in China he would suspect that meant a hole in the ground somewhere, or a maximum security prison. But Americans were different, softer. They made him sick.

"Stay focused, gentlemen," Agent Reed ordered his men. "This must be the asteroid debris field making its way to the West Coast. There have been many large booms across the country already that, while smaller than Memphis, still caused problems. We want to make sure we get our friend here safe and sound behind some really strong iron bars."

"Just a few fireworks, Reed. Don't get your panties in a bunch."

"Holy shit! Look at that."

An extremely bright orange white fireball streaked across the sky due south of them. It was so bright that it lit up the evening as though it were the middle of the day. Then it hit the surface of the Earth some-where not that far from them.

The light was so bright that it nearly blinded him. He looked away just as the light of impact erupted into a fireball expanding into a mushroom-shaped cloud. If Feng had to guess, he would have thought the explosion was only a handful of kilometers away if it was even that far. Then the blast wave hit.

It happened too fast to mentally and emotionally grasp what was going on. Almost immediately after the meteorite exploded, cars in front of them on the interstate were being tossed around. A wall of dust, tree branches, glass, house parts, and other unknown shrapnel flew at deadly speeds into the traffic jam and everywhere around them. Zhi Feng's first thought was that he hoped Childers and Stetson were getting hit as well.

The smaller electric and gas-efficient vehicles became airborne projectiles as the supersonic shock wave in the atmosphere ripped across the interstate, throwing them asunder.

"Jesus H. Christ!" One of the agents shouted his last words just before what appeared to be a blue and white Mini Cooper pounded directly through the windshield of the SUV upside down, ripping off the roof of the SUV and taking the driver's head with it. The SUV was picked up and tossed end over end.

Zhi Feng could feel liquid covering him from head to toe as the instant slowed in time to his perception. He could see that the liquid was dark red blood splattering about from the two now-dead agents' horribly mangled bodies in front of him. Agent Reed to his left had assumed crash position and had his head tucked to his knees. His quick reaction had probably saved his life. The pavement of the highway passed underneath them and Feng could see a car pass by and then another as they landed on a third upside down. The torn roof squealed like fingernails on a chalkboard and then the rumble and crashing sounds of metal and glass against more metal and glass was so horrifying as to be overwhelming and indescribable.

Either from sensory overload or an injury, Feng had blacked out for a brief instant. He came to looking through the torn roof of the SUV at the top of another car. The vehicle beneath them was badly crushed. He suspected that its occupants were no longer alive. He turned to his left and saw Agent Reed hanging upside down, his seat belt holding him in place. Feng then realized that he too was hanging upside down and there was a pretty severe pain in his left foot.

Reed seemed to be coming around and Feng realized he only had seconds to act. So he did. Quickly he elbowed the FBI agent in the side of the head, further stunning him. He reached into the man's jacket, going for his gun, but the agent was made of tougher stuff than Feng had given him credit for.

Agent Reed grabbed at Feng's cuffed hands as they struggled for the weapon. Reed yanked the cuffs downward as best he could and threw his right elbow at Zhi Feng. Feng was coherent enough to move out of the way and then use his head and shoulders to pin Reed's right arm against the car's seatback. This put Feng closer to the agent's body, but again Reed was proving to be quite resilient. He managed to work his hand around Feng's neck, grabbing at his throat. He squeezed tightly on Feng's windpipe, choking him.

Feng's adrenaline completely took over. He reactively head-butted the FBI agent square on the side of his face and right on the temple, stunning the man just enough for Feng to work his hands onto the holster snap and release it. Reed punched Feng in the face twice with his left hand and closed his grip tighter around his throat with the other. But Feng had the man's gun in his grasp and pulled the trigger inside his jacket. He pulled it again.

Agent Reed's grip went limp, but there was no blood. Feng pulled the gun the rest of the way from the jacket and looked closer, realizing that the agent was wearing a bulletproof vest.

"I see, Agent Reed," he spat blood from his mouth. "You are quite prepared."

Feng held the gun to the man's head and pulled the trigger as he turned his own head away to avoid the bright pink and red blood mist and gray brain matter from splattering on him. He then pulled the keys from the agent's belt and fiddled with the handcuffs while accidentally dropping the gun. The gun went off as it hit the top of the car the SUV was upside down on. Feng wasn't sure where the bullet had gone. He had been lucky the misfire had missed him.

Finally, he found the right key and the handcuffs were off. He rubbed at his wrist and then braced himself for a fall as he unbuckled his seat belt. Feng crashed to what was left of the roof of the SUV and the roof of the car they were on top of. He fumbled around in the bloody wreckage until he found the gun and then he engaged the safety and stuck it in the back of his pants. He rummaged through Reed's jacket and found his badge and his extra magazines for the pistol. He took his wallet as well. Then he reached over into the front seat and scrounged for the two dead agents' wallets. He took them.

"Thank you, agents," he said. Then he looked about the mangled vehicle, doing his best to figure a way out. He kicked at the window, hoping to break it, but instantly realized that his left foot must have several broken bones in it. Feng squealed in pain and cursed in Chinese. Once the pain subsided a bit he tested whether he could stand on his broken foot and kick with his good one, but that was no good either. So instead, he pulled the pistol and shot out the window. He grinned and nodded approvingly at his handiwork. Feng was going to survive his capture at the airport. He was going to escape. And he was going to find Childers and Stetson and he was going to kill them.

Carefully he let himself out of the broken window, cutting himself superficially on the shards of glass. Blood oozed down his wrists to his elbow with a slight tickling sensation. There was little pain from the cuts. He knew they meant nothing. Finding Childers and Stetson was all that mattered. He had made it out of the FBI's grasp. He was free.

CHAPTER 44

PAUL NEARLY JUMPED OUT OF HIS SKIN. THE ALARM on his touchpad rang loudly and echoed through his personal area and certainly permeated the zippered closed curtains so the rest of the crew would hear it. He carefully slid his arms out of the sleeping bag and tapped at the screen Velcroed just above his head. He called that direction up anyway.

"God, I'm still tired. Seems like I just went to sleep," he muttered to himself, but the time showing on the touchpad made it clear that eight hours had passed. "Uhgg," he grunted. At least it was easier to pull one's self up or at least out of bed in microgravity.

"Bozhe moi! Eight hours was not enough!" Rykov complained. "Reset it for eight more."

"I'm sorry, comrade, I need to check on our status," Paul said. "But there is no need for the two of you to be in any hurry right now. You might as well stay put until I give the command capsule an assessment."

"I'm awake," Hui said. Paul could hear her rustling

297

about. "I'm going to take a shower if I am not needed this minute."

"Go ahead," Paul replied. Then he got a whiff of himself. "Think I will too when you are done. No hurry."

"Very well," Hui said as she poked her head out of her personal space. "I will let you know when I'm done."

"For God's sake, would the two of you hold it down?" Rykov grunted.

Paul was still wearing his Liquid Cooling Ventilation garment or LCVGs that astronauts wore underneath their EVA suits. Once he was certain Hui had entered the shower he decided to pull the thing off. A couple of times he spun about out of control like a whirling dervish, but he finally managed to right himself and then stow his LCVG in his garment bag attached to the wall. He pulled on a pair of shorts and a T-shirt and some socks. Then he noted that the temperature in the cabin was a very comfortable twenty-three degrees Celsius. The environment control system for the *Tamaroa* was functioning fine. In other words, he was quite comfortable and it was a warm balmy morning inside the spaceship.

Paul tapped at the icons on his touch pad as he floated toward the front hatch into the command capsule. The reactor was humming right along. The pressure sensors throughout the ship showed normal. Fuel levels showed zero. And the communications system still showed the high gain and low gain feeds were offline, but there was an icon blinking on the digital transceiver menu bar.

"Now what?" Paul muttered as he pressed the hatch open button on the wall and then tapped at the icon on his touchpad.

The door opened with only a slight humming of an electric motor. There wasn't even the hiss of pressure equalization. That was a good sign that the capsule hadn't leaked any over the sleep cycle. Then the touch-pad dinged at him and a popup window appeared on the screen.

Incoming message received and stored.

"What!?" Paul excitedly played the message. Once he had listened to it in its entirety, he then piped it through the ship's intercom so Rykov and Hui could hear it.

"Spaceship *Tamaroa*, this is Mission Control. We are so glad to hear from you guys up there! We are tracking you with the Deep Space Network and will be able to communicate with you as long as you can broadcast in the way you are doing. As of the moment we sent this response we are still receiving your repeated broadcast. Please be advised that the Russians had attempted to launch a nuclear weapon to divert the asteroid, but that mission has failed. We desperately need to understand your present status and if you were able to fire the main engines of the *Tamaroa*. We await your response."

"Holy shit! It is about time, comrades!" Rykov practically flew out of his cube, seemingly wide awake. "Paul! We need to respond to them immediately."

"Yes, I know. I'm connecting us now." Paul tapped the microphone icon and the tablet showed it was recording. Then he nodded to Mikhail that it was on.

"Greetings, Mission Control! Boy are you guys a sound for sore ears. We are all alive and well here on the Sutter's Mill asteroid." Paul paused, not exactly sure what to say. "We attached the *Tamaroa* to the asteroid and fired her engines until the fuel was exhausted. We need to know if we were able to push the asteroid enough to miss the Earth. Also, be advised that the *Tamaroa* is grounded, but the crew transfer vehicle is fully capable. We sure hope the engineers back home can figure out a way to get us off this rock and safely to Earth. *Tamaroa* out."

"Very good, Paul," Rykov said as he rolled his eyes up in his head as if he were thinking deeply or calculating numbers.

"I'm hitting the send button," Paul said.

"Yes, yes." Rykov sounded distracted. "If I did the numbers in my head right, we are about eighty-seven light-seconds from Earth. If they got our message, we should hear from them in about three or so minutes."

"Shower is all yours, Paul," Hui's voice startled both of them. Paul turned and could see Hui drying her hair with a towel as best she could while floating about. "Did I miss something?"

"You most certainly did." Paul smiled.

It was the longest three minutes the crew had ever spent. They watched the clock on Paul's touchpad until it had passed the three minute mark. Then thirty seconds more passed. Then another thirty seconds more. Then...

"*Tamaroa* Spacecraft, this is Mission Control! Great to know you are still with us up there. And we have news for Paul. Your wife has come out of her coma and is recovering well. She will be happy to know you are alive and well."

Paul's heart skipped a beat and he felt as if the weight of at least half of the world had lifted from it. Hui patted him on the shoulder reassuringly.

"Great news, comrade." Rykov smiled at him.

". . . initial calculations suggest the asteroid's trajectory may have changed, but it is still too early to know for certain. We will keep you apprised and please update us with your ephemeris tables as often as you can. At this time we are still working the issue of getting you home with just the CTV, but we will figure something out. Just hang in there. Also note that we will follow this transmission with a continuous audio news feed to keep you posted. We would like for you to start an update of your status at least every four hours. Hopefully by tomorrow we'll have some better news on your trajectory and on getting you home. Also note that medical is wanting a list of your food, water, and air stores. If there is anything else you think of that we can help with, we are all ears. Good luck and we'll talk in four hours. Mission Control out."

"Mikhail, we're sending and receiving digital audio, right?" Paul asked.

"Yes."

"Can you rig us up a way to send text? It would be easier to get them data that way rather than having to read it all," Paul explained. He knew they had to get control of their situation if they were going to get home. NASA's statement that they were "working" the problem concerned him that they might not be able to "work it out."

"Very easy, Paul. We'll just need to tell them what we are doing and when we are planning to do it. I'll set it up on a sideband so it doesn't interfere with the audio band. You'll be able to text and talk simultaneously if you like. Just as we could before. I'm afraid at the power we are able to put out right now, though video is out of the question," Rykov replied.

"Good. And, understood on the video. Don't really need it right now. Getting the radio and texting set up is your number one priority starting right now," Paul ordered. "Hui, start taking inventory on the food and water and air as they asked. Anything else you can think of type it up. What about the fuel on the CTV? Any way to take the fuel from the attitude control system of the *Tamaroa* and transfer it to the CTV? Ask them?"

"What are you going to do, Paul?" Rykov asked.

"Well, my friend, I stink. And not being too blunt I hope, so do you." Paul grinned at Mikhail. "I'm taking a shower and I'd suggest you follow suit when I'm done."

Rykov sniffed under his armpit and made a face. Hui did her best not to chuckle but couldn't stop herself. Paul handed Hui his touchpad and kicked off the wall aftward.

"Hui, be subprocessing the whole getting-us-home problem."

"Of course. I have yet to stop doing so."

"How can we not?" Rykov sniffed himself again. "Do I really smell that bad?"

"Yes, you do. And the worst part is, I didn't even notice until after I had showered," Paul could hear Hui tell him as he passed through the hatch into the bathroom area. He smiled. Not because of the banter with Rykov. But because Carolyn was alive and recovering well. And now she knew he was, too.

"She's alive," he whispered to himself as he started the shower system. "Somehow, I'm coming home to you."

CHAPTER 45

SUTTER'S MILL HAD NOT YET ENTERED INTO WHAT was known as the Earth's gravitational sphere of influence. At that point on the asteroid's trajectory, the Earth's gravitational attraction would become noticeable and influential on its future path.

The large cookie-shaped rock, two kilometers in diameter and half a kilometer thick, hurtled flat-side-first toward Earth. After a week since the *Tamaroa* had pushed the large rock at a vector away from Earth, the trajectory analysis was still "iffy." The odds were getting larger that the asteroid would miss the planet, but there was still an equal and quite significant double digit percentage showing impact. There were just too many variables to calculate to get a precise trajectory calculation as of yet. Soon the Earth and the Moon would be coming into play in the equations as well. The multi-body problem was almost beyond predicting a solution without having several days of trajectory position data. But at that point it would be too late.

The asteroid was only nineteen days out from impact

or its closest approach to Earth, whichever it was going to be. It was still up in the air if destruction from near Earth space was going to happen or not. Just to top off the anxiety of not knowing what was going to happen, the people of Earth were licking their rather large wounds from the debris cloud impacts, and the crew of the *Tamaroa* still had no clue how they were going to get off that rock and home, assuming the asteroid didn't take them home the hard way.

". . . and the combined loss of life in Memphis, Cincinnati, and Los Angeles is expected to be in the many tens of thousands, possibly even as much as over one hundred thousand. It will be weeks before the casualties will be accounted for, if ever. There were several impacts in the Pacific at lower latitudes causing small tidal waves from Hawaii to the Philippines but there has been much less reported damage as the warnings of the impacts in the U.S. likely scared the Pacific coastal nations and cities to react and prepare better than expected. There was some damage, but minimal compared to the U.S. The president said today on . . ."

"My God!" Rykov exclaimed. "We have no business moving these asteroids around until we understand the consequences better."

"I'm afraid, comrade." Paul frowned. "We are learning the consequences the hard way. Jesus, the devastation must be indescribable."

"We must hope that we will not learn a much harder lesson," Hui added. "What if the engines did not push the asteroid off course enough?"

"That is in the back of all our minds," Paul agreed with her. What if it didn't work? How big of an impact would it be? Would it kill a country? Worse? Paul didn't like thinking about it, but at the same time he'd been a man who had planned contingencies his entire life. He needed a backup plan. Or at least that was the last thought he had just before the *Tamaroa* rocked hard to his left, slamming against his back.

"What the hell!" Paul shouted, doing his best to find a handhold as the ship lurched again. This time it seemed to be falling, but that couldn't be right. There wasn't enough gravity on the asteroid for that.

"Something is making the asteroid unstable," Hui shouted over the rumbling and metal-on-rock grinding sound that permeated the ship.

"Gravity!" Rykov said. "We are getting close enough to Earth that it is tugging on the rock. No, wait. Not yet, we're still too far out. Hmm."

"Maybe it is heat from the Sun?" Hui added.

The rumbling and grinding noise continued for a few more seconds and then, just as abruptly as it had started, it stopped. The three astronauts looked at each other, briefly stunned, and then their training and survival instincts kicked in.

"Suit up, everyone!" Paul ordered. "We don't know what is going on yet and we need to find out. Let's get suited up and do an EVA."

"I could take the CTV out and look around," Hui offered.

"Not a bad idea. There's plenty of fuel left—we didn't use it as much as had been planned." Paul rummaged through his garment bag for the LCVG and started getting into it.

"Is this rock big enough for tidal forces?" Hui asked.

"I doubt it. It would more likely be a trajectory change imparting a different vector force on the body,"

Rykov said knowingly. "We are still millions of kilometers from Earth. Tidal forces wouldn't be serious until we got to twenty to fifty thousand or so kilometers, I'm guessing. I'm not even sure it could be a vector change causing centrifugal force or something. We are really not even to the edge of the Earth-Moon sphere of influence yet. This is quite perplexing, comrades."

"Let's look around and see what is going on and then we'll send data back to NASA. Maybe they can figure it out if we can't," Paul said.

"Paul, be careful moving in and out between the ship and the rock. If it lurches again it could crush you between them," Rykov warned him over the open mic.

Paul could see him just to his right on his three-nine line and slightly above him using the EVA jets to maneuver about the ship. Paul was following him in general but was doing his own recon of the surface and of the ship. There was nothing he could see that would suggest why the ship had moved.

"Paul, this Hui."

"Go ahead Hui." Paul looked up at the tail of the *Tamaroa* and could see the CTV undocking.

"CTV is free of the *Tamaroa*," she said. "I'm going to swing around the ship once and then I'll make my way up and down the fracture in the asteroid."

"Roger that, Hui." Paul looked about as best he could in his EVA suit and spun himself toward the front of the ship. "I think I'm going to go down the rabbit hole toward Earth. Mikhail, you give the ship a really good once over at least twice."

"American humor," Rykov grunted.

Paul carefully spiraled about the forward section of

the *Tamaroa*, and was astounded and horrified once he reached the command capsule section. The outside of the ruggedized inflatable section of the spacecraft looked like monsters from four different horror flicks had been clawing at it trying to get in. The hardened gel layer had many places that were chipped and scraped clean through to the composite fabric. Fibers of carbon filament and composites were frayed loose. Paul's first impression was that the front end of the ship looked like a deranged Chia Pet that was just starting to grow in. Spacecraft were just not supposed to have fuzzy exteriors. Paul forced himself to move on. Rykov would check it out with engineering rigor.

"Paul, Hui."

"Go, Hui."

"So, from this distance it is hard to tell even that the ship has shifted. However, there are several places where the fault line along the surface appears to have blown outward," Hui described to him.

"What do you mean, blown outward?" Paul wasn't so sure he liked the sound of that.

"Well, there are several points along the fault that looks like something inside the fracture exploded." Hui sounded as perplexed as Paul felt.

"See if you can get some closer imagery and maybe some radar data," Paul told her. "I'm pushing on through the hole."

"Roger that," Hui replied.

Paul fired his rear thrusters with a very short burst pushing him into the cavern in front of the ship. The ship had apparently poked through a thin section in the fault and was currently sticking out into a cavern about the size of a basketball half court. He carefully and slowly pressed forward toward the light at the end of the tunnel. He turned his focus about the walls of the fault line, and as he passed through he saw several veins of silvers, reds, and golds flicker in the sunlight.

Paul fired his forward thrusters and brought himself to a relative stop compared to the wall of the asteroid fracture. He shone his helmet lights at a dark rust red vein in the wall. Sunlight on the wall just above the vein moved down the wall as he watched. The daylight-shadow line on the wall barely touched on the edge of the red. It was enough light that Paul could see the wall above the shadow line like it was daylight on Earth.

He flicked his light off to see if it made any visual differences. He half expected it to be something similar to science fiction movies where something odd would be glowing once the lights were out, but there was nothing. There was nothing but a *ping* against his EVA suit and a cloud of dust bursting in his faceplate.

"Shit!" he yelled. He flicked his lights back on to see if there was any damage. As far as he could tell there was none, but his suit was covered in dust even worse than it had been.

"Paul! Are you alright?" Rykov asked.

"I'm fine. I'm fine," he said as he panned his light along the daylight to shadow line on the wall. As it crossed the red vein to a bright silver vein there were much larger pops followed by dust clouds. "What the hell?"

Paul fired his thrusters, moving him completely into the sunlight. He examined the wall and noticed that wherever there were different colors of material along the rock wall it was pockmarked with divots. The rocks were literally exploding.

"Mikhail, Hui, the sunlight is doing something to the rocks, making them explode," he said.

"What do you mean, Paul?" Rykov asked. "Is it violent explosion or simply a crack?"

"Uh, I'd say somewhere in between." Paul rubbed his fingers about the crater rim of one of the pockmarks. "It is mostly where there are different colored materials in the rock surface. The largest ones are near the silver-looking veins."

"I'm going to push onward and take some more pictures," he said.

It had taken Paul almost thirty minutes to carefully thrust through the opening in the fault. There were never any "tight squeezes" but he went slowly to make certain he didn't lose control and crash into the cavern walls. He also wasn't sure what a lot of the mineral ores were that he was seeing in the rock and so he didn't want to touch any of them if he didn't have too. Who knew? Some of those minerals might be reactive with his suit. He wasn't a mineralogist, a chemist, or even a miner. One thing he was sure of, though, was that this asteroid was filled with minerals and ores. He was very certain that he'd seen gold veins several times and something that was bright silver was in abundance throughout the rock. He was guessing the silver stuff was iridium, but only because he'd read about it being abundant in asteroids and seeing it being silver-colored in movies.

He slowly eased through the cavern precipice into the daylight side of the asteroid. He'd already had to flip his sun visor down. He brought himself to a relative stop on the surface and then fired a harpoon cable into the rock. He reeled himself tight to the surface and then took a breath. He turned a full three hundred sixty degrees to take in the well-lit asteroidscape.

Sutter's Mill was only twenty-five or so million kilometers from Earth and two hundred million kilometers from the Sun. The Sun looked pretty much the same size as it did on Earth to Paul. Maybe it was a bit smaller, but he couldn't tell. The Earth was so small that he could just barely make out its angular subtense and discern it from a point of light—just barely. He could also see a bright point that was clearly the Moon. The sight was breathtaking.

"You guys should come up here and see this view," he said.

As far as Paul could see on the surface of the asteroid, the fracture ran all the way across. He realized then that there must not be much holding the two pieces together. From the full sunlight view he was guessing that the fracture broke the cookie-shaped rock into unequal parts. One side was about two-thirds of the asteroid and the small side about one-third. The small third was on the Earth side of the asteroid and the large piece the space side.

"Maybe that's a good thing," he muttered to himself. "Hui, see if you can orbit this thing and give us a good light side model."

"We did that early on, Paul," she replied from the CTV. "Do you think something has changed?"

"Call it a hunch. I don't know. I'm not sure." Paul was thinking on contingency plans. What if they hadn't pushed the asteroid hard enough to miss the Earth?

"Comrades, my survey of the ship is complete,"

Rykov announced. "There is little holding it in place now. I think we should consider moving it."

"We still have the ACS thrusters. That might be doable," Paul replied. "It might be safer too."

Paul could see a glint in the sunlight rise over the horizon of the asteroid. The CTV slowly approached at about one hundred meters off the surface. Paul wanted the bird's eye view too.

"I see you, Hui." Paul released his harpoon cable and thrust his suit upward and added velocity horizontal to the surface to begin matching the CTV. "Mind if I hitchhike?"

"Careful Paul," Hui said. "I'll reduce my horizontal speed so you can match easier."

"Affirmative."

Paul carefully matched pace with the CTV until he intercepted it. He reached out and grabbed at the landing struts with both hands and then pulled himself to the ladder. He pulled a cable from his belt harness and snapped it on one of the rungs.

"I'm on, Hui. Take us on back."

"Roger that."

"Mikhail, we'll see you inside."

"I'm already in the airlock," Mikhail answered.

Paul took one last look at the Earth as they passed over the edge of the asteroid. *We're going to make it home*, he thought. *Somehow.*

CHAPTER 46

"THE CRACK IS WIDER." HUI POINTED AT THE IMAG-
ery data. "Here is the image of the asteroid when we
first got here. And here it is today. Analysis shows the
fracture is almost two times wider now. And during
my survey I found several places where I could see
completely through the fracture and see sunlight like
the hole here that we are in."

"Well, it isn't gravity," Rykov said. "I double checked
my thinking on that and we are nowhere near the
Roche limit of Earth yet. It is something else."

"Sunlight," Paul said matter-of-factly. "I saw it.
When the light would hit the mineral veins the rock
would pop and crackle. A few times it even exploded
like a firecracker."

"Yes, of course." Rykov slapped his forehead. "The
asteroid is filled with many different minerals and
each of those minerals has a very different coefficient
of thermal expansion. A shadow to sunlight swing in
temperature could be as much as three or four hundred degrees. An iridium vein, which I'm certain is

the silvery metal you saw, would expand almost ten centimeters per couple of meters, and the rock, on the other hand, would only barely expand."

"Ah yes. It is ripping itself apart," Hui added. "I once worked on an optical telescope system that the manufacturers had used the wrong type of metallic bolts in to hold the mirror in place. As soon as we put the scope in the environment chamber and dropped the temperature the mirror cracked. The bolts shrank at a different rate than the glass and tore it apart. This is happening here and getting worse as we get closer to the Sun."

"Well, not closer," Rykov corrected her. "We are and have been for some time about the same distance from the Sun as far as light exposure is concerned. We are getting something like a kilowatt per square meter on the surface. But we moved it and its trajectory is tilting different parts of the asteroid toward the sunlight."

"Before it was spinning like a chicken on a rotisserie," Paul said. He could see in his mind what was going on. "Once they stopped the rotation of this thing it began cooking on one side and freezing on the other. The shear forces must be incredible."

"Yes, comrade, now you get it." Rykov nibbled at a meal bar as he talked. He stopped long enough to take a drink from a juice tube. "We need to either get the ship out of the fracture. Or abandon it. I no longer think it is safe to stay in here."

"I agree," Paul said. "Let's see if the ACS thrusters can move us out. We're still over two weeks out and I don't want to have to stay in the CTV that long if we don't have to."

Neither Hui nor Rykov made mention of the fact that none of them had any idea how they were going to get off the asteroid, slow down to an Earth orbit speed, and then get back down to Earth. Those were just the details.

"Once we're out, then what?" Hui asked.

"I was thinking about that while I was on the light side out there," Paul said. "Look here at the images. The fracture unequally divides the asteroid. The smaller third, here, is on the Earth side of the trajectory. If this thing were to break loose, then this is the side likely to hit the Earth. We should be on it."

"Comrade, I know you want to make it home but that seems a bit extreme."

"No no. I don't want us to hit the Earth. But this is the most likely candidate to get us closest. Somehow we'll have to jump off at the right time," Paul said. "And once we jump off, somehow, we'll have to slow ourselves down to stay in Earth orbit."

"Those are some big somehows." Rykov frowned as he chewed through the last of his meal bar.

"We can certainly use the CTV to jump off, but there will be nowhere near enough delta-vee to slow down for an Earth orbit. We'd need a much larger burn than we have available to us now," Hui explained.

"I know all that." Paul rubbed his chin. He needed to shave the day's long stubble. Carolyn never liked it when he didn't shave. "But this is at least a start to a plan. Let's get the *Tamaroa* out safely and tie it down to the smaller piece of the asteroid on the dark side."

"We'll have to run an antenna relay up to the surface or we'll lose comms," Rykov added. "Why not park in space near the asteroid so I can repair and realign the high-gain antenna? If we need to attach to the asteroid we can do that at the last minute."

"Good plan. Let's do that," Paul agreed. "Mikhail, were there any of the tethers still attached to the ship? I don't want us getting hung up on something when we try to get out of here."

"No, I checked them all. You pulled every single one of them loose when you pushed the asteroid with the main engines."

"All right, I'm going to tell NASA our plans and make sure they don't have any hiccups about it." Paul thought for moment. He wasn't sure if there was anything he was leaving out. "Can the two of you think of anything else?"

"Not really. I'll get started on the high-gain antenna again," Rykov said.

"I think I should detach the CTV when you move the ship. Don't want to damage our only lifeboat," Hui said.

"Agreed. I'm going to update NASA. Let's get started on this."

CHAPTER 47

"WE WERE LUCKY, GARY." BILL WALKED UNDERNEATH the wing of the *Dreamscape* dragging his finger along the leading edge as he inspected the spacecraft. "Los Angeles was hammered and Nevada didn't get so much as a light show."

"It seems as though everything has been working against us on this all along," Gary replied. Bill watched his friend and boss as he limped up the ramp into the vehicle. He was still, after all this time, favoring the leg in which he'd been shot. Bill wasn't sure if it was mental or not, but medical had cleared him for flight. And that was what mattered.

"Have you got all the passengers lined up?" Bill asked.

"You would think, but we're only twelve days out from impact and I still have several multi-billionaires wanting to haggle over price." Gary sounded disgusted. "I told them the price is what it is—take it or leave it. But I don't think some of them have taken me seriously."

"Well, this has never been more serious," Bill started. "As far as NASA can tell, Sutter's Mill is just as likely to impact the Earth as not. Our friend is up there with no way to slow down or get back home. Hell, I'm not even sure they can get far enough away from the rock to avoid impact themselves. I damn near feel helpless and hopeless."

Bill hated feeling that way. He had been in tough situations that only required he keep his head about himself, work through the problem, and come out on the other end alive and kicking. This time there didn't seem like there was any way to keep working through to the end. At least, there didn't seem to be any way that led to a happy end.

"One day, if we keep flying to space, I'm going to have a spaceship like in the movies that can just zip up there, go anywhere, and do anything. Then we could just fly up there and get Paul and the others. I'm not giving up yet, but we are drastically and rapidly running out of time," Gary said as the two of them looked about the ship.

It was a little early to worry about preflight inspections. But Bill had wanted to double check everything since the ship had been repaired. Nobody knew the ship better than Paul and he wasn't there to clear it. He was in deep space over nine million miles from home, hurtling toward the Earth at cataclysmic speeds. And Bill was thinking that he needed Paul's help. He was sure Paul could use all the help he could get.

". . . we sure could use your help on this, buddy," Bill Stetson's image told Paul. Since Rykov had realigned and repaired the high-gain antenna the daily video messages had resumed. Paul stopped the video recording playback for a second to glance over the systems icons.

The *Tamaroa* was purring like a kitten. Well, a kitten that was out of gas. The reactor was continuously pumping out power, the habitat pressure was holding perfect at three-quarters of an atmosphere, the carbon dioxide scrubbers showed the levels were safe, and as far as he could tell both Hui and Mikhail were in their bunks sawing logs.

Paul looked out the window at the fracture in the asteroid about one hundred meters away from the ship. In the sunlight he could see the fracture on the edge of the cookie-shaped rock clearly. For the past two days it had continued to expand and branch out with smaller fractures. In fact, Paul was pretty sure he could have seen through the fracture almost to the other side. The only reason he couldn't was because it was curved. The surface of the asteroid now had several smaller fractures stretching across it. Paul wasn't sure if that was a good thing or a bad thing. But what he was sure of was that the two bigger pieces were barely connected, if at all. He resumed the playback.

". . . But Gary assures me that the engineers have gone over and over the ship and tested it out. I know I'd like to have a test flight before we put passengers on board again. By the way, I've looked over the numbers and data you sent us along with about a thousand million other engineers and orbital mechanics down here. There is just no way to know if that rock is gonna miss the Earth or not. It's gonna be close and that is for dang certain. If only there was a way to give it just a few more meters per second of delta-vee. The current track of probable impact is a zone stretching from Texas westward all the way across the Pacific to Japan and into southern Siberia and northern China. We really needed a 'plan C' I guess. Well buddy, hang in there and don't give up hope. We'll figure something out."

"Figure something out, indeed," Paul muttered, shaking his head back and forth. He wasn't very confident that "they" would figure anything out. They just needed a way to impart a meter per second or two to the rock. The main engines were out of fuel. With the reactor there was plenty of power. There was just no way to convert the heat or electrical energy into thrust without a propellant.

Paul had done countless calculations. In order to impart enough energy to move the asteroid just a few hundred kilometers more, which just might be enough, would require a small nuclear explosion at about three times ten to the twelfth Joules of output energy. That would be just enough to push the rock. The problem was that they didn't have a nuclear weapon. Although they had a nuclear power plant that was pumping out damned near a megawatt continuously for the next hundred and fifty years, he couldn't think of any way to use it.

"If only we had a railgun or a giant magnet or something . . ." Paul stopped talking to himself in midsentence. They did have a very large magnet. In fact, they had six of them, and each one of them could produce more than three teslas of magnetic field strength each. They had up to eighteen teslas available to them.

"Holy shit! Why haven't we thought of this before?" He chastised himself quietly. Paul hurriedly started checking the designs of the magnetic shield system and the six superconducting electromagnet systems. They were modular and they didn't have to work together. But that didn't matter. They looked like they could be reconfigured if they needed to be.

"Let me think... F equals m a, uh, m dv divided by dt." He scribbled with his finger on the touchscreen notepad app. "Okay, separate the derivative and do some algebra... F over m times dt equals dv." Paul scribbled some more.

"Okay, integrate that and I use t naught and v naught for initial conditions and I get delta-tee times F over m equals delta-vee." He thought about the math he'd just completed. "There's some integration constants in here somewhere but with the initial conditions they are zero, I think. So this tells me that if we can create a force from the magnets about equal to the mass of the rock, for every second it works we gain a meter per second of delta-vee." Paul started flipping through the resource materials to find a formula for calculating the force between two magnets.

"I have to get the team up," he said excitedly.

CHAPTER 48

THERE HAD TO HAVE BEEN HUNDREDS OF "WALKING wounded" flooding into the emergency room for almost two full days. There were more serious injuries being ambulanced in, but most of those had been taken care of at hospitals closer to ground zero of the impact zone or had been flown to special care locations. The hospitals twenty and thirty miles radius out from the impact of the asteroid fragment were the overflow for people who managed to drive, walk, or through whatever other means, get themselves to a hospital.

"As you can see, Mr. Chang, your left foot has three broken bones, here, here, and here," the young ER doctor told him. She had done her best to smile but it was clear that she was being pushed beyond her physical endurance limit. "The nurse will be along in just a minute to take you down for a cast."

"Thank you, Doctor." Zhi Feng smiled. "The pain medication is working well. I am in little pain right now."

"Good. If you don't have any other questions, I'll be on my way to my next patient."

"No ma'am. Thank you again." Zhi Feng did his best to smile at her.

"Great. Wait here for the nurse."

Zhi wasn't in any hurry. And, as far as the FBI was concerned, they probably figured he was dead in the aftermath of the impact. If they had figured out that he'd gotten away they still would have no means of knowing in which direction he had headed afterward. He was just another wounded face in the sea of walking wounded that was marching in every direction to hospitals surrounding the Los Angeles area.

He was safe from prying eyes at the moment. And if he was lucky, it would take days or maybe even weeks before they figured out that he was even still alive and at large.

". . . and since the Russian missile has failed, the NASA Administrator Dr. Tara Reese-Walker has ordered the Crew of the ISS be evacuated. With no time to implement a Soyuz or commercial launch for the standard vendors, NASA has contracted with Space Excursions to rendezvous with the International Space Station and extract the crew. Word is that Space Excursions CEO Gary Childers himself will be onboard the evacuation flight."

Feng listened carefully to the television playing in the background. He stretched and leaned to his right to see around a quite hefty woman holding a blood-soaked bandage to her forehead standing in between him and the television. The woman was moaning in pain. Feng paid her little attention. The fat Americans were simply getting what they deserved, as far as he was concerned.

". . . the flight will be piloted by former NASA astronaut Bill Stetson since the company's usual pilot,

Paul Gesling, is still on the Sutter's Mill asteroid.
It is expected that an undisclosed number of multi-
billionaires have also bought seats on the space flight
to witness the asteroid as it comes closer to Earth...
In other news NASA officials will still make no comment on the status of the asteroid other than that it is
still possible for it to impact Earth in a region of the
northern hemisphere stretching from Texas to Russia.
The president is expected to address the nation today..."

"Mr. Chang? Mr. Chang?" A nurse in green scrubs
with an empty wheelchair approached Feng. "Are you
Mr. Chang?"

"Uh, yes ma'am. I'm Mr. Chang," Feng told her.

"Come with me, sir, and we'll get your cast taken
care of," the nurse told him. She was much too happy
so Feng just assumed she hadn't been at the hospital
long. It made sense that at some point the workers
would have to change shifts. His doctor looked like
she'd been there way too long.

"Good. And then I can get out of here?"

"Yes sir. This shouldn't take but another twenty
minutes or so," the nurse assured him.

"Good. I really have some place else I need to be
right now." Feng's foot was not first and foremost on his
mind. Although, having it taken care of would make what
he had to do come somewhat easier, his sole purpose
in life had become finding ways to get his vengeance
against Space Excursions. And he had an idea of just
how to do that in a very poetic manner. As soon as he
got his cast taken care of, he needed to head north to
Nevada. Childers and Stetson were going to pay.

CHAPTER 49

"NO, NO, THAT'S NOT IT AT ALL, COMRADE. THE force from two opposing magnets is found by the square of the field strength times the surface area facing each other divided by two times the magnetic permeability!" Rykov corrected Paul. "You forgot to square the B-field! This is plenty strong enough!"

"Right, I knew that, but somehow I dropped the exponent in my model," Paul agreed. "I see. Hold on."

Paul tapped at the touch screen and fixed his math error. The graph of force versus area plotted across the screen in front of them. All three of the astronauts gasped with excitement. The function of force vs. area of the permanent magnet plotted on a logarithmic scale. As the surface area of the magnets approached ten thousand square meters the magnitude of the force went above a teranewton or ten to the twelfth newtons!

"Is this right?" Hui asked, astounded.

"Yes. We have a total of eighteen tesla field strength. The ground-penetrating radar shows that the iron ore veins spread out across this thing in every direction across the fracture and on both sides of the asteroid. There is well over twenty thousand square meters of surface area of magnetic ores spread about that are facing each other. This baby can be magnetic," Paul explained. "The key is, there is nothing to push against but the asteroid itself."

"I say we see if we can push it apart," Mikhail said, motioning with his two fists separating. "We push the smaller piece off the larger piece. At least then we can keep the bigger chunk from hitting the Earth."

"That is what I was thinking," Paul agreed. "But I was hoping we could come up with a way to keep either from hitting. Maybe keep bouncing them into each other?"

"That'll never work," Rykov shot it down. "Once that thing is separated we're never getting it back together. Besides I'm not so sure how long we can drive the superconductors at full power."

"I looked at that. We should be able to run them for several minutes before we overheat the coils and they shut down," Paul replied. "But if we can't play billiards with the pieces, then what do we do? We don't have time to cut up smaller chunks and make a mass driver propulsion system."

"We'd need more explosives or bulldozers or something like that," Rykov agreed. "No time."

"Paul, could we split them now and have the two pieces go on either side of the Earth?" Hui asked skeptically.

"I don't know? I hadn't thought of that." Paul quickly tapped at the screen and adjusted his dynamics model. He ran the algorithm and had the computer plot the simulated trajectories.

"It might work." Rykov pulled his floating body in over Paul's shoulder to get a closer look at his touchpad.

The model showed the rock splitting apart and the smaller piece accelerated faster—almost three times faster. As the Earth got closer, the two pieces of asteroid continued to separate and then pass by—with the Earth in the middle and no worse for wear. The numbers were tight, but they worked out. The smaller chunk would still pass dangerously close within the calculation and implementation error bars, but it was a better situation than doing nothing at all.

"We have to call NASA," Paul said.

CHAPTER 50

"... AS IT STANDS RIGHT NOW WE HAVE NO OTHER action alternatives. Anything that you can do up there is the only thing that can be done other than civil defense preparations here on Earth." Paul, Hui, and Mikhail floated about the viewscreen listening to the NASA administrator. "Our team here has verified your idea. It will at a minimum, assuming it works, push the larger two thirds of the asteroid clear of Earth. The smaller third is still within the error bars of clearing the planet or impacting it. The longer you can maintain the magnetic field, the better your chances are of successfully missing Earth. Also note that our simulations show that the force must be imparted to the asteroid before you are eight days out. The magic number is eighteen point five meters per second of relative delta-vee between the pieces of the asteroid no later than the eight-day mark. You have less than four days to get this done. We will be continuously sending updated information and specifications. If you need any technical analysis or details that we haven't thought of and supplied then just ask. Three days and seventeen hours and ticking according to the countdown clock running here. Telemetry has time-lag corrected the clock and are uploading the countdown to you now. So get with it."

Administrator Reese-Walker paused for a second and looked up from the script she was reading. She removed her reading glasses and massaged her nose a bit and then sighed.

"The three of you deserve more than this. I'm hesitant to tell you, but you deserve to know. We honestly have no idea how to get you home. I'm truly sorry. Every scientist and engineer in the world is thinking about this problem but nobody has even a wild idea that is feasible."

"You must know that I've spoken with the president, I've spoken with leaders of Russia and China, and I've spoken with several philanthropists who have been involved with this effort. I assure you that your families will be well provided for. Hopefully, there will be time in the last day or two to have near real-time video communications with your families and friends. If you have any particular requests, then please do not hesitate."

"Again, I can only thank each of you for your sacrifice. God speed. Good luck. And God be with you."

Neither of them spoke for several moments. The three astronauts even hesitated to trade glances. In essence, NASA had just told them that they were going to die at some point in the next week or so.

"So that's that then, comrades." Mikhail broke the silence. "We're going to die. So be it. But we've got work to do first."

"Right." Hui nodded. "Our lives will have had purpose. Great purpose."

"We're not dead yet. And, until I'm dead, I'm not dead," Paul said. "But you're right comrade! First things first. Suit up. I want you two to take the CTV and go and retrieve the tethers from the fracture. While you two are on EVA. I'm gonna see if the big side of the asteroid can hold its magnetization."

"What will we do with the tethers, Paul?" Hui asked.

"We're going to tie down the ship to the smaller chunk of rock." Paul looked at the countdown timer that had started on all the screens in the ship and on his touchpad. "I'll explain as we move. We have three days seventeen hours forty-four minutes and thirty-seven seconds and we just lost another second."

"Roger that," Hui nodded and pushed herself backwards toward the command capsule hatch. "Let us go, comrade. We must suit up."

CHAPTER 51

IT HAD TAKEN PAUL THE BETTER PART OF A DAY directing the superconducting electromagnets at the surface of the large part of the asteroid to magnetize the metal ores, but it was working. After a while he realized that if he traced the iron dense regions from the ground penetrating radar maps that he had the most success. He also figured out that the magnetization was stronger on the sunlight side. He suspected it had to do with the hotter side being closer to the Curie temperature, near which the magnetic domains would more easily align.

Hui and Rykov had done their jobs. They retrieved all of the tether materials that they could manage and brought them back in tow behind the CTV. All in all, it had been a hard day of work for all of them. But they still had more to go.

Paul needed to continue to magnetize the large portion of the asteroid in order to create as large a permanent magnet as they could manage. His current approach was to place the north pole of the magnet on the fracture side. Then, at the last moment, he would align all the field coils on the ship such that the nose of the *Tamaroa* would be the north pole. Then they would tether themselves to the smaller part of Sutter's Mill, with the north pole facing the fracture as well. When they flipped on the strong magnets of the shield system, the two large magnets would be pushing north poles against each other with a force of nearly a teranewton.

Paul sat in the crew quarters seat-belted into a chair, drinking a cup of coffee through a straw. Hui was free-floating and so was Rykov. The two of them were jabbering about the work and eating various meals.

Paul thought about their resources for a brief instant and realized they had enough food, air, and water to last them for another couple months if they had to last that long. Paul didn't want to think about that because if they were still on this rock in a month it would mean they were headed into deep space and there wasn't a spacecraft on the world that could get to them before they ran out of something vital to life.

The sheer morbid reality of it all was setting in on him. While they had to do all they could to save the Earth—to save his wife. All of humanity's brightest could find no scenario within which the crew of the *Tamaroa* would survive. Paul didn't like that. He wanted to see Carolyn again. He wanted to hold her in his arms and feel her next to him as they told each other everything was going to be okay.

"I want each of us to record a letter to our families," he blurted out, interrupting Hui and Rykov's conversation.

"Sure thing, comrade," Rykov said nonplussed.

"No, I'm serious." Paul said it more as an order this time. "We may get too busy in the next few days to do so. I want each of you to do this tonight before the sleep cycle."

"Are you alright, Paul?" Hui asked him.

"I just want everyone to record their farewell videos tonight," he told them.

"Okay, Paul," Rykov replied. This time he was more placating than serious.

"Good, then." Paul unbuckled from the seat and pushed himself toward his quarters in the habitat section.

". . . I don't know what to say. I just want you to know that the last couple of years have been the most exciting of my life and it isn't because of going into space or to the Moon or out here. It, well, it has been because of you. I've never felt so in love and so helpless and so . . ." Paul broke down and started crying. He did his best to cover the sound but the privacy curtain was just that, a curtain. He stopped the recording.

"I can't do this," he told himself. "I just can't."

His touchpad dinged at him telling him he had an incoming message. Paul tapped the icon and opened the download. Carolyn's face popped onto his touchpad screen.

". . . am I on?" she asked.

"Yes, ma'am. Just say what you want to say."

"Paul, it's me. I hope you get this." Her voice sounded a bit scratchy and horse.

"I've got it, baby." He wiped tears from his face. "I'm here."

"I'm getting better. I can breathe on my own. I'm

walking around now. I'm alive and well. And I miss you." Carolyn paused for a moment. It was clear this was hard for her too. Paul hated himself for putting her through this.

"Paul, I understand what you are doing up there. I mean, you had to do this. It had to be you. There is nothing you could have done for me here and I know you are doing all you can do out there."

"Oh, my God," he said through his teeth, holding back his sobs.

"You can't be sad. You can't be angry. I want you to come home, baby. I love you."

"I love you too!" He touched the screen accidentally pausing the video. "Oh shit." He started it back.

"But if you don't make it back, you can't feel guilty. I will not allow that. You are doing what you have to do and what nobody else but you can do. So do it. Do it with all your heart and be proud to do so. Do it for humanity. Do it for, well, do it for me, Paul."

"I will, baby." Tears stuck to the corners of his eyes. He wiped at them causing them to ball up and float away in the microgravity.

"I love you. I will always love you. Know that. Now go do what you do." With that Carolyn got up and walked out of view of the camera. Paul noticed a bag attached to her waist and what appeared to be drainage tubes poking out from underneath her blouse. He wasn't sure what that was about, but he suspected they hadn't given him complete details about her health status. But she was up and walking around and she was alive.

It was just like her. She wasn't feeling guilty or allowing anybody else to. She knew that Paul had to do a job and she was telling him to do it and there was no need to feel guilty about the outcome—whatever it may be.

Paul stopped crying. He replayed the message a few more times before he drifted off to sleep whispering to himself at the end of the video each time it played.

"I love you too, baby."

CHAPTER 52

"IN ORDER FOR THIS TO WORK RIGHT, WE'LL HAVE to take the bottom booms off and mount them on the surface of the asteroid or elsewhere to the ship." Paul pointed at the 3D representation of the ship on the viewscreen. "These two here will have to be removed."

"I see." Hui nodded that she understood.

"Wait, Paul." Rykov pointed at a spot on the side of the *Tamaroa* where there were several bare struts. "Why not just mount them here and here? It would be way easier to bolt them down on the *Tamaroa* than to figure out a way to hammer them into that surface out there."

"Good. Make that happen as soon as I finish my last pass over the ore veins of Sutter's Mill A this morning," Paul said. Since the rock had finally broken free overnight they now had two asteroids. They were calling the largest chunk Sutter's Mill A and the one a third the size of the other Sutter's Mill B.

"Roger that, comrade," Rykov said, as the engineer started scribbling at a touchpad with his finger. Paul

335

could tell that he already had an idea of how to install and implement the magnets on the new location. He was an excellent engineer.

"As soon as I'm done with the final magnetization run over A, we need to dismantle these two magnets and move them. Then we'll make one last video call to Earth, park on the back side, and tie her down," Paul explained, but they already understood the plan. Astronauts were famous for repeating the checklists over and over just to be certain they were following all the steps and in the right order.

"Once we are tied down, I'll use the CTV as a low-gain relay antenna," Hui said. "We'll have to figure out a schedule for communications."

"Paul, I could rig a higher-gain antenna if you think we need video," Rykov said as he chewed through his morning meal bar. Paul preferred the pressurized breakfast drinks and the eggs. The meal bars made him feel like he was eating candy for breakfast. And he really didn't like what they did to his bowel movements. Going number two in microgravity was difficult enough as it was.

"Maybe later, if there is time or a need," Paul ordered. "Right now, we focus on the day's work. What is your estimate on how long it will take to reconfigure the magnets?"

"I was timelining that last night," Rykov answered as he let a piece of his bar float in front of his mouth. "I'm guessing somewhere around four hours each. I'll need an hour or so between each EVA to rest and recover before going back at it. So nine to ten hours."

"It will take me four hours this morning. That's downtime for the two of you." Paul didn't like wasting time. He looked at the countdown clock. "Two days and two hours. We're cutting it close."

"It doesn't have to be complete downtime," Hui said.

"How so, Hui?"

"We could either sleep or we could work on the high-gain antenna problem," Hui explained.

"I can't sleep." Rykov chomped at various bits of floating yellow and chocolate brown foods floating in front of him. "I'm wide awake for the rest of the day."

"Hui?"

"I honestly am not sleepy either."

"Well, then, I changed my mind." Paul slurped at his empty coffee tube. "The two of you work on the antenna issue while I'm finishing up the magnetization of Sutter's Mill A."

"Sounds like a plan, comrade!"

"Sounds like a plan, Gary." Bill looked around the cockpit of the *Dreamscape*, finishing out a preflight simulation. There was a flashing yellow indicator icon on the touchscreen to the left, but it wasn't an emergency. He'd check it later. "I'm all set here."

"So, the *Dreamscape* can handle the mission?" Gary asked.

"Come on, Gary, you know as well as I do that we designed the *Dreamscape* to do ISS resupply and rescue if we needed to." Bill tapped at the yellow icon just to read it. The toilet door was open. He chuckled to himself.

"There is no time to get another rocket up there to evacuate the station. Something went wrong in the schedule and they won't make their launch window. So, of course I volunteered us to go and get the three astronauts that are up there." Gary smiled. "For a price."

"Why don't they just evac on the Soyuz capsules they have up there?" Bill asked.

"They can, but the *Dreamscape* is a much cheaper option for them." Gary smiled again. "Cheaper is relative of course."

"So that moves our timetable up by a couple of days?" Bill asked.

"We need to be ready to go by tomorrow afternoon. NASA is working the orbital dynamics with the ground control team here. We'll have all of that figured out in the next couple of hours." Gary looked at his watch. "That doesn't give us a lot of time."

"What about our paying customers?"

"Oh, they're on their way here and should arrive in a few hours. We just need to plan for a longer trip and for more people. This will be a good dress rehearsal for carrying a full crew to the Moon. It is short notice, though, and because of that we had some back out on us." Gary frowned a bit. Or at least as far as Bill could tell it was as close to a frown as he'd ever seen Gary make. "Four of them have backed out and we only had seven to start with. So, we'll have you, me, three customers, and three astronauts. We are running three short, assuming I sit in the copilot's seat. And our flight has now gone from three days to nine. I've already got the crew working the timeline and supply chain. You want me to have Becca flown out to see you off?"

"No. She's going to want to stay with Carolyn and I don't think we need to move her again yet. I'll just video chat with her later about it. I suspect I'll be too busy to spend any time with her anyway." Bill chewed at his bottom lip a bit. "Any ideas on Paul? What is NASA saying?"

"There seems to be nothing that can be done." Gary cleared his throat and for a moment there Bill thought he was going to break, but he didn't. "There is no way to get to him and he has no way to slow down to get to us. I know you know this better than I do, but NASA has spent all their resources at this point. They have no other arrows left in their quiver."

"There just seems like there has to be something more we could do." Bill could not stand the thought of leaving an astronaut crew to float free in space until they died of dehydration or starved or ran out of air. He understood making a sacrifice to save humanity or even some of humanity but it was a hard sacrifice to deal with when it was so torturous. And when it was his friend.

"I'm all for it, Bill," Gary told him. "If you can come up with even the craziest idea, I'll move Heaven and Earth to make it happen."

"I've got nothing," Bill sadly replied.

CHAPTER 53

THE CAST HAD MADE THE LONG DRIVE IN THE HEAVY traffic difficult. Although it had been a few days since the impact, travel out of the Los Angeles area was still moving at a turtle's pace. Zhi Feng had been living on fast food, coffee, and painkillers for almost twenty-seven hours. It had taken that long to make the two-hour drive from southern LA to Nevada. Feng's route had been circuitous at best, and he had been forced to travel all the way south to Anaheim and then turn north and east to San Bernardino before he could get back on course toward Nevada. He had stopped in Anaheim at a hospital.

After spending the night in the hospital and having seen the whereabouts and plans of Space Excursions on television, he now had a plan and a schedule. The damned traffic was not helping. Due to damaged gas lines or power lines or accidents or twenty other reasons, his route was being continuously altered by public safety, rescue workers, and the police. He did his best to avoid the police when he could manage.

The four-wheel-drive pickup truck he had acquired closer to ground zero had served him well. It was the only vehicle not damaged off the highway as he had made his escape from the FBI agents following the impact of the asteroid fragment. For whatever reason, it was sitting running at a stoplight with the door open as if it had been left there just for him. So he had taken it. There were several other vehicles crashed in front and behind it and Feng had been forced to push them out of the way with the truck, denting the front bumper and quarter panel and tearing the grill in places. But the damage had only been cosmetic, because the truck had been functioning flawlessly throughout the journey.

Zhi Feng finished off his coffee and downed another pain pill as he exited at the Nevada Spaceport. He could see the Space Excursions hangar in the distance. It was by far the largest of the newer buildings along the runway. But Feng was exhausted and in pain. He wanted to get himself cleaned up and rest from his journey, but was concerned that he wouldn't have time. The nurse had cleaned the dried blood off his face in the emergency room but it was still on his clothes. He was glad the nurse hadn't realized it wasn't his blood. His face was bruised yellow and blue and scratched up enough from his fight with Agent Reed that having more blood on his face wasn't out of place. Besides, most of the walking wounded who had found their way to the hospital had been battered, scratched, cut, and bloody. Feng had fit right in. Now he needed to figure out how to fit right into the Space Excursions hangar.

As far as the information he'd been able to gather from the television and the radio during his long arduous trek to the spaceport, the *Dreamscape* would be taking off within an hour or so. Zhi Feng knew that he had to move quickly if he was going to exact his revenge in time.

CHAPTER 54

"MAGNET ONE IS IN PLACE AND CONNECTED, PAUL," Hui announced over the radio. "What is our clock time?"

"It took you over seven hours to do that one," Paul answered Hui. "Mikhail, your estimate was off by nearly a factor of two. It took twice as long as we planned. That puts us up against the clock big time."

"Get in here and start your rest cycle now." Paul adjusted the activities timeline schedule on his touch pad for the longer modification time. The schedule still had them about twenty-two hours ahead of the eight-day mark. That was a decent margin, but there were still a whole lot of tasks to be accomplished. Once the magnets were modified, then it would take the entire crew a good eight hours to tie the ship down as planned. Add a sleep cycle and an eating cycle and an hour or so for suiting up and down there was only about four hours to spare. Paul didn't like cutting it that close.

"I hate cutting things so close, Gary." Bill Stetson told his boss as he was doing the final checklists on the

Dreamscape. "Alright, we need to get the passengers suited up and briefed, and start loading for launch. We are at T-minus, uh," he looked at his watch.

"Relax, Bill, we are on schedule," Gary assured him. "The NASA clock has us airborne in T-minus six hours and counting. Give or take a few minutes."

"This is rocket science, Gary. We don't 'give or take' anything for granted. We must be more precise."

"Well, Bill, then just be more precise is all I know," Gary told him. "The customers are paid up in full and are in the briefing room ready to suit up."

"Good, then get in there and suit up with them. I'll be along in about ten minutes." Bill turned back to the touchscreen console. The piston pumps on the oxidizer tank had been yellow and were showing a lower than usual head pressure. "I still need to purge the pressure heads for the LOX pumps."

"That's it. Break's over, guys." Paul floated into the crew habitat. Rykov was sound asleep. He wasn't sure if Hui had been asleep or not. She almost instantly responded to his presence.

"Roger that, Paul. I'll start suiting up," she said.

"Mikhail, time to get up," Paul said a little bit louder. There was no response. "Mikhail! Time to wake up."

There was still no response. Paul banged his hand against the bulkhead several times.

"Bozhe moi!" Rykov cursed several strings of Russian obscenities. "Good thing you two do not understand Russian!" He cursed some more.

"Time to get up, Mikhail."

"Alright, alright. I will get suited up just stop making such noise."

"We are cutting it very close, you two. I don't like our margin. If there is a way to make things move smoother on this EVA we need to do so." Paul thought but didn't say, *if we're going to die we should make it worth something and save a few million lives.*

What he did say was, "Let's move. The clock is ticking."

"Affirmative," Rykov grunted as he floated from his private area in his LCVGs with a meal bar in his mouth.

CHAPTER 55

THE TWO BUSINESSES ON EITHER SIDE OF SPACE Excursions were smaller and slightly older, but they were the same construction as everything else at the spaceport. They were tall, white sheet-metal buildings with large hangar doors on the runway-facing side. The only security would be that you had to go through the road-facing side to get through the airport fencing. In honesty, the Mojave spaceport was nothing more than a runway where spacecraft flew into and back from space with the apparent ease of a commercial airline. The actual number of true spacecraft that had launched from there could be counted on a single hand. And not all of those had actually made it to space. The *Dreamscape* was the only one that had done it repeatedly and had made it all the way to the Moon and back.

Zhi Feng passed the Space Excursions entrance and parked the truck two buildings down. While that building didn't look abandoned, it also didn't look as if there was anybody inside it at the moment. He would break in through there. He used the handle of Agent Reed's pistol to break the glass. Scanning about to make certain nobody had noticed him, he then reached through and unlocked the door.

The building was filled with derelict rocket parts, composite wing structures, and machine tools. Were Feng not on a specific mission he might have been interested in the commercial rocket memorial. As it was, he was centrally focused and very close to his target.

The back room was a hangar with two bay doors chained together and padlocked. There was a standard exit door just to the right of the hangar doors. Feng pushed at the handle and the door opened, letting in the bright desert sunlight, almost flash blinding him for an instant.

After letting his eyes adjust, he stepped outside and turned toward Space Excursions. The hangar doors were open and he could see the nose of the *Dreamscape* protruding just beyond the hangar exit out onto the taxiway. Two steps further and he saw Bill Stetson walking down the loading steps of the spacecraft. Zhi Feng hugged the metal wall of the hangar between himself and Space Excursions.

There were no security guards and no fences. He could see another prototype spacecraft several hangars down just sitting on the taxiway with the doors open. These stupid American commercial space companies were too lax in security. Feng could do pretty much whatever he wanted to with these spacecraft and nobody could stop him.

There was a mockup of some sort of spacecraft sitting on the pavement before the hangar he was currently hiding in front of, but there were no people milling about. There was nobody there to stop him.

Feng saw his opportunity. As soon as Stetson was out of the Space Excursions spacecraft he would make his move.

Zhi Feng took a couple of slow even breaths and carefully made his way to the edge of the open Space Excursions hangar. He leaned his head around and saw Stetson going into a door at the front of the hangar. As far as he could tell, the ship had been left unattended. Feng took a quick breath and bolted for the steps leading into the spacecraft. He stumbled several times, dragging his cast as best he could. Once he made it to the bottom of the steps he grabbed the handrail and pulled himself up and into the ship.

The little ship wasn't at all what Zhi Feng remembered it to be. It looked more like a luxury jet with seven seats than it did the spacecraft that had been to the Moon and rescued him and his crew. He surmised that his memories of that embarrassing and humiliating rescue were clouded or they had upgraded the ship. He poked his gun through the cockpit door but there was nobody in the two-seat control center of the spacecraft. He turned and made his way back, looking under seats and out the windows.

Once he reached the rear of the ship he found the galley door and opened it. The door led to a small flight kitchen on one side and a toilet and shower on the other. On the right side of the room was an airlock. Feng played with the controls for a moment and managed to cycle the airlock. He recognized the international docking ring design on the outer door. It looked like as good a hiding place as any for the time being.

CHAPTER 56

BILL STOOD IN THE DOOR OF THE *DREAMSCAPE* AND looked about the cabin at his passengers. Gary was already seated in the copilot's seat with specific orders not to touch a damned thing. In the first row on the pilot's side in seat 2A was a fortyish-year-old woman named Maya Press—a multibillionaire from Texas. Her family had been in the oil business for several generations. Apparently, there was a story between her and Gary, but neither of them were talking.

The older man in Seat 2B was Elliot Harbor, a software designer in the previous decade and had long since moved into global philanthropy. Bill knew of the man before he was a customer and as far as he was concerned, the phrase "global philanthropy" just was a fancy way of saying he was a busybody trying to stick his nose in everybody else's business.

For weight and balance seats 1A, 1B, 3A, and 3B were empty. Customer number three was seated in 4A. Katsuo Satou was a Japanese entrepreneur. Bill knew little about him other than he was a paying customer and had dealt with Gary before. Seats 4B and 5A were also empty. There was no 5B because that's where the spacesuit locker was.

Bill looked around and made eye contact with all the passengers and then keyed his headset microphone so his voice would sound over the intercom and in the suit helmet radios.

"Alright. If everyone will be seated we'll soon be getting underway. You don't need to lower your face shields unless I tell you to over the headsets. Please buckle up and we'll start through the countdown procedure in about five minutes. You've all had the preflight training so there shouldn't be anything unexpected for you. So get ready for an exciting ride." Bill pulled the doorway closed and dogged it down. Then he crawled into the cockpit and into the pilot's seat.

"Alright copilot, let's do some preflight checks and then bring mission control online," Bill said and then tapped an icon labeled "Preflight Checklist."

"Passenger Briefing. Check." Bill tapped the first box on the touchscreen.

"Seat sensors. Check."

"Seat-belt sensors. All fastened. Check."

"Vehicle hatch closure?" Bill tapped the next box. "Check. Pressure status is in the green."

"Brakes. Check." He pressed the pedals with his feet. They indicated proper performance.

"Master circuit breakers armed. Electrical equipment indicators are green. Check."

"Avionics Power Switch on and indicator is green. Check. Secondary circuit breakers are on and all panels are hot and green. Check." Bill compared a picture of the secondary breaker indicator lights and colors that popped up on his touchscreen with the actual lights touching each one on the picture as he looked at the panel.

"Stall Warning indicators in the green. Check."

"Landing and taxi lights on. Check."

"Comm panel master switch on. Radios on. Check." Bill clicked a switch on the stick and looked at Gary. "Pilot to copilot, do you copy?"

"Uh, I copy." Bill could hear Gary's voice but not over the radio.

"Gary, we've been through this. Click the voice activation switch on your right hand panel marked pilot channel there." Bill pointed to the appropriate switch.

"Uh, sorry. Got it. Copilot copy," Gary said after frantically flipping the switch into the on position. "But remember, you told me not to touch anything."

"Ha ha, yes I did. That right there is the only switch you can touch. Copy?"

"I copy, Bill."

"Good. Gary. Try to relax. This is supposed to be fun." Bill toggled the icon on the checklist. "Pilot to copilot channel, check."

"Alright, next." Bill toggled a different channel on the radio. "Ground Control, Ground Control, this is the *Dreamscape* performing radio check, do you copy?"

"Roger that, *Dreamscape*, we copy."

"Ship to ground radio test. Check." Bill swiped the screen a bit. "Alright. That is the minor stuff. Now we actually start in on the spacecraft stuff. You paying attention, Gary? You might have to fly this thing one day." Bill laughed, but Gary didn't see the humor.

"Let's see, what's next? Got it. Weight and balance?"

Bill tapped the second box. "Chec— Uh, wait a minute; that's not right."

He tapped the icon again and opened the advanced menu. He pulled down the list until he found recalculate. A task bar started across the icon turning green from left to right showing a one hundred percent completion after a couple of seconds. The results were the same as before.

"What the hell?" Bill hit the recalculate button again. Same result. "Am I going crazy? I just checked this thirty minutes ago and with the presets for the passengers it was fine."

"What's the problem, Bill?" Gary asked. Bill could tell that Gary was already nervous enough. He didn't want to start with problems that might make him freak out. But, this was starting to freak Bill out just a bit.

"Our weight and balance are wrong." Bill was perplexed. It didn't make any sense. He'd gone through a pre-preflight checkout already and the ship was in the right condition for flight. Now, for whatever reason it wasn't. "We've got an extra seventy-four kilograms in the back somewhere that wasn't there thirty minutes ago."

"How is that possible?" Gary asked with a shaky voice.

"I don't know. Nobody is in the bathroom. All the passengers are in their seats. I just did the seat sensor checks. And they're all buckled in. Hold on a moment." Bill switched screens to the main menu and scrolled to the internal cameras. He brought all of them up on the screen in a multi-image split view. There was a camera for each seat, one in the galley, one in the toilet and shower area, and one in the airlock.

"What have we got here?" He nearly jumped out of his seat at first. There was a person in the air lock. Bill tapped the airlock camera and expanded it to fill the screen. "Holy shit!"

"Zhi Feng!" Gary almost shouted. "Look, Bill, he has a gun in his hand."

CHAPTER 57

ZHI FENG SHOOK HIS HEAD AS HE REALIZED HE had nodded off to sleep briefly. He had been sitting in the airlock as patiently as he could, but his foot was starting to hurt him, and exhaustion from the previous three days was catching up with him. His body was going to force him to go to sleep soon no matter how hard he fought it. He was beginning to realize that his anger had forced him into a situation where he was quickly losing the upper hand. He was afraid that he would not be able to stay awake long enough to complete his plan. He had to complete his plan. Bill Stetson and Gary Childers would pay for what they had done to him. They would pay for the shame that he felt and for the shame that they had brought upon China.

His plan was to cause a catastrophe on launch that would kill everyone on board. His life no longer mattered to him as long as he took out Space Excursions with him. He knew it was time to act. It was right then or never. He had heard the door to the spacecraft close and heard Stetson's voice over the intercom. They were about to take off. They were all closed up inside. He could wait until they took off, but he might pass out before then. No, they were all captive inside and likely buckled in. He could go in and kill them all with the gun and then open the throttle on the spacecraft's engine. From what he had read about the ship, it flew like an airplane at takeoff. Feng was pretty sure he could manage to get it off the ground by himself.

Zhi Feng forced himself up and then checked to make certain there was a round of ammo in the chamber of the pistol. For a second he saw stars before his eyes and it was difficult to catch his breath.

"I'm very tired. I must move now," he said to himself. Then he cycled the airlock. The red light on the door flashed yellow and then back to red. He cycled the airlock again—same effect.

"That's not right," he said sluggishly. "Again. I'll try it again."

He started working through the process for opening the universal airlock controls in his mind. He'd done it many times before, but years ago when he was a taikonaut for the Chinese space program. He'd been to the International Space Station once and he'd been to the Moon. He was pretty sure he was doing it right. His head felt so foggy and he was so tired he could barely hold it up. For a brief instant his vision tunneled in and he had to shake himself awake. His hands felt like they had lead weights attached to them and his broken foot throbbed as if it would burst from the cast. Then he realized from his astronaut training that he was going through the stages of hypoxia. He also quickly realized why the airlock wouldn't cycle open. There was a pressure difference on either side of the door. The safety feature built into the system prevented the door from being open while there was a pressure differential in order to avoid an explosive compression or decompression, depending on which side you were on. Somebody had slowly let the air out of the airlock and Feng was succumbing to the low pressure and low oxygen level.

"Damn you, Bill Stetson!" He could barely mutter the words as he raised his pistol, intending to fire it at the airlock window, but couldn't manage to raise his arms all the way as he fell backwards to the airlock floor. His head hit the docking ring exit door with a *thud* and the world tunneled in on him and faded to black.

CHAPTER 58

"WE NEED TO FIRE THIS THING OFF IN LESS THAN eight hours. I don't think we have time for a break, guys. Sorry," Paul replied. "Would an extra set of hands be of any use? Or could I swap out with one of you?"

"Sorry, comrade. This job requires certain skills. Don't ask to do the engineering EVA and I will not ask to fly the ship." Rykov grunted. Paul wasn't certain if his grunting tone was humor or annoyance or pure exhaustion. He didn't care as long as they could keep working. They were tired, very tired. The sleep and eating cycle he had to cut from eight hours to six. It was taking them longer than they had expected. There was a scheduled one-hour break presently, but there just wasn't time for it. "Roger that, Mikhail. Seven hours, fifty-seven minutes, folks. I'm here to help if you need me."

Paul had plenty of time to do his part. All he had to do was to reconfigure the magnetic field controls so that he could ramp the magnetic field strength up rapidly without blowing out the coils or tearing them away from their moorings. That was a simple graphical user interface job. Toggles and dials on his touchscreen were all he had to manipulate. Then he would run simulations to double check and optimize his settings. He also kept the radio open and listened to Hui and Mikhail's progress and banter just in case they needed him.

After about three hours he had the field coils reprogrammed and the simulations showed that they should be able to get the push between the asteroid pieces that they needed. On his last pass over Sutter's Mill A over thirty-six hours ago he had measured the field strength to be on the order of a tenth of a tesla. The large rock was highly magnetized. With the superconducting field coils on the *Tamaroa* and the iron ore deposits throughout Sutter's Mill B, there should be more than ten or fifteen tesla field strength permeating the smaller chunk's surface once the equipment was ready and turned on. The combination of the two magnets pushing against each other should be just enough to push the asteroid parts free of the Earth—each part passing the planet on opposite sides. He hoped.

All the simulations still showed that the Sutter's Mill B piece would approach very closely to Earth or hit it. The latest models he ran suggested that if he could keep the field coils on and at significant strength for more than fifty seconds, then they should at least clear the Earth by two hundred kilometers. That was scary close and they would be slowed down some as they ripped through Earth's atmosphere.

Paul had originally gotten excited at that result, hoping he could slow the asteroid down by aerobraking in the atmosphere enough so that it would be caught in an Earth orbit. But the rock was just too big and it was moving way too fast. It had only been a fleeting moment of hope that physics and orbital mechanics had shown was a false one. But, Paul still couldn't let himself accept that they were all going to die on this stupid rock. Somehow he was going to find a way off. Somehow he was going to go home. He just could not accept death that easily.

He wasn't sure how Hui and Rykov felt about it, as they had all been too busy to discuss it much. But if the magnetic push worked, they would have a long eight days with nothing to do but talk. He figured there'd be a lot of soul searching then. And he also planned to spend as much of that time as he could sending and receiving messages from Carolyn. He so wanted to see her, to touch her, and to feel her embrace just one more time.

Paul wanted to go home. Somehow. Someway. Paul told himself that he was going to survive this. Somehow he and his crew were going to get home safely. Somehow.

"Paul, Paul, you copy?" Hui said over the radio.

"Roger that, Hui. I'm here. What's up?"

"What is our clock status?" Hui asked. Paul glanced up at the screens they had reattached or repaired about the command capsule. All of them were tied into the countdown clock.

"Four hours thirty-nine minutes," he said. "What's our status?"

"Mikhail is moving like a whirlwind out here. In less than an hour we will be finished," Hui replied. She sounded confident in her answer. Paul looked at the external camera feeds and could see several tethers staked into the asteroid's surface holding the ship down. Paul hoped the magnetic field would hold the ship in place, but just in case they needed the tethers.

"That's great news. Wrap up then and get in as soon as possible," Paul said. "We're not going to have time to call NASA before we fire the magnets. The clock is burning down on us and I don't want to take any more time than we have to."

"Understood."

CHAPTER 59

"WAKE UP, YOU SON OF A BITCH!" BILL SLAPPED
Zhi Feng across the face and then poured water from
a bottle on him. "I want you to be awake when I
punch you in the freakin' mouth."

"He's coming around, Bill," Gary said as he pocketed
his cell phone. "The authorities are on their way to pick
him up. You don't think he can get loose, do you?"

"Not a chance in hell." Bill almost laughed while at
the same time he glowered through his gritted teeth
and snarl. "That is two hundred mile an hour duct
tape. And I used three rolls."

Bill watched as Zhi Feng's eyes opened and he
gasped for breath and then cursed something in
Chinese once the man realized he couldn't move.
Finally he became coherent enough to realize that
he was duct taped to the security light pole outside
the hangar bay doors of Space Excursions. One of
the technicians sat on a folding chair holding the gun
Feng had been using. Feng was going nowhere, and
Bill Stetson was glad of that.

"You think we wouldn't find you back there in the airlock, Feng?" Bill taunted him.

"To hell with you, Stetson!" Feng spat at him. The man squirmed but Bill had him taped so tightly to the pole that he couldn't move a millimeter. "You too, Childers. The two of you should die."

"We might someday. But not today and not by your dumbass hands." Bill punched the man in the nose. "Ever heard of weight and balance, Feng?"

"Bill," Gary said as Bill punched him in the face again. "Take it easy. Don't break your hand. We still need you to fly."

"Break something on him? Why, it looks like he already broke something." Bill kicked Feng's cast pretty hard with his flight boots. "Did you hurt yourself, Feng?"

"Ahhh! Stop," Feng shouted in pain. Bill kicked the man's foot again, twice.

"That's for Carolyn, you piece of shit." Bill kicked him again as the man screamed in agony. "That is for my wife."

"Stop, please," he screamed.

"You are such a big strong man when you're facing pain, aren't you, Feng?" Bill spat on the man's face. "Coward."

Bill elbowed him on the side of the jaw with a crack. He hoped he broke the bastard's face.

"That's for Gary here. I've got a good mind to let you go just so I can shoot you as you run away."

"Bill." Gary put a hand on his shoulder. "He's about had enough."

"Has he?" Bill looked at the man as dark red blood trickled from his swollen nose and mixed with sweat glistening on his upper lip. His jaw was swelling and there was no telling what had happened to his foot. But Bill didn't care. All of the delays caused by Feng could have been part of what was keeping Paul from coming back. Feng's actions had likely given Gary a permanent limp. Who knew how well Carolyn would recover? Her wounds would bother her for years, probably. And his wife Becca had her hand blown off. Only through miracles of modern science might she regain use of the rebuilt pieces. Bill kicked him again. The man screamed again. This time the pain in his scream was even too sickening for Bill.

"But I'm not going to kill you, Feng. Oh no. That would be too good for you. I want you to rot in prison for the rest of your life as we here at Space Excursions go on to do great and wonderful things and there is nothing you can do to stop us." Bill turned to Gary. "We better move. This jerk altered our timeline. We'll just make our launch window today if we get going and cut a few corners."

"He's not going anywhere, Mr. Stetson," said the tech holding the gun on him.

"Great. Thanks." Bill nodded to the tech. "Have fun in prison, Feng. Better hope you go to an American jail. I suspect the Chinese will execute you if they extradite you."

"Well, Gary . . ." Bill turned and put his arm on Gary's shoulder. "Let's go rescue some astronauts on the International Space Station."

"Bill, are you okay?" Gary hesitated. "I, well, I've never seen you like this."

"He messed with my family, Gary," Bill said. "You don't mess with my family."

"We'll see to it that he doesn't mess with anyone ever again," Gary assured him. "I'm glad to get real closure on this."

"Closure?" Bill could hear the sirens from the police cars. "I guess."

"Well, we at least don't have to second guess that he is somewhere looking at us through the scope of a rifle."

"Uh, yeah right. Agreed. We really need to go." Bill turned and started toward the *Dreamscape*. "You coming, copilot?"

"You gonna let me touch anything?"

"Yeah. The radio button."

"Great. I'm right behind you."

CHAPTER 60

"THREE HOURS TWENTY-SIX MINUTES AND COUNT-ing," Paul told his crew as they cycled through the airlock. "Let's get your gear off and get you strapped in. We need to hustle. I want to fire this thing up within the next twenty minutes," Paul said.

"Paul," Rykov said with heavy breath, "do not wait on us. We will hold on if we are not strapped in yet. But we should go now."

"I agree, Paul," Hui said. "Go now."

"Okay then. Hold on when I tell you to. I'll give you a ten-second countdown over the intercom."

"Roger that. Go, Paul." Rykov pushed him forward. "Go."

Paul grabbed a handhold and pulled himself through the aft hatch of the habitat section and then kicked off with his legs. He pulled his way into the Command Capsule and into his captain's chair. He quickly strapped himself in and then took a deep breath.

"Alright, let's see how we're doing," he said to

himself and tapped at icons on the touchscreen in front of him.

He pulled the magnetic shield system menu to the top level and then loaded the algorithm he'd been working on. The superconductor field coils were brought online with a very low current to start with. He didn't want to shock them with full strength and risk ripping them apart. But once he toggled the current ramp up program the field strength would jump to maximum via a steady climbing ramp function that would take about ten seconds to reach peak value. Simulations of the system suggested the coils could handle that quick of a field buildup. He hoped the mooring booms could take that type of stress as well. Again, the simulations said they would, but simulations were never exactly right. There was always some unknown unknown that got left out of every model. But none of that mattered as long as they reached eighteen and a half meters per second of relative delta-vee between the rocks before the eight-day mark ticked by.

"Field coils are coming online and will be ready for implementation in about thirty seconds." Paul watched patiently as the current flowing through the superconductor coils slowly increased to about two percent of maximum allowed. It was a long slow thirty seconds. He looked at the countdown clock and there were still over eight days and three hours left before the asteroids hit the Earth.

"External cameras are online. Doppler radar is online." Paul waited until the warming sequence for the coils was completed and then it was go time.

"Hui, Mikhail, hang on back there. Here we go

in ten, nine, eight, seven, six, five, four, three, two, one, engaging!" Paul tapped the icon that started the system algorithm. The current flow rose quickly from two percent of maximum to one hundred percent in ten seconds. Then once the fields reached one hundred percent and held, a clock started. Paul could feel about a half of a gee push his body forward against the seat restraints. They were accelerating.

"We're moving!" Paul shouted over the intercom. "Doppler relative velocity at four point six meters per second."

The clock showed ten seconds had passed.

"Come on, baby!" Paul shouted. "Relative velocity at seven point three meters per second. Twenty-one seconds and counting."

"Twelve meters per second!" Paul kept one eye on the radar readout, one eye on the clock and scanned as best he could the magnetic system health status. "Field coils still at one hundred percent."

Looking out the window of the Command Capsule Paul could see the gap between the two asteroids spreading significantly. There was no noise throughout the ship as with a rocket engine. And there was no debris or signs of action other than the fact that the distance between Sutter's Mill A and B was increasing steadily.

"Fourteen point eight meters per second! Clock is at thirty-three seconds." They had reached a point that Paul had seen in the simulations where the velocity increases would start dropping off nonlinearly as the two rocks were pushed further apart from one another and the magnetic field strength between them dropped off.

"Fifteen point two! Come on. Hui, Mikhail, are you all right back there?"

"We are fine, comrade!" Rykov replied. "Everything looks good from back here."

"Fifteen point nine. Clock is at thirty-nine seconds." Paul held his breath unconsciously. Finally, he let out a deep exhale. "Sixteen point six. Forty-five seconds."

The models had shown that somewhere between fifty and sixty seconds was the sweet spot. The magnetic system seemed to be working fine. There were no systems outside of the green.

"Seventeen point two meters per second. Clock is at fifty seconds."

Clang, clang, clang. Something hit the side of the *Tamaroa* making it ring like a bell. Then it stopped with a final metal on metal *clang*.

"What was that?" Paul shouted.

"Paul. One of the mooring cables has come loose. I can see it through the aft port side window. It looks like from back here that the cable's hasp has stuck to one of the magnets," Hui explained.

"Nothing we can do about it now. Seventeen point nine!" Then one of the field coil icons turned red and the magnetometer showed a one sixth reduction in field strength.

"Shit! We've lost coil number four. Eighteen point one. Come on baby! Come on!" Paul checked the clock. "Sixty seconds."

"So close. Keep climbing, baby, keep climbing." Paul watched the graph of their relative velocity as it approached the demarcation line they had to cross. They had to reach eighteen point five meters per second. The line was barely moving now but at the same time it was flirting closely with that line.

"Eighteen point two. Come on!" Paul sat glued to the touchscreen. The curve of their relative velocity was leveling off right about eighteen point two five or so. It wasn't quite eighteen point three and it damned sure wasn't eighteen point five. Losing coil number four might have been all the difference.

"We've leveled off at eighteen point two five or so. We're done. I'm going to bring the system down as it seems to be having no further impact on our delta-vee," Paul announced. "Shit."

"That may be enough Paul. We are three hours ahead of schedule and there was error margin. I think we have done it," Hui said.

"We'll see. If it worked, it worked. If it didn't, then, well, it didn't. For now, the two of you did an outstanding job. Mikhail, you're off duty until further notice. Hui, I need you to take me out in the CTV to send a signal to NASA. Then we'll sleep as long as we want."

CHAPTER 61

"... THE FBI HAS HIM IN A HIGH SECURITY HOLDING cell. He's going nowhere for now. State Department isn't quite sure if the Chinese government wishes to extradite him or not. But the best part about this is that Zhi Feng is incarcerated indefinitely and all of you are safe from him now."

"Roger that, Houston Control." Bill smiled and he could tell by the look on Gary's face that he was quite happy with the end of the someone-trying-to-kill-him ordeal. "What's the word on the *Tamaroa*?"

"You'll also be happy to know that it looks like the magnetic push concept that Paul Gesling came up with has appeared to do the job. While all the models do show the smaller piece of the asteroid will pass as low as fifty kilometers through the atmosphere, it does look like it is going to miss the Earth. That does assume that it doesn't break up or explode against the friction of the atmosphere."

"Roger that, Houston." Bill muted the radio and turned to Gary. "He's a glass half empty guy, ain't he?"

Gary chuckled at Bill's comment. But only briefly as he had to grab his barf bag. The microgravity was a bit rough on Gary and the Japanese businessman, but the woman oil baroness and the philanthropist seemed to be taking it just fine. Nobody could ever know how their body would handle microgravity until they were in it. Bill knew that it was very common for astronauts to spend their first day or two sick as a dog and acclimating their body, and in particular their inner ear, to the weightless feel.

"It'll pass in a day or so Gary," Bill assured his friend. "It'll pass."

"God, I hope it doesn't take an entire day of feeling like this," Gary said around heaves into his bag. Bill did his best not to laugh. He knew that while it might seem funny, a health issue in space could be a nightmare. He toggled the switch back on the radio.

"Uh, Houston, we're ready for those ISS rendezvous burn numbers whenever you are," he said.

"Roger that, *Dreamscape*. We'll be uploading the navigation package within the next ten or so minutes. We'll keep you posted. In the meantime, you are cruising just fine and your orbit looks good."

"Roger that, Houston. We'll be waiting on that package. *Dreamscape* out." Bill unbuckled himself and worked his way out of the pilot's seat. "I'm going to check on the passengers. You need anything, Gary?"

"I'm good," Gary said around tightly clenched teeth.

Bill floated into the passenger cabin and let out a sigh. While they were safe from Feng, most likely safe from the asteroids, and going to have the best seats in the house for the near miss, Bill couldn't shake the thought of Paul having put in so much effort to save everyone back on Earth and now there was nothing that Earth could do for him. He felt helpless.

"Everything going alright, Captain Stetson?" Maya Press asked him as he hovered between seats 1A and 1B.

"Yes. All is good. The ship is purring like a kitten and all systems are green. I also thought I'd let you know that the crew of the *Tamaroa* has performed a miracle and it looks like they've managed to push the asteroids just enough that they will miss the Earth," Bill said.

"Asteroids? I thought there was just one of them," Elliot Harbor replied.

"Oh, I'm not sure what all has been said on the news or how much y'all have kept up with it. The asteroid Sutter's Mill broke into two pieces a few days back and they are being called Sutter's Mill A and B. B is going to come very, very close to the Earth but it should just miss us thanks to the brave crew of the *Tamaroa*. NASA tells us that there is still the slight possibility that Sutter's Mill B can break up in Earth's atmosphere and cause some problems, but let's keep our fingers crossed that they are just being worry warts," Bill explained.

"I see." Maya Press seemed impressed.

"So, I wanted to let all of you know that we are at least an hour away from any flight corrections and that we'll be floating along in our orbit for a while. Now would be a great time for you all to unbuckle and play around in the microgravity. You might wear your helmets for a few minutes until you get used to it. You don't want to bump your heads." Bill pushed himself back to the man in seat 4A.

"Mr. Satou, how are you feeling?"

"I've been better." The way the man looked, Bill hoped he'd been better. His skin tone was pale and his jaw was clenched so tightly that Bill was afraid the man was going to break his rear molars.

"Mr. Childers is having a similar time so don't think this is unusual. Many people take a day or so to get used to the microgravity. We were all trained on this, but until it happens to you, it is difficult to really understand what it's like. Hang in there." Bill put a hand on the man's shoulder for reassurance. "You'll be fine in no time."

CHAPTER 62

"... AND BILL AND GARY HAVE PICKED UP THREE astronauts from the space station and now have three days to wait out until the event. Bill says that Gary was very sick his first two days up there but now he is taking to it like a duck to water. Those are his words."

"Sounds like Bill," Paul muttered. He was hanging on every word of the message, not because it was important information, but because it was his wife speaking. He hadn't seen her in many months and hadn't been able to speak with her even longer than that. Paul could see the sadness in her eyes and could hear her doing her level best to mask it from her voice. Carolyn was strong—way stronger than him.

He was a total mess. In the five days since they might have saved the Earth, Paul had slept. Barely eaten. Slept some more. And sat at the touchscreen playing videos of his wife talking to him over and over. He recorded hours of himself talking to her but had only chosen to download a few minutes. Paul sat with tears balling up in the corners of his eyes so bad that he had to continuously wipe at them. Crying wasn't designed for microgravity.

"You should see Rebecca's hand. It is almost completely healed. The pins and halo wires have been removed and she's in a normal cast now. Once she gets that one off, the doctors are telling her she'll have some months of physical therapy and possibly some skin grafts may be needed, but it is a fully functional hand. That is a miracle, Paul. I wish you could see it."

"Me too..."

"They're telling us down here that Sutter's Mill A is going to miss the planet by thousands of kilometers and is likely to even miss all the satellites. Sutter's Mill B on the other hand, well, it's gonna be close. They're really worried about it blowing up in the atmosphere and they keep talking on the news about it destroying satellites and maybe even the space station. I hate that you are stuck on that thing. They did say on the news that it was your idea how to use the magnets to push the asteroid and how you and your crew have saved millions of lives. I'm so proud of you, Paul Gesling. I am so proud to be your wife."

Paul touched the screen and paused it for a second. He wasn't so sure how much more of the martyred hero part he wanted to play. As the days ticked down they were no closer to having any hope of getting home. Oh, they could likely get off the rock using either the *Tamaroa* or the CTV and go kilometers away from it, but they would still be on an Earth fly-by trajectory with a relative velocity of over fourteen or fifteen kilometers per second. It would be like falling in a broken elevator and jumping right before you hit the ground. You'd still be falling at the elevator speed minus your jumping speed. In other words, you'd still die.

Every astronaut knew that the escape velocity of Earth was eleven point two kilometers per second. They'd have to slow down an extreme amount, almost four kilometers per second, and they just didn't have the fuel to do it. The attitude control thrusters of the *Tamaroa* and the main propulsion of the CTV weren't even close to enough thrust to give them the delta-vee needed to slow down and attain an Earth orbit.

"I get my lung drain tubes out next week. The doc says at that point I can start doing some very light exercise to build my lung capacity back up. I'll start on the treadmill under supervision, but soon after I'll be able to go for walks. Also, the doc tells me I need to move to a dry climate. We still have our place in Nevada. I'm thinking I'll move back out there after all this is over. Gary says I don't have to come to work ever again, but I'd like to."

"Gary is good people." Paul spoke as if she could hear him.

"Gary is good people. At least he has always been good to me. Oh hey, I found this here at Gary's bunker. Well, 'Gary's Bunker' is what we're calling it although it is more like a fortress or an underground castle. Anyway, look. Your favorite childhood book, *Ender's Game*. I thought I'd read it just to see what you like so much about it. I like the bit about not knowing which way is up or down in space. Do you really do that? I bet you pick some place that you call up and one down and one front and back and so on."

"Huh, how about that." Paul almost smiled at the sight of his wife holding up a copy of one of his favorite books. "Why would there be actual books there? I haven't seen the actual book in decades."

"Well, dearest husband, I'm running up on my clock limit so I'll let you go until tomorrow. I love you Paul. I miss you. Bye for now." She blew a kiss at the camera. Paul sat frozen in his seat mortified by the video. He knew she wanted to tell him to come home, but she managed to keep herself from saying it. Carolyn was such a trouper.

Paul hit replay on the video file and watched it again.

Hui and Rykov had taken their turns at recording video messages for home and had watched their own messages from loved ones over and over, but Hui could tell that Paul was having the hardest time with it. Hui had been close to death in space before. She had been stranded on the Moon and had fully expected to die there until she heard a voice trying to reach her. That voice had been Paul Gesling. Had Gesling not found them and discovered they were alive, she would most certainly be dead now. He had saved her. Well, it had taken Bill Stetson and a few others to save her, but she had been saved and it was all initiated by Paul. Somehow she felt responsible for him. She felt like she should help him if she could to move past his grief. She wasn't sure how.

"It is your move, comrade," Mikhail told her in his parody of his own Russian accent that he had adopted over the past several months. "Check."

Hui looked up at the touchpad that Mikhail handed to her and realized that she had not been paying close enough attention. Rykov had her in a Fool's Mate scenario, of all things. Most kids learned that as the first strategy in chess and most seasoned players spot the strategy quickly.

"How did I not see that? You are too good for me today, comrade," she said jokingly. Her attempt at the Russian accent was destroyed by her Chinese accent, which made it all the more hilarious when she said it. The two of them chuckled half-heartedly.

"Yes, I have you. You are much distracted, Hui. Are you okay?"

"I am. But, I am worried about Paul," she said. "I'm not so sure how he is doing."

"I think he is fine. We all must make our peace with what is ahead of us in our own way." Rykov sounded like a life coach rather than the burly Russian engineer and astronaut that he was.

"I get that. But, you don't think he is closing off to us and isolating himself up front too often now?"

"No. I don't. Or, I don't think it really matters anymore. Face it, Hui my dear, we are not long for this world. That countdown clock on the top of every screen in the ship and on that touchpad is our life expectancy. Three days seven hours thirty-two minutes and some seconds that just keep on ticking by very fast." Rykov frowned and then reset the game on the touchpad to single player. "Why don't you go talk to him? I think I want to retire to my cube for a bit."

"All right then," Hui told him. She oriented herself headfirst toward the front of the ship and kicked off the wall, pushing herself along. As she passed by the window she rolled over and looked at the edge of Sutter's Mill B. It was jagged, like the wall of the Grand Canyon and stretched out to the left and right across her horizon. The horizon was filled with familiar stars. In the distance she could see Mars glowing red.

"Sure wish we would have just been going to Mars."

CHAPTER 63

"... AND BE ADVISED THAT THE LATEST MODELS show that if a significant amount of micro-debris is released during the fly-by that most of LEO will be filled from pole to pole for several days. It turns out that evacuation of the ISS was probably a really good idea. This is going to give NORAD and the Space Command folks a helluva headache trying to track all this stuff. Orbital maintenance recommends a fifteen hundred kilometer perigee minimum and they also suggest circularization. We are uploading the burn package now. With that you should be fine; though you can come on home, if you'd prefer."

"No chance of that, Houston. Remember our first goal was to be out here. Your rescue was added to the plan later. What about Sutter's Mill A?" Bill asked.

"Looks like A will be approaching closest at about twenty-three hundred kilometers and we'll get phasing burn calculations as soon as we can so that you can put it on the opposite side of the planet from you."

"Roger that, Houston. Fifteen hundred kilometer circular orbit sounds great to me. Anything else?"

"Not at this time, Bill."

"All right then. *Dreamscape* out."

Bill let out a long exhale and stretched his arms above his head. He had the cockpit to himself for a while as Gary was in the back having dinner and drinks with the paying customers. As far as Bill knew he was probably back there cooking up his next big business venture. Bill hoped it didn't have anything to do with damned asteroids.

Bill tapped at his console touchscreen and found the file for the asteroid trajectories. He ran the simulations and watched them. The newest data was fairly accurate now that the asteroids were close, there was radar and telescope data from Earth, and there was star tracker and navigation data from the *Tamaroa*. After several days of watching the rocks, the models were getting more and more accurate. As long as B could hold itself together, the Earth would be spared any problems bigger than it had already seen.

But Paul and crew on the other hand, well, there was still no solution for them. Bill watched the model over and over looking for some loophole in the situation. He did a few calculations to see if the *Dreamscape* could fly to the asteroid and get them, but they'd need a much larger engine to create that type of delta-vee. While they could fly to the Moon if they wanted to, that only required about a fourth of the thrust that would be needed to catch up with the asteroid and then slow back down again. Rescuing them with the *Dreamscape* was not a viable option.

"Dammit. There has to be a way," Bill said to himself. "It's like jumping off a damned falling elevator."

CHAPTER 64

"IT'S JUST LIKE JUMPING OFF A FALLING ELEVATOR!"
Paul sounded excited. "We're gonna jump off this
rock as hard as we can right as it hits the bottom."

"What good will that do us, Paul? We'd have to
jump with a relative velocity of over four kilometers
per second," Hui interrupted him.

"Perhaps you need to rest, comrade," Rykov said.

"No no. I'm not nuts. Of course we don't have
conventional propulsion to do it. But we do have the
superconducting magnets!" Paul explained. He pointed
to the 3D touchscreen display and started waving his
hands rapidly. "I'll need to remagnetize the rock. The
magnetometer shows we are down to a thousandth
of a tesla. Not sure why it lost its magnetization the
way it has. But no matter. We wait till we get right at
the bottom and we do a magnetic push just like we
did with the asteroid chunks. We should be able to
slow down just enough to get caught in an extremely
elliptical orbit."

"Of course, Paul. Why have we not all already thought of this?" Rykov slapped him on the shoulder hard. "You've done it, my friend."

"Not so fast, comrade." Paul held up his hand. "Look at the countdown clock."

The three of them looked at the clocks all around them on every screen in the ship. There were twenty-one hours and five minutes until closest approach. It had taken them more than eight hours to tie down the ship and several more to adjust the magnets for their last push. And Paul would need several hours to remagnetize the asteroid as best he could. They were just about to go on a sleep cycle so they had been up a long time already. Paul knew they could do it. He now had faith that they could get home. If only there was time to figure it all out.

"There is time, Paul. What first?" Hui asked.

"First, Mikhail get out there and get those tie downs off this ship." He looked at the Russian who was becoming one of his close friends. "Make it fast."

"I'm on it," Rykov said.

"Hui, take me out in the CTV. We have to contact NASA now and get them on the calculations and timing. If I don't have to do this myself I'd rather not," he said.

"Great, Paul. Let's go."

"I knew Paul would come through for us!" Gary almost shouted as NASA relayed the news to them.

"He hasn't come through yet, Gary. There is a lot that has to be done in the interim." Bill did his best to stay calm himself.

"Now who is the glass-half-empty person?" Gary replied.

"Right, I just don't want us putting our cart before our horse. Let's do the work we need to do to help them," Bill warned.

"What do you mean, Bill?"

"Gary, that spaceship was not designed to use an asteroid as an aerobrake, fling itself madly off of it with superconducting magnets, and then manage itself into a sustainable orbit. Also, they are going to be so low when they approach the Earth that if they do survive the first go-round it will be because they have that big rock as a heat shield. On their second orbit as they scream back down into the atmosphere they'll burn up and fall apart."

"Jesus, Bill. What do we do?"

"Well, we're going to catch them. If we can." Bill thought about that for a moment. "And if we can we'll push their perigee up out of the atmosphere. If we can't, we'll just grab the crew and run."

"What is the advantage of saving that ship?" Gary asked.

"I've been thinking about that also. There is no way NASA would ever reuse it. I'm sure it is banged up all to hell and gone." Bill rubbed at the stubble on his chin. He hated shaving in microgravity. "There is the issue of the nuclear reactor on it. We don't want it falling back to Earth in the wrong place. It could spread radioactive material into a populated area and that wouldn't be very good for the people or the future of space travel."

"So what do you suggest? What would NASA normally do?"

"Gary, honestly, I'm not sure. I suspect that in a normal situation NASA would be able to control the reentry and put the craft right where they wanted it. Perhaps Paul and crew could put the reactor in a 'safe mode.' I am pretty sure the control rods can be lowered to shut the reactor off, but it still has fissile material in it that we don't want to fall just anywhere uncontrollably."

Bill pulled up a simulation on the main screen and pointed out to Gary the details of his plan. The Earth was rotating in the center and as the asteroid approached he pointed out the closest approach point.

"The perigee will be here somewhere between fifty and a hundred kilometers. Thick atmosphere to a vehicle moving at that speed. It'll be a helluva fireworks show for people on the ground. Right here Paul will have to jump off and do it carefully. If they accelerate too fast they'll pull so many gees it will kill them. I'm guessing they'll have to accelerate for almost a minute at about eight or nine gees for this to work. That ship was not designed for those types of fighter-planelike forces." Bill paused to see if Gary was understanding him.

"I'm following you. The ship will be scrap if it holds together at all," Gary acknowledged. "And eight or nine gees for a minute will be brutal. Can they survive that?"

"They will survive it, but they will most likely black out for a moment or two. They better hope nothing needs their attention on board the spaceship while this is going on."

"Bill, I get it. We have to rescue them and we need to somehow push the ship into a safe junkyard orbit," Gary said. "Can you do it?"

"Do we have a choice? We must do it, Gary. We must."

CHAPTER 65

"THOSE BOOMS ARE GOING TO RIP RIGHT OFF AFTER about three gees," Rykov explained. "We have to take the magnets off the booms or retract the booms and override the interlocks so we can run them when they are not deployed."

"Which is quickest?" Paul asked. "We do whatever is quickest."

"I think we unbolt the booms here at the base and just lay them over on the structure and bolt them down, strap them down, duct tape them, and anything else we can think of," Rykov said.

"Figure it out. As soon as the magnetization run is complete you go." Paul thought about it briefly. "How long, Mikhail?"

"Four or five hours, probably."

All three of them looked at the clock. There was less than ten hours to go. Paul tapped at the magnetometer icon and opened the readings on the asteroid.

"Zero point one tesla. This isn't going to work in

time." Paul rubbed at his head and grunted. "Dammit! We are so close."

"We have to do another run over the asteroid," Hui said. "We just have to hurry."

"It's not going fast enough, Hui. We need to rethink this for a moment." Paul took a deep breath. "The problem is we are having to not only remagnetize but change where the north pole is. So, we're working against the previous magnetic field. Can't be helped."

"Maybe we could magnetize the CTV and leave the ship behind," Hui suggested.

"Not enough iron in the CTV to do that," Rykov pointed out. "And there is not enough power to run even one of the electromagnets on the CTV."

"No, we just have to stick with our plan and just move faster," Paul said. "We don't stop no matter what."

Paul brought the *Tamaroa* closer to the asteroid and pinged the ground-penetrating radar to get an updated map of the iron ore deposits. He brought the ship so close that a few times he was certain he was going to drag one of the habitat modules off the ship. He looked for the largest vein of iron he could find and focused on magnetizing the hell out of that spot.

"Here, we'll launch the ship from this location. It should give us the biggest push," Paul said, marking a spot on the video image so he could find it again.

It took three more hours, but finally Sutter's Mill B was a permanent magnet with a field strength on the order of one tesla—in places. As soon as he turned off the magnets it was time for Rykov and Hui to get to work. Paul still had to work on loading the algorithm into the computer to drive the magnets. If he drove them too hard too fast it would produce enough gees that it would turn their internal organs to soup. He didn't want to do that. But if he didn't drive it fast enough they would be too far away from the asteroid's magnetic field to get enough push. He also had to keep in mind how many gee forces the *Tamaroa* could take. It was a fine balancing act.

Paul hoped he could manage a profile that would allow them to stay conscious for the maneuvers, but the best he and NASA had been able to work out was about eight gees for right at forty-three seconds. That was *really* not going to be pleasant. But compared to the alternative of dying on an asteroid in deep space, Paul decided he'd take it.

CHAPTER 66

"THREE HOURS, MIKHAIL! WE HAVE TO MOVE IT."
Paul was looking at the clock and getting concerned
that they were not going to have the booms lowered
in time. Rykov and Hui were working as fast as they
could, but they only had two of the four booms moved.

"We're working as fast as we can, Paul."

"I know you are. I'm just saying." Paul really didn't
know what to say. They *were* working as hard as they
could.

They had already moved two of them before the
last push on the two asteroid parts. There were six
total magnets, but they had lost one pushing Sutter's
Mill away from the Earth. Five were functioning.
Presently, they had hard-mounted three of them to
the ship and there were two to go. Paul ran through
the numbers in his head and he wasn't quite sure if
three or even four of the magnets would be enough.
They needed all five of them.

Earth was large enough now that he could see it

peeking out over the limb of the asteroid. He was getting nervous and he had hoped to get to call Carolyn and speak to her real time once they had gotten this close. But there was just no time now to speak with anybody but his crew. They had to focus on the task at hand if they had any chance of survival. And of course, everything depended on Sutter's Mill B not exploding when it smacked into the atmosphere at fifteen kilometers per second.

While they had mapped the asteroid with the ground penetrating radar and made as many measurements as they could, it was difficult to determine how well the rock's internal structure would hold together. Just from sunlight heating the thing had already broken into two different pieces. Paul hoped that what really had broken the asteroid was some larger impact with something else years ago.

"Completing phasing burn number three now." Bill said over the radio to Houston Control. "How does it look, Houston?"

"If the orbital mechanics down here did their math right, Bill, you should be perfectly lined up to see Sutter's Mill B on its final approach."

"Great. Have you got the burn package calculated yet for matching orbits with the *Tamaroa*?" he asked.

"We're working on it and constantly updating it. We will not have it complete until we see which orbit they actually make it into."

"Uh, roger that, Houston." Bill looked out the window and expected to see two bright spots in the sky headed toward them, but he could see no such thing. "Are we good for now?"

"Affirmative, Bill. There's nothing to do right now but sit tight and watch the countdown clock."

"Alright then. Houston, *Dreamscape* out." Bill toggled the microphone off and looked over at his anxious copilot. "Well, Gary, nothing we can do now but relax. Maybe we should go hang out with the passengers."

"I'll do that. Unless you just want to get up, I think you should stay right here and keep an eye on things," Gary told him. "But, of course, since you're the captain, all that is your call."

"I appreciate that, Gary. I do. But, honestly, I think I'll relieve my bladder before we start chasing a dragon's tail." Bill winked at Gary and unbuckled himself. "Probably wouldn't hurt business either to do a last-minute brief."

CHAPTER 67

"TELL ME NOW, MIKHAIL. ARE WE GOING TO MAKE it on number six?" Paul looked at the countdown clock. They were at twenty-one minutes and counting. They had entered deep into Earth's gravity well and before long would start feeling the atmosphere.

"Seven more minutes, Paul!" Rykov said nervously. "Six if you'll shut up."

"In seven minutes you are coming inside one way or another." Paul did some quick timelining in his head. In seven minutes they would be only fourteen minutes from perigee. They would pass through Earth's atmosphere for about three minutes. Paul had planned to get as much aerobraking out of the atmosphere as he could before he jumped off the asteroid. So, they really had twenty-four minutes before firing the engines. But he imagined that the ride through the atmosphere would be quite bumpy and he wanted the crew safely buckled into their seats long before any of the fun started.

He watched the clock tick and tick and tick down.

There was nothing he could do but sit and wait and pray. Paul thought of Carolyn and wished he could tell her what was going on. He wanted to at least tell her goodbye if it didn't work out right. There was just no time.

"Fifteen-minute mark!" Paul said. "You have two more minutes out there and that is all!"

"Almost there, Paul," Hui said. "We just have three more bolts to go."

"Move fast." Paul bit at his lip and fidgeted against the restraints on his seat. For a brief moment he thought he felt something pulling him into his seat. "We are about fifteen thousand kilometers from perigee. I'm feeling some acceleration I think. You two need to get in here now before it is too late."

"Two more bolts, Paul," Hui said.

"Hui. I have this, comrade," Rykov told her. "Get inside. It will be quicker for me to cycle through the airlock if you have already gone through."

"Are you sure?" Hui asked.

"Go."

"You heard him, Hui," Paul agreed. "Now get in here. I'll meet you at the door!"

Mikhail could see the Earth looming at the edge of the asteroid to his right and could see that Hui had made it to the airlock. She would be fine. He placed the large centimeter diameter bolt into the hole on the superconductor magnet's mounting bracket and pushed it through. At first the bolt hung on the mounting hole in the *Tamaroa*'s external scaffolding structure.

"Bozhe moi! The bloody damned holes aren't

lining up!" he said to himself. He pounded it with the butt of the cordless screwdriver as best he could in the microgravity and EVA suit. But each move was difficult and each blow bounced him away from the ship.

Rykov held tight with one hand and worked the bolt with the other. Finally, it managed to push through the hole. He grabbed the "nut gun" as they called it from the tool clip at his waist and slid the socket onto the back side of the bolt with his left hand. Once he was sure the nut was lined up with the threads on the bolt he slid the socket from the cordless in his right hand onto the head of the bolt. Gently he depressed the button and the bolt started threading. Once he was sure it wasn't cross-threaded he squeezed at the trigger harder. He could feel the bolt pull tight against the bracket.

"That one's in. One more to go."

"One minute, Mikhail." He could hear Paul's voice. He also knew that it had taken him over three minutes with the last bolt and that the bolt had to be put in place. While the three bolts holding it right now might hold it, they might not. His calculations showed that all four bolts were needed in order to have a good safety margin. He was going to put the last bolt in. There was time.

"There's time," he almost whispered to himself.

He worked himself into position around the structure so he could line up the nut and bolt driver guns just right. He felt himself gently falling onto the boom structure. He realized they must be starting to brake slowly against the extreme upper atmosphere of the Earth. He put it out of his mind and started working the bolt into position through the superconductor magnet's mounting bracket. While the last bolt had been difficult to force into place this one popped right in. In fact, it slipped in so easily that it took Rykov off guard and his hand slipped off the head of the bolt.

Newton's third law got him. For every action, the bolt slamming into the bracket, there is an equal but opposite reaction, the bolt bouncing out of the bracket and flying through the space in front of him.

Mikhail saw the bolt as though time had slowed down. He reached for it and grabbed at it with his gauntleted hands but the spacesuit was just not flexible enough. The bolt drifted past him slowly and out of his reach.

Thinking quickly, Rykov disconnected the carabiner on his tether and kicked out in front of the bolt. He used the thrusters on his suit to turn himself such that he was facing the ship. He tracked across the space between him and the ship as best he could and there it was glinting in the light.

"Mikhail, I want you inside now!" Paul told him. "That's an order."

"Uh, not now, Paul." He fired his thrusters and moved toward the bolt, grabbing it with both hands. He carefully placed it in his left hand and held onto it with all his might. He used his right hand to drive himself back to the rigging. He was moving a bit fast and hit the ship with a *thud*. It wasn't fast enough to hurt. He grabbed the edge of the magnet and pulled himself back to the ship. He found his tether and snapped it in.

"Mikhail! We are at ten minutes and counting. Get your ass in here!"

"Almost there." He quickly slid the bolt in the hole, but this time made certain to keep a gloved finger on top of it. He reached to his tool belt and pulled the "nut gun" around to the backside of the bolt and threaded the socket over the end. He held his finger against it tightly and spun it as best he could to make certain it bit against the nut. He didn't want to lose it again.

"Nine minutes, Mikhail!"

He grabbed the cordless driver with his right hand, dropped it in place over the bolt's head, and started it up. It zipped in tight and he was done.

"Finished, Paul!" he shouted. "I'm on my way."

Mikhail unsnapped his tether and kicked aftward toward the airlock. He used his thrusters several times to correct his path. He was coming in hot but he was also in a hurry. He hit the edge of the airlock door and grabbed the handholds with both hands. His arms yanked tight with his momentum and he could feel a bit of a tweak in one of his biceps, but he'd live.

Rykov cycled the door and pulled himself in. He turned and pulled it shut behind him and sealed it off. The lights on the panel flashed red, then yellow, then green. The door opened and Hui reached in and grabbed him.

"We must hurry," she told him, like he didn't already know that. Mikhail did his best to shed the thruster pack on the EVA suit. With Hui's help it took almost a full minute to get out of it.

"Eight minutes!" Paul shouted. "You two move it."

Rykov turned and dogged the door down to the airlock and then secured the EVA jet pack to the wall. He disconnected the hasp for the tool kit and then snapped it to the EVA pack. There was no time to put things in their proper places.

"Go, Hui. Let's go," he said.

CHAPTER 68

"THERE IT IS!" MAYA PRESS SHOUTED FROM SOME-where in the back. Bill could recognize the only female voice out of the group.

"Yes. I see it!" one of the NASA astronauts shouted.

"Holy Christ, it is bigger than I expected."

Bill used the external spotting scope on the *Dream-scape* to find it and then he set the center of the asteroid in the center of the field of view of the camera and turned on the autotrack function in the software.

"While there is nothing like seeing it with your own eyes, I'm tracking it with the ship's external telescope and you can see the video on your monitors if you like," Bill announced over the intercom. "Now, I need all of you to do me a favor and buckle into your seats. We are going to be firing the engines soon in order to rescue the brave astronauts that are currently riding that monster."

"This is scary, Bill," Gary told him.

"You think it's scary for us. Imagine what it must be like for Paul, Hui, and Mikhail," he replied as he fiddled with the controls on his touchscreen. "Now get buckled in. We've got work to do."

Bill turned on the FASTEN SEAT BELTS sign and there was a *ding* throughout the cabin. That was a feature Gary had insisted on early on so that it would make the occupants feel as safe as on a commercial airline. Bill almost chuckled out loud every single time he heard it.

"Okay, Gary, we're on." He nodded to his copilot and then toggled the radio. "Houston Control, this is *Dreamscape*."

"Go ahead, *Dreamscape*."

"We've got visual on Sutter's Mill B and I'm relaying video now," he said.

"Roger that, *Dreamscape*. Appreciate the video. We've got several large ground scopes tracking it, but nobody is as close as you are." There was a brief pause. And Bill thought that there were three people much closer than they were but he didn't say anything. "Be advised that NORAD is tracking and as soon as we have the burn package calculated for you; we'll get it up there."

"Roger that, Houston. *Dreamscape* is standing by."

CHAPTER 69

"IS EVERYONE BUCKLED IN?" PAUL SHOUTED. "HUI?"

"Affirmative!" Hui replied.

"Mikhail?"

"I'm in. I'm in."

"Three minutes!" Paul had the planned trajectory overlaid on their screens and their actual path was plotting along on top of it as they went. "Should start feeling the aerobrake acceleration anytime now. I'm expecting about two-thirds of a gee."

"Paul, will the attitude thrusters be able to orient us against two-thirds of a gee?" Hui asked.

"Jesus! Why are you just now thinking of that? I hadn't even considered that." Paul thought briefly about flipping through the manuals on his pad to see if he could figure it out but there was really no time.

"Either it will or it will not, comrades. It is too late to worry about things now." Rykov grunted.

"I'm feeling the gees," Hui said.

"G-meter at zero point two seven gee and moving," Paul announced. Then something shook the ship with a violent jerk that ended with a dampening vibration. The ship rang like a bell.

"What was that?" Hui asked over the noise.

"I don't know. Maybe there are parts of the asteroid popping loose," Paul guessed. He looked at the clock and the trajectory map. "One minute to perigee! G-meter at zero point six one gee."

"Any idea what our relative velocity is with Earth?" Rykov asked.

"Only what the sims say. The star trackers are offline while we're in the aerobraking blackout." Paul looked at the sim. The screen seemed to be bouncing back and forth in front of him and his teeth were chattering. While the overall gee load was very weak, the quick jerks and vibrations were unnerving and they made it difficult to focus on a single object.

"We're at perigee!" Paul said. "Starting the countdown clock for the magnets. We are at T-minus two minutes and counting."

The ship continued to vibrate and ring. Occasionally there would be external pings against the hull of the ship. Paul assumed that debris was shaking free from the surface and they were flying into it. He wasn't sure.

"Okay, initiating attitude control thrusters." Paul brought the thrusters online and started flying the ship.

In two-thirds gravity the hundred-meter-long ship was very sluggish. It flew almost as if it was swimming in water. Paul kept an eye on the fuel for the thrusters. There would be enough. There had to be.

"Forty-five seconds to push!" Hui told him. "Come on, Paul."

"She's fighting me!" he said as he worked the thruster controls. As the ship pitched up, he finally had a good view behind them at the asteroid's path. There was a bright orange and blue glowing ionization trail stretched out for kilometers behind them. Paul used that as a focal point and worked the stick to tilt the ship upward and hold it in place.

"Fifteen seconds! Come on, Paul, you are still off by ten degrees," Hui shouted.

"You can do it, comrade!"

Paul fired the aft port thrusters to kick the bottom in and then slightly overcompensated with the nose thrusters. He cursed under his breath a bit as he watched the attitude readouts and the countdown clock.

"Ten seconds, Paul!"

"Count it from five!" he said as he continued to fight for the correct attitude of the ship. Paul knew that if it wasn't pointed upright enough that when he turned on the magnets the opposing fields would align the ship upright. But if the angle was too steep the generated off axis forces would be more than the system was designed for and it could rip the magnets right off the ship. Or worse, rip the ship.

"Five," started Hui.

"Go, Paul!" Rykov cheered him on. "You got this."

"Four."

"Come on, baby!"

"Three, two, one. Now!" Hui shouted.

Paul slapped the icon to fire the magnets. The algorithm kicked on and started driving power from the reactor to the superconductors. The current ramped up and almost instantly they went from two thirds of a gee to eight gee.

Paul felt like he'd been hit by a train as he was slammed into his seat. He squeezed his thighs and stomach muscles as best he could. Breathing was extremely difficult.

"Hang on!" he shouted through guttural grunts. He could barely focus on the clock at all. He breathed like a woman in labor.

Paul wasn't sure, and for a second he thought his mind was playing tricks on him, but then he realized the Command Capsule walls were flexing out and the nose was moving toward them. It was as if the capsule was a can and a giant were stepping on it. Paul had been through this before. He knew what to expect.

"Visors down everyone!" He lifted his arm to his face. It took all his strength since his arm weighed about fifty kilograms. He tapped the visor lever and it slammed shut. It was just in time too. A bolt popped free from the front of the capsule and shot across the cabin, glancing off the side of his faceplate.

"Fifteen seconds in! Hang on!" he said.

The ship creaked and groaned against the force load on it. The flexible walls of the capsule squished inward, popping loose any of the riggings that Paul hadn't torn loose previously when he'd pushed the asteroid with the main engines.

"Warning. Warning. Reduction in cabin pressure." An alarm started sounding throughout the ship. "Warning. Warning. Cabin pressure rapidly falling."

"Aaahhhrrrgghh! That's uggg"—he grunted against the gee load—"why we're in the suits!" His stomach hurt and his back ached and his limbs felt like they were being ripped off at the joints.

"Warning. Warning. Reactor thermal exchange malfunction."

An icon popped up on all of their screens showing

a red spot on one of the large radiators. The temperature of the cooling liquid was rising, but was still in the safe region.

"Rykov?"

"It will not blow with just one radiator out!" How he managed to speak without grunting amazed Paul. But Rykov was an old-school *Russian* astronaut. Paul guessed that the Russians had him up in MiG fighters doing high gee maneuvers for training not unlike his own while in the Navy. They just probably weren't as safety conscious in their training as the American military.

"Thirty-three seconds!" Hui said as best she could.

"Almost there! Five, four, three, two, one!" And then instantly the gee load dropped to zero. They were in microgravity again. Paul heaved twice and almost vomited in his suit, but he somehow managed to keep it down. He took several deep breaths until he could regain his composure.

"Did it work, Paul?" Rykov asked.

"I don't know."

"*Tamaroa, Tamaroa*, do you copy?" The radio nearly caused Paul to jump out of his suit. He looked up and the Earth was right there in plain sight. The radio antennas had line of sight and they could talk to NASA now.

"*Tamaroa*, this is *Dreamscape*. Do you copy?"

"Bill!" Paul was too excited for protocol. "Bill, is that you?"

"Roger that, Paul. Listen. It looks like you did it. You managed to bleed off enough velocity that you're in an Earth orbit. But you ain't out of the woods yet."

"Warning. Warning. Reactor thermal system failure imminent."

CHAPTER 70

"PAUL, ALL THREE RADIATORS HAVE STOPPED FUNC-tioning!" Rykov was tapping wildly at his console. "We're venting coolant fast."

"How long, Mikhail?"

"Warning. Warning. Reactor overheating imminent."

"Five minutes at best," Rykov replied. "And, I don't think we can stop it. It is going to overheat and explode."

"Then we need get the hell out of here and fast," Paul said. "Alright, everyone in the CTV now!"

Paul unbuckled and waited until Rykov and Hui had made it through the hatch before he left the Command Capsule.

"You did us proud, girl." He patted his captain's chair and then kicked off.

The three of them floated, swam, kicked, and bounced to the aft docking hatch as fast as they could. Rykov in first, then Hui in the pilot's seat, and then Paul at the hatch.

"Hatch is sealed," Paul said as soon as the light turned green.

"Internal lights, on," Hui said. "Master switches on, Check."

"No time for checklists, Hui," Paul said. "We've got to go *now*!"

"Right." Hui flipped the breakers and switches from memory as fast as she could and then grabbed the stick. "Okay, hold on."

She pushed the docking ring release mechanism and they popped free of the *Tamaroa* for the last time. Hui masterfully fired the attitude thrusters, spun the CTV around, and fired the main thrusters full throttle. The three astronauts were pushed gently into their seats by about a half a gee of acceleration.

"How long, Mikhail?"

"About two minutes," he said after looking at his touchpad.

"*Dreamscape. Dreamscape*, do you copy?"

"Roger that, *Tamaroa*?"

"Bill, the reactor on the *Tamaroa* is going to blow. We're in the CTV and making distance from it as fast as we can," Paul explained.

"Roger that, Paul. I see you. How long do we have?"

"A minute and a half or so." Paul looked back as the CTV was slowly pulling away from the *Tamaroa*. "Are we going to get enough distance?"

"It is not a nuclear bomb, but it will be a sizeable thermal overpressure bomb," Rykov said. "I just have no idea what a safe distance in space will be."

"Right. You heard the man, Hui. Keep the pedal to the metal."

The CTV continued to thrust at its very modest top acceleration. The main thrust for the vehicle was measured in the upper hundreds of newtons. The ship was never designed to provide more than a few tens of meters per second of delta-vee. Hopefully, it would be enough.

"Ten seconds!"

The three of them sat quietly for the next fifteen seconds, and then thirty seconds, but there was no explosion. Paul knew that the warning system could only estimate the explosion time. He was just about to ask Rykov a question when he saw the aft section of the *Tamaroa* fly apart into multiple pieces.

The ship spun as the reactor components exploded and coolant fluids and gases escaped. There was no ball of fire or blast wave. The *Tamaroa* just *looked* as if it were flying apart.

"Brace for impact in case we get hit."

They waited for several minutes, but there was no impact.

"Paul, this is Bill. You copy?"

"Roger that, Bill. We're all good here." Paul looked at his crew and they all nodded in agreement. He breathed a sigh of relief.

"Paul. Y'all ready to go home?"

"You bet we are."

EPILOGUE

"... AND THE GOVERNOR OF TENNESSEE TODAY HAS issued a warrant for the arrest of Anacleto Rosalez for three-hundred-ninety-four counts of unlawful death, destruction of property, and wrongful endangerment. It is expected that the governors of Ohio and California will follow suit. These actions create an interesting diplomatic problem for the State Department as Rosalez is not an American citizen nor was he on American soil when these crimes were committed. In other related news, the president of the United States, the president of Russia, and the president of China are presenting the brave crew of the *Tamaroa* with each country's equivalent of the Presidential Medal of Freedom. The medal is the highest honor given to civilian..."

"I can't get this damn bowtie right." Paul fidgeted with the thing as he looked at himself in the mirror. Carolyn stepped in behind him and gently pushed his hands aside.

"Hold still. You're doing it all wrong," she told him.

"I save the world but can't figure out how to tie a dang bowtie," he grunted.

"You're just nervous," she said as she straightened it out and pulled it tight. "There, see. I'll make a deal with you."

"What's that?" Paul turned and pulled her close to him.

"You fly the spaceships and I'll tie the ties."

"You have yourself a deal, Mrs. Gesling." Paul kissed his wife and held her tight against his body. All was right with the world.

AFTERWORD

WE ARE NOT AGAINST ASTEROID MINING. IN FACT, we believe that we must mine the asteroids if were are ever to be a prosperous, interplanetary species. We just believe that we need to be very careful when we start moving space mountains around, especially when they are near the Earth. Can it be done? Yes, and this book only looks at a few of the many ways asteroids can be safely moved to new orbits. And you never know when you might want to move an asteroid...

As Tunguska and, more recently, Chelyabinsk, have taught us, the solar system can be a dangerous neighborhood. There are thousands of near-Earth asteroids, some of them will eventually be in the wrong place at the wrong time—at the same time and location as the Earth—and that day will be catastrophic. (Just ask the dinosaurs.) Fortunately, we are now mapping the population of these asteroids and will soon have a good understanding of which pose a risk of collision. But can we do more? What if one of them is headed our way?

If we have enough lead time, then we can move the mountain—the space mountain—literally. All it will take is a small nudge using one of many promising and technologically doable techniques and an impact can be avoided. But it will take time and a space access infrastructure that we currently lack. We need to do more than map asteroids; we need to make sure we can move one of them to a slightly different orbit should it be coming our way. The time to build this infrastructure is now, not when disaster is imminent—for then it might be too late.

Remember, the dinosaurs did NOT have a space program.